Return to DEATH'S PROVINCE

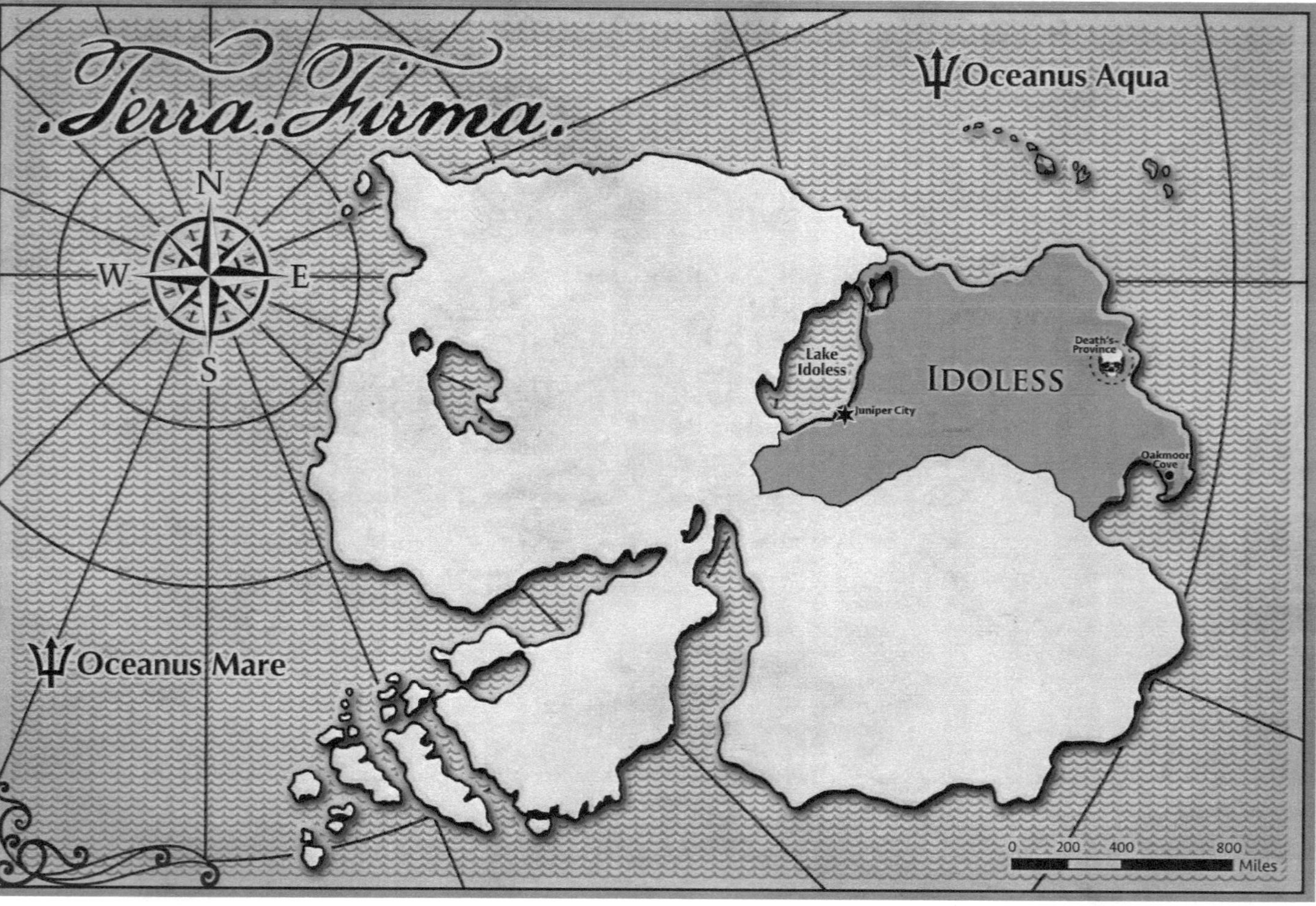

Terra Firma.
Oceanus Aqua
Oceanus Mare
N
W E
S
IDOLESS
Lake Idoless
Juniper City
Death's Province
Oakmoor Cove
0 200 400 800
Miles

BY. KEITH JAMES

ISBN-13: 978-1-7337042-0-5

SOMEONE TO WATCH OVER ME

Music and Lyrics by GEORGE GERSHWIN and IRA GERSHWIN

Song entered public domain January 1, 2022

Cover and all illustrations by Keith James
Visit www.thegeekcanpaint.com

For my family,
I pray in time you can understand me.
I hope this story can help.

Contents

Dear Reader,

If you've read *Return to Death's Province* before and this message was not in it, you read the original release of the book. While I'm proud of that version, I ended up having a couple regrets about it after it was published and have made a few changes.

My first regret was a lack of diversity in the cast. I think, I thought I was being diverse as I wrote it. I mean, if you've read the story, you know in the world I constructed the issue of race isn't significant. Yet, once the book was published, I was able to take a step back and realize. . . all the lead characters (and then some) were white. It made me uncomfortable to realize I'd done that. Maybe race isn't important in the story, but it should have been more important to me. The problem was, by then people had bought and read the story. So, at the time, I was prepared to leave it be, but vowed to myself to work in more diversity as I continued writing the series.

My second regret was a bit more specific but also related to a racial issue. In the story there is a black man who, at one point, is referred to as a *thug*. Now, the character fits the definition of the word (a violent, aggressive person, especially one who is a criminal) but I've come to learn that *thug* is a particularly derogatory word when used to depict a black man. So, for all the old copies of the book still out there in the world with that word in it, I want to own up to my mistake and apologize.

To be honest, I was just going to go in and change that one word without saying anything, but there's a new development. I've decided I'm going to create graphic novel adaptations of *The Secret War* stories. The thing is, with such a visual format, I couldn't ignore the lack of diversity the way I was going to. And since I want the novel and graphic novel to complement each other, I decided to go ahead and repair both of my regrets.

However, as I started going through the story, I began to feel I'd grown as an author. So, I figured as long as I was making the other changes, I'd allow myself to make even more; why not make this book as good as it can be? So, I cut some superfluous lines, and refined others, creating the version of the book you are looking at now.

In closing, please understand, despite all I've just said, not much of the actual story has changed. This isn't a second edition of the book. In theory, anyone who's read the original release shouldn't notice too much of a difference in this one. It's just a tighter, cleaner read now. Sure, some characters look different, but they're still the same people, doing the same things that they had before.

Whatever the case, whether you've read it before or not, I hope you enjoy the definitive version of *Return to Death's Province*.

~ Keith James

Chapter One
Looking for a Man Named Jack

W e're looking for a man named Jack," bellowed Private Daniels as he entered the tavern.

He and his team had been sent to collect Jack from the small town of Oakmoor Cove, an isolated ocean-side village on the eastern peninsula of Idoless, as distant from the capital as possible. None of the soldiers thought anyone out here could possibly be so important. The lieutenant didn't give them a mech-pad or even a poster—just a scroll of all things. Daniels had a feeling it was a joke, but the commander himself had come on this mission, and the name on the scroll told them all they needed to know. They'd heard the rumors.

An elderly man started to stand, timidly saying, "M-m-my name is Ja—"

"Not you, old man! Sit down!" Daniels clarified, "Jack *Waramond*. He was last seen in the year 575. He's thirty years old, has a tan or olive complexion with dark hair, brown eyes, and has been seen with an army-issued sword like this." He jerked a thumb at the hilt protruding behind his shoulder.

One of the other soldiers had pulled out the scroll and was showing it to the surrounding patrons. There was a photo of a young man in a military uniform laden with medals and the hint of a smile.

"He has two tattoos. One is a band around his left ring finger. The other is a symbol on the back of his right hand." Daniels pointed to the scroll. Next to the photo of Jack was an illustration of the tattoo: a triangle pointing down with a circle inside it, with another triangle inside the circle, pointing up.

Daniels studied the faces in the tavern. Most wouldn't meet his eyes. Then he noticed the bartender's gaze drifting to a man in a hooded cape at the far end of the bar hunched over a drink. The bartender's eyes darted up when he realized he was being watched. Daniels began to make his way toward the hooded man while saying, "He's not in any kind of trouble. We just need him for some questioning."

Greasy, shoulder-length hair hung from the hood, concealing the man's face, but an Idolessian Army sword hung at his side. As Daniels approached, a voice under the hood grumbled, "Thanks a lot, Ernie."

"I'm sorry," apologized the bartender. "But they were gonna notice ya themselves."

Now standing over the hooded man, Daniels said to him, "Excuse me, sir, I was wondering if you've seen the man we're looking for?"

The hooded man didn't look up, just shook his head and said, "I don't think so."

"If you didn't hear, his name is Jack."

"There's an old guy over there named—"

"Don't get smart." Daniels grabbed the man's shoulder and forced him around. The stranger's face bore the scruff of someone who shaves only every other week—and this wasn't the other week. Daniels compared him to the picture on the scroll and noted, "That's a nice sword you've got there." Then added darkly, "I never caught your name."

The man responded, "Of course you didn't, *Private.* You haven't even asked for it."

Private Daniels was shocked by the man's nerve, but persisted, "So . . . ?"

"So . . . next time, we need to talk a bit more. You know, you try to get my name, but I cleverly avoid it. We exchange some witty banter, *then* you can say all intimidatingly, 'I never caught your name.'" The man in the hood looked to one of the other soldiers and said, "He's got the theatrics down, but his dialogue is all messed up. Honestly, I don't even know how to proceed from here. I mean," he turned back to Daniels, "have you ever even done this before?"

A couple of suppressed snickers came from the back of the tavern.

Trying to regain control of the situation, Daniels asked the bartender, "How much has he had to drink?"

Ernie responded, "I don't know, five, maybe six." Daniels began to smile knowingly, but then Ernie finished, "But it was just water."

Ignoring the bartender, Daniels demanded, "I want to know your name."

The man looked him in the eyes and said, "You didn't say please," then turned back to the bar.

Daniels ordered his men, "Take him. Even if he isn't who we're looking for, I want to bring him in. For sheer impudence."

Two of the soldiers grabbed the man, each taking an arm. Markings resembling the tattoo from the scroll could be seen protruding from under his fingerless gloves. With incredible speed the man hooked his arms around one soldier, slamming his head on the bar, and then kicked the other's legs from beneath him.

Daniels attempted to grab the man's shoulder, but before he made contact, the hooded man gripped Daniels's hand and twisted it in a way that made his whole body submit. The man steered Daniels outside, then released his hand and kicked him in the backside, which knocked him to the ground.

Daniels bolted up and drew his sword, prepared for the fight he was sure to follow. However, all he saw was the door of the tavern closing.

He stomped to the door and kicked it open to see the hooded man casually getting back onto his barstool. The other soldiers all stood stunned, unsure what to do.

"What is the matter with you?" Daniels yelled. "Get him!"

Drawing their weapons, the soldiers surrounded the man, who said quietly, "I don't want to fight you. And believe me," he put his hand on the hilt of his sword, "you don't want to fight me."

The team looked at each other, assessing their numbers, and charged. The man sighed in resignation as he drew his sword to deflect the first round of assaults. He countered the attacks, swinging his sword in an almost casual way as he fought his way past the group and sprinted out the door.

"Don't let him get away!" roared Daniels.

They ran after the man but were surprised to find him standing in the square outside, waiting for them. They looked around, trying to understand why he wasn't running.

The man explained, "I didn't want any damage to come to the tavern—I like that place." He flung off his cape, revealing a blue shirt with rolled sleeves under a leather vest with a high collar. "Now, can we get on with this?"

With the skill of a battle-hardened warrior, the man moved through his attackers, using his sword only for defensive moves; any attack he made was with his fists and feet.

Townspeople began to gather in their doorways to watch the spectacle, encouraging the man with shouts of "Go, Gabriel!"

One boy, eager to help this Gabriel, approached a soldier from behind and kicked him. The soldier backhanded the boy in response. Seeing this, Gabriel pummeled the soldier so soundly it revealed that, until now, he'd been holding back, sending a clear message to the soldiers: Leave the townspeople out of this.

Daniels had been content to let his subordinates take the worst of the assault, but with all of them now unconscious on the ground, he stepped forward.

The clanking of their swords reverberated off the cobblestones as Daniels and Gabriel attacked and parried. Daniels wiped perspiration off his forehead, grasped his sword hilt with both hands, and swung dramatically, but Gabriel simply stepped aside and disarmed Daniels with a single upward strike of his sword, sending the private's weapon sailing across the square. Daniels grunted with rage and began to swing his fist, but Gabriel gave one final punch to the center of the private's nose, knocking him down flat.

Gabriel shook the pain from his hand as he strolled over to the unconscious soldier who had backhanded the boy and plucked the sword from his hand. He walked a little farther and called into a dark alley, "Tim, is that you?"

A freckled boy with brown hair, and a rapidly swelling eye, stepped out from the shadows. "Yes, Mr. Gabriel, sir."

"How old are you now, Tim?"

"Eleven, sir."

"Well, Timothy Grant," Gabriel knelt down and held out the sword, "this is for you."

"Um . . . what?"

"Thanks for the help."

"But . . ." the boy stepped forward, eager to take the precious weapon, but clearly unsure if he should. "But I didn't help."

Gabriel smiled. "But you tried. And more so, you survived, which means you'll live to try again. And next time, you'll have this to help."

"But . . ." Tim paused again. "It's his." He looked at the unconscious soldier.

"Not anymore. Not after he hit you. He lost the right to it."

Tim took the weapon by the hilt—his muscles quivering under its weight—and looked at it with awe. "It's not a toy, Tim. Learn how to use it. Find a teacher, practice every day, and only use it for good."

A baritone voice from behind them said, "Those are expensive, you know."

Gabriel and Tim spun around to see two more soldiers approaching. Believing the fight wasn't over, Tim dashed back into the shadows of the alley with his new sword.

The front man had dark skin, and his head was shaved along the sides. Gabriel recognized him as Mike Church. Like the other soldiers, Church wore a standard army uniform made up of an earthy green shirt with brown trim, brown pants, and a black beret with a maroon band and a dogwood leaf pin on it. He also wore numerous decorations, including golden epaulettes, ribbons, shoulder cords, and even a red cape. Most notable was a golden oak leaf brooch at his collar, meaning he'd been promoted to the commander.

To Church's right stood a tower of a man, with girth to match. He had short brown hair, a thick red beard, and dense eyebrows. On the collar of his uniform were the hickory leaf pins of a lieutenant and a helicopter seed pin, indicating he was a pilot. Like the other soldiers, he wore his sword strapped to his back, but it was not a standard-issue weapon. He had a large broadsword, ornamented with a pommel in the shape of a pinecone. He would be an imposing person to encounter in a dark alley, if not for the warm grin on his face. Gabriel knew him too. He was Jack's brother, Frank.

"You can't just go giving away my soldiers' weapons like they're trinkets," said Church, though his tone implied he didn't really care.

Gabriel wasn't startled by their approach. He sheathed his own sword and answered, "He didn't deserve it, and I think Idoless can afford the loss."

"Yes, I suppose it can," Church agreed. A wide, toothy grin broke out on the commander's face. He beamed as he put out his hand. "It's good to see you again."

Gabriel shook the commander's hand and smiled, but not as effusively. "So, what's going on?"

"We need your help," Church answered.

"So I'm not under arrest?"

"After all these years, you think we'd come after you now?"

Gabriel raised his eyebrows in doubt, but Mike reassured him, "You aren't in any kind of trouble."

"Fine. Let's go talk."

Gabriel led Mike and Frank into the forest that lined Oakmoor. After about ten minutes of walking in silence, they arrived at a tiny log cabin near the cove. The cabin didn't have electricity, and Gabriel apologized for the lack of light. "I just need a minute to build a fire."

Mike smiled and said, "Allow me." He raised his hands, and a fire blazed to life in the fireplace and all the candles lit up, giving the room a warm, comfortable glow.

Gabriel was impressed. "You're a wizard now?"

"Oh, no, nothing like my father. Just a few parlor tricks, mostly stuff with fire. I've done my best to master it, because you never know when it might come in handy." Mike made a gesture at the light in the room.

Now that it was lit, the cabin's interior wasn't much to see. A bed and a trunk filled one corner. Above the bed hung three drawings with creases from where they'd been folded at one time. A ratty recliner faced the fireplace, and a small dinner table with a single chair next to a basin and counter acted as a makeshift kitchen.

Eyeing the oak leaf brooch on Mike's collar, Gabriel said, "So, you're the commander now."

"Yes, well, someone had to be. When Ryan Marks retired, the king asked, and I accepted." He paused like he was trying to think of small talk. "So . . . 'Gabriel'?"

A gruff voice answered, "It's his middle name, sir." It was Frank, standing at attention in the background, waiting patiently.

Mike looked back. "Ah, what was I thinking? Go ahead, Lieutenant. I'm sure you've been looking forward to this moment more than anyone."

Frank broke attention and stepped forward. "Hey, Jack."

"Hey, Frank." Jack smiled back warmly.

They looked at each other for a bit, neither knowing what to say.

Commander Church broke the silence with laughter. "I was expecting a better reunion than that. Lieutenant, how long has it been since you've seen your brother?"

His eyes on Jack, Frank answered, "Five years, give or take a month, sir."

Jack Waramond exhaled and said to his brother. "Frank, you know I'm thrilled to see you. But let's face it. This . . . it's just weird. What's going on?"

Frank answered, "Jack, something big is going down, and we need your help. The king needs your help."

Jack sat on the trunk in front of his bed and asked, "What is it?"

Frank shrugged helplessly. "Oh, I don't know."

"That big, huh?" Jack rolled his eyes.

"Forgive your brother, Jack. I brought him along because you haven't seen each other in so long." Jack shot him a look of disbelief. Church bowed his head and put up his hands. "*And,* because I thought he'd be the most suited to appeal to you."

"That still didn't answer my question," Jack persisted.

"No, and Frank couldn't answer, because he's not privy to all the information. But he's a good soldier, and trusts those of us in command when we say . . . it's important."

"Well, as I think everyone knows, I'm not like him. I'm not a good soldier."

"You were the best, Jack," said Frank earnestly.

Jack put up a hand, "Yeah, yeah. You know what I mean." He looked at the two men. "When I first saw you, I really did think you'd come to arrest me. I assumed Frank was along so I'd go quietly."

"No, Jack. After what happened, King Hawthorn had ordered to leave you be," explained Church. "And we were going to. But we didn't foresee what was coming. So, we're here to get you to come back."

Jack stood up. "Come back?"

Neither Mike nor Frank responded, they just peered back at him with the most serious of expressions.

Almost laughing, Jack said, "You can't be serious."

Mike turned and said, "Frank, I'd like to talk to Jack alone for a minute."

A soldier once again, Frank stiffened and saluted, "Yes, sir," then left the house.

Jack watched his brother leave, wanting to follow. And he would have, except he knew Frank would've marched him right back in to take care of business before they did any catching up.

Jack turned to Mike and asked, "So?"

"I'm sure you remember the Death's Province mission?"

"Of course. We lost a lot of good men there."

"Modest," Mike responded. "I believe we lost all our men on that mission. All but one."

"They were a bunch of barely trained kids, Mike. Get on with it."

Dropping all pretense, Mike said, "You're the only man who's been to Death's Province and lived."

Jack crossed his arms. "Yeah. I was lucky to get out. What of it?"

"We need to go back in."

Jack stared at Mike in disbelief. Church let him process the information. Jack began pacing, stopping for moments, then resuming again. Finally, he stopped and murmured, "You know they call it Death's Province for a reason, right? Why would you willingly go into that place? There's nothing there but death."

"Death . . . and a very valuable artifact."

Jack sneered, "This is about treasure?"

"Do you really think I would come all this way to get you and go into that place, for mere treasure?"

"Well then, what?" asked Jack. "Because I really can't fathom why anyone would ever willingly go in there again. There's nothing that important."

"What about someone?"

"What?"

"Is there some*one* important enough to you that you'd take on such a mission? Maybe Frank, or . . . ?" Mike trailed off and raised an eyebrow at Jack.

Jack took a step back. "Don't. Don't you bring her into this."

"I'm not. She's already in it," explained Church, "thanks to her father."

That meant this had something to do with Hershel Nickolie.

It happened often enough: a monarch, official, or—in Hershel's case—a dignitary, got in a spat with someone from a different nation. Threats were made, attacks waged, and battles fought. And for a short time, everyone would wonder if the five nations of Terra Firma would become four. But in the end, level heads prevailed, peace was made, and people got on with their lives.

But Hershel was one of the level heads, hardly the type to start a war. He was an ambassador first and foremost, and he prized peaceful resolutions. It was one of the main reasons his daughter had such a passion for making the world a better place. Things didn't add up. Jack looked at Church with confusion.

Mike said, "Look, I'm not going to try and blow smoke in your eyes and trick you. You're too smart for that. And I know I can't wave the flag to inspire you, like I could with your brother. I'm not going to lie—we need you, and I would do just about anything to get you back. And that includes using Eliza." He sighed, and his shoulders sagged with the weight of regret. "I believe you told me you made a vow to keep her safe."

"Yeah, I made that vow. Among others. And we both see how well that's turned out." Jack exhaled. "Mike, you can't use something you don't have. Eliza is perfectly safe where she is."

"Is she?" Mike tossed a folder on the dining table.

Jack picked it up and looked inside. It contained a stack of photos. He asked, "What is this?"

"Keep looking."

Jack sifted through the pictures. They showed a rugged tract of land where everything had been burned down, smashed, and destroyed. He began to ask again, "What does this have to do with . . . ?" but Mike just eyed the pictures, suggesting Jack keep looking before asking anything else. When he got to the end of the stack, Jack understood. "This . . . this isn't . . . ?" He now recognized where the photos had been taken. One showed a sheer rock face inscribed with a symbol that matched the tattoo on Jack's right hand.

He knew the place well. It was where he had spent the best days of his life.

"Who . . . ? What happened?" Then he flipped to the last and worst photo of them all. It was of a tree, nearly unrecognizable now. Squinting, Jack could just make out a heart carved in its flank.

Mike clenched his fists. "Attacking the island was a message. They will use anything to get to Hershel, even his daughter. Something is coming, Jack, and we need to be prepared."

"Prepared for what?" Then the questions began flooding in, "What could Hershel have done? Who could he have pissed off so badly? How would they even know about the island?"

Church explained, "Ambassador Nickolie stumbled on some information about something located inside of Death's Province, and it has upset . . . some very important people."

Jack closed his eyes, trying to concentrate. "And what exactly is it we . . . you, want to get? What did Hershel discover?"

Mike had another folder in hand, and he pulled out some of its contents. "We've been gathering intel for some time. Our best researchers have studied ancient texts and records, and it looks like it's an item of great power. I hesitate to use the term, but the best word we have for it right now is . . . well, we think it's a weapon."

"What do you mean? You aren't talking about something magical, are you? Do you know how bad an idea that is? With your father . . . you've never heard about that stuff corrupting? And if this . . . *thing* is so powerful . . ." He scratched the back of his head and looked over the files, sighing. "I don't know, maybe it's best if it's left where it is. Death's Province has to be the best protection it could possibly have. Besides, how do you even plan on getting in? Last time, we made it in because of some lucky information. That kind of thing doesn't come along every day."

"Actually, we got lucky again. There's someone who knows where the doorway currently is. We just need to find him before it moves again." Mike closed the file so Jack would look at him. "I understand your fears, Jack. But we know that," he stopped for a beat, then spoke carefully, "another group . . . is also trying to get the weapon. We don't want them to get to it first. I'd much rather," he stopped again and looked Jack over, as if he were trying to decide, just now, if he could be trusted. After a moment of consideration, he finished: "I'd like to make sure the right people have control of this power."

"I've seen power corrupt the best of people," said Jack skeptically. "Who is it that we don't want getting it?"

Mike shrugged and said, "That's classified."

Jack threw the file back at Mike in disgust. "You want me to go back in there, but you won't give me all the information? Just get out of here!"

"Jack, please—"

"Tell Frank it was good to see him again, and now *he* knows where to find me." Jack stormed over to the recliner in front of the fireplace and threw himself into it.

Mike gathered up the papers and files. "Jack, I'm just trying to do the right thing."

"Good-bye, Mike."

"You have to underst—"

"I said *good-bye*."

The silence lasted for so long Jack thought that somehow, in his anger, he'd missed hearing Mike leave. But then Mike tossed the photos in his lap. "You can keep those. They're just copies." Then Church walked to the doorway and left.

Jack glared at the pictures. On top of the pile were the ones he'd recognized, placed there on purpose, he was sure. He knew he was being played, and he didn't want Church's scheme to work. *Damn you, Church,* Jack thought, as his eyes floated over the images. He saw the design etched in the rock and then looked down at his hand, only a part of the tattoo showing, the rest covered by his glove. Jack pulled it off, looked at his tattoo in full, and began to feel an old pain in his heart.

Jack stood up, grabbed the photos, and chucked them into the flames. He watched the photo of the rock curl and then crumble to ash under the logs.

He cursed himself and ran to the door, flinging it open to chase after Mike and Frank—but they were standing just outside, waiting for him. Mike said, "I'm sorry, Jack, I really am. I'll have Frank collect you in the morning."

They turned and left, though Frank glanced back with an apologetic look in his eyes. Jack just closed the door.

Chapter Two
Return of the Prodigal Son

At dawn the following morning, Frank came to get Jack. He arrived earlier than expected, so Jack brewed a pot of coffee as he packed his few belongings. "You really don't have much, do you?" asked Frank as he looked down at Jack's single bag.

Not looking up, Jack replied, "I've never really needed much."

Frank continued to drink his coffee in silence while he looked over his brother's dwelling. "How much of this stuff did you make yourself?"

"Um," Jack looked around the room, "well, I didn't make those." He pointed to the recliner and trunk.

"But the rest . . . ?"

"Yes. It was all trial and error," Jack smirked. "But it was all right. Gave me lots of extra firewood."

"And you always thought you didn't have an artistic bone in your body," Frank chuckled as he admired the craftsmanship.

"Not like you," Jack said and pointed to the drawings tacked to the wall.

Frank felt blood rush to his face. "Oh, Jack . . . you don't have to keep those."

"No. But I want to."

"Yeah, but I did them so long ago, they aren't very good. I can't believe you still have them."

In his youth, Frank had often been teased for his interest in art. While most of the other boys were outside playing sports, Frank was content to be sitting with a sketchbook. The castle maids blamed his ample weight on this lack of activity, and often shared their theory with his mother, Hazel, a fellow maid. But she defended Frank and said she loved him no matter what his size. And she told Frank she knew he wasn't heavy due to laziness; his father had sported the same large frame, and it hadn't stopped him from becoming a major in the army, destined for greater things if he hadn't died.

Hazel knew Frank was courageous and strong when he needed to be. She said so every time she gave him fighting lessons. Though it was against the law for women to practice the martial arts in Idoless, Hazel was a master. Frank and his brother didn't know how she knew what she did. "A story for another time," she would answer when they asked, but she taught them what she knew in secret.

Five years younger, Jack had watched Frank train until he was old enough to join in. Those years of observation, combined with natural talent, allowed Jack to pick up the skills quickly. Their mother taught them fighting techniques unlike anything they learned in the army, which gave them an advantage over their peers and forged a special bond between them.

Jack threw their coffee cups in the basin, saying he'd take care of them when he got back. So, they put out the fire and left.

As they began their trek out of the forest, morning dew still hung on the leaves and a briskness filled the air, both of which would soon be abolished as the sun rose in the sky.

Jack told Frank he needed to make a stop before leaving and led them to a home on the edge of town. Frank stayed back to give his brother privacy as Jack went up to knock on the door.

A thin, older man with scratched spectacles answered the door. Jack spoke with him for a minute, then a younger woman with brown hair joined them. As soon as she saw Jack, she hugged him. Jack gestured to Frank to join them and said, "Phil, Maria, this is my brother, Frank. Frank, this is Philip Campbell and his wife, Maria Grant."

Philip shook Frank's hand, but Maria gave him a hug and said, "Your brother is an amazing man."

"Well . . . yes," Frank began. "That's why King Hawthorn needs him."

Philip gasped, "The king? Gabe, you didn't mention anything about the king!"

"Yeah, well . . ." Jack didn't say more.

"Still our man of mystery, eh?"

Maria then asked them to wait, ran off, and returned with a gift: a leather cord strung with multicolored beads held at the center by knots on either side. Jack bent down so Maria could loop the cord over his head. She kissed his forehead as she spoke so softly to him, "This town owes you a great debt. Thank you. And be safe."

As the brothers left, they passed a young boy with a swollen eye, up in a tree, clutching his new Idolessian army sword. Walking past, Jack gave him a wave and said, "It's up to you to protect Oakmoor while I'm away, Tim."

Eyeing Frank, Tim replied, "He's your brother? He doesn't look like he could be."

Jack answered simply, "I was adopted."

As they walked to the transport vehicle, Jack told Frank about his years in Oakmoor, explaining that before he'd arrived, pirates used to visit the town regularly. Rather than pillage the town broke, they'd extorted money and goods, leaving enough to ensure there would always be new bounty when they returned.

"Pretty advanced thinking for pirates," said Frank.

"I guess, as far as banditry goes. To me, it was just more proof that, in general, people suck."

"I suppose. I take it you rescued the town?"

Frank noticed Jack thoughtfully touching his leather vest as he looked back and sighed, "I hope they'll be all right. It's been a while since we've seen any pirates, but without me here . . . They don't really have any warriors."

"I'm sure they'll be fine." They walked in silence for a minute or so before Frank said, "You know, I've missed you, bro."

Jack gave his brother a pat on the shoulder and replied, "I've missed you too, Frank."

The brothers joined the rest of the soldiers at the transport vessel that would take them back to the capital. There was a hiss of the propulsion systems coming online as they began to climb aboard, but Jack suddenly stopped.

Frank asked, "What?"

"I just thought of something."

"What?"

"Jas . . . the prince."

Frank understood. "Oh, don't worry about that. Commander Church took care of it. Prince Hawthorn is at a diplomatic conference with the new king of Mechina. He'll be gone for well over a month."

Frank could see that relieved Jack and the brothers hopped aboard. It wasn't exactly spacious, but military vehicles like this rarely were.

"Are these guys yours?" Jack nodded at the twelve soldiers who'd been sent to collect him. Most of them were now sporting black eyes, split lips, and other bruises from last night's fight.

Frank smiled, "Yeah. They're a little cocky, so I figured rounding you up would be a nice lesson in humility."

"Careful. You're sounding like Captain Nelson from the academy," chuckled Jack. "They did pretty well. I could tell you trained them. Keep it up and you could be a head trainer like your old man was." As the airship lifted off the ground Jack noticed, "Hey, where's Mike?"

"Oh, he left last night right after we talked with you," Frank explained. "He's become quite important. He was the only clear choice to become commander when Marks retired."

"What about you?"

Frank laughed.

"Don't even, Frank. You're a fantastic leader." He looked at Frank's hickory leaf pins and said, "I'd have thought you'd be wearing the sassafras by now."

"Me, a captain? Naw, I'm still only a lieutenant."

"I was only a lieutenant, and considered for commander, so why not you?"

"Look, I know I'm a good trainer—a better pilot—but I don't think being commander is ever going to be in my future. Enough about me though," said Frank. "Besides building log cabins, crafting furniture, and saving towns from pirates, how've you been?"

Jack gave a weak smile. "Nothing else to tell, really. I've been . . . I guess the best way to say it is . . . I've . . . I've been on a quest for inner peace."

"And?"

"And what?"

"Did you find it?"

Jack looked at Frank then said, "I found a purpose."

"But . . . not the peace you were looking for?"

Jack just turned and looked out the window. The sun was now full in the sky, its golden brilliance lighting the land beneath them. Jack never answered the question, which was itself an answer of sorts. And the brothers sat in silence for the rest of the ride.

They arrived at Juniper City a few hours later. Towering over the city, with its parapets stretching to the sky, Castle Idoless appeared to grow out of a shoreline cliff along the largest body of water on the continent of Terra Firma: Lake Idoless.

As they got closer, Jack scanned the approaching fortress. He noticed some improvements but had the feeling that nothing significant had changed. It was the same old castle he knew and, though he'd never admit it, adored.

As the airship landed, Jack began searching the surrounding field, wondering if he even wanted to see . . . her. He felt eyes on him and turned to see Frank smirking.

Jack asked, "What?"

Frank just shook his head.

Jack felt exposed. Was he that obvious?

A line of soldiers stood at attention to receive them, and at the entrance a man waited to escort them. He was a major with salt-and-pepper hair and a bushy walrus mustache that couldn't distract from his missing ear. He smiled and said, "Greetings, Mr. Waramond. Welcome back, Lieutenant." He nodded at Frank, but then suddenly threw a punch at him. Jack began to react, but Frank was ready. The two exchanged a series of punches and kicks that ended as quickly as it began. They smiled and shook hands.

"I almost had you that time," claimed the major.

"No you didn't . . . sir," Frank said with a wink.

"No, I guess not." Major Smith smirked. "Tried to catch you off guard. Maybe next time I'll use some of those new moves you showed me."

Frank gave a nervous glance, then in a hushed tone said, "Now, Larry, you know I only share those moves with a select few."

"I know, I know," said Larry.

"You're showing improvement though. I can tell you've been practicing. Those last kicks were really good. We can start moving on to the next form soon. And if you think those last moves were special, just wait till you see what's next!"

"I look forward to it." Major Smith bowed to Frank like a student does to his sensei. He then resumed his courtly manner and gestured to the doors, "Please, gentlemen, follow me."

Jack raised an inquisitive eyebrow at his brother. With a grin, Frank shrugged and motioned that they should follow the major. Then in low tones, he explained that while he taught advanced training classes for soldiers like the ones who tried to collect Jack in Oakmoor, there were some, like Major Smith, who took private lessons on the side. He whispered to Jack, "Larry is one of my best students. He doesn't get to go on assignments anymore since he lost his ear. But I think he likes to feel like he could still kick some ass if needed."

As they followed Smith through familiar staircases and halls, Jack noticed more guards than he remembered, as well as extra security cameras sprinkled throughout the halls, and all the doors had locking security panels by them now. But the security upgrades didn't distract Jack for long. He couldn't ignore that he was filled with an excitement so powerful it hurt. He kept glancing down hallways and through open doors, both hoping and fearing to see Eliza. Anytime they passed someone new, Jack felt butterflies in his stomach until he confirmed who it was—or wasn't.

When they reached the throne room, the large double doors were closed. Major Smith went in to announce their arrival. As the doors opened to let them in, Jack could hear shouting.

"How does he keep getting past you all? How can we possibly—"

The doors closed.

Jack had recognized the voice. "Was that Vergo?"

Frank scowled. "Yeah. He's a captain now."

"What was he going on about? Who keeps getting past what?"

Frank explained, "We've been having trouble with a thief. Fancies himself a Robin Hood type—you know, stealing from the rich and giving to the poor. Calls himself—"

"The Cardinal."

Frank looked stunned. "How did you know?"

"Seriously? The Cardinal's been around for ages. He's like, a legend." Jack looked for some kind of recollection in his brother's eyes. "There was even someone doing the same thing when we were kids. Don't you remember?"

Frank scratched his beard. "I . . . I don't. I feel like I should. It seems familiar, now that you mention it." He shook his head, mad at his faulty memory. "I'm sure you've noticed some of the improvements to security. But it seems that no matter what enhancements are made, he still slips by them. The thing is, the rich he's stealing from are . . . well, us. He's pilfering directly from the castle. You and I both know the castle can afford it, but it's gone too far. He's taken . . . well, a lot."

Jack made a noncommittal sound. Even though the Cardinal was generally known as a thief, he had always idolized the bandit.

Frank continued, "I'd be more annoyed if it wasn't for the fact that Vergo was put in charge of catching the Cardinal. He's no closer to apprehending him today than the day he was assigned the task." Frank tried to suppress a laugh. "And since Vergo was put in charge, the Cardinal has taken to leaving messages, to make sure we know when he was here."

Frank couldn't contain it and released a single, hearty guffaw. Jack couldn't help it and laughed too, which seemed to give Frank permission to laugh even more. When the brothers realized where they were, they composed themselves, but just then the sounds of Vergo's shouting grew loud enough to hear through the heavy doors ("And another thing!") causing a second volley of laughter from the brothers.

As they regained themselves again, Jack said, "It's got to be someone on the inside. Surely Vergo realizes that. There's no way, even before all the security upgrades, for it not to be."

"For a short time, he thought it was you." Frank explained, "It was Vergo who found you in Oakmoor in the first place. King Hawthorn was very firm about just letting you be, but Vergo was so certain you were responsible, he did a search anyway. And when the king found out, he let Vergo have it." Frank put his hands in the air like a frame for his mind's eye, "Oh, Jack, you should have seen it. It was beautiful. But then they knew where you were and well, here we are today."

The subject of Jack's disappearance sobered them. Frank turned to his brother and said, "You know, I still have the note you wrote me the night you left."

"Frank, I—"

Suddenly Major Smith opened the doors and motioned for them to enter while Vergo was finishing, ". . . and I assure you, Your Majesty, I *will* capture this bandit!"

King Hawthorn replied from his throne, "You'd better, Captain. Dismissed."

Vergo bowed, turned, and stormed down the aisle, followed by the team of soldiers he'd been upbraiding in front of the king. Jack thought Argus Vergo hadn't changed much; he had the same sharp, angular features and long blond hair that he kept pulled back into a tight ponytail. Vergo stopped for half a second when he realized Jack was there, then blew past with a sneer plastered on his face.

In the wake of Vergo's departure, the Waramond brothers bowed to King Hawthorn. He had a tan complexion, similar to Jack's, and sported a well-trimmed chin curtain beard with shoulder-length gray hair. He was tall, thick, and muscular for man of his age, though Jack noticed his hair looked lighter and wrinkles seemed deeper than he remembered. The king wore a polished golden crown adorned with jewels centered on the national emblem of Idoless, the dogwood leaf.

When he noticed Jack, the king's entire demeanor transformed. He all but leaped from his throne, beaming, "Jack! Are you truly standing before me? What has it been—three, four years since I last saw you?"

"Um, five actually."

"By the gods, has it been that long? Time flies when ruling a nation." The king embraced Jack warmly. "I've truly missed you, Jack."

"And I you, King Hawthorn," Jack said sheepishly.

Jack *had* missed him. King Hawthorn had always treated him like another son, which meant a lot to Jack, since he didn't have a father of his own. Frank's birth father, Jacob Karr, had died before Jack was born. And though Jacob's brother, Joseph, was like a father to Frank, he never seemed to treat Jack like true family.

The king looked around the room as a smile spread across his face. "This calls for a feast!"

Jack winced. "Oh, please, no, I—"

"I won't hear of it. The Prodigal Son has returned, and I want to celebrate!" There was a sound from somewhere in the room—a cough, maybe a gasp, distracting everyone but the king. "It's done, then."

Jack took a breath to protest, but Frank slapped his back and said, "Jack is honored, Your Majesty, truly."

The king smiled mischievously and said, "No, he isn't." Jack returned the grin, knowing that the king understood him. "But I'm in the mood for a feast, and Jack's return seems like a good reason." King Hawthorn returned to his throne and sat down. "Now, as you know, I wasn't here the night you were hurt."

Jack looked up. "Hurt?"

Frank and several others in the room shifted uncomfortably. The king picked up on the tension. "And apparently the subject is still a little tender. I know better than anyone to just leave it alone. Jack, we'll talk at the banquet."

Jack was stunned. But before he even knew what had happened, Frank had thanked the king for his time and ushered Jack out of the room.

Once they were back on the other side of the throne room doors Jack demanded, "What was that? What was he talking about, 'the night you were hurt'?"

Frank looked uncomfortable. "Look, Jack, no one knows exactly what happened that night. Jason was raving about you trying to murder him, and we had to tell the king . . . something, so . . ."

"You lied to him."

Frank gave his brother a determined stare and said, "Tell you what, you want to set him straight? Let's go back in there right now and you can tell him exactly what happened. I know *I'd* love to hear it."

"Excuse me, I don't mean to interrupt," said a voice from behind.

Jack and Frank turned to see a man whose face was young but tired. His light brown hair hung like curtains over his eyes. He wore priestly robes of white with gold trim and carried a staff with a glass orb at the top.

"Albert!" exclaimed Jack.

"He's a kirk now," said Frank.

"Kirk? You made it!" Jack shook Albert's hand. Then he marveled, "Five more years, and you *still* look the same age."

Albert proceeded, "Jack, may I ask you something? The king just referred to you as 'the Prodigal Son.'"

"Um, yeah?"

"Well . . . what does that mean to you?"

What a weird question. It had been years since Jack had seen Albert Larson, and this seemed an odd greeting. "Oh, um, I'm not sure. I mean, it's just an old saying, isn't it?"

"Indeed, it is."

An uncomfortable silence followed as Jack and Frank waited for the kirk to elaborate. But Albert said, "Indeed," again and just walked away, deep in thought.

"Well, that was . . . odd," Jack noted.

"He's been like that lately," said Frank. "I'm not sure what happened. He worked so long and hard to become a kirk. Despite his . . . *condition,* he finally earned the title. And about a week later, he started acting . . . well, like that. He got better for a bit, but recently it's gotten worse."

They discussed Albert a little longer, but in time the kirk and the subject of Jack's disappearance was forgotten, and the conversation shifted to what was new in the castle. Frank steered Jack down the halls, pointing out the various improvements, and any soldier he had trained in his official classes or private ones; there were quite a few. He then led Jack toward the most significant change. "Come on, I'll show you the paddocks."

"Paddocks? What kind of paddocks?" Jack asked. "You don't mean . . .? From Phlogiston?" Frank gave him a knowing grin. "Since when?"

"Since last year. But it's all still in the trial stages. Obviously, it's very new to us, so it's not like there'll be much worth seeing, but still . . ."

Jack probed, "How many breeds did they get?"

"Just a handful."

"Unicorns?"

"Oh, yeah. But don't be too impressed—they're basically just extremely high-end horses."

"Wait, you wouldn't be telling me this if . . . no." Jack eyed his brother and demanded, "Dragons?" Frank's great beard couldn't hide his grin. "Frank! How long have we . . . has the army been trying to work out a deal with Phlogiston so it could get tamed dragons?"

Frank bellowed a laugh so loud it turned heads. "I know! Obviously, they didn't sell us many. Just four: a male and three females. But over time, they'll turn into more. They also sold us two dozen unicorns, a couple of griffins—who've already had a litter—and a sphinx." Frank puffed up proudly, "With my flying experience, I was even put on the committee that decides who will be most suited to ride each of the creatures. You know, if you stayed, I might . . . Jack?"

But Jack wasn't beside him anymore. He'd stopped several paces back and now stood motionless, gazing down the hall leading to the treasury.

He'd been talking to his brother about . . . something, he couldn't remember what, because it finally happened.

He saw her.

Eliza.

Just the sight of her transported him in time. He smelled the beach, felt the sun on his skin, and heard waves crashing on the shore.

Unlike those days on the beach, today Eliza looked entirely regal. Her viridian green gown, made of the finest dupioni silk, had a high neckline and fitted waist that cascaded into graceful folds that trailed behind her. She also wore a massive wig of wavey ombré hair that began as white at the roots and gradually transitioned to a vibrant green as it trailed down her back. Atop it all rested a polished gold crown with a great emerald jewel that marked her as royalty.

On top of her right hand was the only unusual element, a tattoo of a triangle within a circle, within another triangle. Jack knew there was a second tattoo, a band on her left ring finger, though it could barely be seen peeking out from beneath the enormous diamond-studded wedding ring she now wore.

Perched on her shoulder was a creature that resembled a cat. It had a long tail and pointy ears and gray fur that looked like crushed velvet. Unlike a cat, however, this creature had white feathered wings. It wore a permanent scowl, but when Eliza reached up and scratched its chin, it reacted with what could only be described as happiness. "Meh," it mewed with a bored, raspy, but feline sound.

Aside from the tattoo and unusual animal on her shoulder, Eliza looked like the embodiment of style and sophistication.

Nevertheless, in between blinks, Jack saw her as he remembered: the young girl on the beach . . . no royal gown or tiara, just a vibrant tropical flower in her long, straight raven hair, flowing in the wind . . . soft russet skin, kissed from so much time under the sun . . . deep brown eyes taking his measure.

Eliza stood in the treasury's entrance hall, looking at one of the paintings on the wall. *Of course, there's a portrait of her father in this corridor.* Several handmaidens accompanied her, which, when grouped with her dazzling attire, made her look like a bride on her wedding day.

It was a gift to be allowed to gaze upon her uninterrupted for those moments.

He didn't duck away or try to hide; he just stood there and beheld her. After a slight glance to her right, she saw him too. Her face didn't change; she just looked back.

In a shy, cautious tone, Jack said, "Hello."

Eliza answered, "Hi." Her voice was like music to him.

The cat on her shoulder squawked more enthusiastically, "Meh!"

"Hey, Oliver," Jack replied.

"Meh," responded Oliver, content now that he'd been acknowledged.

Jack had spent countless hours and sleepless nights thinking about what he'd say to Eliza if he ever saw her again. He'd dreamed up grand exchanges that brought them back together; or sometimes he got to tell her off perfectly for how she'd wronged him. But now that she was standing before him, he was at a loss for words.

Jack fought with himself, thinking he needed to say something. *Anything.* "So . . ."

"Yeah," she responded.

"You're . . . ?"

"Yeah."

"And you, you look . . ."

"Thanks." There was a pause, and she added, "And you. You're . . ."

"Naw, I . . ."

Jack realized just how much he'd let himself go. He was still lean and muscular, but that was hard to appreciate under the dirty clothes and long, unkempt hair. It made him self-conscious. He pulled some of the locks back behind his ears, not knowing what to say. Eliza didn't either. They just stood there, acting like a couple of shy teenagers on their first date.

"This is just . . . pitiful," said Frank, blank-faced, watching the exchange from a short distance.

Oliver seemed to agree. "Meh," he stated.

Frank's voice snapped Eliza from her daze. "Frank!" She smiled and ran to hug him. He picked her off the ground and spun her around as she giggled. Her maidens shuddered at the sight, not sure how to respond to such inappropriate conduct. Meanwhile, Oliver took flight and circled above them, countering the spin. Once Frank set Eliza back on the ground, the animal resumed its perch upon her shoulder.

Jack felt a twinge of jealousy toward his brother. Frank and Eliza had been close in school, and it appeared they had grown even closer during his absence. Finding her voice, Eliza said, "So . . . Jack, they . . . they got you back."

"Just for one mission."

"Yeah," said Frank, "when the fate of Idoless hangs in the balance, there's only one person we can turn to!" He put his arm around Jack shoulders, "Only the best will do!"

"I have to confess, I didn't think you'd agree," said Eliza. "How did they persuade you?"

Jack wasn't sure if Eliza knew about the island's devastation. And if she did, did she even care? He figured she had to at least know something about her father's involvement, unless Hershel had made a point of keeping her in the dark. Jack tried to read her, but his emotions were clouding his judgment. "It was . . . it was something Mike Church showed me." Jack looked into Eliza's dark eyes. He thought about how everything he was doing now was to ensure her safety, and added, "It just really made me appreciate the importance of the situation."

She shifted her weight and suddenly had a difficult time keeping eye contact. "Well . . . I think that's brilliant. They're lucky to have you."

"They?" asked Jack.

"What?"

"You said 'they.' Don't you mean—"

"We really should get going," Frank interrupted with concern in his voice.

Eliza stiffened and met Jack's eyes. "No, you're right. *We*, the nation and all who stayed, are lucky to have your services." She cleared her throat. "Hopefully this will go quickly, and you can go back to . . . wherever it was you were."

"Oh, it was nice, Eliza," said Frank. "Very nice indeed. Jack, we really need to get going."

"Well, *Princess*," Jack said irreverently, "If there's a problem with me being here, why don't you just say so, and I'll go."

Frank groaned.

"Oh no, come and go as you please," said Eliza. "It's one of the things you're best at."

"What's that supposed to mean?" Jack demanded.

Frank put his hands over his eyes. "Oh, dear." Oliver, too, gave a moan of discomfort as he brought his tail up to cover his eyes.

"Nothing at all. I was just observing that you've mastered the art of leaving." Eliza abandoned propriety, hands on her hips. "I look forward to seeing you demonstrate your mastery again."

"I'm not sure I understand what you're getting at, *Your Highness*," Jack replied. "It sounds like you might be mocking my oath as a soldier. But I have to tell you, I was taught rather harshly that around here, oaths and promises don't mean too much."

"Is that so?" said Eliza between gritted teeth.

"Yes. So, if anyone is a master of leaving, I'd say it was——"

Without warning, Eliza slapped Jack across the face. He stood there, shocked as the sound echoed through the hall.

Eliza adjusted her dress and wig. "Now, if you'll excuse me, I have a number of things to take care of before dinner. Frank, I'll see you later. Good day, *Mr.* Waramond." Without a backward glance, she strode down the hall with her handmaidens in tow. One, a young girl with umber skin and a halo of curly hair whom Jack recognized but couldn't place, kept glancing back at him as they left.

Jack stood there, holding his cheek as he watched Eliza leave. Frank broke the silence, "Well . . . that went better than I thought it would."

"She hits harder than she used to."

12 Years Ago

568 AR

S moke was beginning to fill a number of the ship's passageways. Jack was heading for the bridge, running as fast as he could with the limited view. He came across the captain and a handful of soldiers running in the opposite direction. "Who attacked us?" he asked breathlessly as he joined them.

"We don't know, Your Majesty, but whatever hit us was, wait—you aren't the prince!"

Jack retorted, "How do you think we fooled everyone into thinking we were brothers all these years?" He looked around. "So wait, Jason isn't with you?"

"No, but the ship *is* going down. We need to find him and evacuate."

They arrived on the upper deck, greeted by rain. The sky had turned a sickly green and the clouds were moving fast.

"Just perfect," exhaled the captain. He turned to the crewmen and yelled to be heard over the pounding rain. "You two, come with me. You two, go that way. Make sure people get off the ship and on the other two."

Suddenly a great explosion rocked the water. The Idolessian ship furthest from them had blown up. All that remained was a large burning framework, sinking fast.

Banging his fists on the ship's gunwale the captain growled, "Who is attacking us?"

"That was no torpedo hit," said Jack.

"It doesn't matter—just get the people off the ship," commanded the captain. "The prince is our primary concern. Once he's saf—"

BOOM!

The second ship burst like an overripe melon, and its shattered debris rained down upon them. When it was over, Jack found the captain's lifeless body lying next to him, impaled through the heart by a massive piece of shrapnel.

The crewmen stood there, stupefied.

Jack shouted, "All right, guys, listen up. Hey, you with me?" Dazed, they looked up from the captain's body. "Do as you were ordered! Get the prince to safety and spread the word to abandon ship!"

The soldiers were so shocked they didn't notice Jack was merely one of the academy graduates that the ships were full of, and they spoke to him as if he were a commanding officer. "Off the ship? Where to? The other ships are . . . are—"

"We have lifeboats, right?"

"Yeah, but—"

"No buts. If we stay, we die. If we leave, we at least have a chance." Jack pointed down the passageway, "Get going!"

The crewmen did as they were ordered. Jack ran in the opposite direction, toward the civilian area, hoping the prince was there with Eliza because he knew he would only have time to find one of them.

Jack felt the ship rock in the escalating storm. He figured that if the attacks didn't sink them, the storm would finish the job. Water was already beginning to spill over the side of the ship and onto the deck.

As Jack turned a corner, before him stood a tall, imposing man. The roar of wind and rain made it difficult to hear anything, but Jack shouted to him, "Sir, you need to get off the ship! It's going down. Do you know where the rest of the civilians are?"

The man lazily turned to look at him. At first, he seemed to recognize Jack, but just as quickly, he turned away and said, "You should get off this ship." Jack heard the man clear as a bell, as if the voice were inside his own head.

Jack followed. "Yeah, I know. That's what I was trying to tell you." He noticed how difficult it was to hear even his own voice over the storm, wondering how this man had spoken so clearly.

There was something odd about the man. His long hair and lengthy beard were unaffected by the squalls that tossed the ship around. Jack was slipping and sliding, struggling to stay upright, while this man walked as if he were on a pleasant stroll. "Hey, what's going on here?" said Jack as he grabbed the man by one of his arms.

The stranger's eyes blazed with a light that was so white it appeared blue. As the man turned, a force radiated from his eyes and threw Jack into a bulkhead, which cracked and dented from the force of the blow. The figure bellowed, "You dare lay hands on me, mortal?" He seemed . . . no, he *was* larger than before.

Jack's vision blurred, and his hand felt numb. He looked up at the stranger, who was now pointing a great golden trident squarely at him. "Oh, my . . . you, you're a . . . you're one of them!" Jack bowed. "I didn't realize. Forgive me," he ventured a guess based on the weapon, ". . . Lord Poseidon."

With bored indifference, the god answered, "Call me Aegir." The god must have been satisfied by Jack's submission, considering he didn't kill him, and just continued on his way with near disinterest. He peered into a room but moved on after finding it empty.

Jack had never seen a god up close before. Aegir had looked human at first, but now that Jack recognized him, he noticed that the god's skin glowed with a slight blueish-green cast. Seaweed was entwined in his hair, which flowed like it was underwater. Jack wondered if he was just now noticing this, or maybe Aegir had, only at this moment, *allowed* himself to be seen this way. The experience was utterly surreal.

Jack sprang to his feet. "Please, Lord Aegir. The people of this ship they . . . they need your help."

Once again, Aegir's voice rang clearly in Jack's head. But instead of offering compassion, in a lazy drawl he answered, "I have greater concerns." Jack saw the god's lips moving, but the sounds didn't match the words.

"But, my lord, this ship, it's sinking—you could save it if you wanted!"

Aegir stopped just long enough to look over his shoulder and say, "*If* . . . I wanted." He locked eyes with Jack and said, "Get off the ship or perish with it." Then proceeded down the deck.

"Please! I . . . I'll do anything! Please! Just save this ship!" The god continued to walk effortlessly down the passage, while Jack held onto the bulkhead for support. He called after, "Hey, wait. Hey! Are *you* doing this? Is this your storm? Answer me!"

As if in answer, the ship gave a great heave and Aegir was gone. Jack began to chase after the god, but when he rounded the stern, Jack practically ran into Eliza. She had torn the side of her dress so she could walk more easily and was leading a group of civilians up the passageway. "Stay together," she shouted to them.

Jack asked Eliza, "Have you seen Jason?"

"No. We were right by the explosion when it happened. We've been on the move since."

"Good thing you are. We're evacuating the ship." He started back the way he'd come, "This way."

"We can't, we're still missing someone!"

"What? Eliza, the ship is going down! We need to get you off it, now!"

Eliza paused for a moment then turned to the group. "See that passageway? Follow it and you'll get to the lifeboats."

One of the others began, "But what about—?"

"I'll find her," said Eliza.

Jack sighed, "You're not finding anyone, Eliza. The ship is sinking!"

Ignoring Jack, Eliza yelled at the group, "You heard him, get going!"

One of the women struggled to walk in her dress, so Eliza grabbed a bit of shrapnel from the ground and slashed the side seam of the woman's dress as she had done to her own. The woman looked scandalized but walked freely now. After the group passed, Eliza turned to head back into the ship, but Jack grabbed her by the wrist. "Eliza, no!"

"Jack! Let me go." When he didn't, she swung a fist into his stomach. He doubled over but refused to let go. Instead, he pulled her arm and hoisted her up over his shoulders. "Hey! Put me down!"

"We're getting off this ship. Now."

Eliza writhed against Jack as he attempted to cross the rain-soaked deck. The churning waters heaved the ship up at an impossible angle, and Jack fell to the ground. He twisted so he'd break her fall, and she landed on top of him. Eliza gave a roar and slammed her palms across Jack's chest before picking herself up. "Dammit, Jack!"

She began to make her way back, but Jack chased after her. "Eliza, I said—"

"Ugh, save someone who needs saving, Jack!"

"That's what I'm trying to do!"

Eliza clutched Jack's uniform. "Listen. It's Emily that's missing. Her . . . her parents were killed. We were separated by the blast, and I've been trying to get to her, but all the routes are blocked."

Emily was only nine years old. Her family had joined the cruise as guests of Eliza's father, since he couldn't be there himself. Jack had warned them not to come, but Eliza had talked them into it. "Eliza, how do you even know—?"

"I saw her, Jack. On the other side of the rubble, I saw her moving. She's alive, and *I am not leaving without her.* She and her family came on this cruise because of me. And now, they . . ." Eliza couldn't finish.

"I'll make you a deal. We both look for her, for the next . . . five minutes."

"Fine," she said, though he could tell she was not really listening.

"But," said Jack, demanding her attention. "You go this way." He pointed up the passageway that led toward the lifeboats.

Eliza looked disgusted, "No."

"I," he emphasized, "will go back that way." He pointed down the passageway Eliza had wanted to search. She looked down the passageway, considering the proposition but didn't answer, so he reasoned, "I don't even have to make this offer, Eliza. I could just knock you out and carry you to a lifeboat now!"

Eliza shot him a look of defiance then said, "Fine!" And without so much as a good-bye, she spun around and began her search.

Watching her leave, Jack muttered, "You're amazing."

CHAPTER THREE

A LACK OF INNER PEACE

Jack's mood sank after his less-than-ideal reunion with Eliza, and the stares and whispers from castle personnel weren't helping. Frank suggested he could get cleaned up for the feast as a way to remove himself from the line of gossip, and Jack agreed.

Frank's rank as lieutenant offered the perk of living in the castle. It was a step up from the barracks, offering a semblance of privacy. As he walked into Frank's modest stone room with a single window, Jack saw a cot had already been rolled in for his use. "You can put your stuff in there," Frank said, pointing at a small wardrobe.

Jack started unpacking his bag. When he opened the wardrobe to put away his things, he smiled to see Frank's box of pencils, paints, and brushes on top of a tidy stack of sketchbooks and canvases.

Frank asked, "Ready to get cleaned up?"

Jack nodded, and they headed to the showers. The best part of being a ranking officer was the private showering facility—not the large communal showers that privates, corporals, and sergeants had to endure.

A young woman dressed in a maid's uniform was stationed outside the shower facility, and she offered to wash Jack's clothes. The sight of the maid's uniform brought Jack a twinge of pain as memories of his mother surfaced, but he agreed to let her launder his clothes anyway.

Jack didn't want to admit it, but the shower felt good. While part of him preferred looking like an outcast, it felt great to shed the dirt and grime. He thought about how he'd be seeing Eliza again at the party and washed a second time, then he shaved for the first time in weeks. When he got out, Jack found a uniform waiting for him to wear until his clothes were ready. He turned it down, preferring to wait with just a towel wrapped around his waist. The steam was still rolling off his shoulders as the maids scurried to get the laundering done, though a couple of the younger ladies didn't seem to be in as much of a hurry.

Now clean, his shirt was a more vibrant shade of blue and his leather vest no longer held its stiff shape after months on his shoulders. The maids had even cleaned up his fingerless gloves and cleaned his boots. The shower, shave, and fresh clothes made him almost unrecognizable. He even pulled his hair back into a ponytail, though he couldn't help but roll up his sleeves the way he liked.

Jack began to hook the scabbard of his sword to his belt when he noticed Frank looking at him with a worried expression and asked "Surely, you don't plan on wearing a weapon to the feast? And you should unroll your sleeves."

Jack had grown accustomed to being accountable only to himself the past five years, and reasoned, "I always carry my sword. And I like my sleeves this way."

"You don't think it would be, I don't know, kinda rude to arrive armed to a feast in your honor? Seriously," said Frank, "why would you need it in the castle?"

In the end Frank won; the sword was left behind, and Jack's sleeves were unrolled.

From the tall windows in the castle's main hall, Jack caught a glimpse of the setting sun. Servants were already lighting the hundreds of candles, providing a warmer ambience. Groups of guests congregated around tables laden with roasted joints of lamb, steak and kidney pies, freshly baked bread, and tankards of ale. Jack had forgotten how quickly a feast could be put together at the castle, and he was surprised at the number of guests, given the short notice. *I suppose if the king calls for a party, you go to the party.*

The king's feast made the parties back in Oakmoor pale in comparison. Still, he preferred Oakmoor's celebrations, if only for the music. Music was rare in mainstream Idoless, but Jack had found that wasn't the case in the outer regions. There, people often brought out their instruments and sometimes even sang at parties. The only background music at the king's feast was the low murmur of people chatting.

Most of the guests didn't even know why they were celebrating, which was fine with Jack. He stayed close to Frank, who was better at small talk and handled most of the conversations. As the guest of honor, Jack tried to put on a pleasant face, but it wasn't easy. All he saw were a bunch of phonies, lavishly attired in robes, gowns, jewelry, makeup and wigs. They were only out to impress the king and each other, and Jack had no interest in reciprocating their false pretenses.

He rolled his sleeves back up.

Scanning the room, Jack finally encountered one welcome face. "Hi, Albert!"

"Hello, Jack. Enjoying the party?" asked the kirk.

"Umm . . . well . . ."

Albert smiled. "Me neither. I've never been particularly interested in events like this."

Frank joined in, "You're looking more like yourself, Kirk Larson."

"Honestly, Franklin, how many times do I have to tell you? Just call me Albert. And yes, I *am* feeling better, thank you. I've . . . well, I've had a lot on my mind lately."

Jack said, "You've been working toward becoming a kirk for as long as I've known you, Albert. Now that you've finally made it, I'd have thought you'd be able to, I don't know . . . relax a little?"

Albert sighed. "I suppose I should try."

Jack asked, "So, did you ever figure out what was bothering you about that 'Prodigal Son' thing?"

Albert's smile faded. "I'm afraid that was only one piece, a very small piece, of a much larger puzzle."

Frank asked, "Is there anything we can do to help?"

The smile returned to Albert's face as he put a hand on each of the brothers' shoulders. "Hazel would be so proud of you two. Thank you, but unfortunately, this is something I have to figure out by myself . . . at least at this point."

Frank said, "Well, the offer stands."

Jack nodded in agreement, then took a shot at small talk and asked, "So . . . um, now that you're a kirk, do you see the gods all the time?"

Again, the smile on Albert's face dropped, but this time his expression held a darkness about it. "Not as often as you'd think."

Jack exchanged a look with his brother, who tried to move the conversation along, "I . . . I've seen a couple. Poseidon's been to Idoless several times."

"He likes to be called Aegir," said Jack.

Albert rolled his eyes. "Oh, he has been in Idoless frequently. When I encountered him, he said he favored the name Dylan. But I'm sure that if I had called him that, he'd have said he favored Brendon, or Neptune, or any of his other names."

"Wait a sec," chuckled Frank. "Jack, how'd you know that?"

"Because I met him," said Jack.

"I didn't know that," said Frank, eyes wide.

"I met him at a time when he could have used his power to save a lot of people, but he didn't do a damn thing." Jack gave a disappointed sigh. "It seems to me that the gods are just out to help themselves." Jack shot Albert a glance. "Sorry."

Albert, however, gave him an interested smile, as if he were just now recognizing something about Jack for the first time. Then he gave a single nod, which Jack took as agreement.

Frank tried to lighten the mood, so he laughed and teased, "Oh, ye of little faith."

Albert stepped close to Frank. "Why did you say that? What did you mean by it?"

Frank backed away. "What? I . . . I don't know. It . . . it's just a saying. Jack made that comment about the gods, so I—"

Albert gasped, "It's still there!" He became agitated, pacing and gesturing wildly as he rattled off unrelated thoughts and questions, sometimes directed at the Waramonds but mostly to himself. "There *is* truth to it. It's part of our vernacular. But then, what does that mean? What am I supposed to do about it?"

Jack set down his glass of water and tried to calm Albert, "Whoa. Slow down. Are you all right?"

"It's still *there*."

"What is? What's still there?"

For a moment, it seemed that Albert was going to answer, but he faltered. "I . . . I . . . can't explain. I'm sorry. Excuse me." Then he pushed his way out of the room.

Jack asked, "What was that all about?"

"I told you he's been acting weird. It's just never been *that* bad." Frank crossed his arms. "Maybe I should try and get him to see someone. A doctor or something."

Before Jack could respond, the master of ceremonies announced the royal family's arrival at the feast. Jack's eyes immediately went to Eliza, and Albert disappeared from his thoughts.

She wore a more extravagant gown than before, with a massive wig, that faded from a dark auburn to a rosy pink, all pulled up into elaborately looping knots. Jack thought she looked equally amazing and ridiculous. He could hardly reconcile the grandiose woman entering the room with the girl he'd known.

And he couldn't decide if he should go to her—maybe apologize for before—or wait for her to see him and come over. When she finally looked his way, her eyes didn't even pause as they passed over him, and her blatant disregard left him feeling sick. From that moment on, Jack spent the rest of his time at the feast trying to look as if he weren't watching her. It frustrated him that every time he snuck a peak, either she was doing a better job of acting like she wasn't looking at him, or worse, she really wasn't.

Jack tried to make sense of the changes he saw in Eliza as she worked her way around the room. He looked for any trace of the charming, complicated young woman he'd fallen in love with, but it appeared she'd transformed into a socialite, reveling in her high-profile role as princess.

Had he idealized her in his memory? Or, had the Eliza he knew only been an act?

After an hour of discreet surveillance, Jack had a revelation: if this were the real Eliza, he might finally be able to move on.

Just the thought made something inside him explode. He wanted to run over, shake her, and demand to know the truth. He left Frank in the middle of a conversation with some wealthy pretender and started toward her, but at the last second thought better of it, and left the room.

Getting away from the crowd felt good. It gave him time to cool down, and removing Eliza from his sight made it a little easier to think. Jack wasn't sure how long he had wandered the castle when he noticed a pair of guards relieving two others. That would likely make it an hour until midnight, if he remembered the castle schedule correctly, and so the feast would likely continue for another couple hours.

Jack eventually found himself outside, in an unfamiliar area. He caught the distinct odor of hay and animals, and realized he'd found the new animal paddocks Frank had intended to show him earlier.

Just then, something the size of a large dog leaped high into the air but fell back to the earth with a thump. Jack turned toward the sound and saw a young griffin, still shedding its youthful down from the eagle-like front of its body, tethered to the ground by a long leash. While its brothers and sisters were sleeping, huddled by their parents, this griffin experimented with its wings. Using its strong lion hindquarters, the creature sprang into the air and flapped its wings. But just when it started to gain any kind of momentum it would hit the end of its tether and tumble back to the ground.

Jack felt a strange tugging at his heart as he watched the creature struggle and walked so close to the fence, he could feel

46

the gusts from the young griffin's powerful wings. And a lump formed in his throat as he recognized the freedom the griffin longed for. Freedom its instincts knew it deserved . . . but would never get.

Before he realized what he was doing, Jack had climbed over the fence and stood before the griffin. It looked up at Jack with its round, golden eagle eyes and whimpered. Its deep brown feathers shimmered in the moonlight, revealing flecks of amber, green, and gray. Time seemed to move outside of Jack's consciousness, and the next thing he knew, he was working at removing the collar.

While Jack concentrated on releasing the griffin, a guard on his rounds came around the corner. "Hey, what are you doing over there?"

Fortunately, Frank had been searching for Jack since he'd disappeared from the party and found him just in time. "Ease off, soldier." Then Frank called to him, with a calmness that made Jack feel worse than if he'd been shouted at, "Jack, please get out of there."

Jack turned to see Frank just outside the fence, motioning for him to come out. He felt embarrassed, like a child who'd been caught sneaking cookies just before dinner. He stood up and began to walk toward his brother. He'd almost made it to Frank when he heard a terrible shriek. He turned and saw the griffin chasing him. When it reached the end of the leash, the griffin snapped back with such force that it fell to the ground. It picked itself up and looked at Jack while tugging at its restraints.

The lump returned to Jack's throat.

"Come on, Jack," said Frank.

Jack took a couple more steps toward his brother when the griffin began to writhe on the ground, kicking up dirt and the last of its remaining down as it screeched and groaned. He stopped and looked back at the sad creature. "He . . . he just wants to be free," Jack said, more to himself than Frank.

"I get that, but it won't be good for him," Frank reasoned. "He's too young to survive on his own. We're thousands of miles away from any other griffins. If you set him free, you'll be doing him more harm than good."

He knew his brother was right; and though it pained him to do it, Jack walked away from the griffin's cries and crawled back over the fence. A couple guards made as if they were going to take Jack into custody, but Frank shooed them away. "Back to your posts."

"But sir—"

"I said, back to your posts. I've got this." The guards did as they were ordered, but Frank watched to make sure they did. Once they were alone, he turned to Jack, who was looking back at the griffin. "Jack, what in Hades were you doing?"

"Frank, I'm sorry. I . . . I don't know what happened. I . . ." And he didn't know. Or at least, he couldn't explain.

"It's all right. I'm sure this day hasn't been easy for you. Look, just come with me back to the feast, and—"

"No. No thanks," interrupted Jack. "I think I just need to go to bed." Frank gave him a suspicious look. "Honest, I'll head right there. I just can't go back in that room."

Frank took pity on his brother, agreeing that it was probably for the best.

They walked back inside the castle together but took different paths: Frank back to the party and Jack to the lieutenants' dorm.

Jack passed the hall leading to the treasury, where he and Frank had met Eliza earlier. He paused at the spot where they'd had their exchange and put his hand to the cheek she'd slapped.

That was the Eliza I remember. He stood there, cherishing the moment, causing things to stir inside him once more.

When Jack had left the castle five years ago, it had been a bad parting, and it still tainted the way he saw everyone and everything. In his search for peace, he had met with specialists, healers, and spiritual guides, trying all kinds of different training and meditations to control his rage. While nothing had worked entirely, he had mastered a handful of exercises to calm himself. He knew he needed to try one now.

So, he sat on the floor, crossed his legs, rested his hands on his knees, and closed his eyes. He steadied his breathing, focused on feeling the air fill his lungs, and held it for a moment before exhaling. *Eliza.* He calmed his mind and tried to channel his energies. *Eliza.* He took a deep breath. *Eliza. Eliza.* He brought his arms in the air and slammed a fist into the palm of his other hand. *Eliza.* "Focus," he told himself. *Eliza, Eliza, Eliza.* "Damn it!" Jack shot to his feet and began pacing. He was tempted to get his bag and make his way back to Oakmoor, but then he thought about the reason he had returned. He threw his hands against the wall and dropped his head, closing his eyes tight as he tried to quiet his rage.

And it was then that he felt it. A slight vibration in the wall, that ended almost as soon as it had begun. He hadn't felt that since he was a child, playing with Jason in the castle. But there was no mistaking it; he remembered that tremor and knew exactly what it meant. Jack ran down the hall to the treasury doors. The guards, already perplexed by his peculiar behavior, readied their spears at his approach. "Someone is in there," Jack told them.

"What?"

"Someone is in there. You need to open those doors right now, before whoever it is gets away." The two soldiers looked to one another, not sure if they should believe him. Jack sighed in annoyance. "Fine, don't. But when the king finds out tomorrow that the vault has been robbed under your watch, don't say I didn't try to warn you when Argus Vergo is tearing you a new one." Jack turned to leave.

One of the guards shouted, "Wait!" He turned to his partner. "It doesn't hurt to at least check."

The other guard eyed Jack. After a moment, he said, "Yeah, all right." He pulled out his keys, thrust one into the lock, and turned it, never taking his eyes off Jack. Hearing the bolt unlatch, the first guard swiped a card through a security panel and then entered a code. There was another clicking sound of the backup lock, and finally they spun the great dial on the front of the door. They opened it and went inside.

Shelves lined the walls of the large room, and an island in the center held low cabinets full of drawers. The shelves overflowed with valuables: jewels, gold bars, and bundles of paper money, bonds, and deeds. The room also housed ancient artifacts and statues alongside technological devices whose purposes Jack couldn't even begin to guess. But for all the room's wealth, the most glaring element was the large empty space on the middle shelf and a message painted on the wall behind it:

The lettering was elegant and was signed with a sort of stamp, red and in the shape of a bird: a cardinal. They'd only glanced at the empty spot when the first guard turned back to Jack and pointed his spear at him. "Freeze!"

"What?" said Jack.

"I said *freeze*. We're taking you in. I don't know how you did it, but . . . you . . . you distracted us."

"I distracted you and then told you to check the vault?"

The guards didn't answer; instead, the second guard just turned his spear on Jack as well.

Rolling his eyes, Jack said, "I don't have the patience for this right now."

With amazing speed, Jack snatched the weapon from the first guard, twisting it from his hands and then tossed it at the second, who instinctively dropped his own spear to catch it. Jack punched the second guard, knocking him out cold, and finished with a spin kick to the first guard's stomach. The soldier fell to the ground with a great thud, gasping for air.

Jack ran out of the room and down the hall. As he turned the corner, alarms began to ring, and red lights high on the walls flashed. He cursed under his breath, thinking he could really use a sword right now.

Chapter Four
A Cardinal Pursuit

With folded arms, Jack leaned against the stone doorframe at the end of the corridor and waited. A dim glow from the torch on the wall provided the only light. Jack's eyes had adjusted to the dark, and he thought he could just make out a figure headed toward him.

The darkness didn't seem to bother the man, who ran with grace and ease among the shadows, but skidded to a stop at the sight of Jack Waramond.

"I was wondering when you were going to get here," said Jack, with a nonchalant air about him.

The figure remained in the shadows, but close enough that Jack could see he was dressed entirely in crimson, not an iota of flesh showing. His hooded cloak split along his back and frayed at the tips, making it look like a set of bird's wings. The only parts of his disguise that were not some form of crimson were a silver belt buckle and the solid black visor on his helmet containing two glowing yellow lights where his eyes should be.

"So, you must be the Cardinal?"

The Cardinal didn't respond.

"Where's the money? You stash it in another part of the passages to go back for later?"

Again, the Cardinal didn't answer. He just stood silent and motionless.

Jack stood upright and took a step forward. "So, how'd you find the secret corridors? Me, I—"

The Cardinal shifted into a defensive stance.

"Whoa, whoa!" Jack put up his hands. "No need to start anything. We're just . . . well, *I'm* just talking." The Cardinal continued to hold himself ready while Jack kept his posture casual and confident. "Look, we're not going to get anywhere just standing here, so why don't we—"

There was a flash of crimson as the Cardinal emerged from the shadows and swung a kick at him. Jack deflected the blow, along with the several others that followed.

The Cardinal then backed off, retreating back to the dark. Jack didn't retaliate but stayed close. The Cardinal let loose another onslaught of punches and kicks, and as Jack blocked them, he tried to explain, "Look, I don't want to sound full of myself or anything, but you aren't going to beat me. I'm . . ."

Suddenly, the Cardinal leaped in the air, hooked his leg around Jack's neck, twisted around him, and sent him twirling to the ground with a crash. He then leaped over Jack and dashed out the door.

Jack grumbled, then bounced to his feet and ran in pursuit.

Palace officials had silenced the alarms and reassured guests that all was well. Most of the people were still at the feast, and that seemed to be right where the Cardinal was headed. Jack realized his opponent's wisdom; as soon as they reached the feast, the Cardinal's escape was almost guaranteed in the chaos of a frantic crowd. Jack knew he had to catch up before that happened.

As the Cardinal rounded the last corner before reaching the banquet hall, he ran into two guards. The Cardinal knocked the first guard to the ground and took his sword before he knew what was happening. As the Cardinal fought the second soldier, Jack noticed something familiar about his style of fighting. *The sweep kick could have been a fluke, but not this.* The fighting form the Cardinal was using was unlike anything Idolessian soldiers learned, but Jack knew it well, and seeing it stopped him in his tracks.

The Cardinal looked back at Jack. For a moment, they scrutinized each other before resuming the chase.

Jack tried to close the gap, but it was too late; they had arrived at the banquet hall. He expected the Cardinal to charge the crowd, then slip out in the commotion, but he didn't. Instead, the Cardinal leaped into the air, hopping across tables, pillars, and statues until he finally landed on the mantel of a massive fireplace at the end of the banquet hall, a tapestry of the Hawthorn royal crest as his backdrop.

Jack watched as the Cardinal looked down at the people from his little stage. The room went silent, waiting for the Cardinal to say something. He didn't, but Jack sensed an air of contempt as the Cardinal turned his head slowly, looking out at the crowd. Then he raised his stolen sword and slashed the tapestry. The crowd gasped as a portion of the drapery fell to the ground.

Captain Vergo's voice rang throughout the hall, "What are you all gawking at? Get him! GET HIM!"

As ordered, the soldiers in the room rushed toward the thief. With that, the Cardinal put two fingers to his forehead, saluted to Vergo, and with a great swoosh, took off like a bolt toward the largest window, his cape flapping behind.

Jack could see the soldiers weren't making much headway weaving around the party guests, so he snatched one of their swords ("Thank you") then leaped up and across the room, using a similar path as the thief's. He was annoyed with himself for trying to find Eliza in the crowd as he passed, but the distraction didn't slow him down. He caught up to the Cardinal, grabbing hold of his cape just as the crimson bandit threw himself through the window, shattering it completely.

The two of them tumbled toward the earth; both looked down and then at each other. Jack yelled over the sound of the wind, "I don't suppose you can fly?" Suddenly, the Cardinal stopped falling, and Jack watched him sail away. "Huh."

For a flash, he fantasized Eliza was screaming in distress for him as he fell to his death. A sudden tightening around his waist jerked him back to reality. He looked up and saw a cord running from him to the Cardinal. Unfortunately, the cord snapped under the force of the fall, and he continued his plummet.

Focus, Jack.

He swung his body upright, steadied himself, and stabbed the sword against the castle wall. At first it just bounced off the stones in a shower of sparks. Jack tried again and hit a gap in the mortar between the stones, and the sword began to dig into the wall. The muscles in his arms burned under the strain, and Jack began dragging his heels against the wall to try and slow his descent even more.

As he approached the ground, Jack flung himself away from the sword, aiming for the straw roof of a nearby storage shed. He felt another sharp tug at his waist before falling straight through, landing with a thud on the shed floor. The wind had been knocked out of him, and he was seeing stars . . . actual stars, as he looked through the hole in the roof he'd just created. For a second, he thought he saw the Cardinal peeking through, but he blinked, and the outlaw was gone.

Jack rolled over and pulled himself up onto his feet. His hands went to his waist to unravel the cord which the Cardinal had used to save him. *Is that what had happened? Did the Cardinal just save my life?* He stumbled out of the shed, leaned against the doorframe, and looked around. He'd landed in the griffin paddock, of all places.

He saw the young sleeping griffins huddled by their parents. Close by was the young griffin from before. It looked pitiful, lying in a heap by itself. Jack approached it, but it didn't beg for his help like it had earlier. Their last encounter made it clear; Jack wasn't going to help. So, it just laid there, despondent. To its right were the remains of the sword Jack had used, with only a shard of the blade left, the rest lost to the side of the castle.

Jack looked up to see if he could tell where the Cardinal had flown off to, but all he saw was the groove he'd dug into the castle wall with the sword. He looked back down at the young griffin, which still didn't look back. It just heaved a deep, sad sigh.

After his tumble out the window, Jack was quickly located in the griffin paddock and brought to the throne room, where the conversation had been going in circles for over an hour.

"I'm telling you, Your Majesty, it was him!" Captain Vergo screamed as he pointed a finger dramatically at Jack. "Just after Jack Waramond . . . *left*, this Cardinal started appearing. I'm telling you, it's been Jack this whole time. I've said it all along, especially when I found out who the previous Cardinal was. It's obvi—"

The king raised a finger to silence Vergo. Jack couldn't help but be interested. This was the first hint of something different. Apparently, the previous Cardinal's identity was known, and a closely kept secret. But what did that have to do with him?

Commander Church repeated, "Captain, it's just not possible. I personally collected Jack from Oakmoor Cove, which is as far away from this castle as one can get without going into one of the other nations."

"Yeah, besides, you all saw the guy!" Jack added.

"How convenient," spat Captain Vergo. "The perfect way to get yourself off the hook—staging that little show!"

"*Staging?*" gasped Jack. "Are you *kidding* me? I fell out of a castle window chasing after *your* thief!"

"And survived," retorted Vergo.

The king was sitting on his throne, eyeing Jack. His face remained calm, but his knuckles were white as he clutched the remains of the mutilated tapestry. "You must admit, this . . . this *spectacle* tonight happened with most unfortunate of timing for you, Jack. Until now, we've never seen the Cardinal. But the same day you come back, he reveals himself quite dramatically."

"It wasn't his choice," said Jack.

"How so?" asked the king.

"I cornered him."

Vergo snapped, "And how did you corner him, exactly? Shouldn't you have been at your own feast?"

"I never wanted that feast." Jack gave the king an apologetic glance. "I needed to get away from the crowd, so I went for a walk. You can ask my brother. He came looking for me and found me out by the animal paddocks."

"See! See! He admits it!" raged Vergo.

"Admits *what?*" asked Jack, incensed.

Vergo turned back to the king. "Sire, not only was the treasury robbed tonight, but one of the young griffins has been taken as well!"

"Oh," said Jack sheepishly.

King Hawthorn turned his gaze on the Prodigal Son. "What is it, Jack?"

"Well, that was sort of my fault. After I fell, what was left of my sword landed right on your missing griffin's collar . . . cut right through it."

Vergo sneered, " Your sword hit it at the neck and didn't kill it? You really expect us to believe that?"

Jack shrugged.

"So where is it now?"

"I dunno, he took off like a shot."

"A likely story. Those creatures are far too young to fly!"

Jack crossed his arms and challenged, "What are you, the griffin expert?"

Vergo tried to sound as friendly as he could. "Just admit to your crimes, and we'll be more merciful with you. The longer you hold out, the more trouble you'll be in."

Jack just kept his arms crossed and looked at Vergo as if he were crazy. Vergo exhaled and turned back to the king. "Sire, if you'd just let me question him properly, I swear I could get to the bottom of this."

"Okay, you got me." Jack raised his hands in the air with a slight wince. Everyone turned to look at him, the guards readying their weapons for an arrest. "Just go to my brother's quarters, and you'll find my bag. In it is your missing griffin."

Vergo's face twisted. "Oh, shut up."

"No, it's true, I've always wanted a pet. All the other kids had one growing up." Jack sighed. "I guess I thought I could make up for lost memories. I was planning to smuggle him out after this mission was completed. Till then, I was going to sneak him scraps of my dinner."

"This is not a joke, Waramond! I want the truth!" demanded Vergo.

"All right, all right! Jeez. The truth is, I want to be a great chef, and griffin is a rare delicacy."

Though none of the other men were brave enough to do the same under the serious circumstances, Mike Church smiled. "I think Mr. Waramond is trying to illustrate that Captain Vergo's allegations are . . . well, a little farfetched."

Jack jeered, "Ya think?"

"Fine," snapped Vergo, "he doesn't have the griffin. But that doesn't explain how he knew the Cardinal was in the vault. And what he was even doing at the treasury? He just said he was at the animal paddocks."

"I *was* at the paddocks. And as I told you, Frank can vouch for me. He'll also tell you that we parted ways because I wanted to go to bed. And it was on my way to the dorms that I . . ." Jack hesitated. The secret passages were, well, a secret. As far as he could tell, only he, Jason, and now this Cardinal character knew about them. He didn't want to let the secret go just yet. "I, I . . . sensed it."

"You *sensed it?*" chided Vergo.

"Yeah."

"How? What exactly did you *sense?*"

"I don't know how to explain it."

"The guards tell me you knew the Cardinal was inside," the king stated.

Jack sighed. "Sire, the guards are afraid of getting in trouble. Look, if I had anything to do with this, why would I have said anything to them? Wouldn't I have just let the place get robbed?"

"Yes," said the king. "While the timing is unfortunate, nothing else makes sense." Vergo began to protest, but the king interrupted. "I know you are doing everything you can to catch the thief, Captain. But the evidence suggests that Jack isn't the culprit."

"He has an accomplice, then. I tell you, Your Majesty—Jack Waramond is involved, just as—"

The king raised his hand. "That's *enough*, Captain. I don't want to hear another word. Jack is here as a favor to me and not for any other reason." He took a breath, rising from the throne, still gripping the tapestry. "It seems this . . . *Cardinal* has become something more than a minor nuisance." He squeezed the cloth and let it drop to the floor. "I'm going to assemble a special task force to capture and bring this bandit to justice."

Vergo stepped forward. "I assure you, Your Majesty, with that kind of enforcement, I am certain to capture—"

"You will not be leading the task force, Captain," the king said flatly.

"But . . . Your Highness . . . I—"

"That is not a comment on your abilities, Captain. But as you know, we have a more important operation coming up, and I'm going to need you for that."

Both Vergo and Jack grunted; Vergo with resentment and Jack with nausea.

The king approached Vergo and snapped, "Do you have a problem with my orders, Captain?"

"Of course not, Sire. Wherever you need my skills, there they will be."

Jack groaned again. The king looked at him pointedly. Jack gave a small cough and lowered his head. "You'd all best get your rest," said King Hawthorn. "We have a long day of work tomorrow." He walked back up to his throne and said over his shoulder, "Dismissed."

Jack and most of the others walked out, though Commander Church stayed behind. The throne room doors clanged shut behind him, and all the men scattered. Vergo shot Jack a dirty look as he passed.

Frank, who had been pacing outside, ran straight to his brother. "Jack, are you all right? What happened? What's going on?"

Jack grabbed him by the arm, "We need to talk." He led Frank down an empty hall away from the throne room, looked around to make sure no one else was in earshot, then rounded on his brother. "Is there anything you want to tell me?"

Frank looked confused. "What are you talking about? Are you okay? Jack, what's going on?"

"I had a little run in with the Cardinal."

"Yeah, I know. I mean, everyone saw you two, at the party." Frank took a step toward his brother, his brow creased with concern.

"Don't worry, Frank, I'm fine."

"Jack, when you . . . when you went out that window . . ."

"I'm fine. Really. But when I fought the Cardinal . . ." he looked suspiciously at Frank. "It's just, you and I . . . we made a promise to each other."

"Jack, what are you talking about?"

"I know how much it must mean to you to do a good job training the soldiers."

"Yeah? What of it?"

"Well," said Jack, "the Cardinal, he was definitely one of your guys. He was using your moves."

"Well, it's like you'd said before—it had to be someone inside the castle. This just narrows the search." Frank stepped back.

"Wait—you don't think . . . *I'm* somehow involved with the Cardinal?"

Jack waved his hands in the air, "No. No, Frank, forget the Cardinal. I don't care about the Cardinal. Just . . . what are you teaching these guys?"

"I don't understand."

Jack was somber. "Frank, he was using Mom's moves. He used one on me."

"What? No. That's impossible. Maybe it just looked like—"

"No, it wasn't chance." Jack's tone was heavy with disappointment. "We made a promise, Frank. There was stuff that was only hers to give, and she gave it to us alone. She didn't want these skills spread to too many people. Only those responsible enough to use them."

Frank looked dumbfounded. "Honestly, Jack, I haven't been teaching Mom's moves to the men, I only . . ." He stopped, and his eyes widened.

Jack looked at him, and while he was still upset, it was without accusation that he said, "You know who he is, don't you?"

Frank said, more to himself than Jack, "But it couldn't be."
"Frank. Who?"

"No, really, it couldn't be." He collected himself and then explained. "Look, Jack . . . I *did* share Mom's training with someone."

"How? Do you happen to have a son I don't know about? Cause it was only meant to be taught to *family*."

"Yeah, well, I'm not likely to ever have a family, so I figured Mom would be okay with me passing it on to someone else." Jack's eyes went wide, but before he could say anything, Frank continued, "I didn't make the decision flippantly, Jack. I taught it to someone I trust."

With a hint of self-righteousness, Jack snapped back, "Yeah, and how did that turn out?"

Frank got defensive. "Well, I'm sorry I didn't run it by you first, but you weren't exactly around for me to ask."

"Don't put this on me, Frank. And besides, how do you know you won't ever have a family? You're only thirty-five. There's still plenty of time."

"No, Jack, it's just … I …" Frank stumbled with his thoughts for a moment, but then rested on, "Look at me."

As long as Jack could remember, Frank had always been uncomfortable with his appearance. By no means was he ugly, he was just … large and furry. As a soldier, that could be regarded as a badge of masculinity, but somehow Frank carried the shame it had brought him in his youth. Jack scoffed. "Oh, not that old self-image crap. I thought you outgrew that."

Jack's anger ignited Frank's the way only a brother can. "And what do *you* know about it?"

Though the things he was saying about his brother were kind, Jack shouted angrily, "I *know* that you're a great guy, and the best person I know—even if you don't, can't, or won't see it yourself! And someday, you're going to make some woman very happy!" Frank's shoulder's sagged and he turned to leave but Jack pressed on, "And she's going to be the luckiest woman on the planet, Frank."

Frank turned back and looked his brother in the eyes. They stood there for a few moments, both trying to decide if they should continue the argument. Finally, Frank broke the silence. "Jack, I *do* see myself for what I am. That's one of the reasons I've dedicated my life to the army."

Jack tried to reason with his brother, "Frank, lots of soldiers have wives, especially the ranking officers. Look at your uncle.

You have options. And the sooner you realize that the sooner you're going to find love."

Frank's sadness could not be hidden and with a tone that suggested he wasn't going to say more, apologized, "I'm sorry for sharing Mom's skills without your blessing." He walked to the doorway and turned back again. "Look . . . I'll get to the bottom of this Cardinal business. You're here for more important things."

Then Frank turned, took a deep breath, lifted his head, and headed back into the castle.

12 Years Ago

568 AR

A steady splash of ocean waves slapped Jack to consciousness. He rolled over, his whole body aching from trying to stay afloat for so long. He didn't remember when he'd given up trying. Obviously, he'd held out long enough to survive and wash up on shore. He didn't know where he was. It had to be some island far off the coast of Idoless. Whatever the case, it felt good to rest. He relished the stillness until his mind caught up with his body.

Eliza!

Jack bolted upright. Every inch of his body throbbed as he forced himself to move again. The previous night's attack had sunk three of the king's imperial vessels and left hundreds of people dead or injured. Jack was concerned for them all, but his mind kept circling back to his friends: Eliza and Jason. Jack's sense of duty told him to secure Jason's safety first since he was the prince, but his only real concern was for Eliza. *Why had he agreed to let her go off alone?*

He reckoned there was nothing to do but start moving, but the sight before him stopped him in his tracks. Bodies of passengers from the ships littered the seashore. He inspected each one, looking for survivors. It was a grisly task. With each body, he felt a twinge of guilt at his relief that it wasn't Eliza.

He hadn't realized just how much she meant to him until now. Her flowing black hair and hourglass figure had made her popular with all the guys in school. Jack figured she had to realize that, though she never let on that she did. She hung out with the same people he and Jason did, and it wasn't a stretch to imagine her dating one of them. But she wasn't interested in that, which only made her more appealing to him. She certainly found both him and Jason amusing; she even appeared to enjoy the way they competed for her affection.

As Jack searched the shore, his mind kept racing through the events of the previous night. He couldn't escape the overwhelming feeling of guilt. He'd literally had her in his grasp and let her go.

Jack had a bit of luck when one of the bodies he checked turned out to be alive. It was one of his fellow graduates, Eric Hullet. He didn't know Eric well, but he was glad to find another survivor. Minutes later, Eric and Jack put their military training to work when they performed CPR successfully on another survivor they found together, Gary Finzer. Jack knew Gary; he was a better student than warrior, but a decent guy. Jack felt things were turning around as he watched Gary coughing up the sea water from his lungs.

Eric stayed with Gary as Jack continued searching the bodies which, after a while, all began to look the same. Jack's sense of panic grew until he finally saw her. Eliza was alive and checking bodies like he was. She still wore the bodice from her dress, but she had torn off the sleeves and the cumbersome skirt and wrapped some salvaged cloth around her waist offering her better maneuverability. As her makeshift dress billowed in the wind, she smiled when she saw Jack, showing no shame that so much of her skin was exposed. They ran to each other and embraced, exclaiming simultaneously, "You're alive!"

Jack went in to kiss her, but she pulled away. "Whoa! Back off, soldier." She pushed Jack away, "I'm happy to see you too, but it's not like that."

"Sorry . . . I just—"

"Yeah. Emotions. I get it." She dusted herself off, as if a simple shake would make her clothing clean again. Changing the subject, Eliza asked with a note of trepidation, "So, did you find her?"

"Who? Oh, Emily? Yeah, I did."

Eliza gave a breath of relief, and then asked, "Where is she?"

"She was with the other civilians."

Eliza beamed, "They're all right?"

"Well," Jack began, then cut his eyes toward all the bodies on the beach. "I don't know yet."

Eliza seemed to understand and glanced away, "Oh. I see." Looking for something to occupy her, she leaned over yet another body.

Jack wanted to comfort her, but the best he could do was give her a little hope. "After I found Emily, we jumped into the ocean. That's when we found the civilians you had sent to the lifeboat."

The soldier Eliza was examining was dead, but she continued looking him over, unable to face Jack as he told his tale. "I don't need to hear the gory details, Jack."

"What?"

Eliza looked up at him, tears glistening in her eyes. "Well, you said you were on the boat with the civilians, and yet you're here and they aren't."

"Well, I wasn't . . . *on* the boat, exactly."

She stood up, "How exactly were you not, *on* the boat?"

He wasn't sure why, but she seemed irritated with him. "Well . . . you weren't there."

"So?"

"So . . . I left Emily with the civilians and swam back to look for you."

Eliza started smacking Jack repeatedly. "You mean you left them?"

"Ouch, hey . . . stop that! Hey . . . ow, you're welcome, ow!"

Eliza quit her assault and turned away with an exasperated sigh.

"Eliza, I'm sorry, but they were safe, and I was worried about you!"

"Yeah, I get it," she said, crossing her arms.

Jack took a step toward her. "You keep saying you get it, but I don't think you do." He took her shoulder and turned her around to face him. "I didn't realize . . . not until . . ." He stumbled for words. "When Emily and I found the lifeboat, and you weren't on it . . ." He took one of her hands, cupped it in both of his, and looked down, unable to say more.

Suddenly Eliza's face lit up and she exclaimed, "I can't believe it, he's alive! Jason's alive, too!"

There in the distance was Jason, followed closely by another soldier. Eliza ran to him, and they embraced just as she and Jack had. Jason looked up, saw Jack, and waved. Jack waved back.

She didn't get it. Jack wasn't just another guy competing for her attention. She was no longer some kind of prize to win. It had been growing in him for some time, and now he knew it with certainty. For the first time in his life, Jack was in love.

Chapter Five
The Best of the Best

The next morning, Jack startled awake from a bad dream to find Frank had already gotten up and left. They hadn't spoken since their fight last night, and Jack was anxious to apologize. Jack figured Frank had gone off to draw, something that had always brought him solace.

As Jack looked around Frank's room, he noticed the absence of artwork. Frank had only one of his sketches out, a drawing he'd done of their mother, framed and on his nightstand. Jack had only been just shy of eleven years old when Frank drew it. He'd only had one year of art lessons, but he'd captured their mother's likeness well.

Neither Jack nor Frank had an actual photograph of her, and the drawing pulled at Jack's heart. He picked up the frame and outlined the shape of her face with his finger. Frank had even drawn in her necklace, with the silver pendant shaped like a lowercase *t*. Jack jumped when the door opened, and Frank entered with a sketchbook under his arm. They gazed at one another, both unsure of what to say.

Jack noticed their mother's *t*-shaped pendant hanging around Frank's neck, now on a leather cord rather than a chain, like in the drawing.

Frank looked at the picture Jack was holding and asked, "Would you like me to draw a copy for you?" Jack didn't say anything, he just nodded. He set the drawing back on the

69

nightstand and offered his hand. Frank took it, but only shook it once before pulling Jack in for a hug. He patted his back, pulled away, and, still holding his hand asked, "Are we good?"

Jack smiled. "Yeah, bro, we're good."

"Good." Frank ended it with a smile and a wink. "Look, we've got a little time before breakfast. There's something I want to show you."

They left the castle and hiked down a hillside that wrapped around the cliff the fortress was perched atop. Along the way, Jack said, "I noticed you're still wearing Mom's necklace."

Frank took hold of the *t*-shaped pendant. "Yeah. Outside of the drawing, I didn't really have much else to remember her by, and—"

"What is it?"

Frank looked up, like he was trying to recall something. "It's just, I actually remember her placing it in my hands, but . . ."

"But what?"

Frank rubbed his head. "That's just it, I can't remember."

"It's okay. I was just making conversation."

"But . . . I think it's important."

Seeing his brother's frustration, Jack tried to offer questions to help dig up some answers. "Didn't it used to be on a chain?"

Frank's eyes narrowed, as he tried to scan his memory. "Yeah . . . I remember putting it on the cord, because . . . did it break?"

"I don't know, did it?"

"No, I remember—it *did* break. I mean . . . I think." Frank grunted in frustration, "Why can't I remember?"

"How about the *t*, what's it mean, anyway? I always assumed it was a gift from your dad."

"That would explain why she cherished it. But his surname is Karr and there's nothing in his family line that has anything to do with the letter *T*."

"I wish I could have met your dad."

Frank agreed, "I wish I could have known him longer. I was so young when he died."

The necklace was forgotten when they arrived at the base of the cliff, and Frank ushered Jack into a cave large enough to house what he'd brought Jack to see.

"Frank! When did you get it?" exclaimed Jack at the sight of a large biplane, its pontoons keeping it afloat on the water.

Frank answered, "It's the plane I used to get you off that island. It was the only one they'd let me borrow to go looking for you, 'cause it was in such shoddy condition. It was actually decommissioned shortly after I brought you home."

"I thought it looked familiar," said Jack as he admired the plane.

Frank looked at the aircraft like a father would look at his child. "Ever since the first day I flew a plane, I've wanted one of my own. Someday, when I retire from the army, I'm gonna live in this."

"Live in it?"

"Yeah. It's big enough—there's a space that I could easily clear out and turn into a small living compartment with plumbing for a sink and toilet even. I figured I could earn a living by making deliveries with it."

Jack studied the plane. It was old. Most of the paint had worn off, and many areas had begun to rust. He didn't know much about engines, but one of the turbines was exposed and looked like it had already undergone some repairs. "It definitely needs some work."

"Absolutely," replied Frank. "I work on it in my free time. No one ever comes down here. So, I get time to myself and fixing it is cheaper than buying a new plane. I've got big plans for it. The only thing I'm not sure about yet is what to name it."

"Name it?" asked Jack.

Frank enlightened his brother. "Sure, all the best airplanes have names. I have to find the perfect one for her." He patted the hull.

"'Her,' huh?" smiled Jack.

Frank shrugged with a smirk of his own. He gave the hull another loving pat. "We'd better get back. I don't want to miss breakfast. I have a feeling this is going to be a long day."

After breakfast, Frank received his orders: assemble a company for the mission. His only parameters were to pick 150 of the "best of the best" soldiers. His task was complicated by the perplexing fact that Lieutenant Lewis Patrick received the exact same orders for the exact same mission.

Frank and Lewis worked together to make both teams balanced, but they suffered the collective headache of battling for their choices with General Marcus Long. Long oversaw the soldiers staying to guard the castle and the king. With casualties a certainty in Death's Province, Long wanted to be sure the castle would still have capable soldiers after the mission was over. Frank and Lewis had to make deals with Long to get certain men, which also meant taking others they didn't want.

"No, not them," Frank protested. "Anyone, *anyone* but them!"

"They aren't bad soldiers," reasoned Lewis. "They're actually quite good when properly motivated."

"They're the worst," muttered Frank. "And we shouldn't have to motivate them to do a good job."

"You don't want them coming because they teased you in school," retorted Lewis.

"No. I don't *like* them because of that. I don't want them to come because they're bad soldiers. These groups are supposed to be the best of the best."

"I agree with Lieutenant Waramond," interjected General Long. "They *are* bad soldiers, and with so many good men gone, I don't have the time to put up with their antics." He sighed with a sacrificial tone, "I'll have quite a lot on my plate trying to make use of those I have left."

"Have left?" exclaimed Frank. "You'll still have most of the men! We're only taking three hundred. And only a third of *them* are actually going into the Province."

"Frank," Lewis began. Frank cursed under his breath. "It's for the best. Besides, the rest of the soldiers love them. On a mission like this, they'll be good for morale."

"Not mine," returned Frank.

"Frank," Lewis pleaded, "they can be in my group."

"Ugh, fine. Just keep them away from me."

Lewis assured him, "You won't even see them."

General Long smiled. "Good! Corporals Hawk Taylor and Joss Huntsman will go with you two on the *big mission*," he said with a hint of sarcasm. "With that settled, I think we're done here. Good day, gentlemen." He collected his files and left.

"He's got it easy," Lewis remarked. "Tomorrow when we leave, he just has to organize the soldiers left over." He let out a deep sigh then turned to Frank. "Let's just get on with this. The sooner we get this paperwork finished, the sooner we can get everyone their orders and be done . . . at least for tonight."

Jack had spent the morning in the castle's conference hall with King Hawthorn, Commander Church, and the other high-ranking officers, plotting out the mission.

The bulk of the morning was devoted to the challenge of entering Death's Province. Though it was located in Idoless, an enchanted barrier sealed its entry. Only a handful of wizards knew the ancient spell that opened the deathly realm. Although only one was technically required, Commander Church didn't want to take any chances, so he summoned six of the nation's most accomplished wizards.

Of the six, only one was there by choice: Eli Warren. Like his fellow wizards, Eli wore a baggy sleeved tunic with ornate trim, but that was where the similarities ended. While the other wizards were stuffy intellects, Eli was brash and spoke with unrestricted language. It put some off, but Eli was unquestionably the most skilled wizard in Idoless, and possessed the same authoritative presence as his son, Mike Church.

Eli was also alone in his support of the mission. The other five wizards believed it was an enormous risk. The "doorway" of Death's Province was a difficult access point to locate because it moved frequently. They argued that this meant the doorway was not meant to be opened.

After hearing this reasoning several times, Eli slammed his fists on the table and bellowed, "If that were true, there wouldn't even be a fucking doorway. Now shut your mouths unless you have something useful to say."

Undaunted, the wizards tried to explain that calling it a "doorway" created a misconception about the access point, arguing that it was more like an exhaust valve to release the overwhelming negative energy in Death's Province. But Commander Church and even King Hawthorn were unwilling to hear the warnings. They would wave their hands dismissively and say, "We are aware of the risks," and move past like they hadn't heard a word.

After hours of debate, one of the wizards rose and in an aggravated voice asked, "Why are you so desperate to go in there, anyway?"

Jack was surprised. *So, they don't know why we're going in either.*

Commander Church told them what he'd told Jack back in Oakmoor: they were after an object that was a weapon of some sort. This provoked even more complaints from the wizards, who felt the same as Jack had—anything powerful enough to be protected by Death's Province itself should be left alone. But their warnings were dismissed again.

In exasperation, one wizard asked, "How do you even know where this . . . *thing,* is? It's not as if Death's Province is mapped!"

Commander Church explained, "Upon discovering the object's existence, we also found a device that will lead us to it once we're inside." He clutched a silver pendant hanging from his neck. "That is our first advantage. Our second is our guide." Church nodded toward Jack. "We have the only person who has ever been to Death's Province and survived to lead us through." Church moved on before any of them could argue further.

"The first leg of the mission will be to gain our third advantage: the doorway's current location. As the wizards here will confirm, when the door of Death's Province changes locations, it arrives at its new position spectacularly. We've discovered that someone witnessed the most recent doorway shift. Our only challenge will be finding him—he's off the grid. We have an idea where he lives, but we'll need to find him quickly before the door moves again."

The king left the room twice to receive communications from the prince, who was currently on official business in neighboring Mechina. Every time it happened, Commander Church asked a group of people, including Jack, to leave the room so those remaining could discuss confidential information. Jack didn't think anything of it at first, but after the king returned the second time and asked what had been accomplished in his absence, Church carefully worded his answer in a way that seemed to imply Jack and the others had been there all along. It then occurred to Jack that both times he was asked to leave the room, he was invited back just before the king returned.

Close to the end of the day, the king was called away a third time, and once again, Church asked for the room to be cleared after. Jack asked if he could stay this time. He tried not to let it bother him, but when Church said no, the hairs on the back of his neck stood up. Something was going on.

Once the doors closed behind him, Jack told the guards he was going to use the restroom.

"Our orders are that you are not to be left alone. A guard will have to come with you," said one of the men.

But Jack took off at a sprint, saying, "Sorry guys, there's no waiting for *this*."

Jack ran down several corridors while the soldiers clambered after, demanding he stop. Once he was at a bathroom with access to the secret passageways, he turned to his sentinels and said, "I'm sorry, guys, but I've really got to go."

The men were visibly annoyed but had no reason to doubt him, considering that they watched the door shut after him. He shouted, "This may take some time!" hoping the ruse would ensure his privacy.

Jack went to the stall at the far end of the room and locked the door behind him. He pressed on a stone in the wall, which receded until he heard a faint click. He was then able to push on a larger section of the wall, revealing the hidden passage behind it.

The existence of the secret corridors had been lost until Jack and Jason stumbled on them in their childhood. However, now there was this Cardinal person. *How did he learn about them?* For a moment, Jack entertained the notion that Jason was the Cardinal, but the idea was ludicrous. For one thing, Jason was in Mechina on a diplomatic mission. And for another, why would the prince steal from his own treasury? In any case, Jack had a more pressing matter at hand: *What was Mike Church hiding?*

He crawled into the dark passage, closed the entry, and took off in the direction of the conference hall. The hidden corridors had a limited number of entrances but had observation points all over the castle. He knew he wouldn't have much time. He'd only be able to listen for a minute or so before the guards grew impatient and started looking for him.

Arriving at a spot where he could see the conference hall, Jack threw himself on the viewing ledge. He tried to steady his breath so he could hear the conversation clearly. The first voice Jack heard he didn't recognize.

". . . and how are we supposed to keep it away from him once we have it?"

"We can't worry about that now," replied Church. "We don't have the resources to get it, the way it's currently protected. So we have to stay undercover and utilize the army while we still can."

"But once he's gotten his hands on it, we'll never get it away from him," countered the unknown voice.

Jack wondered who they were talking about. *Could it be me? Was that why they asked me to leave the room?* He knew a cloud of mistrust surrounded him, and perhaps the only reason he was here at all was because King Hawthorn had insisted upon it. Maybe that's why Church only included Jack when the king was around.

"Well, I have an idea about that," said Church. "After last night's little show, perhaps the Cardinal can take it from him."

Are they somehow connected with the Cardinal? Jack strained to hear. It was difficult to make out anything over the erupting protests of the other voices in the room.

Church's voice climbed over them. "It's one of the best ways we can do it and still stay off their radar!"

The unknown voice returned. "It's perfect, actually."

Mike said passionately, "It's imperative that we stay hidden until we're ready." Jack wanted to stay to learn more, but he knew the guards would be looking for him soon. He was just about to pull himself away when Church added, "But when we *are* ready, we'll take control."

Jack couldn't believe his ears. *Are they plotting to overthrow the king?* Forgetting he needed to leave, Jack continued to listen, but then someone entered the conference hall. He couldn't see who it was, but Church looked annoyed and asked, "What are you doing here? You're supposed to be watching Jack."

"We were, Commander, but he got away from us somehow, and now he's . . . well, we can't find him."

"Dammit!" hissed Mike and Jack simultaneously.

One of the soldiers must have checked on him. Jack launched himself from the viewing ledge and ran back toward the bathroom. His mind went back and forth between trying to think of an alibi and processing everything he'd just overheard.

He was at full stride when he remembered another exit just ahead of him. He had no idea how he was going to explain his disappearance from the bathroom, but knew he had to risk it. He opened a door behind a tapestry hanging in the kirks' oratory and was about to head back to the bathroom when fortune smiled on him. His friend, the newly appointed Kirk Albert Larson, was there sitting deep in thought, staring at one of the statues of gods that lined the room.

"Albert?"

The kirk slowly turned and, in a monotone voice, said, "Yes, what can I do for . . . ?" He stopped speaking when he realized it was Jack.

"Are you all right, Albert?"

Albert studied Jack for a moment, and said, "You know, Jack, you're probably one of the few people to whom I can openly admit that no, I am not." He paused, taking in Jack's tension. "But I'm guessing you're not here to hear about my problems."

"Normally, Albert, I would be. Really. But I'm actually in a little bit of trouble right now."

"Is there anything I can do to help?"

Jack smiled with relief. "Actually, there is."

Mike Church burst through the bathroom door and was greeted by the sound of a toilet flushing as Jack emerged from the farthest stall.

Jack approached the row of sinks to wash his hands and feigned jolting in surprise at the sight of him. "Mike?"

"Where were you, Jack?" demanded Church.

Jack glanced back at the stall.

"You know what I mean. You disappeared."

"I'm sorry if there's some confusion, Mike. Yeah, I ran off. But I had to," Jack put on a self-conscious smile, "well, I had to *go* pretty bad, and—"

The commander threw Jack against the wall with a forearm against his throat. "Don't play games with me, Waramond! Where did you—?"

"Commander," came the voice of King Hawthorn, "what is the meaning of this?"

Church's eyes grew wide for a moment. He released Jack and turned to find King Hawthorn accompanied by Kirk Larson. "Your Majesty, allow me to explain. Jack was missing and—"

"So you attack me?" Jack coughed melodramatically while rubbing his throat.

Church stammered, "No. I was just—"

"Morning coffee and the castle's breakfast burritos don't mix—what was I supposed to do? Besides," Jack said pointedly, "I only left the room because you asked me to."

"What's that?" inquired the king.

"Sire," Church took a step forward and raised an eyebrow, "we needed Jack to step out while we discussed certain . . . *details* that he was not cleared to hear."

"Ah, I see," answered the king with a nod.

For a moment Jack wondered if he'd misunderstood what he'd overheard. *No, not after Church said he would take control.* Jack turned his attention back to Church, who still had anger glinting in his eyes and snapped, "That's still no reason to attack me."

"He has a point, Commander," the king agreed.

Church gave an exasperated face. "You must forgive me, but after last night and this business with the Cardinal . . . when Jack went missing—"

"I was cleared of all that last night," stated Jack. "You defended me yourself."

"Yes, I know, but we need to take this mission seriously. I apologize if I took things too far, but I don't want anything to go wrong." Looking at the king, he added, "Sire."

King Hawthorn looked at Jack and smiled, "You just can't seem to get a break, can you? Wrong place at the wrong time," he chortled.

Jack forced a smile, and tried to go with the flow, "No, I guess not. Look, I'm sorry about this. I guess I'm just not used to the way things work around here anymore. I got used to doing things my own way."

The king waved his hands in the air. "Think nothing of it. You two shake hands and make up, and we'll go."

The king left the room, the door slowly closing behind him. Jack put out his hand, "Sorry, Mike."

Church took it. As the door clicked shut, he squeezed Jack's hand. "I don't know what you're playing at, Jack, but I *will* find out where you were and what you were up to."

Jack felt the pressure on his hand, but he didn't let on that it hurt. He dropped his smile and looked Church in the eyes. "Seems like we're all hiding something."

Mike's eyes widened, but he didn't respond.

Late in the afternoon, Jack found Frank, slouched and distracted, outside the conference hall doors and said, "Frank, I need to talk to you, I just . . . What's up with you?"

"Nothing," Frank answered.

"You sure?"

"It's dumb. I'm just," Frank took a breath, "disappointed." He sighed and wiped his face with his hands as if he were rubbing the worry away. "It'll be fine. What were you going to say?"

Jack pulled Frank away from the other soldiers outside the door and asked, "What's Mike's deal these days?"

"Church? What do you mean? Nothing. I mean, obviously he ranks pretty high for someone of his age, but let's be honest— if you hadn't left, it would've been you, and you're even younger."

"Not that. I mean, do you trust him?"

"Why wouldn't I? He's the commander, and a damn good one. I mean, he asked that Seth be on the mission, which I didn't feel great about. But that's a minor issue. Seth is his brother; I'd do the same for you. Anyway, Church is doing a far better job than Commander Marks ever did, and I think the king is happy with him. Why?"

Jack couldn't think of a way to tell Frank about what he'd heard Mike saying without revealing the secret of the hidden passageways. "I don't know, there's just something . . . off about him."

With a sly smile, Frank asked, "Is it because you got in trouble with him today?" Jack looked at him with wonder. "Yeah, I heard about it. News travels fast around here, especially when it's *you* who's gone missing and the commander who finds you."

Jack tried to clarify. "It wasn't like that."

"He's a real hands-on commander, Jack. It's one of the things that makes him so good. He's leading the mission into Death's Province himself."

"So, King Hawthorn . . . he trusts Mike?"

Frank recoiled slightly and laughed, "Of course he does."

"More than he should?"

"Jack, where'd this come from? You know him. One of your greatest missions was under his charge when he was still a general. You know he's a good guy." Frank grabbed Jack by the shoulders, looked him in the eyes and asked, "What's with the paranoia?"

"I . . . I can't explain it. I thought Mike was a good man. We got along really well on that mission. It's just . . ." Jack considered telling Frank about the secret passages, but knew his brother was always out to do the right thing—and in Frank's mind, the right thing would be to report the passages. It was the only reason Jack had never shared the secret with him before. And even though Jack didn't live in the castle anymore, he still didn't want to let the secret go. "Something is going on, Frank. We're not being told everything."

Frank clenched his fists and put them at his hips, "Hogwash! Of course we're not being told everything. We don't need to know everything. We're just soldiers."

"*You're* a soldier," Jack reminded him, "not me."

"You know what I mean. So we're not being told every detail of the mission. That doesn't mean something sordid is going on. Try and remember what it was like to be a soldier, Jack."

That was part of the problem. For years, Jack had just done what he was ordered. He was a good soldier and a great warrior, so it never surprised him that he was sent on so many dangerous missions. He was almost killed numerous times, the most recent and final being when he was sent to Death's Province. Then he discovered that he wasn't sent on all those missions because he was so good at his job. They were attempts on his life.

"Jack," said Frank, "nothing's changed."

The doors of the conference room opened, and Mike Church emerged. He and Jack locked eyes, glaring at each other.

"That's what I'm afraid of, Frank," Jack said quietly.

Chapter Six

Easy Target

Jack tossed and turned all night. He'd been plagued by nightmares ever since the first time he went to Death's Province. Just before dawn he woke with a gasp so loud it woke Frank. "Wha . . .? What . . . what time is it? Are you all right?"

Jack sighed and said, "Don't worry about it. Go back to sleep."

Frank didn't need to be told again and was snoring before Jack finished his sentence.

Jack got up and looked out the window. In the distance he saw the griffin he'd freed, soaring over the forest, catching bats for its breakfast as the sun slowly crested the horizon. Once sunlight filled the room, Jack woke Frank and the brothers headed down to the mess hall.

The king had ordered a special breakfast for all the soldiers going on the mission. It was no banquet feast, but it was a step up from the standard grits and scrambled eggs. Cooks prepared made-to-order omelets, and platters overflowed with crispy, thick-cut bacon, juicy fruit, and freshly baked cinnamon rolls dripping with glaze. As the soldiers dug into their meals, gratitude quickly became suspicion.

"I can't remember the last time we got treated so well."

"I know this is an important mission, but why all the fuss?"

"What, don't they think we're coming back?"

"Yeah, is this our last meal or something?"

Frank told the table, "Just enjoy the treat, guys." He turned to Jack and said, "Not a good idea, making a big deal out of this. We've got good soldiers, but they tend to get suspicious when things deviate from the norm." Jack was listening but didn't respond. "Don't get me wrong, they'll do their jobs, and I'm sure they'll do them well."

"That's right," said a voice from behind the brothers, "haven't you heard? We're the best of the best!"

Frank's face fell. "Hello, Corporal Taylor."

Hawk Taylor sat down with a tray full of food. "Oh, Frank, why so formal?"

"Yeah, we go way back, old pal," Joss Huntsman said, as he sat down with his own tray.

"That's right, fellas," Hawk announced to the table. "Joss and I were in school with your lieutenant here. We knew Franky in his youth, when he was just a little thing . . . only a little bit bigger than you and I are now."

There were a handful of snickers from the table.

"Ha. Ha," Frank said flatly.

Unimpressed with the others' reaction, Hawk continued. "Oh, come on, guys, it's all right to laugh. If we can't laugh at ourselves, and especially Frank, who *can* we laugh at?"

"That's *Lieutenant* Waramond," Frank said without his usual confidence.

"Oh, that's right, I forgot, you're a *big man* now. Well, you've always been—"

"Still telling fat jokes, Hawk?" interrupted Jack. "Maybe you should move on to bald jokes. I'd think you'd be an expert on those."

Hawk was, indeed, quite bald. A ring of hair grew around the sides of his head, but he kept it cropped and usually wore a hat. He had thick eyebrows over close-set eyes that looked small next to his bulbous nose. Ignoring the bald crack, Hawk exclaimed, "Jack! I heard you were back. How ya been? Try and kill any princes lately?"

The jab had a pronounced effect. One man choked on his juice, while another let his bacon drop to the floor. Yet another looked around, gave a weak "Ha," then got up and left. But most of the men just went quiet. The only two unfazed by Hawk's comment were Joss, who erupted in laughter, and Jack, who just smiled and answered, "Naw. I thought I'd start small today, maybe just a corporal or two."

Joss's laughter fizzled, but Hawk grinned wider. "Come on, Jack, lighten up. You don't need to keep looking out for your brother. He's a big boy ..." he raised his thick eyebrows at Frank, then looked back to Jack. "Very big." He chortled at his own joke. "He can take care of himself—right, big guy?" He gave Frank a wink.

"Yeah, we're only having some fun," echoed Joss. Though Joss liked to joke, everyone knew his strength came from Hawk, who was the front man of their duo. Joss's appearance was unassuming. He had a round head with black hair, which he kept short, and heavy-lidded eyes.

"Oh, hey, Joss, you grow a thought of your own yet, or do you still let Hawk do all the heavy lifting?" asked Jack.

Joss laughed good-naturedly. "I've had a couple."

"See now," Hawk pointed at his sidekick as he spoke with a mouthful of omelet, "*That* is how you take a joke. We're only having a little fun with ya."

The soldiers liked Hawk and Joss. They were easy to talk to and found humor in everything. They weren't afraid to make fun of themselves—there were even a few bald jokes—with jester-like timing in their delivery. Even Jack cracked a smile once. The only one at the table not enjoying their humor was Frank, who was frequently the subject of their hilarity.

When Jack challenged them about it, Joss had a response at the ready. "It's just, he's such an easy target."

"Yeah, you can try, but it's near impossible to miss one so large," chuckled Hawk.

Frank bided his time, enduring the volley of jokes at his expense, until a momentary lull provided an excuse for him to leave. Unfortunately, Hawk had an uncanny way of seeing through him. "What, you're leaving already? But you didn't even finish your food! How will you stay in shape?"

On cue, Joss asked, "He's in shape?"

"Well, *round* is a shape," replied Hawk, with timing as precise as if they'd rehearsed it.

Frank spun around to give them a piece of his mind.

WHAM!

He slammed into a young soldier passing by with a tray full of food. Both trays flipped into Frank before they crashed to the floor.

After a moment of silence, the hall burst into laughter. Everyone applauded, while jeers came from multiple directions, Joss shouting, "Gravity check!" and Hawk roaring, "Clean up on aisle Waramond!"

Frank's face and ears turned apple red. He turned on his heel and headed out of the mess hall. He looked down at the slop running down his body and grumbled, "So flipping cliché," and headed for the lieutenant's dorm.

Once in his room, Frank began to change his clothes. He saw that some of the spill had even seeped through to his undershirt, so he pulled that off as well. He opened his closet to grab some clean clothes. A mirror hanging inside of it cast his reflection, and he stepped back to see more of himself. He turned sideways, examining his extra weight, and sighed. He picked up his belly and let it drop. It wasn't like his weight was a problem; he was able to keep up with and, in many cases, outdo his peers. He put his arms out, and then pulled them back in and cupped his pecs, thinking they looked more like a woman's breasts than a man's muscular pecs, muttering with disappointment, "Moobs."

There was a knock at the door, and Jack walked in. "Am I bothering you?"

"What—oh, hey, Jack. No, come on in." He tried to smile as naturally as he could, turning to put on his clean undershirt. "This is your room too. You don't have to ask to come in."

"Yeah, well, I wasn't sure if you wanted to be alone."

"Why would I want that?" asked Frank, putting on the rest of his clothes, avoiding Jack's eyes.

"No reason." Jack dug in his bag, but he didn't take anything out. "So . . . I see Hawk and Joss are still the same."

Frank tied the laces of his boots still not looking at his brother. Trying to sound as lighthearted and jovial as Hawk and Joss, he replied, "Yeah, well, I never said life was perfect."

"I would have thought a couple of asshats like them would have been kicked out by now." When Frank didn't respond, he continued, "Look, Frank, try not to let what they say bother you. I don't think they mean any harm."

"Yeah, well," Frank was still not looking at his brother. He had all his new clothes on now and was just strapping on his belt and sword. "Just because harm isn't intended doesn't mean it hasn't been done."

Once he had everything on, Frank finally faced his brother and smiled—a smile so sincere, it wasn't.

Jack said sympathetically, "You don't have to put on a brave face with me, Frank."

Frank brushed past him. "I don't know what you're talking about. I'm fine. I've endured far worse from them in the past. And like they said, I'm a big boy—I can take it. And truthfully, I barely see them—maybe once or twice a month at the most these days."

"You know you're a hundred times the soldier they'll ever be," said Jack, taking a step toward Frank.

"Jack." Frank groaned and sat down hard on his bed. "I don't need cheering up."

"I know you don't." Sounding annoyed, Jack said, "What you need is more confidence in yourself."

"I'm plenty confident."

"Then what do you care what they think of you?"

"I . . . I don't."

"Bullshit!"

Frank stood up and stared down at his brother. "I don't!"

"Well, then, when are you gonna start showing it?" demanded Jack.

They stood so close Frank could smell the coffee on Jack's breath as he looked down at him, hollering back, "I show it every single day! Dozens of soldiers are under my supervision!"

Jack yelled, "Damn right they are!"

"So why are we shouting at each other?"

"I don't know!"

They laughed.

After a minute, their laughter subsided. Still chuckling, Jack asked, "By the way, what are *moobs*?"

Frank stopped laughing. "What's what?"

"I thought I heard you say *moobs* or something when I walked in."

Frank shuffled sheepishly and said, "Oh uh . . . it's, well . . ."

"What?"

He felt his face heat again, and Frank explained, "It's short for . . . well . . . man-boobs."

Clearly not expecting that as an answer, he replied simply, "Oh." But a moment later sputtered.

Frank let out a snort of his own. Suddenly they were laughing, harder than either had in a long time.

Frank wiped the tears from his eyes and said, "Oh, Jack, I don't know why I still let them get to me. But really, I'm fine. I'll be fine."

Still chuckling, Jack said, with a note of trepidation in his voice, "But they're on the mission."

"Yeah, I know. I approved it."

"You did?"

"I didn't want to. Believe me. And not just because they're a couple of grade-A jackasses. It was just part of the process. Don't worry. Lieutenant Patrick is taking responsibility for them, and he promised I won't even have to see them."

Later that morning, all the transports were packed and ready to leave, and the soldiers stood assembled outside in the courtyard facing a stage with a podium, set in front of a castle terrace. Upon the stage stood the king, the commander, two generals, and Captain Vergo. The wizards stood at the back, except for Eli, who remained at the front with his son Mike Church.

Directly in front of the stage stood the mission's two leading lieutenants, Frank and Lewis Patrick.

Vergo spoke into a microphone explaining, "Obviously we're all on the same mission and going together for the same purpose. But if there's ever a need to split up or divide, it will be into these platoons." He began to read off the names of the soldiers going on the mission. As each name was called, the soldier went to stand near his assigned lieutenant.

Jack watched Frank's face twitch after Vergo read, "Joss Huntsman: Waramond's platoon." He thought that it might not be so bad; Joss wasn't quite as obnoxious if separated from . . . "Hawk Taylor: Waramond's platoon." Jack grimaced and glanced at his brother again, who looked straight ahead, trying to appear unfazed. He watched Frank glance at Lewis Patrick, who mouthed the words, "I'm sorry," and shook his head to show he hadn't known about the reassignment.

When Vergo finished, he added, "Oh, and, Jack, you'll be riding with us in the commander's vessel."

Jack shouted up to Vergo, "Actually, I'll be with my brother."

Irritation dripped from Vergo's voice as he replied, "No, the commander wants you with him."

"I don't care what he wants," Jack yelled back. "I'm going with my brother. If the commander needs me, he knows where I am."

Vergo steadied himself, but he couldn't hide the contempt in his voice. "If you won't do as you're told—" he began, but Commander Church approached and whispered something in his ear.

Frank said out of the corner of his mouth, "What are you doing? We don't disobey orders."

"Maybe *you* don't."

"Soldiers can't—"

"I'm not a soldier anymore."

Frank gave an annoyed sigh, but Jack ignored it.

Vergo and Church finished their discussion. "Fine." Vergo turned to the soldiers, "Jack, you can stay with Lieutenant Waramond's platoon. If you're needed, we'll call for you." Back to the soldiers as a whole he shouted, "All right, let's move out!"

Everyone scattered, going to their assigned ships. Frank rounded on Jack. "What is wrong with you? If you want to go rocking your own boat, don't let me stop you." Frank thrust a finger at Jack, "But don't do it to mine!" He turned and trudged ahead to his ship.

Jack followed, calling after, "Frank, I'm sorry. I didn't think—"

"No, you clearly didn't."

"I just wanted to—"

"Oh, I know exactly what you were doing," said Frank as they approached the vessel.

Hawk and Joss arrived at the same time. At the sight of Frank, Hawk hollered, "Lieutenant Waramond, I'm so honored to be a part of your platoon." Then with an air of mockery, he saluted and went through the door.

"Yes," followed Joss, "It's a pleasure to be under the direction of the great Lieutenant Waramond," Joss gave a similar mock salute, "whose reputation precedes him." Then he boarded the ship as well.

Hawk's head popped back through the doorway, "Only just after his stomach!"

Frank heaved a great sigh and turned back to Jack, "Look, despite what I said, I appreciate what you were trying to do for me. But we aren't kids anymore, and I don't need you watching out for me."

Jack looked at him blankly and said, "I don't know what you're talking about, Frank. I just didn't want to spend days on end with Argus Vergo for company." And he climbed aboard.

Weighed down by the gear and personnel, the massive hover crafts inched along the route for a couple days. They reached a remote area where they landed and began the remainder of the journey on foot.

Their first assignment was to find the man who knew the location of the entryway into Death's Province. The only intel they had was that he lived off the grid, though the commander thought they had isolated his location to a 60-mile radius of terrain.

Each morning the search began the same way. The transport vehicles moved ahead to set up a temporary camp while the soldiers divided into their platoons and combed the land for the person of interest, meeting at the camp by day's end. As they cleared each area, they set up motion detectors called boundary pylons. The pylons registered any activity between them, creating a sort of detection net, alerting the soldiers if anyone passed through ground they had already covered.

Most of the soldiers found this to be an unbelievable waste of time. Many wondered aloud what kind of information the person could have that was so important. Jack figured they'd have a fit if they knew it would not only take them right up to Death's Province, but inside of it.

After a week of searching, the men's patience began to wear thin. The trekking was monotonous, and each day the hills grew steeper and the ground more uneven. Even Commander

Church was getting frustrated, snapping at the men for the smallest of issues. And after enduring days of endless heckling from Hawk and Joss, Frank's patience was nonexistent.

Close to midday, more than a week into the search, Frank's platoon found themselves atop a massive, treeless hill. Hawk commented on how the only thing large enough for a person to hide behind was Frank, and Joss pitched in, "How about it, Franky? Is he behind you?"

Trying to ignore them, Frank didn't answer.

"I'll take that as a no," said Hawk. "Let's head to camp, boys."

After a cheer of approval from the others, Frank rounded on them, "Don't drag the rest of them down to your level."

The two of them kept right on smiling. Hawk said, "Oh, come on! You have to admit this is a waste of time. Tomorrow, we'll breach the forest line and there can be some genuine searching. But look." He spun in a circle on the spot, "There. I just searched the entire area. There's no one out here."

At the end of his rope, Frank snapped, "I don't know why we're doing this, Corporal Taylor. I don't ask questions. I do what I'm told. That is a soldier's job. But I can't do my job with you two running off at the mouth. If you two don't shut up, I'll personally see to it that you get extra duties from now until this mission is over. Do I make myself clear?"

Hawk and Joss looked at Frank defiantly.

Normally Frank would have walked away at that point, but he saw Jack watching. So he turned back and repeated to the pair, "I said, *do I make myself clear?*"

By now the rest of the platoon had stopped what they were doing and were watching the scene. Hawk and Joss both muttered a begrudging "yes."

"I didn't hear you."

Joss said much clearer, "Yes," while Hawk glared around at the others watching.

Frank rounded on Hawk. "Yes, what? Corporal Taylor?"

Hawk whined, "Come on, man."

Frank repeated, *"Do I make myself clear, Corporal? I will not ask again!"*

In all their years, Jack had never seen Frank with the upper hand over Hawk and Joss. Somehow, Hawk's charisma had kept him out of trouble, but now he was dealing with someone he'd made an enemy of. He wasn't used to his charm failing him, and being disciplined like this, in front of so many peers, he clearly didn't like it at all.

"Hey, chill out, Frank, you're embarrassing us," he muttered.

Frank gave a hearty but equally exasperated laugh. "Well, now! I wonder what that's like." He crossed his arms and continued to wait for his answer.

Jack thought he could actually see Hawk swallowing his pride before saying, "Fine. Yes, sir."

"Yes, sir, lieutenant," Joss echoed weakly.

Go, Frank! Jack turned away and continued helping set up the boundary pylons, occasionally looking up to check on his brother. He smiled when he saw Frank now carrying himself taller and proud. However, he didn't like the way Hawk seemed to be stalking Frank, or the way Joss was acting like some kind of lookout. Jack left a soldier to finish the pylon they were working on by himself, and he began making his way toward Frank.

But it was too late.

Hawk and Joss had stealthily set a stack of the boundary pylons just behind Frank back at the edge of the hill, then screamed, "Lieutenant! Lieutenant Waramond, sir, quick!"

Frank turned right into the pylons, tripping and falling over them, and they spilled in every direction as he tumbled out of sight, falling over the edge of the steep hill.

Jack got to the edge in time to see Frank's roll down the hill come to a finish. Hawk and Joss looked surprised, as if they hadn't expected this outcome from their prank, but as soon as Frank picked himself up, they erupted with laughter.

Hawk cried, "Did you see that? He looked like a beach ball!"

Jack advanced on Hawk, punching him square in the nose.

"Ow! Hey!" Hawk yelped, clutching his face as blood pooled between his fingers.

"Don't worry, I didn't break it. Yet." Then Jack pulled back a fist and turned to Joss, who flinched so hard he fell backward. He began to pick himself up, but Jack pointed at him and ordered, "Stay."

"What?" asked Joss.

"You heard me." Jack looked down the hill to check on Frank. He was at least on his feet now. "Frank! Frank, are you all right? Frank!"

"I'm fine," came a quiet response from Frank, and then more clearly pronounced, "I'm fine."

"Can you get back up here?"

"Yeah." There was a pause, then Frank said, "But I think it'll be easier if we just meet up ahead. I think the land flattens out some."

"But that isn't for miles. You'll probably be on your own for most of the day."

"I know."

Jack worried about Frank. Being humiliated in front of his platoon had to sting. He heard the slightest trace of giggling from behind, turned and saw Hawk still holding his nose and Joss on the ground, but both with smiles on their faces. He glared at Hawk, who replied, "What? He's not hurt."

Then Jack yelled down, "Do you want me to throw one of these losers down the hill to help you?"

After a short pause Frank answered, "Naw. I'll just have some words with them later."

"All right. We'll meet you up ahead at camp."

"See ya then."

Jack then turned back to Hawk and Joss. "You hear that? And any words he forgets, I'll make sure to remember and add a few of my own."

He turned his back on them and walked away as the two exchanged a nervous glance.

12 Years Ago
568 AR

J ack sat on the shore, watching the sun rise. He tried to ignore the sunburn on his forehead, or how sweaty and hungry he felt. He reminded himself that as soldier he would likely endure far worse in the years to come. As a distraction from his discomfort, Jack replayed the attack in his mind because he couldn't make sense of it. The cruise wasn't even an official military exercise; it was simply a celebration for the graduates of the academy, the ladies' finishing school, and their families. At first Jack assumed the attack was because Jason was one of the graduates on board. Except Jason's presence at the academy had been a well-kept secret. He had attended the school under an assumed identity to assure equal treatment. No one, not even the academy's staff, knew that the prince was in this class until the graduation ceremony, on the evening they left.

The hoot of a jungle bird roused Jack from his thoughts. He looked toward their camp to see if it had woken the other survivors, but they slept undisturbed. Jack's stomach rumbled. While they had been drinking coconut water to slake their thirst, Jack craved clean, fresh water. He thought about waking Lieutenant Rob Brown, the only experienced soldier among the survivors and thus their commanding officer, except of course, Jason outranked him as the prince. So he roused Eric and Gary instead, asking them if they'd be interested in looking for some water. They left Jason, Eliza, and Rob to sleep by the remains of the previous night's fire.

The hoots and chirps of animals grew louder as the three privates pressed deeper into the jungle. And even though they only saw brightly colored birds, they couldn't shake the feeling of danger. For a moment they thought they heard what sounded like the static of a radio.

"What was that?" gasped Gary.

Jack turned and hissed, "What?"

With some panic in his voice, Gary said, "Over there. Look!"

Jack looked. "I don't see anything."

There were only two swords among the group of survivors. Jason had his, which Jack regretted not borrowing, and Eric had the other, which he held drawn and at the ready. That didn't stop him from suggesting, "Maybe we should just head back."

A loud shriek sent all three men ducking for cover as something burst from the shadows. They chuckled at their shared cowardice when they realized it had only been a harmless toucan. The bird landed a few yards away, dipped its head, then tilted back its enormous orange beak and swallowed.

Eric spoke louder than any of them had since they entered the jungle, "Wait! I think it's drinking!" He sheathed his sword and dashed toward the bird.

The discord of the jungle birds' hoots echoed as they ran toward the toucan. Jack let out a hoot of his own when he laid eyes on a babbling brook. Dropping to their knees on the rocky bank, the privates cupped their hands and drank greedily.

Jack felt the cold water run down his throat and fill his stomach. He grinned as he stood and wiped his mouth dry on the sleeve of his uniform. For half a moment he thought about giving a prayer of thanks to one of the gods, but then thought about Aegir and withheld his gratitude. He could hardly wait to share his discovery with Eliza and Jason.

Gary asked, "Now that we know this is here, do we find some kind of containers to transport some back, or—"

"Too much work," interrupted Jack. "We'll be rescued soon. Probably today even. Let's just bring the others here."

"Sure," said Eric. "We'll just make sure one of us stays behind in case a rescue party shows up."

Gary tilted his head and said, "Yeah, I guess you're right. I was just think—"

Shuck. Shuck. Thuck. Shuck.

Two arrows struck Gary in the chest, one missed, and a fourth lodged in his head. He collapsed, dead before even hitting the ground.

Jack and Eric began to move when they were pelted by another set of arrows. Jack yelped in pain as one hit his left shoulder. The second arrow missed, while two hit Eric in the back. He fell forward and leaned on Jack, coughing blood. Eric tried to grab the sword on his back, but it was too much effort. Jack watched him give one final panicked look before he felt Eric's body go limp. As his comrade slumped in his arms, Jack reached over and pulled Eric's sword from the sheath. He felt a twinge of guilt when he looked at Eric's dead body on the ground, but there wasn't time to mourn as a third set of arrows whizzed toward him.

Leading with his good arm, Jack ignored the pain in his left shoulder and instinctively swung the sword around, stopping all four arrows with the blade, except one that missed completely.

Crack. Thwack. Snap. Thump.

It wasn't dumb luck. Jack had proven to be capable with a sword and had done similar in training at school. He'd never been in actual danger then, let alone with a wounded shoulder, so he was unable to contain a chuckle at his success.

Then four grungy pirates burst out of the brush. The man at the front shouted, "He's wounded, this won't take long." He tackled Jack, kicking up clouds of dirt as they rolled. The pirate was wiry but strong, and Jack lost his grip on the sword. A moment later, he found himself under the pirate, holding back a knife that hovered only inches from his throat. When the pirate cocked his arm to complete the job, Jack bolted upright, knocking the pirate off his body.

They both scrambled to their feet, paused, and eyed Eric's sword a couple yards away. The pirate darted for the weapon, but instead of running, Jack picked up a rock and launched it. The rock hit the man's skull with a dull crack, and Jack heard him fall to the ground with a thud.

As Jack surveyed the area, no one else was in sight. The other three pirates had vanished. Fearing the worst, he took off toward the campsite. Running with all his might, Jack leaped over the growth of the jungle, swallowing the throbbing pain in his shoulder. As he neared the camp, he began to shout cries of warning.

Then he saw her. *Eliza.*

She ran toward him, concern all over her face. "Jack! What's going on? I woke up and you and the others were gone and—"

Jack didn't stop. He grabbed Eliza by the wrist and pulled her with him. Seconds later, an arrow struck the tree Eliza had been standing in front of.

As they ran toward the jungle seeking cover, the wiry pirate reemerged in front of them. He had Eric's sword strapped to his back, and a stream of blood running down the side of his head. The pirate wasted no time, tackling Jack again, knocking Eliza from his grasp. He growled in rage, tearing buttons off Jack's uniform as he grabbed it and slammed him on the ground. Jack felt the world spin as he gasped for air.

Eliza charged at the pirate, trying to help Jack, but her small frame did little damage to the bandit. As she went for a second attempt, she was pulled backward into the arms of a giant, bald man, who called to the other, "Hey, Beauregard."

Even with no fight in him, Jack couldn't help but titter, "Beauregard?"

Beauregard, the wiry pirate, slammed Jack into the ground and barked at the other, "What are you doing here? You should be with the others."

The enormous man tipped his head down at Eliza who he held, despite her writhing, without much effort, and dumbly said, "They weren't there."

"So find them you idiot! Just make sure not to kill the prince."

"The others are looking for them. I came to help you."

"I told you, I got this," snapped Beauregard.

The giant moaned, "Doesn't look like—ow!"

Eliza had bitten the large man's hand. Reeling from the pain, he let go of her, but she didn't run. She grabbed a fallen tree branch and swung it at Beauregard's head. He laughed as he caught the branch with one hand. "Oh, she's feisty!" He pushed back on the branch, sending Eliza tumbling to the ground. "Try not to kill her either. We'll have some fun with her later!"

Jack's good arm shot up and grabbed Beauregard's throat. "Have fun with this!" Using his good arm, Jack punched the pirate, sending one of his teeth flying.

Breathing heavily, Jack stepped between Eliza and the bald pirate, ready to fight.

A voice called out, "What's all this then?"

Jack watched as three more pirates arrived. Distracted, he didn't notice Beauregard had gotten up, until he snatched Eliza away.

She screamed, "Jack!"

"No—Eliza!"

When the pirate held a knife to her throat Jack opened his fists, raised his hands and took a step back in submission. "All right, all right, just don't hurt her."

As Jack surveyed the five men, he glimpsed Jason approaching from behind them. He didn't see Rob but was certain the lieutenant and the prince had a plan. Jason probably meant for Jack to see him, so he decided to try and stall the pirates. "Why did you attack our ships?"

Beauregard spat blood on the ground. "We didn't do that. This was just luck," he said. "The radar showed a royal ship was in that big storm. We came to salvage the wreck, but all we found was you little shits." He laughed, "But imagine our surprise when we realized that one of you was the fucking prince!"

The pirates all chuckled with victory in their bellies. "Yeah, turns out there was something to salvage after all," cackled a greasy-haired pirate.

Jack laughed incredulously, "So, what—you're going to try and ransom him?"

Beauregard scowled at Jack and snarled, "You laughing at us you little prick? Huh?" He grabbed Eliza's cheek and squeezed. "When we've got this pretty little thing in our possession?"

Eliza tried to speak, but all she got out was, "Jack!"

Jack tried to stay focused. He needed to keep the pirates talking, but seeing Eliza in this animal's clutches enraged him, and he couldn't stop himself. "You . . . you keep your filthy hands off her!"

"Or you'll what? Huh," the pirate mocked, "*Jack?* Just what are ya gonna do about it?" He turned and ran his tongue up the side of Eliza's face.

She groaned in disgust, and Jack muttered, "The minute she's out of your grip you're going to find out."

"What's that? Huh? What'd you say to me?" The wiry pirate grabbed Eliza by the hair and yanked her back, while pointing the knife at Jack. "You know what? I was going to save her for later, but the way she's got you all riled up, I can think of something better to do with her now!"

He pulled Eliza forward and swung the knife at her, but before it connected, Rob burst from behind a tree, grabbed the pirate's hand, shoved Eliza free of his grip and kneed him in the gut.

Rob began to shout for Eliza to run, but his eyes widened, and his body tensed, just before falling at Eliza's feet, with Beauregard's knife stuck in his back.

Beauregard pulled the knife out, but it was knocked from his hands almost immediately. Jack had cleared the space between them and began to pummel the pirate.

Jason had sprung out from behind a tall bush attacking the remaining pirates. Three stayed on him but the greasy-haired pirate broke off toward, "Jack!" yelled Jason.

Seeing the greasy man approaching, Jack let Beauregard's beaten body drop, then grabbed Eric's sword and began parrying with the pirate. Adrenaline numbed the pain in his shoulder as he blocked strikes. When he finally saw an opening, Jack heaved his sword into the pirate's skull, leveling him. Jack then joined Jason, making short work of the remaining pirates—killing them all.

But it wasn't over. Jack and Jason spun around when they heard Eliza scream. Beauregard was stalking toward her, a bloody mess, but still alive.

Jack cursed, "Don't you ever die?"

Jason bellowed, "Give up, pirate! It's just you now."

Beauregard stopped moving but began to chuckle. He turned toward the boys and spat, "It isn't just me you little shit! We're just the search party."

"*Right*," mocked Jason, "And that's why you attacked us."

"We only advanced on you because your group divided," growled Beauregard. He looked at Jason, "But we're coming for you. And when we do, mark my words," he snapped his head, "*Jack—* you and this little bitch are as good as dead!"

He tossed a grenade in the divide between them, far away enough that the prince wouldn't be harmed, but close enough to distract them while he made a getaway.

Jack picked himself up and ran after the pirate. Dashing past bushes with large leaves and whipping by tall grass, they passed the brook where Gary and Eric's bodies still lay. Soon they rounded to a rocky edge of the island, where the pirate search party must have landed.

He knew he was too far away to catch the pirate, but Jack didn't stop running until he skidded to a stop right at the rocky edge.

Huffing to catch his breath, Jack watched the pirate zooming away on a motorized dinghy, hearing Beauregard's shouts faintly over the motor, "You're dead! You hear me—dead!"

Jack winced. "Sorry," Eliza apologized as she cleaned the wound on his shoulder later that evening.

"It's okay. Just took me by surprise."

As she wrapped Jack's shoulder, Eliza said, "I'm no doctor. We'll have to watch it, make sure it doesn't get infected. But the wound looks pretty clean."

Jack craned his head to peer at her work. "You did great. It feels fine." He looked at the cloth she was using to wrap his shoulder. "That was a good idea, salvaging the shirts off the others before we buried them."

"I had to make myself useful somehow, since you guys wouldn't let me help you dig the graves."

Jack replied, "Sorry, but that's no work for a woman." Eliza gave an exasperated grunt as she tied the knot of the makeshift sling quicker and tighter than needed. "Ouch!" he yelped. "Well, it isn't."

"You two could have at least let me help dig Rob's grave. He saved my life, you know. If he hadn't been there . . ." She sighed deeply, containing her tears as she looked at the blood on her clothes that she knew was Rob's. "I wanted to honor him somehow."

"You honor him by still being alive," Jack said firmly.

She grunted irritably.

Jason had been silent for some time, staring off into the night sky. Jack and Eliza weren't even sure he was paying them any attention until he said, "Don't worry, Eliza. It's been three days. My father must have the army looking for us. They'll probably be here tomorrow. Just relax."

Jason returned to his stargazing, while Jack and Eliza looked at the fire. Eliza picked up a stick and prodded it irritably. Jack inquired, "What is it?"

She exhaled, "I just feel so useless."

"Useless?"

"Yes, useless. I couldn't do anything in the attack." She threw the stick into the fire. "You and Jason fought those goons, while I was just a . . . a hindrance."

"Women aren't supposed to fight," Jason stated.

"Jason, if I hadn't been captured, maybe Rob would still be alive. Maybe I could have even helped you."

Jason maintained, "Women don't fight. If you *had* helped, you would have been breaking the law."

"Two words, Jason: *Worth. It.*" Eliza threw another stick into the fire before continuing. "A life is more valuable than some archaic, ridiculous . . . *manmade* law about what a woman should or shouldn't do!"

Jack tried a calm voice, "Eliza, maybe—"

"It is *so* important that you don't finish that statement," she warned. "Do you have any idea what it's like to be a woman in Idoless? If I'd been trained, I could have helped fight those pirates today. Instead, I was helpless." She looked at Jack and Jason, and roared, "Helpless!" She threw an arm at Jason. "And he's the flipping prince!" She gave a great growl and turned to Jason. "You had no right putting your life in danger like that!"

Jason remained calm, but there was a definite edge in his voice as he replied, "Excuse me, but I had every right. As you just pointed out, I am your prince. It was my duty and frankly, I'm a more than capable warrior."

Jack stood up. "I think we all need to just take a breath and calm down."

Jason protested, "I'm calm."

Jack rolled his eyes and groaned, "Don't aggravate the situation."

"What do you want me to say?"

"Just say something nice."

Jason then spoke in a friendlier voice. "Look Eliza, you're among friends. We . . . we haven't even made one comment about your inappropriate attire."

There was fire in Eliza's eyes, so Jack jumped back in and said to her, "Tell you what. Um, next time . . . we'll let you help dig the graves."

Eliza's eyes bulged. "Next time?"

"No we won't," said Jason.

"Not helping," said Jack.

Eliza shook her head and shouted, "It's not about the graves, Jack!" then got up and stormed off.

Jack gave Jason an exacerbated look and said, "What's wrong with you?"

Jason just looked in the direction Eliza had left and shrugged, "Far too emotional. It's no wonder they aren't allowed to fight." Jason leaned back and grinned as he closed his eyes to rest. "And I wasn't actually complaining about her clothes, or lack thereof. Gives me something much more interesting to look at than palm trees."

"That's not really helping," said Jack. And for a moment, he wondered if the law about women's clothing was put in place because of the women or the men. Jack got up, and said, "She, um . . . she probably shouldn't be alone."

Jack headed out in the direction Eliza had fled. After only a few minutes of walking, he found her on the edge of a clearing lit by the cool moonlight. She either didn't hear him approach or didn't care; she just stared at the jungle's edge. Jack inched up to her and was about to say something when she groaned, "What do you want?"

"Nothing. I um, just figured . . . you shouldn't, you know . . . you shouldn't be out here alone, is all. There could be more pirates."

With her arms crossed, holding herself in a sort of hug, Eliza kept her back to him and said, with a sort of sad sarcasm, "My hero."

"Eliza, I'm sorry."

She turned and faced him, her brow furrowed. "For what?"

"Huh?"

"You said you were sorry. What are you sorry about?"

"I . . . um. I'm sorry you're mad?"

"Exactly. You don't even understand." She turned away again. Jack allowed silence to swallow the conversation until finally she sighed and murmured, "Jack."

"Yeah?"

"There's just so much . . . *wrong* with this world. And it doesn't seem like anyone is willing to do anything to fix it. Everyone is just content to let the bad things be bad."

"It's not *all* bad. And some things change."

"Oh sure, small things. But . . . nothing that really matters."

"Well," Jack began, but stopped. He pondered a moment, then said the only thing that he knew to be true. "If anyone could make the kind of change you're talking about, Eliza . . . it's you." She turned to Jack and considered him. "I mean, I don't think the world is all *that* bad a place. After all, it has you in it."

"Oh, shut up," Eliza said, annoyed by his sappy choice of phrase. "You're just trying to make me feel better."

"No, I'm not. And I can prove it." He stepped alongside her and led her further into the clearing.

Eliza narrowed her eyes, challenging his mystery. She followed with friendly suspicion, then stood where Jack stopped, her makeshift dress billowing in the breeze.

Jack began, "All right, this is pretty basic, but you're just starting out, so . . . if someone is throwing a punch at you—"

"Wait, what? What are you doing?"

"I'm going to show you how to fight."

"What . . . what about the law?"

He grinned. "Well, I've been changed. Today I learned that a life is more valuable than some archaic, ridiculous, *manmade* law about what a woman should or shouldn't do."

Eliza's face changed. *Was that a smile?*

"And," he added, "if Jason and I aren't around, I want to make sure you can defend yourself." Jack took her hand and brought it to where it should be for a ready stance. "Because your life is pretty valuable to me. Much more valuable than the law."

Chapter Seven
Frank's Discovery

Frank's ears were still ringing from his tumble down the hillside. He felt heat crawl up his face, a mixture of anger and embarrassment flooding his thoughts. He was brought back to reality as he became aware of a cold, wet sensation spreading across his hip. He looked down and realized his canteen was as broken as his pride.

The terrain he was on rose and fell in an irregular rhythm. It was more demanding than the trail the platoon was following, and he already felt the heat of the sun on the back of his neck, but Frank had endured worse. And now, by himself, he could at least be at ease. He was able to enjoy his surroundings—and they were beautiful surroundings indeed. The rolling land may have been difficult to trek, but it was a feast for his eyes. The breeze made waves through the lush green grass, and the forest he was walking toward formed the perfect backdrop. He was so taken with it all that he began to forget about his recent humiliation.

But as the day passed, Frank's attention shifted from the pleasant landscape to his growing thirst. His mouth became increasingly dry, and he felt as if his throat was sticking to itself each time he swallowed to try and create some kind of moisture within it. As the day wore on, he began to feel dizzy, and his head ached. He knew it would be at least another couple of hours before he'd meet up with the group. Two hours turned to one, then one turned to only half, but by then, he couldn't think of anything but his thirst.

To distract himself, he mentally went through all the potential names for his plane and weighed the pros and cons of each. As he discarded the most recent option, Frank heard the faint whoosh of running water. At first, he thought his dehydration was causing him to hallucinate. Frank stopped walking and strained his ears. The sound seemed to be coming from just ahead in the forest, so he turned off the trail to investigate.

Frank followed the sound until he found himself in front of a cascade. The verdant foliage lining the shore formed a palette of dusky olive and Brunswick greens, freckled by lively orange, yellow, and crimson flowers. Sunlight cut through the canopy of trees in sharp, dappled beams. A torrent surged down the side of a jagged ledge, emptying into a large pond and filling the space with mist. A vibrant rainbow glowed where the spray collided with the sun.

Frank knelt down, cupped his hands into the water and slurped the cool, fresh liquid, quenching his thirst. Once he'd had his fill, he splashed some water on his face, then got to his feet and looked around once more. He wished he had the time draw this splendor—or better yet, to paint it.

He turned to leave but froze at the unexpected sound of another person's voice. Who could it be? It was a man, though young by the tenor of his voice, and he was *singing*!

"There's a saying, old, says that love is blind.
Still we're often told 'seek and ye shall find.'
So I'm going to seek a certain man I've had in mind.
Looking everywhere, haven't found him yet.
He's the big affair I cannot forget.
Only man I ever think of with regret."

Singing was such a lost art in Idoless. Beyond the lullaby his mother (who'd been anything but traditional) had sung to him as a child, Frank had only heard singing a handful of times.

The pool twisted behind a stand of tall bushes, hiding a cove just beyond, and whoever was singing was just on the other side. Frank peered around the ledge, and gasped. The singer was bathing in the pond.

> *"Oh, I'd like to add his initial to my monogram.*
> *Tell me, where's the shepherd for this lost lamb?"*

The word *lamb* was held with such a clear and perfect note, it transfixed Frank.

The man dove under the water for a moment and then burst through the surface, his body now glistening in the sun, and continued.

> *"There's a somebody I'm longing to see.*
> *I hope that he turns out to be*
> *Someone who'll watch over me.*
> *I'm a little lamb who's lost in the wood.*
> *I know I could always be good*
> *To one who'll watch over me."*

Frank's artist's eye traced the contours of the singer's lanky yet toned frame. He had a mass of curly hair that was uncommonly blond considering he was dark skinned. He ran his hands across the tight coils, squeezing out excess water, as he sang with growing passion.

> *"Although he may not be the man some*
> *Girls think of as handsome,*
> *To my heart he carries the key!"*

The singer must be parroting something he'd heard a woman sing; but Frank didn't care, he didn't want the moment to end. The thought startled him. Something felt wrong about what he was doing so he decided to leave, but absentmindedly emerged from behind the bushes instead.

They stood there for what, to Frank, felt like hours, just staring at each other in complete silence, except for the sound of the running water and the birds chirping around them. Frank kept thinking he should say something, but all that came out of his mouth was, "Um . . ." Without warning, the singer sprang from the water and took off like a shot. "No! Wait!"

The singer was fast, but Frank was skilled and, despite his large frame, swift. He caught up with the young man and grabbed his left arm, "Wait, I just—" The singer turned and swung his right fist, which Frank blocked with his other hand. "Listen, I just wanted to—" but the young man jumped in the air, kicking Frank in the gut. Frank's grip loosened, and the singer fled.

Frank scrambled to his feet and sprinted though a dense patch of undergrowth to cut the man off. The singer skidded to a halt and Frank winced at the man's bloodied, bare feet. "Oh! Are you all ri—?" but the singer took off again, leaping through the undergrowth, leaving Frank wondering what had just happened.

Just then, Frank heard raised voices in the distance and sprinted toward the sound. It was the army campsite, and by the time Frank reached it, chaos had erupted. In his attempt to flee from Frank, the singer had unknowingly charged into the camp like a wild animal. Many soldiers had their weapons out, thinking they were under attack.

While assessing the scene, Frank spotted Jack hopping across the tops of the transport vessels, likely to get an aerial view of the situation. They made eye contact, and after exchanging a couple hand motions, Frank knew what to do.

He instructed the men nearest him to form a perimeter, blocking escape, then dashed toward the chaos where the singer punched, kicked, and scratched at the soldiers like a rabid animal. Frank charged toward him like a bull, herding him away from the soldiers, right to where Jack was now hidden.

Jack stepped out and kicked the man in the gut with all his might. Having been running at full stride, the blow took all fight out of the singer. He laid on the ground, holding his stomach, gasping for breath.

"It's just . . . I feel responsible for him," explained Frank.

"Why do you feel responsible for him?" asked Church from behind a desk in the tent being used as the command center, where Frank was now being debriefed.

"It's like I told you, sir, I found him. None of this would be happening to him if not for me."

"Yes, and it's a good thing you did."

"Sir?"

"Lieutenant, what do you know about this mission?"

"Just that we're going into Death's Province to get something important for the king."

"Yes, it's very important . . ." Church oddly glanced at one of the guards in the room then finished, "to the king."

Jack, who was lurking in the back, made an audible noise of irritation and stormed out.

Frank watched anger flash across Church's face. He knew if Jack were still a soldier, Church could discipline him for showing such disrespect, but Jack's special status gave him the freedom to act as he pleased. Still, Frank wondered if Church was going to have Jack dragged back in anyway. Instead he asked for the room to be cleared.

Once they were alone, Church turned to Frank and asked, "Lieutenant Waramond, have you heard of . . . the Secret War?"

"Of course," answered Frank.

"What do you know of it?"

"It's an old myth, or myths really. I've heard tons of versions but basically, the kings of Terra Firma are all fighting with each other for ultimate power." He shrugged, "But they're just stories, mostly to villainize the kings. They're nonsense." When Church didn't reply, he asked, "Aren't they?"

The commander looked at Frank thoughtfully. "Actually, there is some truth to the stories. They've been distorted over time, but the Secret War is real." Frank's mind flooded with questions, but he could feel the commander watching him carefully, so he didn't dare move as he was being trusted with such critical information. Finally, Church continued, "It's a weapon. An ancient and powerful weapon the king has asked us to find in Death's Province. And it's imperative that we find it first."

Before he could stop himself, Frank responded, "First?" Commander Church didn't answer, he just wore a grave look on his face. Frank nodded in understanding. "I see."

Church confirmed, "Yes, there are others who know about the weapon, and we are essentially racing to get to it. We know it's inside Death's Province. That's why we're going in, and that's why we needed your brother. He's the only man who's been there and survived; he'll be our greatest advantage. But we need to get inside first. The entrance to the Province is hidden and moves frequently, but our sources discovered a person who knows where it currently resides. That's who we've been looking for."

Frank's eyes widened. It hadn't even occurred to him. "The captive!" He felt his face heat with regret for speaking out of turn again.

But the commander nodded and patted Frank's shoulder. "Yes, it's him, and thank the gods you found him first. He isn't talking though. We're not even sure he can. We knew he lived off the grid, but nothing like this. He behaves more like an animal than a human. I tried talking with him myself, but he just glared at me." Church looked at Frank pointedly and asked, "You're positive that in your encounter with him he didn't say anything? Anything at all?"

Frank hadn't said anything about the singing yet. It had felt like a private, intimate moment to him, and couldn't bring himself to disclose it for some reason. So far, he'd just omitted the information, but now that he was asked directly. . .

"No sir. He . . . he didn't say a word," he lied.

Commander Church sighed regretfully. "I'm certain he's the one who can help us find the entrance. We're going to have to hold onto him until we find a way to get it out of him. Maybe I'll send for a telepath or something." He sighed again. "I'm having him officially questioned now to see if—"

"Questioned? By whom?" Frank knew he'd spoken out of turn yet again, but he couldn't help himself. "Not Vergo."

The commander raised his hand and said emphatically, "It is—*so important* that we get to that weapon first, Frank." He turned to head back to the desk and said, "You're dismissed, Lieutenant."

Frank braced himself and said, "Sir, one last thing. May I try talking with him?"

"I just told you, he—"

"I know, but I . . . it's like I said, I feel responsible and would just like to try."

"All right. Just, if he does talk, come right to me."

"Yes, sir. Of course."

"Dismissed."

"Yes, sir."

When Frank got outside, shame flooded his body. He'd lied. Right after the commander had entrusted him with classified information, he lied right to his face.

Frank turned to go back in and confess when a voice from behind said, "He's not telling you everything."

Frank spun around to find his brother standing in the shadows. He scolded, "Jack! What was that in there? What's the matter with you?"

"Frank, something odd is going on. They aren't telling us everything."

"Bah, you're paranoid!"

Frank turned and began to stomp away, but Jack chased after saying, "Listen—right now, you're the only person I trust."

"Why did you even come on this mission?"

"What?" Jack looked stunned, "Because you asked me—"

"Bull!" Frank stopped and faced his brother. "You had quite firmly given up on the army. Hades, you gave up on pretty much everything!" Frank composed himself, but his intensity remained. "But you came back. And you came back for a reason, and I know that reason wasn't me."

"Frank, I . . ."

"Jack, I know she's special." Jack began to look away, but Frank grabbed his shoulders so they were face-to-face. "Hey! So you came back. And you came back because you knew this was important. So stop being such whiny brat and start being useful." Jack dropped his defiant expression in favor of something that looked like, Frank hoped, regret. "And I know you've missed it. This life. The job." Frank paused, "You know, after this mission is over, King Hawthorn would probably let you come back, no questions asked."

Jack took a deep breath and looked up at the sky. "Frank . . . You're my brother, and I love you. But there are . . . there are things you don't know about."

Frank's eyebrows turned up and his forehead creases showed as he told his brother the plain truth, "She chose someone else, Jack. She chose Jason."

"Jason!" Jack spat on the ground.

"Hey, show some respect. He's going to be your king someday."

"Not mine. He will never be my king!" With that, Jack turned to leave.

Frank yelled after him, "What happened that night, Jack? When you left. What happened with Jason?"

Jack stopped, turned and said, "I don't know what it is, but there's something Church isn't telling you." And then he walked away.

CHAPTER EIGHT

THE DEAL

As evening fell, a cool breeze blew through the camp, so Frank put on his coat before making his way to the camp's mess tent. In the prep area, he found Hawk and Joss dicing onions, tears streaming down their cheeks. "Hey, you two are doing good." Hawk scowled, and Joss refused to look up from their growing mountain of onions.

"You know we have machines that can do crap like this," groaned Hawk.

Frank raised his eyebrow. "Oh, you want me to find something different for you to do?" When the two wouldn't answer he said, "Tell ya what, why don't you stick around and clean up after dinner too."

Hawk stood up. "What? Why?"

Frank approached Hawk and Joss, stopping just inches away. His large frame, the butt of so many of their jokes, now towered over them. With his brow furrowed and eyes unblinking, his face radiated anger as he explained, "It's called a *punishment*."

"Look, we're sorry," muttered Joss.

"Joss, no!" hissed Hawk under his breath.

Frank turned to Joss. "What was that?"

Joss's face reddened. "I said we're sorry. We're sorry for tripping you." Hawk gave a low moan of disapproval, but Joss continued, "We didn't mean for you to fall down that hill like that."

Frank sighed. "It's not just the hill. You shouldn't have tripped me to begin with. I know cadets who have more discipline than you two."

Looking down to the ground, Joss said, "Yes, sir."

Frank looked at Hawk, who reluctantly said, "Yeah, fine we're sorry."

As Frank walked away, despite the apology, he felt defeated. No matter how hard he tried, he always felt like he was back in school when he dealt with those two. It didn't matter that his military rank was higher than theirs; they had a sort of social rank that seemed to outdo him at every turn. He'd often considered reporting them, but snitches didn't get much respect in the army. He could dispense minor punishments like this, but if he wasn't careful, it would prompt them to seek out revenge. *Yup—just like school.*

Concerns of Hawk and Joss vanished as the interrogation tent came into view. Argus Vergo was emerging from it, wiping his hands on a rag, with four other soldiers following behind him. Frank cursed under his breath and sped up his pace.

As Frank approached Vergo drawled, "You needn't bother yourself, Lieutenant. The prisoner is feral and cannot speak. And believe me, if he had anything to say, he would have."

"Vergo!"

"Trust me. I've questioned him for the last hour, and—"

"The last *hour*? He can't be much older than a cadet. What did you do to—?"

"I was told by the commander," interrupted Vergo, "to do whatever I had to, to extract the information we needed." Vergo threw the rag, reddened with blood, to the ground.

Looking at the rag, trying his best to remain calm, Frank replied, "Well, if you don't mind, Captain, the commander said I could try."

"You're wasting your time." Vergo turned on his heel and strode toward Commander Church's headquarters.

Two of Vergo's soldiers began to follow Frank into the tent, but he stopped them. "Thanks, guys, but I won't be needing any help." They nodded and took their positions guarding the tent.

Frank pulled back the tent flap and entered the shelter. It appeared empty until he heard the sound of chattering teeth coming from a corner, where the singer huddled in the dark. The man was still practically naked; they'd only given him a pair of boxer shorts to cover himself. *He must be freezing.*

The man was filthy, covered in scratches and cuts from the chase. Frank also noticed a number of scars from old wounds and wondered, *How did I miss those before?* But he knew why and cursed himself for it. And then there were the fresh wounds; signs of Vergo's "questioning."

Frank took off his weapon and beret and left them by the entrance, then sat in the chair closest to him. "They tell me you aren't speaking," he said, but the singer didn't react. "They're saying it's because you *can't* speak." Still there was no reaction. "Look, I'm sorry about all this. We only wanted to ask you some questions." The man continued to stare at nothing, like he didn't hear or understand a word. The silence made Frank uncomfortable. "Hey, you were the one who threw the first punch ya know."

Still the singer didn't speak.

Frank felt a surge of annoyance. "Don't sit there pretending like you're some kind of animal when I know you can talk. I heard you singing!" The prisoner's eyes flickered at Frank. With a feeling of triumph, Frank leaned in and said in a hushed voice, "Ahhh, there it is."

But the singer flinched at Frank's proximity. Pity overcame him. He sighed and leaned back in his chair and pinched the bridge of his nose. "I . . . I'm sorry. I didn't mean to scare you."

A quiet mumble came from the man.

"What was that?"

The singer sat tall and threw his shoulders back in defiance. "I said, you didn't scare me."

Frank paused a moment, but then said, "No, of course not. I'm just some strange man who appeared out of nowhere along with a platoon of soldiers. We captured you and tied you up, and now we are holding you here against your will. Then the others, they . . . they . . ." Frank faltered at the thought of what Vergo had done, and guilt swept over him. "Nothing to be scared of at all."

Frank slouched in his chair. This was a very different type of interrogation than he was used to. Were the captive a criminal, Frank would have been aggressive. But this stranger had done nothing wrong, and it was Frank who had brought this disruption to the man's life.

The young man stood and began pacing as far as his restraints allowed, looking like a tethered dog. "Let me go, or I swear you'll regret it!"

Frank smiled sympathetically at the bravado, which he was certain was just posturing.

"Do you think I'm joking?"

"Not at all." Frank got up from his chair and unsheathed a small knife he wore on his belt and stepped forward to cut the bonds on the captive's hands, but at the sight of the blade the singer pulled away. "No, here, I just want to make you more comf—oof!" Before Frank even knew what was happening, the stranger had thrown his entire body at him, knocking him to the ground.

Frank jumped back on his feet. He turned to find the stranger clumsily cutting his hands free with his knife. Frank yelped, "Hey, I was just going to—Hey!" The young man lunged at him with the knife, but Frank blocked the strikes. "Stop it. I was—Hey! I was trying to help you!" Finally, Frank blocked an attack and knocked the blade out from his hand.

Though he was now weaponless, the prisoner continued to fight. He was fast and wiry, but he left himself wide open for attacks. Frank didn't take advantage of the openings though. He only deflected each blow, all while trying to reason with the man.

But the singer just wouldn't listen.

Finally, Frank had enough and took the offensive, quickly pinning the man to the ground and growled, "I was trying to help you. But if you're just going to act like a maniac, I'm going to treat you like one." In moments, Frank had the man in new bonds and turned to go report to Commander Church.

He snatched his beret and sword, grabbed the tent flap, and was about to exit when he heard a sob. He looked over his shoulder at the singer, back in his corner, head turned away.

Frank asked, "Are you . . . ? Did I hurt you?"

Trying to control his voice so that it wouldn't reveal that he was crying, the young man answered, "I'm fine."

Regret flooded through Frank. He set his hat and sword back down and returned to the corner. This time the man didn't flinch; he was defeated, which made Frank feel even worse.

"I . . . I'm so sorry for what they did to you." He waited a moment then added, "It . . . it was wrong."

Tears now freely rolling down his face, the singer barked, "I said I was *fine!*"

Frank noticed the young singer had started shivering again. So, Frank took off his coat and draped the garment over him like a blanket.

Blinking tears from his eyes, the singer whimpered, "I just want to go."

Frank had half a mind to cut the bonds and let him. This man wasn't a war criminal and didn't deserve to be treated as such. But Frank was nothing if not a man who lived by the rules, and he wasn't about to change that now. He knew Commander Church wouldn't allow their captive to go until they had what they needed from him. "Listen, umm . . ."

"Peter."

"What?"

"My name is Peter."

"Peter," Frank smiled. "We're on a mission—an important one. I'm sure that's why the others have treated you . . . well, the way they did. If you just help us, they'll let you go."

Peter grabbed the corners of the coat and pulled it tighter around himself. "Do you promise?"

Frank put out his hand, "You have my word."

Peter looked at the hand blankly.

Frank chuckled. "If you shake my hand, it means we have a deal. It's my duty to fulfill it." He smiled. "I promise you'll be released."

Peter looked at the coat on his shoulders, slowly pulled his bound hands out from under it, and cautiously took Frank's hand. After one shake, Peter yanked them back under the coat.

"Thank you, Peter." Frank knelt down and began to cut the new restraints.

"So, what do you need help with, uh . . . ?" Peter looked at him inquisitively.

"Frank."

Peter gave the slightest of smiles and repeated, "Frank. So, what do you need help with, Frank?"

"That," Frank stood up, "is up to my commander."

Peter sat up and with panic in his voice said, "But I made the deal with you. I only want to talk with you."

Frank looked at him with compassion. He picked up his beret again and said, "I'm sorry, Peter. The commander needs to hear from you directly. I don't have the proper clearance." Peter looked like he was going to be sick, so Frank quickly added, "But maybe he'll let me be present."

Peter leaned back, relaxing a little, but said nothing.

In the silence, the sound of scuffling outside the tent could be heard. Frank grinned to let Peter know it wasn't anything to worry about; there was bound to be shouting and yelling at a military campsite after all.

"All right, I'll be right back with my commander." Frank turned to leave, but hesitated at the door and, a little awkwardly, risked saying, "I . . . I liked your singing." Then he left the tent.

Frank had taken only a couple of steps outside when he realized something was wrong. The guards stationed outside of Peter's tent were no longer there. He saw one of them up ahead, lying face down on the ground. He ran to the guard. A long gash zigzagged down the soldier's side, but it was not bleeding badly. A little further away Frank saw the other guard, who hadn't been so lucky. *Who or what could have taken both of these men by surprise?*

As soon as the thought crossed his mind, Frank heard a snort behind him, and hot breath made the hairs on his neck stand. He turned to find himself face-to-face with a massive grizzly bear. The bear stood on its back legs, displaying its full size before dropping back to the ground. Frank could feel the ground tremble as it landed. The great beast then leaned in, nose-to-nose with Frank, who wasn't sure how to react. It smelled him up and down, and after a moment it seemed to find on him the scent it was looking for. The bear made eye contact with Frank, and it delivered a low, rumbling growl.

"Aww, shi—"

The bear smacked Frank with one massive paw, hurling him yards away.

12 Years Ago

568 AR

Jason kicked the sand. "What has it been, three weeks?"

With compassion Eliza said, "Actually, it's closer to, um, four. Or more."

"Of course. I must have . . . I mean . . ." Jason tried not to sound too desperate, "How hard can it be for the army to find one simple island?"

Eliza placed a hand of comfort on Jason's shoulder. "It was a huge storm, Jason. We got blown so far off course—it's just going to take some time for them to find us."

Jason reassumed his confident, princely voice and said, "Yes, of course." He stopped looking out at the ocean and turned to Eliza, attempting to give her a genuine smile. "I'm sure that's it. These islands are virtually uncharted. Who knows how many of them my father has already searched?"

"Well, I think your plan is going to work." She beamed at him. "Then we won't even need rescuing."

The plan wasn't elaborate. He and Jack had set several traps to impede the pirates when they returned. And as they contended with the traps, Jack and Jason would pick them off, one at a time. Once the number of pirates was small enough, Jack would take one of their dinghies and head out to overtake the main ship while Jason would contend with any still on the island. Eliza's role was to hide in a cave at the base of the island's mountain, which they had been using for shelter.

Eliza began, "Hey, about the plan—"

"You're absolutely right, Eliza." His smile became more sincere. "I . . . I hope you can forgive my moment of weakness. I didn't mean to complain."

"Oh, Jason, that wasn't weakness. You were being real with me. It was actually quite nice." She gave him a small peck on his cheek. In that instant, all concerns about their rescue vanished from Jason's mind.

Just then Jack arrived, carrying an armful of branches. "I think we'll have enough for the fire tonight. But there's only a bit more we can use from the jungle's edge. I gathered it together, but I couldn't carry it all in one trip. There's just a little left—"

"I'll get it," exclaimed Eliza, and she tore off before anyone could argue.

Jack smiled as he watched her running from sight and unloaded the branches. He looked at his friend, "You okay?"

Jason realized he was touching his cheek. He snapped awake. "Fine. I'm fine. I was just thinking how nice it is to have Eliza around."

"Yeah, she's amazing," Jack agreed, looking back in the direction she'd headed. "She certainly takes the sting out of our situation."

The affection in Jack's voice fully returned Jason to reality. He measured his friend; then, trying to put the same amount of weight in his tone, said, "I can't think of anyone I'd rather be stranded on a deserted island with."

During their years at the academy, Jason and Jack had playfully competed with each other to win Eliza's favor. Jason's feelings for Eliza had become more authentic after arriving on the island; but hearing the way Jack talked about her now, it occurred to him that he might not be the only one. And the suspicious look Jack was giving him made Jason wonder if Jack might be thinking the same thing about him.

As if Jack were reading his mind, he stated, "She's the best."

"Perfect, really," responded Jason meaningfully.

Eliza's voice surprised them both, "Is everything all right?" She dropped the bundle of kindling on the pile Jack had gathered.

Jack and Jason responded too quickly, as if they had been caught cheating on an exam. "Of course," said Jason.

"Absolutely," said Jack at the same time.

"Good. 'Cause it looked like you were going to start throwing punches or something." She laughed at the absurdity. "I just realized I left the flare gun back at the cave. I'll be right back."

As she ran off again, Jason and Jack stood in an awkward silence. Jason realized he was being ridiculous and smiled. Jack had been his best friend for as long as he could remember. It was one of the reasons the king treated Jack like a second son. And when Jason had to attend the academy, his title was kept a secret from his fellow students, so they told everyone they were the fraternal twins. They looked and acted so much alike; it was more than believable.

Eliza burst back on the scene. "Didn't you guys hear me yelling?"

"Huh?"

"What?"

"Don't you see?" she bellowed. "The pirates—they're back!"

"What?" Jason turned to see a large pirate ship on the horizon approaching the island. "Eliza, go! Get to the caves. We'll come get you when it's over!"

"No," said Eliza as she pulled her hair back into a ponytail.

"What?"

Eliza retorted, "You guys need my help."

Jason scoffed, "And what could you possibly do?"

"If the pirates weren't so close, I'd show you exactly what." Relaxing the hand she had clenched into a fist, she appealed to Jack. "Tell him."

Jason asked, "Tell me what?"

Jack looked down at his feet and cleared his throat.

"Oh, forget it." Eliza turned to Jason. "Jack's been teaching me how to fight."

Jason began to laugh, but at the sight of Jack's guilty expression it faded.

Jack tried to explain, "It's just, after what happened before . . . it didn't feel right. I mean, what if something happened to her and we're not there to help? At least now she'll be able to defend herself."

"Fine," said Jason. "Eliza, you can defend yourself . . . at the caves."

Eliza snapped back, "That's not what he meant, Jason, and you know it."

More to himself than Eliza or Jack, Jason grumbled, "We don't have time for this!"

"You're right, we don't," stated Eliza. "You also don't have the manpower to take on a full crew of pirates."

Jason half laughed, "Yes, the *man*power."

"Listen, you—!"

"No, you listen! You've had what, a few weeks of training? Jack and I have had years. I know what to expect from him." He shot Jack a look of disappointment. "Or at least, I thought I did."

"I'm sorry we kept this from you," Jack groaned. "I just didn't think you'd underst—"

"I repeat—we don't have the time!"

"Then just let me help you!" demanded Eliza.

Jack offered, "You know, she's not half bad. Maybe—"

With a grunt of revulsion, Jason roared at Jack, "Are you seriously going to argue in favor of putting her in danger? I thought you cared about her."

When Jack couldn't respond, Jason glanced at Eliza. Her arms were crossed, and she wore the most stubborn of expressions. "Understand—the only reason I am not fighting this, the absolute only reason, is because we truly don't have the time. You two are forcing me to make this decision, and I hate it." Jason paused and as he second guessed himself, but then decided, "The plan stays the same. The only difference is, now I'm the one going to the ship. Since you two are familiar with each other's skills, you will stay behind and . . . contend with the remaining pirates. Eliza, you stay close to Jack. Jack, it's on you to finish what she can't."

Eliza began to say something, but before she got a word out Jack nodded and said, "I understand."

Jason looked meaningfully at his friend. "Keep her safe. All right, let's move."

Jack and Eliza dashed into the jungle, setting the traps they had made. Jack felt Eliza in his peripheral, hot on his heels, just as she was instructed. The further they got, the more he began to feel the weight of her life, and the situation suddenly felt far more real to him than it had earlier. He stopped.

She asked, "What is it?"

"It's just . . ." It was the worst time for it, but when Jack looked at Eliza, he couldn't help but think how beautiful she was. "Jason was right, this is incredibly dangerous."

"I know."

How strong she was. "No, you don't. And you aren't as good as you think."

"Excuse me?"

How amazing she was. "I don't have the time to sugarcoat this. Jason was right—you've only been training for a couple weeks. You aren't anywhere near ready to go into battle like this."

Eliza shook her head. "What are you saying? I'm not going to the cave."

"I'm not asking you to, Eliza." He almost laughed, "I'd never ask . . . I mean I want you to, but I wouldn't ask you to. Look, it's just, all I'm saying is . . ." What he truly wanted to say to Eliza stuck in his throat. He finally took a breath then blurted, "I want you to change the world, Eliza. So I need you to stay alive."

The urgency in his voice threw her. Barely knowing what to say, she squeaked, "Jack, I—"

"I can't do what you can. But what I can do," Jack drew his sword, "is this. You aren't ready, so please, stay close and just help me."

Eliza nodded silently, and they trekked further inland to take their position. They didn't have to wait long before they heard the buzzing of boat engines. The noise grew louder until the engines finally shut off. Echoes of numerous male voices filled the silence left by the motors. Jack couldn't tell for sure how many there were, though unquestionably more than last time. A lot more.

Suddenly, the ground trembled as he heard an explosion from the beach. They'd salvaged a few grenades from the pirates they'd killed before, and used them in their first and grandest trap, designed to take out a large number in one blow. After that, they were simpler, more primitive setups, made only from what they had to work with on the island.

Jack motioned for Eliza to follow him, and they began creeping through the jungle, looking for any sign of movement. When they finally encountered some pirates, Jack was thankful; there were only two. He sprang out and leveled the men before they could make a sound, and Eliza didn't have to do anything.

As he wiped their blood off the blade of his sword, he looked at Eliza. She wore a serious expression as she watched—as if she were running numbers in her mind or something. He wanted to ask her what she was thinking but talking would have to wait, he didn't want to give away their position.

So, Jack and Eliza continued to make their way through the jungle, slowly and silently until they encountered more pirates. There were three this time. Jack gutted two in rapid succession, but before he was finished with them, the third had broken off and gone for Eliza.

With a stony expression on her face, Eliza drew back and took the ready position, just as Jack had taught her. The pirate laughed at the site. Jack felt it was probably Eliza's saving grace that the pirate hadn't taken her seriously. He didn't even try to fight, he just reached for her. But she grabbed his wrist, pulled him forward, and kneed him in the gut, forcing all the air out of his lungs. He made a stronger effort after that, but by then, Jack was done with his opponent and threw himself on the pirate, grabbing and twisting his neck in one fluid motion. With a crack, the man fell to the ground, dead. Jack looked around, ready for more, but no one was there. He looked at Eliza, who was staring at the dead pirate.

Eliza's brow furrowed. "That's what he was talking about, isn't it?" She kept staring at the body on the ground. "Jason—when he told you to finish what I couldn't. He meant killing them." She looked up at Jack. "We aren't just beating them up."

"We can't," confirmed Jack. "There's too many for us to manage by ourselves. It's either us or them."

"Jason was right. I'm not . . . I can't." Eliza looked at Jack and with a serious, unblinking expression. "Look, I get it now. What you were saying—I get it. I'm not ready for a battle like . . . like this." A twig cracked somewhere deep in the jungle and the pair froze. When no one turned up, Eliza finished, "I can still help. I can't do . . ." she gestured at the body, "that." Then she looked back at Jack. "But I can still kick them in the nuts . . . really hard."

Jack couldn't help but grin. "Works for me."

They began to walk again when suddenly, a lone pirate burst from some thick brush just between them, shouting, "Here! I found them! They're he—!" Jack winced as he watched Eliza's foot (as promised) swoop up between the pirate's legs. The man dropped his weapon and doubled over in agony. Jack then put the pirate out of his misery with one slash from his sword.

They knew there wasn't time to doddle, but still breathing heavily, they paused and nodded to each other. Then, as they'd expected, the rest of the pirates swarmed them.

Jack felt the pressure of both fighting the pirates and protecting Eliza. But somehow, her being there gave him something to fight for. His focus sharpened and he fought better than he would have under any other condition. His strikes were calculated and precise, and he leveled the assailants quickly and efficiently. From the corner of his eye, Jack saw Eliza fending off attacks, slowing them down until Jack could get there to finish the job.

Jack lost track of how many pirates he'd slain, but things were going far better than he thought they would. He knew the odds were stacked against them. But just when he allowed himself to feel that things might actually work out, his heart sank when he heard a familiar voice, "Hey, Jaaaack!"

He turned to see Beauregard holding a rusty revolver to Eliza's temple. The pirate had cleaned up since the last time Jack had seen him, and he was wearing a tri-cornered hat with a feather in it. He ordered Jack, "Drop the sword."

Eliza whispered, "Jack, don't—"

"I said drop it!"

Without thought, Jack dropped his weapon. It hit the sand with a thud.

Beauregard ordered two of the other pirates, "Hold him."

"Who died and made you captain?" asked one.

"The captain did! And since I got this," Beauregard pointed at his new hat with the revolver, then at a satchel he was wearing, "and this. I think that puts me in charge. Now hold him!"

The first pirate kicked Jack's sword away, then he and the other took hold of his arms.

Beauregard sneered, pointed the gun at Jack, then through his remaining blackened teeth said, "You've got one chance to make this easy. Tell me where the prince is."

Jack scanned the area. *Only six pirates left.*

"Well?" demanded Beauregard.

Jack thought the best chance they had was the truth. "He's not here."

"Obviously. Where is he?"

"Finishing off whoever you left back on your ship." Jack stared at him, shoulders squared.

Beauregard looked toward the main ship, "What?"

Speaking with a bit more bravado, Jack elaborated, "That's the plan anyway. He takes over your ship, while I deal with whoever shows up on land." When the pirate didn't look back at him, Jack snickered, "What's a'matter, *Beauregard?* Don't tell me your whole crew came with you." The pirate scowled. Jack felt Beauregard was too stupid to be bluffing. With any luck, Jason already had the ship under control. He began to laugh, "That's it, isn't it? Everyone came here. Jason must have taken your ship with ease."

Almost an entire minute went by as Beauregard just stared in the direction of the ship, until one of the other pirates asked, "Beauregard?"

"I'm thinking!" Beauregard let go of Eliza and reached into his satchel, pulling out a rectangular device containing a single button under a shield, which he flipped up.

Jack felt one of the pirate's grip loosen as he said, "What are you stupid?"

"I can't let him have the ship." Beauregard shook the device at the pirate and said, "That's exactly what this is for."

"It's a last resort you idiot. If you blow it up, then we'll be stuck here!"

Beauregard turned the revolver on his fellow pirate, "Call me an idiot again! Go ahead, call me stupid! Let's see how smart *you* are with a bullet in your head."

The pirate let go of Jack and stepped forward to counter Beauregard's boast. "You don't have the guts!"

With the two of them distracted, Jack saw his opening. His muscles had only just begun to tense when Eliza grabbed Beauregard and thrust her knee into his stomach, causing him to drop the device. Jack pulled the pirate who still had a hold of him and threw him into the one who'd let go.

With the fight back on, Jack dared to feel a sense of hope again. That hope, however, was tempered by the fact that, while he fought the five others, Eliza was left to face Beauregard alone.

After kicking the detonation device away, Eliza took a second to diagnose the situation. Jack had knocked over two of the pirates, but they were recovering and would be joining the other three attacking him now. She wanted to help, but Beauregard sprang back upright and took aim at Jack with his gun. All five of his fellow pirates stood in the line of fire, but Eliza figured that wasn't going to stop this rabid animal; he'd gladly kill one or more of them to take out Jack. So Eliza kicked the gun from his hand.

"Why you little slut!"

The insult fueled Eliza's rage. She could hear Jack cry out to her with concern, but she hollered back, "I've got this!"

Jack had said she wasn't as good as she thought she was. She decided at that moment that she would show him she was better.

I have got this!

She could tell Beauregard wasn't a trained fighter like Jack or Jason, but his attacks had a vicious brutality nonetheless. With each punch Eliza was forced backward. She shook her hands of the pain, focused, then went on the offensive and began throwing punches of her own. She got in one good strike, but Beauregard rebounded right away. Reaching out with both hands, he grabbed her ponytail and threw her down.

Her head hit the ground and the world began to spin. Her body betrayed her, going limp as she laid there, completely incapacitated. She couldn't see what was happening, but assumed he was kicking her and was surprised at how little it hurt; just a sort of horrible dullness consumed her. She could hear Jack shouting, but all sound seemed to be falling away. There was nothing she could do. She was done for.

And all at once it stopped.

For a moment Eliza wondered if she had died. But when she tried to move, the pain told her she was still alive. She pulled herself up and saw Jack still fighting the other pirates, and then saw Beauregard, arms locked and desperately struggling with . . . Jason?

They were wrestling with one another, and Jason had the upper hand. But he didn't see that one of Jack's foes had broken away and was approaching from behind.

Eliza pushed past the agony she felt and stumbled toward the brawl. She couldn't remember exactly what had happened next. Just . . . ambushing the pirate who was stalking Jason, then it all became a blur. There were shouts, punches, blocks, the sound of the gun firing, and even an explosion at some point. But then the world went black.

The next thing Eliza knew, a voice was calling to her from a distance. She felt the world moving again, all while the voice got closer and closer until finally, she could make out, "Eliza? Answer me, Eliza!"

She winced in pain and asked, "Wha . . . what happened?"

Jason, grasping her by the shoulders, looked at her warily and said, "Well . . . for one thing, you saved my life. Don't look so satisfied with yourself. Before that you were nearly beaten to death until I saved you." He leaned back against a boulder. "I thought you said Jack taught you how to fight?"

Feeling a bit defensive, Eliza declared, "He did! He . . . wait, where is he?" She looked at the bodies of the pirates, then back at Jason. "Where . . . where is Jack? He's not . . . ?"

"He's fine," said Jason, rising to his feet with a wince of his own. "After you stopped that pirate behind me, I was able to take care of the rest. But apparently their captain had a remote switch for an explosive device on their vessel which, once it was clear they weren't going to win," Jason pointed past the shore, where smoke was billowing from the smoldering remains of the pirate ship now sinking into the water, "he used."

Eliza grimaced as she touched her head. "But where is Jack?"

"He's fine, he went to get you some water."

Just then Jack, running as quickly as he could, returned with a canteen. "Eliza! Thank goodness, you're all right!" He scurried around Jason dropped to his knees and practically forced the water in her mouth. "I should never have let you do that, you were almost killed, what was I thinking?"

She was going to protest, but the cool liquid felt wonderful running down her dry throat, and she drank heartily. "Mm, thank you!"

"Do you need more? I can get more."

Annoyed at Jack's doting and hearing him regret letting her fight, Eliza pushed him away and began to stand up. "No, Jack, I'm fine—ah!" Hurting all over, she stumbled. Trying to rationalize that she couldn't possibly have been hit literally everywhere, she tried to distinguish a place on her body that didn't throb. After not being able to find one, she slumped back and decided that maybe a little doting wasn't so terrible. So she asked for more water and drained the canteen.

Jack seemed happy to see her not trying to move anymore and leaned back with a smile. "Good, that's good. Just rest. There's no rush to get up. We'll move when you're ready." He glanced up at Jason and said, "You were right, I should never have . . . wait, is that a bullet wound?"

Adrenaline coursed through Eliza's body, numbing the pain as she shot up, exclaiming, "What?"

With a large red spot on his flank that seemed to keep growing, Jason muttered, "Yeah, well . . ." and staggered back.

Eliza and Jack shot up to help him sit on the boulder she had just been leaning against. Then while Jack went to refill the canteen again, Eliza checked the wound. Worrying it was her fault that he'd been shot, she apologized repeatedly, growing more and more frantic.

Clearly trying to calm her, Jason reminded her, "I've been shot before you know. Remember back in school?" When that didn't work, he grabbed her hand, looked her in the eyes and said, "I'll be okay. If you hadn't hit that bastard when you did, this could have been much worse."

"But you said—"

"Look, Eliza, I . . ." He cringed in pain, then admitted, "If you had done what I said, I'd probably be dead right now. We all would." Eliza looked up at him wide eyed. Now that she was calm again, he felt safe to add, "But you were completely outmatched. Just because you know how to throw a punch doesn't mean your opponent doesn't know how to take one. And being a woman, you aren't as strong—"

Eliza pulled away and snapped, "Just because I'm a woman doesn't mean—"

"I didn't mean that as an insult, Eliza! It's just a fact." Jason exhaled slowly, giving them both a moment. "I know you don't like your . . . *restrictions,* as a woman in Idoless."

She gave a snort.

He continued with sincerity, "But that pirate was stronger than you, and more accustomed to fighting. Even if you had been training for a year, you still would have been outmatched. You need to learn your place." Feeling Eliza's rage flare again, Jason raised his hands and defended, "Not as 'a lady,' but as someone who is a woman. I just meant that you need to understand your limitations."

Eliza looked at him, not sure how to take that statement. Was he being kind or condescending?

As if in answer Jason said, "Knowing your limitations is part of being a good warrior."

"You . . . you'd consider me a warrior?"

"Eliza . . ." He chuckled, which caused him to cough and then wince, clutching his side. He took a few breaths then continued, "Even before today, I knew you had a warrior's spirit. If willpower were a more tangible thing, you'd be the ruler of the world."

Eliza sniffed, "Thanks, Jason," and tucked a loose strand of hair behind her ear.

When Jack returned with the water, they cleaned Jason's wound as well as they could. It looked like the bullet had gone clean through, only slightly tearing the flesh in his side.

When they finished, they just sat in silence and looked out at the ocean. Their escape plan now sat at the bottom of it, and with it, their hopes sank too.

CHAPTER NINE

KODIAK ATTACK

After his exchange with Frank, Jack made his way to their tent, taking a longer route to avoid as many people as he could. All he wanted was to climb into his sleeping bag and shut out the world for the rest of the night. He arrived and began to roll out his sleeping bag on a cot when he felt the back of his neck prickle and he bolted upright. Without understanding his unease, Jack drew his sword and barreled out of the tent; the closest guards tensed at his sudden arrival.

Then without warning, several enormous bears burst from the edge of the forest. Their swift, efficient swipes made quick work of the guards as Jack ducked behind a nearby stack of crates. He watched the bears rear on hind legs, teeth bared and claws slashing wildly as they systematically attacked the soldiers.

From his hiding spot, Jack counted more than two dozen of them methodically invading the camp from different directions. They seemed to be scouring the camp for something specific. Something, or someone!

Jack raced toward the prisoner's tent, using the trees as cover. Out of the corner of his eye, he noticed a bear, larger than the others, with a patch of dark fur on its chest, barreling toward a soldier. Jack turned, sped up, and threw all of his momentum into a strategically placed kick in the bear's flank, knocking it off its course.

As Jack drew his sword, the bear reared back onto its hind legs, striking a sort of fighting stance. Jack squinted as he thought about what to do, then slid his sword back into its sheath and took a fighting stance of his own.

The rescued soldier gasped, "What. Are. You. Doing?"

Without taking his eyes off the bear, Jack said in a slow, calm voice, "Go warn Church. We need to fight as a unit, or we'll be flattened." He looked at the soldier and hissed, "Go!" The soldier didn't need to be told twice.

Jack looked at his opponent, and muttered, "All right, let's do this."

Without any hesitation, the bear swung a long, muscled arm at his face. Jack ducked and kicked. When he made contact, the blows had little effect, so he used momentum to leverage the bear's weight against itself, causing it to fall over. Each time, Jack was tempted to draw his sword and end it, but the bear was fighting him evenly and fairly. It wasn't using its razor-sharp claws or massive teeth; it seemed to be fighting . . . with honor, which in Jack's mind dictated that he did the same.

Jack's theory was reinforced when a small female bear with lighter colored fur lunged at him from behind a tent. Jack jerked out of the way and fell on his back. The female took advantage of Jack's folly, her front paws raised in the air ready to slam down on him when the larger bear blocked the attack. The two animals roared at each other, but the female reluctantly moved on. When the large bear turned back, it waited for Jack to get to his feet before resuming the fight.

Jack took a wild risk and drew his sword dramatically. The bear stopped short and gave him a look. *Was that . . . disgust?* The beast's tone changed, and it charged at Jack with a new ferocity. Jack knelt and laid his sword on the ground just as dramatically as he had drawn it, then extended his empty hands and bowed his head in submission.

He stayed in that position for what felt like hours. When he dared to look up, the bear was only inches away, reared up on its back legs with one great paw extended, ready to strike. Jack kept his hands raised in submission but rose to his feet. Looking the bear in the eyes, he said, "I don't know if you can understand me. I'm hoping you at least recognize that I don't want to fight you." The bear didn't move, its paw still raised. Jack ventured a question: "So, are you looking for the boy?"

Immediately the bear dropped to all fours, now at eye level with Jack. It sniffed him angrily and then softened its demeanor, sitting back on its rump. "I'm going to take that as a 'yes.'" Still unsure if the animal truly understood what he was saying, Jack continued, "I can take you to him." He waited a moment, then the bear leaned down, picked the sword up in its mouth, and gave it back to Jack. "I'm going to take that as a 'yes' as well."

Jack began walking toward the captive's tent with the bear scampering closely behind him. Along the way Commander Church and a group of soldiers carrying guns arrived. They aimed their weapons at the bear. Jack knew that if bullets began to fly, there would be little hope of salvaging the situation. He threw a hand in the air and yelled, "Don't! I'm taking care of it."

Church looked at him as if he'd lost his mind, but he lowered his weapon and let Jack proceed.

They made their way across the camp, amid the fighting soldiers and bears. Occasionally, the bear he'd been fighting would bellow at the others within earshot, who would then stop fighting and join them. Soon, Jack found himself leading twenty-some giant bears through camp. *This has got to be one of the weirdest things I have ever done.*

Not far behind this odd parade were the commander and his group, still holding their weapons at the ready.

They were approaching their destination when a large figure came crashing down, sliding to a stop just a short distance away. Frank propped himself up and coughed, ". . . it!" He coughed some more and gasped for air.

"Frank!" Jack took a step forward but stopped as the bear that had attacked his brother appeared. It was on all fours, head held low, and stood right over Frank and glared at the group. It was smaller than the other bears, but still much larger than an average grizzly with russet fur that looked coarse and bristly.

Jack wasn't sure what to do, but the bear he'd been fighting, who was the largest and appeared to be the pack's leader, stepped out and began to circle the smaller one, still standing over Frank. The small bear growled at Frank, smelling him. The leader leaned down and sniffed Frank as well.

"Jack?" asked Church.

He could feel the guns behind him aimed over his shoulders at the bears. "Not yet," he said, without taking his eyes off the scene.

The large bear lumbered calmly around occasionally moaning and snorting, which only seemed to agitate the smaller one. After a few tense minutes, the larger bear made a final, decisive grunt and the small bear roared. It reared and lifted its paws.

Jack shouted, "Now, Church! Do it now!"

Church and the others took aim, but before they could get a shot off, a voice rang out. "Terrie, no!"

The captive appeared draped in Frank's coat, running toward the bear.

"Hold!" ordered Church.

The bear—Terrie—jerked away from Frank and dashed toward the captive, who jumped into Terrie's waiting arms, and the grizzly gathered him close, giving him a literal bear hug.

The prisoner climbed down and ran to Frank's side, kneeling over him and asked, "Are you okay, Frank?"

"I've been better, but I'll survive." Frank groaned, got to his feet.

"I tried to warn you."

As he dusted himself off Frank said with a tongue-in-cheek tone, "No, it was my fault. When you said that I'd be sorry, I should have known that it meant a drove of enormous bears was going to attack the camp."

The captive answered matter-of-factly, "That's okay."

Frank chuckled, but it turned into a cough.

Jack went to Frank and asked, "You all right?"

Frank replied, "Yeah, I'm good. So . . . what's going on?"

"Big bears."

"Yeah." They looked around at all the soldiers and animals, neither group really knowing what to do now. "Weird."

"Very," agreed Jack.

Commander Church gestured to Jack and Frank, and the three approached each other, walking as if they were in a minefield.

"Lieutenant Waramond, Jack. Do either of you know what in Hades is going on?"

Frank replied, "Well, I'm not sure, but the answer, as crazy as it seems, is becoming clear. I think Peter—"

"Who?" asked the commander.

"The prisoner—his name is Peter. And, well, I think he . . . belongs to, or is a part of, or . . ."

"They raised me." The group turned to look at Peter, who was scratching the bear's chin. "They're my family. They're called the Kodiaks. When I didn't come back to the pack tonight, they came looking for me. They followed my scent here and . . ." Peter looked back at all the destruction, but smiled as he rubbed Terrie's belly, "They came to get me."

Amused, Jack said, "I'll say they did."

Though the bears had become docile, most of the soldiers were still afraid to lower their weapons.

So Jack asked, "Will they leave if we release you?"

Church grumbled, "But we need him."

"Explain that to the bears."

Just as Church opened his mouth to rebuke Jack, Peter said, "I'll explain it."

"What?" said both Jack and Mike at the same time.

"I'll explain it to them," Peter repeated.

"You can do that?" asked Mike.

Like it was obvious, Peter replied, "Uh, yeah."

Unsure, Church asked, "And why would you do that?"

Peter looked at Frank and grinned. "I made a deal with Frank." Frank's ears grew red. Then Peter looked back to the commander. "And I promised to see it through. You're looking for that thing I saw, aren't you?"

Church's focus sharpened. "I don't know. What was it you saw?"

"Deep out there." Peter pointed in the direction of Death's Province. "Where the world stops. I saw a bright light across the unseen wall."

Trying not to sound too interested, Commander Church responded, "That sounds about right."

Jack thought Peter didn't like something about Church's response. He crinkled his nose at it, like he smelled something foul. But then he just turned and joined the group of bears and began . . . *talking* with them.

Taking advantage of the break, Jack questioned Mike, "So, you brought guns?"

The commander stood fully upright. "Not that I have to explain anything to you, but yes, we did. I would think the only man who's ever survived Death's Province would appreciate being sufficiently protected when going back in."

Unfazed, Jack continued, "Not with guns. Did you even read the debriefing about my first time there? The sounds they produce draw far too many creatures. I wish someone would have mentioned that you were bringing them." Jack locked eyes with Mike and said, "Or maybe it was discussed in one of your *private meetings*."

"Jack, shut up," warned Frank.

Church responded without hesitation. "It's all right, Lieutenant. No, Jack, it was clearly stated to everyone, you just weren't paying attention. You were preoccupied with pouting."

Jack began to retort, but knew it was true. In his anger and mistrust, he'd missed that simple bit of information. He was still angry with Church, but now he was also angry with himself for his oversight. "Just . . . don't bring them in. We're better off with only swords and spears."

Church contended, "Maybe you're incredible with a sword, Jack, but some of the others—"

"Look, I may have been the one who walked out of Death's Province, but there was an entire platoon of soldiers who walked in with me. We were *all* equipped with guns, because just like you, we figured we'd be safer with them. But the first men lost were to friendly fire." Jack shook his head and said, "At minimum, lose the guns. The energy blasters are at least quiet and more humane. No one should die slowly and painfully with a tiny shard of metal stuck in his spleen." Then Jack stormed off toward his tent.

Frank and Mike stood silently, watching Jack stalk away. After a few moments, Frank said, "I'm sorry, I'll have a talk with him, Commander."

Church took a deep breath. "He's had a hard time, Frank. I don't blame him for being so . . . well, whatever it is he is. Don't get me wrong, I'd like to have him thrown in the stockade."

"I kinda want to just punch him in the head right now," Frank said, half joking.

Church gazed in Jack's direction, "He's on board. He just needs to blow off some steam. In a few days this'll be over, and he can crawl back beneath the rock he was hiding under."

The comment took Frank by surprise. He knew Church was right, but he was just getting used to having Jack back in his life.

Animated grunts from the bears took Frank out of his musings, and he realized Peter had returned.

"I talked with the Kodiaks. They . . . *agreed* to let me help you," he said, shoulders hunched as he looked back at the animals. There was sadness in his tone, and he was clearly holding something back. Then Peter seemed to summon his nerve and said, "So I'll help you find that light in the wall you're looking for."

Church beamed. "Thank you, Peter."

Peter nodded, but then confirmed, "And Frank will be there?"

Feeling self-conscious, Frank scratched the back of his head and looked away.

"If that's what you want," promised the commander.

"And after, I'm free to go?"

"Absolutely."

Peter put his hand out to Commander Church. "I have your word?"

Frank grinned.

"Yes, indeed." Church took his hand and shook it. "Excellent. I'm so glad you're willing to help us." As Church released Peter's hand, he looked at the bears and the apprehensive soldiers, adding, "If there's anything I can give you, don't hesitate to ask. But, um . . . if it isn't too much trouble, could you ask the . . ." he said the next word carefully to make sure he was saying it right, "*Kodiaks,* if they could perhaps keep a distance from the camp? My soldiers don't know what to make of them, and I worry it might disrupt their work."

Peter agreed readily, promising that the bears wouldn't be coming anywhere near the camp. Frank, Commander Church, and the others watched as he went around and said good-byes to the bears. Some of them he walked up to and pressed his forehead against theirs, while others got hugs. Then all the bears—except Terrie—ambled away into the forest as Peter wiped tears from his eyes.

One of the soldiers muttered under his breath, "What's with the drama?"

Another agreed. "Yeah, it's not like he's saying good-bye forever."

Frank looked at Peter's sad expression, and in a moment of shock, thought, *Actually, I think he did.*

Chapter Ten
Retaliation

Frank had managed only a few hours of fitful sleep after the bear attack. When he awoke the camp was already buzzing with activity as he headed to the edge of the forest to relieve himself. After, he ran into Commander Church who carried a cup of steaming tea in one hand and wore a wide grin on his face. "Good morning, Lieutenant. Got a minute?" Frank nodded and fell in step next to the commander. "I have a task for you."

"Yes, sir," replied Frank and waited for his orders.

Church gestured toward the south side of the camp and said, "I've already had a team assess the damage from last night's attack. It is minimal, mostly cleanup rather than repairs."

"That's good."

Church sipped his tea, then hooked the teabag string by a finger to raise and lower it in the cup a few times. "We have secured everything, and everyone, so it's time to advance the mission."

"That's great."

"Yes, it is." The men continued walking, and Church pointed to a nearby transport vessel, which had beams of honey-gold light periodically emanating from its widows. "Earlier this morning, I gave the wizards the go-ahead to begin the first phase of breaking the barrier into Death's Province." He sighed lightly.

"I've already caught a couple soldiers trying to sneak a peek inside to figure out what they're doing. Rumors are beginning to circulate, and the men are getting restless."

"Yes, sir."

Church switched directions, leading the way to the mess tent. Frank got a tray of breakfast, while Church was content with just his tea. Once they sat down, Church began again, "So, that task. Do you think you might be able to watch out for Peter today?"

Frank gulped his coffee.

Church explained, "The bears agreed to keep their distance, but the men are on edge. And thanks to the attack, many of them already associate Peter with this whole mess. I'd tell them to just deal with it, but . . . I don't know if you've noticed, but there's something . . . *off* about him. Something—unnerving. Anyway, Peter responded so well to you, I thought you could help him fit in a bit. Maybe that will put the men at ease."

Frank had no idea how he was supposed to do that but like a good soldier . . . "Yes, sir, of course. I'll get right on it."

"Good man!" Without another word, Church got up and left.

Last he knew, Peter was still wearing nothing but those boxer shorts and *his* coat. So, after finishing his breakfast, Frank went to find some clothes for Peter; that seemed like a good place to start. Frank asked around and collected a spare white t-shirt and the smallest pair of pants he could find, and brought them to Peter.

Given Peter's small stature, all the clothes were loose. Frank had to cinch the waist of the pants with a rope and trim the legs, which he accidentally cut too short leaving them looking more like oversized shorts. There wasn't a pair of boots that fit him, but Peter claimed he was content being barefoot. Finally, Frank offered him his own zip-up hoodie he'd brought along. It looked a little like Peter was wearing a tent, but he seemed to cherish it more than anything else.

Frank noticed Peter had put on all the clothes with ease and familiarity. That, paired with the fact that he could speak so well, suggested he'd been more than just exposed to civilization before. *So, how did he end up with the bears?*

Once outfitted in his new clothes, Peter made Frank's task easy, because he stayed by Frank's side the rest of the day without even being asked to.

Church had been right about one thing: Peter had a quietly intimidating presence. He seemed to know things—things he logically couldn't. That said, the more time Frank spent with Peter, the less it mattered. They had fun together.

He also admired how Peter remained unfazed when the soldiers mistreated him. Their cruel glares alone would have been enough to crush Frank's own self-worth, let alone when one actually spit at Peter—who was then given Hawk and Joss's onion cutting duties that evening. However, it seemed Peter truly didn't care what anyone thought of him. And to Frank, that was one of the purist forms of bravery.

The camp had a tense, subdued air on the eve of resuming the mission. The men took advantage of their last hours of free time by talking around scattered campfires. Jack had started a cheerful blaze outside his tent, and within a few minutes Frank and Peter joined him at it. Jack laid back on an army-issued blanket, facing the sky with his hands behind his head, while his brother and Peter sat on some logs facing the fire.

Frank prodded the blaze with a stick, then sat back down. "That's better." He looked down at Peter and smiled.

Peter asked, "What do you want to know?"

"What?"

"You want to ask me something."

"How'd . . . I mean, how would . . . what makes you think that?"

"It's obvious," stated Peter.

Frank looked to Jack, then back to Peter and said, "Well, I'm not sure where you're getting that."

Peter sighed, "Whatever."

For a short time, no one spoke. A few moments later Frank got up to stoke the fire again. Sitting back down, he repeated, "That's better."

Peter sighed loudly, and Jack said, "It was pretty obvious that time."

Frank's cheeks went pink. He got to his feet and said, "I'm going to see if dinner is ready," and stormed off.

After another moment, Jack probed, "How *did* you know?"

"What?" asked Peter.

Jack sat up and scooched to where Frank had been sitting. "I see now that something is up with him, but you noticed it earlier. How?"

"It's not just Frank. You all have loads to say but won't for some reason. The bears just say what's on their minds." Peter looked in the direction Frank had gone. "If they had something to say, they'd just say it."

"But they're animals. They can't talk like us."

Peter looked at him blankly for a moment. "Yes, they can."

"I'm not saying they don't have their own way of communicating—"

"Animals are far smarter than people give them credit for." Peter began to trace his fingers across the dirt. "They know and see a lot more than humans ever will."

"So, is that how you do it?"

"Do what?"

"Read people. Were you like, trained by them to see those things other people usually don't or something?"

"I don't know. I never really thought about it."

"That must be what it is. You're interpreting people's body language. By living with the bears, you learned how to pick up on the subtlest gestures without the need for language. You'd probably make an excellent interrogator. You'd know when someone was . . ."

Peter asked, "What?"

"It's nothing."

"No, it isn't."

Jack chuckled. "No, I suppose it isn't. And you would know, wouldn't you? I just had an idea." Jack glanced back at Church's tent. "Peter, do you think you could—?"

"You two are getting along well," Frank said as he returned.

Jack smiled and teased, "What's the matter, jealous?"

Frank snorted. "Whatever. Dinner will be ready soon." He sat down, unaware that he was pouting.

"What are you so upset about?" asked Jack.

"I'm not . . . look, just drop it," he said, and crossed his arms.

Peter sighed, disappointed.

Jack dropped his harassing grin and said, "Actually, we were just talking about where Peter here was raised."

"You were, huh?" Frank said, trying to sound disinterested.

"And I was just about to ask about the Kodiaks."

Peter looked at Jack. "What about them?"

"Well, they raised you, right?"

"Yeah."

"Always?" When Peter shot him an inquisitive look, Jack explained, "It's just . . . I have to say, you look familiar. To have dark skin with blond hair like you; that's pretty rare. That said, I can't figure out where I would have ever met you."

Peter looked at the fire while absentmindedly touching his spongy mound of blond hair and said, "Well, I *have* spent some time with humans. I don't know where I was born, and I don't know who my parents are. The first thing I remember is the bears. They raised me. But they thought I should be raised by humans, since I *was* one, so they gave me to some people."

Jack inquired, "They weren't in a town called Oakmoor Cove, by chance?"

"No, it was . . . it was . . ." Peter's voice grew quiet, ". . . it didn't work out."

Jack could tell Peter was upset. Frank shifted uncomfortably and gave him a single pat on the shoulder.

Peter glanced at Frank, sighed again, and said, "Humans really don't know what they want, do they?" Jack looked at Frank, who wore a face that suggested he didn't understand the ambiguous statement either. "That's why I like the bears. I went back to them, and they welcomed me with open paws."

There was a snigger as Hawk and some of the other soldiers arrived with trays of food.

"Can we help you with something, Hawk?" Frank asked, not hiding the irritation in his voice.

Hawk smiled, "Naw, I was just listening to the moving tale." He laughed. "'Open paws' . . . I don't even have to comment— that's funny by itself!"

The new group of soldiers laughed.

Peter's eyes flashed with bitterness. "Well, they did."

"I'm sure, I'm sure," replied Hawk flippantly.

Another soldier took the reins from Hawk, asking, "Tell me, is one of the female bears betrothed to you yet?"

The laughter grew.

Peter crinkled his nose with dislike for their new company and Jack said, "Knock it off, guys."

Just then a tall, muscular soldier with a surly expression and a thin goatee, whom Jack recognized as Church's brother, Seth Warren, chimed in, "Yeah guys, he's still a young pup. He's not ready to fuck yet," and laughed boisterously. The others around joined in, laughing louder than before.

Peter jumped up.

Seth chuckled, "What up, Pup?"

"You're disgusting, that's what," replied Peter.

Seth stood up to face the challenge. Jack and Frank started to get up as well, to diffuse the situation, but didn't get the chance before Terrie leaped from the cover of the forest, slammed Seth to the ground, and stood muzzle-to-face with him, snarling.

"Terrie, no!" yelled Peter.

Terrie glanced at Peter and snorted. He shifted his massive weight, turned, and walked away as Seth picked himself up and shouted after, "That's right, you dumb animal, run away!"

Terrie stopped, looked over his shoulder, and bared his teeth. In that moment, they all realized Terrie had understood every word. In one effortless movement, Terrie turned to face the men, rose on his hind legs, showing his incredible size, and bellowed. The men drew their weapons, led by Seth who wore a wicked grin, and goaded, "Come on! We're ready for you this time, you fucking beast! We owe you for the men you killed!"

Frank shouted, "Seth, stand down! All of you, stand down *now*!"

Seth called back, "Don't listen to him. You know who my brother is."

Many of the men obeyed Frank but a few looked at each
other, uncertainty written on their faces.

"Do not aggravate this situation any more than you already
have," warned Frank. "Peter, could you get the bear to . . ." but
as Frank looked over his shoulder, Peter was already on Terrie's
back and riding away into the brush.

"That's right, run away you fucking coward!" spat Seth. He
picked up a rock, but as he wound to throw it, Jack slapped him
across the rear with the flat side of his sword, causing Seth to
drop the rock on his own foot. "Argh!"

Jack said coolly, "I believe a superior officer has given you
an order." He turned to his brother. "Go ahead, I've got this."

Frank nodded to Jack and chased after Peter and Terrie.

Frank followed their trail easily and found them beneath the
umbrella of a sizeable willow tree. Terrie had his head bent
toward Peter, who was in a rage, kicking the ground and
swatting at the branches hanging over them, stopping when he
noticed Frank's presence. Terrie stood squarely on all four legs,
facing Frank, but Peter put his hand on the bear's massive head
and said, "It's all right, Terrie. He's the one I told you about.
The good one."

Terrie sat back down, becoming quite docile.

Frank took a couple of steps and said, "I just . . . I . . . I
wanted to make sure that . . . that you were all right."

"I'm fine, Frank." He moved next to the bear and put his
hands on its chest. "But I think I'm going to stay with Terrie. I'll
talk to your leader tomorrow morning and point him in the right
direction."

"Um . . . I'm not sure the commander—"

"I'll stay close enough that you can yell if you need me. But I won't be much use until we're closer to that door-thing he wants to find."

Frank was pretty sure Church wasn't going to like that, but that wasn't what he was worried about. "Hey, look, Peter, I'm sorry about the guys. I'm sure they were just, uh, blowing off steam. I don't think they . . ." he couldn't complete the sentence with much conviction, "actually meant any harm."

Peter sniffled and wiped a couple tears from his eyes as the bear gave a soothing coo. "It's okay."

There was another rumble, but it wasn't coming from the bear. Frank smelled ozone. "Hey, I think it's going to—"

"Rain, I know."

"Well, maybe you should—"

"I'll be fine, Frank," said Peter, struggling to contain his tears. The bear wrapped one of its massive forelimbs around Peter to comfort him.

Frank had never seen anything like this. Wild animals were . . . well, they were wild. To see one behaving like this, so human, was surreal. Yet instead of wonderment, all it made Frank feel was a sort of loneliness. He said numbly, "Okay. Well, I'll see ya," and waved good-bye as he turned and ambled back up the path. The song he'd heard Peter sing began echoing in his memory.

Terrie made a low sound that could be mistaken for a growl, but Peter knew better. Looking in the direction Frank had left, he said, "It's okay, Terrie. I'm just frustrated with people."

Peter had only spent a few days with humans again, but most of them had done nothing but frustrate him—or worse. The Church guy was working some angle, and it wasn't to fulfill the grand mission he claimed. Jack was the only one Peter respected; he was at least saying what he thought and felt, though it was mostly that he was unhappy and didn't want to be there.

So why does he stay?

Peter got mad at himself, realizing he was pretty much in the same situation.

Why do I stay?

Right away, these people had demonstrated they only wanted one thing, and they didn't care how they got it. He grew more upset when he thought about those men just now, some of whom had blood in their eyes. He knew that Seth guy would have killed Terrie if he could have. Peter didn't like a single one of them except . . .

Frank, who had been so kind to him when no one else was. He had no ulterior motives, plainly doing what he thought was right. Even though he couldn't fully understand it, Peter admired Frank's devotion to his duty. He felt Terrie's great paw across his back, comforting him as he remembered that moment only a day ago, when Frank had appeared out of nowhere, standing at the pond's edge in a daze. It had been clear what Frank was thinking then, and since. But like all the rest of these people, he wasn't saying what he wanted. Wishing it were a hand on his back instead of a paw, Peter knew why he stayed.

With tears forming in his eyes once again, Peter turned into Terrie's embrace. More calming rumbles came from the enormous animal as it held Peter until they both fell asleep beneath the tree.

A few hours later, Peter woke to a slight tugging on his leg. As he opened his eyes, a rope tightened around his ankle and yanked his entire body into the air. He hung upside down, from a limb of the willow tree by a rope tied around his ankle. Terrie chased after him, but a massive net had ensnared the bear, and he was hung from the next limb over.

"Terrie!"

Seth and small mob of men surrounded the bear, jabbing him with spears and swords. Peter tried to loosen the rope fastened around his ankle, but there was a drizzle making the rope slippery.

Peter had just gotten a grip on the rope when Seth grabbed him by the hair and pulled him back. His slimy voice came from behind. "Don't worry, Pup. We'll save you from this dangerous monster." Peter felt his hands shaking with fear as he tried to strike Seth, who released the rope with a shove. Peter swung wildly through the air, the tree limb groaning under the stress. He used the power of the returning momentum to strike Seth in the back of the head. Seth reeled from the attack, and turned to retaliate as Peter swung back again, this time scratching across the soldier's face, drawing blood. Seth roared in pain and held his face in his hands.

Peter went back to work on the rope around his ankle as he swung back and forth. Grabbing hold of the rope with one hand, he raised himself up to give him the slack to work on the knot with the other hand. Rain fell heavily now, and the blood rushing to his head throbbed against his skull. He finally freed himself and dropped to the ground with a thud. He wanted more than anything to run, but he knew that if he left, Terrie was as good as dead. With more boldness than he felt, Peter faced Seth and raised his fists.

"Hey, Seth, we gonna do this or what?" one of the men called out.

"Hold on a sec," he yelled back. "Pup wants to play."

Seth was the leader of the gang for good reason. He was as tall as Frank, but he was all muscle. He smiled, put up his fists, and motioned for Peter to advance. Peter charged and swung his fists fiercely, but Seth effortlessly blocked each strike. Seth then punched Peter square in the gut, sending him flying backward. Terrie thrashed and roared, powerless to help.

The day Peter had first encountered the soldiers he'd been a force of nature they couldn't contain. But under these circumstances—fighting, not running—he was outmatched. Peter dropped his fists and beseeched Seth, "Please! Please, don't hurt him. He, he's my friend." He tried not to cry, but he felt so helpless.

Seth just laughed. "Well, I hate to tell you this, Pup, but your friend is a dangerous beast. It hurt a lot of good men." He walked over to Terrie and drew his sword. "And it needs to be put down."

Peter ran to Seth. "No! P-please, no! I . . . I'm sorry!"

Half laughing, Seth looked down at Peter and prodded, "What are you sorry for?"

Peter cried desperately, "I—I don't know. Please, just please!" He grabbed Seth's sleeve, shaking uncontrollably and screamed to the sky, "Creator, please!"

Seth just laughed, "'*Creator*'? Who's that, Pup? One of the gods? Think they'll save your friend?"

"Just don't," Peter begged, "Please, don't."

"What? You don't want me to . . . put my sword . . . like . . . this?" Seth touched the blade's point to Terrie's side.

"No! No! Please, no! Please, please, please." Peter sobbed, gasping for air between his cries. He turned to the other men, begging them, "Why are you doing this? Please! Please, stop him!"

"Or maybe it's . . . *this*," Seth thrust the blade into Terrie's side, "that you don't want me to do."

Terrie roared in pain and Peter fell to the ground, splashing in a puddle as he screamed, "No!"

"You thought that was something?" Seth laughed and leaned over Peter. With a wicked smile he whispered darkly, "Watch this."

Frank had been asleep in his tent when he felt a hand shake him awake. "Frank. Wake up. Please, wake up . . . sir."

"What?" Frank looked up to see Hawk and Joss standing over him.

Jack woke too. "What's going on?"

Frank looked up at Hawk and Joss, wary that they'd called him *sir* voluntarily. "What's wrong?"

Hawk and Joss looked at each other. Then Hawk said, "It's Seth."

Instantly Frank understood. He shot up and started gathering his gear. "Where?"

He ordered Hawk to brief Commander Church and round up more men. Then they all departed without another word, Frank leading the way.

As they neared the willow tree where Frank had last seen Peter and the bear, Frank could hear the sound of Peter's pleading. "Peter!" He ran toward the sound so fast that Jack and Joss had difficulty keeping up. Reaching the crest of a hill, the full scene appeared below him: the bear suspended in a net, Peter on the ground just below, Seth driving a sword deep into the bear's flank.

Frank ran at Seth, throwing his entire body into the man, sending him soaring through the air before sliding to a stop a few yards away. Frank heard Jack say, "Heads up," as he jumped, sword drawn, slashing the net to free Terrie. Jack landed on his feet, but the bear fell with a lifeless thud.

Frank, Jack, and Joss wedged themselves between the men and the bear, whose head was now cradled in Peter's lap.

Frank shouted at Seth and his group, "How stupid are you all? Do you realize how much trouble you're in?" A couple of the men looked around nervously.

"Don't worry about him!" Seth snarled, wiping mud from his face and body as he rejoined the crowd. He spat blood on the ground and reminded them, "You all know who my brother is! This operation might as well have been sanctioned by the commander himself!"

"Operation? There's no operation." Frank looked around at Seth's gang. "You should all know better. Just because Seth is the commander's brother doesn't mean he has any kind of special authority."

With that, two of the soldiers broke away and ran back toward the camp, but it didn't sway the rest of the gang. Frank watched as Seth counted the men who remained, smiling at his odds.

Frank gave them one last chance, "Here and now, *I* am the superior officer." He drew his sword, holding it with both hands, and with his shoulders hunched and brow furrowed so low his eyes were mere specks of anger, he roared, "and you *will* stand down!"

Seth chuckled. "Don't listen to him. He's just trying to intimidate you."

"And you *should* be intimidated," Jack said.

"What would you know, Waramond? You're just as much an outsider as Pup over there." Seth looked to his gang and said, "These men hold no power over you. Besides," he smiled, "we outnumber 'em. It's no match."

"He's right," said Jack. "Hey, Joss."

"Yeah?"

"Why don't you run along so we can make this a little more even?"

"Funny man," sneered Seth.

"I wasn't being funny."

And with that Frank and Jack moved. Joss backed away, guarding Peter and the bear, and got to witness something that hadn't been seen in years: the Waramond brothers in action.

Jack took on most of the soldiers, while Frank faced Seth and a few of the others. They fought for a bit and then, without a word of communication, the brothers switched opponents.

"I owe you for that swat earlier," Seth snarled.

"Yeah, I'm terrified," Jack retorted as he threw his elbow into the bridge of a soldier's nose, bashing him unconscious.

"Damn, you're arrogant! You need someone to put you in your place!"

"Just let me know when you've got your dress on straight," replied Jack, sweep-kicking another soldier's ankles and knocking him to the ground. "We'll start when you're ready."

Seth bellowed in rage and charged.

Frank attempted to move the fight away from Peter and Terrie, seamlessly swapping opponents with Jack several more times along the way. With each switch, the gang dwindled, until only Seth and two others remained.

When the two soldiers realized their situation, like the first pair, they fled, leaving Seth to face the Waramonds alone.

Outmatched, hate flashed in Seth's eyes as he tossed a small metal ball with a blinking light at the Waramonds.

"Charge orb!" shouted Frank.

"Where'd he get one of those?" exclaimed Jack as they both dove out of the way.

Strands of white-hot electricity shot in all directions. With all the rain and water on the ground, the electrical charge surged through the grass and caught both of them. Jack took the worst of it and was laid out cold on the ground, smoke rising off his body. Weakened but conscious, Frank tried to lift himself up.

Seth had jumped up and grabbed a low-hanging tree branch to avoid the shock. He dropped down and triumphantly ambled up to the Waramonds, standing just out of Frank's reach—not that it would have mattered, he could barely move. Seth laughed and spat on him. "Not out? Looks like all that extra padding helped you out this time, eh, Waramond?"

Frank saw Seth draw his leg back and grimaced as he waited for the strike, but it never came. He heard a loud thud and looked up to see Terrie clutching Seth's foot in his jaws, dragging him across the muddy path.

The bear swung Seth's body around like a rag doll, water and mud flying in every direction as he was repeatedly slammed to the ground.

When Terrie was done, Seth just laid there, coughing up blood.

Still too weak to move, Frank could only watch as Peter walked up to Seth. Frank called after him weakly, "Peter." Peter stopped but didn't turn around. He just stood over Seth's crumpled body. For a moment, there was nothing but the sound of the rain tapping on the ground and rippling through the trees. Frank called again, "Peter, please."

Peter growled at Seth, "You tried to kill him." Lightning flashed and thunder followed. "You . . . you stuck a sword in him—you didn't even care!" Another flash and boom. Peter crouched down, silhouetted eerily by the lightning in the sky, and said, "You . . . deserve . . . to *die!*"

Flash! Boom!

11 Years Ago

569 AR

Returning from another day's exploration, Jack and Eliza arrived at a small pond near their camp. They agreed to walk around it and look at the wildflowers in bloom, then call it a day and go back. Jack smiled coyly and said, "We'll need to mark where we've started so we know when we've made it all the way around." He pointed to a magnolia tree standing at the edge of the pond, its branches hanging over the land on one side and water on the other. He ran up to it, scaring off a small flock of parakeets that left in noisy protest. He turned his back to Eliza and pulled out his pocketknife and leaned in, pressing the blade into the trunk, which released a green, earthy scent.

Eliza protested, "Jack, what are you talking about? We've been here before; I know exactly where . . ."

Jack turned back to Eliza with a self-satisfied smile, revealing a heart he'd carved into the tree's flank. She rolled her eyes, but smirked and began walking.

Jack jogged to catch up with her. "What?"

"Just walk."

They turned toward the edge of the trees at the sound of rustling leaves, not far away from the area they'd just left.

"I wonder what that is?" Eliza said.

Jack glanced back. "Dunno. Probably just some animals." He waited a beat, then said with a grin, "Maybe it's mating season, and the males are fighting to woo their mates."

"Ease off, soldier boy," Eliza chided as she sped up, creating space between herself and Jack.

Rather than chase her, Jack walked at the same pace but called ahead, "I don't know why you can't do it."

Eliza stopped and turned around, "Can't do what?"

"Tell me how you feel about me," Jack said, as he walked past.

Eliza's tone landed somewhere between angry and defensive. "I . . . I don't feel anything for you."

She started walking again, but Jack stopped and turned, blocking her. They stood face to face, eyes locked in a silent duel. "Really? You don't feel *anything*?"

Her eyes darted away, and Eliza said, "I mean . . . I *like* you." Jack smiled, and she shoved him out of her away. "But not in the way you think. Especially since you won't train me to fight anymore."

"Look, Eliza, after what happened with the pirates—Jason getting shot—I gave him my word I wouldn't anymore." He leaned toward her, grinning. "But go ahead and use that as an excuse all you want, to cover up your feelings for me."

"Stop that," she snapped.

"Stop what?"

"You . . . you're too close."

"But I need to be close."

She shook her head, "What? Why?"

"So I can do this," he leaned in close enough to kiss her.

Eliza yanked her head away. As she did, Jack gently pushed a peachy-orange tiger lily into her hair.

Stunned, she touched the flower gingerly.

Jack's self-assured smirk returned, and he said, "There. A beautiful flower for a beautiful woman." Then he continued along the shore as Eliza pulled the flower from her hair, ready to toss it to the ground.

He walked at a steady pace and was just about to look back for Eliza when she caught up with him. He noticed she had tucked the flower properly behind her ear. She seemed to stare straight ahead to avoid his obnoxious grin, which had grown wider than usual.

They heard the noises of the animals again and stopped to listen. Now on the opposite side of the pond, they noticed a tree near their starting point, shaking violently. "Looks like some birds," Jack said, then halfheartedly added, "I think."

They scrutinized the tree in silence for a few moments.

Eliza said, "I'm pretty sure you're right. I think I hear wings flapping . . ." But there were screeches, too, and suddenly one pierced the air. They both winced. "But it doesn't sound like birds."

They continued their walk in silence, and with each step the silence grew into a looming presence of its own. Finally, Eliza cracked. "Oh, shut up."

With a chuckle, Jack said, "I didn't say anything."

"Yeah, but you were thinking it. And wipe that smile off your face."

Jack stopped laughing, but he couldn't remove the smile. "What? What was I thinking?"

"I . . . I don't know."

Jack started laughing again.

"Shut *up*," Eliza pressed.

"Eliza, I'm not saying anything. But if you really want me to, I won't say anything else." Then Jack looked at her and waited until he knew he had her full attention. "I won't talk about your beauty, or how much I enjoy these days I get to go exploring with you. I won't tell you what an amazing person I think you are, proven by the fact that you've managed to do the impossible."

"The impossible?"

"Yeah." He took a step toward her. "Every day, you manage to make me stop noticing how beautiful you look, because I'm too busy noticing how beautiful you *are*." Eliza blushed. But then Jack finished, "I won't say any of that." They stood still, unable to move or look away from each other. After a few moments, Jack added, "I won't tell you how I love you."

Eliza said sharply, "Don't."

"Don't what?"

"Don't say that so flippantly."

"I wasn't."

"Jack, my father told me that when things were getting serious between him and my mom . . ."

"Things are getting serious?"

Eliza smacked him across the head. "Pay attention. When they were getting serious, they agreed not to say those words until they really meant it."

Jack considered her story, and then asked, "What words?"

"Jack," she warned.

"No, really. Was it the stuff about your beauty?"

"Jack!"

"Or . . . the stuff about how amazing you are?"

"I'm being serious."

Jack went on, mischief sparkling in his eyes. "What? I need to know that we're talking about the same thing."

Eliza pursed her lips and exhaled through her nose. "I mean it, Jack. People throw those words around too loosely. How many marriages do you know that haven't worked out? If people waited to get married . . . if they waited until they really knew that they . . . *really were,* you know . . ." Then she leaned in closer, "My parents didn't say it until the day they meant it. It was the day my father asked my mother to marry him. So, I won't say it until I know it's true . . . Until I mean it."

Eliza stepped back from Jack, creating space between them. He stood quietly, studying her face but he couldn't suppress a grin. "So you do have feelings for me."

Eliza smacked him across the chest, "Jack!"

He grinned. "It's okay, Eliza, you don't have to say it 'til you're ready."

Exasperated, Eliza grabbed his shirt to let him have it, but a ruckus erupted just ahead of them, and she looked toward the sound.

Jack took her hands off his shirt, held them in his and said, "Eliza, I've been sure of it for a while. So even under your set of rules, I feel quite comfortable telling you that I love you." He gave her hands a squeeze, then headed toward the commotion.

Neither Jack nor Eliza could identify the creatures causing the uproar. At first, they appeared to be cats. But upon closer inspection, they all had . . . wings. A gray one with a wounded wing was being attacked by the others. It sprang from branch to branch of a large rain tree as the others flapped around it, taking turns tearing at it with their sharp claws.

Neither Jack nor Eliza had seen one of these creatures before. Jack looked at them with a bit of wonder, but Eliza just muttered, "Bullies," with disgust.

They watched the gray cat defend itself until it lost its footing and fell. It hit a lower branch and tried to grab onto it, but the creature fell from that one as well and one of the healthy winged cats struck out as it fell past. Eliza hollered for them to leave the wounded one alone and ran to the tree.

Jack shouted after her, "Eliza, no!"

The gray cat lost its grip and fell from the tree directly into Eliza's waiting arms. "Meh," it stated weakly, before closing its eyes and losing consciousness.

As Jack approached the site, the healthy cats yowled, growing more hostile. The cat closest to Eliza made an angry, guttural sound. It hissed and leaped at her, and she turned her back to protect the wounded animal in her arms. As the cat soared through the air, Jack hurled a rock at it and knocked it off course. The cat hit the ground, scrambled in confusion for a moment, then hissed.

Jack made his way between the cats and Eliza, pulling his sword and scabbard off his belt. He took out the blade and jammed it into the ground. The cats' eyes never left him as he swung his scabbard around like a club and said, "All right. Let's do this."

As if they understood, the winged cats leaped at him, attacking from all angles. Jack swung the scabbard, striking with skill and accuracy, hitting them to wound but not kill. Hindered by the animal in her arms, Eliza spent most of her time dodging attacks. After a few minutes of this, the winged cats finally retreated.

Eliza cradled the gray cat in her arms and caressed him. He lifted his head and gave a half-hearted "Meh," in gratitude. Despite the scowl on its face, the cat purred and cuddled into Eliza's embrace.

Eliza asked, "Have you ever heard of a creature like this?" The cat gave another "Meh" and nestled further into her arm.

Reattaching his sword to his belt, Jack said, "Never." He reached down and scratched the cat under the jaw with a finger. It gave a little "Meh" in response. "It looks kind of like a manticore—you know, a lion with wings. But this little guy is clearly no lion. He's like a . . . a miniature manticore. A minicore."

"Meh," agreed the winged cat.

Jack and Eliza chuckled. "I think he likes it." She looked at the little creature and added, "He's pretty cute."

"Meh," the cat agreed again.

"I've never been much of a cat person," Jack replied, "but yeah, he is."

Eliza looked at the cat and asked, "Do you think Jason will mind if we take care of him? At least until he's healed."

"I don't see why not."

Eliza looked up smiling and asked, "What should we name him?"

"Name him?" exclaimed Jack, raising his eyebrows. "I thought it was just until—"

"It is! But we need something to call him in the meantime."

"Okay. Let's see. How about—"

"Oliver," Eliza cut in.

Jack laughed. "You want to take a minute to think about it?"

She blushed, "All right. I just always wanted a pet. I mean, I always wanted a . . ." she looked down at the bundle in her arms and said in a hushed tone, "D-O-G."

"Meh," whined the cat.

"But Oliver, despite being of the feline persuasion, seems like a keeper."

Jack didn't argue. She cradled Oliver in her arms as they trekked back to the caves. After walking in silence for a bit, Eliza asked, "Say, why didn't you kill the other ca . . . minicores?"

"What?"

"Well, you're a soldier. I can't imagine the notion of killing is exactly foreign to you. I mean . . . *the pirates.* But just now you only used your scabbard on the minicores, not your sword."

Jack shrugged. "I'm a soldier, not a killer." He paused, searching for the words to explain it. "Yeah, I killed the pirates, but I didn't take any pleasure in it. I didn't have a choice. But those minicores, they're just animals." Eliza stopped and gazed at him. Unable to read her expression, he asked, "What?"

She walked up to him, and in one fluid motion she lifted a hand to his face and leaned toward him. Before Jack could register what she was doing, he felt her lips on his own. He gathered her closer to him, and he felt Eliza yield to his embrace. How often he had imagined this exact moment—her body close to his, the intoxicating taste of her mouth, the soft brush of her hair against his cheek. But he barely had the time to savor any of that before she pulled away and murmured, "It's because of things like that . . . that I have feelings for you." Then she ran ahead toward the caves.

Jack was going to run after her, but he stopped when he saw the magnolia tree with the heart he'd carved earlier. He pulled out the knife again and approached the tree. This time he added their names to the engraving, the heart now encircling the words *Jack and Eliza.* He kissed his fingers and touched them to the heart. He stood back from his work and felt the strangest impulse to say, "Thank you," but didn't know to whom, exactly.

He closed his eyes, relishing the moment, and smiled all the way back to the caves.

Chapter Eleven

Titles, Monograms, and Marriage

Frank rose shortly before dawn and headed to a makeshift landing pad that a group of soldiers had cleared late last night. Though it was still dark, he could hear the droning of a motor from an approaching transport vessel, which was to take Seth and the other soldiers who had attacked Peter and Terrie back to Idoless. It couldn't arrive soon enough for Frank.

For the past two days, Commander Church had grown increasingly irritable as he attempted to repair the damage Seth had caused. Officially, Church claimed to be upset because the attack had delayed the mission, but Frank believed it was more than that. He figured Church was humiliated by the incident, and even ordered the court martial for the men himself.

The sun began to crest the horizon as the transport touched down, and Frank joined Church in greeting it. Armed soldiers chaperoned Seth and his lackeys as they shuffled toward the vessel, restraints clanging and heads held low.

"Good morning," said Kirk Albert Larson, peering out of the vessel's doorway.

All the men jerked their heads up. They had been prepared for surly guards, not a placid spiritual advisor.

Commander Church ordered the men in custody to halt while he and Frank greeted the kirk as he disembarked. The weak smile on Church's face couldn't mask his annoyance. "To what do we owe the pleasure?"

"The king spoke to me last night, explaining the . . . disruption," said Albert, glancing at Seth and the others. "I offered to give your team some . . . spiritual guidance to help regain focus. It is such an important mission, after all."

Frank noticed something about Albert was different than the last time they'd met; he appeared focused and much more himself now. He still looked tired, but he always looked like that. It seemed that having a purpose distracted him from whatever he'd been struggling with back at the castle.

A small detail of soldiers then poured out of the vessel from behind Albert and escorted Seth and his gang inside. Church had another soldier lead Albert away then turned to Frank and took a deep breath. His voice tight and controlled, he said, "Meet me back at my tent in twenty minutes. Sharp." With that, Church turned on his heel and strode off, not even waiting to watch the ship containing his brother take off.

Frank took a brief break to head to the mess tent and grab a cup of coffee. He sat down at an empty table and tried to sort out the mess of the past two days in his head. After the attack, Peter was ready to call everything off. He threatened to take Terrie back to the Kodiaks; it was only because the bear's injuries made travel impossible that they were still there.

In an effort to reconcile, Commander Church had ordered the head medic to care for Terrie, as best he could. He also declared that Peter and Terrie were officially under the protection of the Idolessian Army. Despite Church's efforts, Frank knew Peter wasn't impressed and leveraged his power by insisting they stay put until Terrie's condition was stable, which only agitated Church further.

Jack wasn't making the difficult situation any easier. Last night after the brothers had climbed into their cots, Frank had been forced to listen to his conspiracy theories. Jack was convinced that Church was ready to leave the bear and force Peter to help resume the quest. Feeling almost as annoyed with the memory as he did when he heard it, Frank thought again of what he'd said to Jack, "Of course, he's annoyed! We're behind schedule. But he's doing what he can to make things right."

Frank drained his coffee cup and headed to Commander Church's tent. He announced himself at the tent flap and walked in, sitting in the small folding chair opposite Church's table. Church glanced up from a map he was reading and didn't waste any time getting to the matter at hand. "We're breaking camp tomorrow—we've wasted enough time. The doorway to Death's Province could move at any moment. It might have already moved for all we know, and this would all be one big waste of time and resources."

Frank sat silently as Church folded the map and slid it into a folder. He then turned to look Frank in the eye, "I'm done with damage control. Peter has no idea what he's costing the mission." Frank shifted in his chair, guessing what was coming next. "We need to move on. Can you talk to him, get him to see how important this is? I'd do it myself, but I don't have much influence with Peter. But you're a different case. He listens to you."

Frank fought the heat rising in his cheeks. He felt special and wasn't sure if it was just because this task made him more useful to the mission. He was flattered that Peter trusted him, but Church recognizing it gave him a feeling he'd not felt before— something like pride, but different. Whatever the case, the commander had asked, so he promised to do what he could.

Later that evening, Albert joined the Waramonds at mealtime. He and Jack did most of the talking, each getting caught up with what the other had been doing in the years of Jack's absence. Frank sat in silence, looking off into the forest. He'd spent the entire day working up the courage to talk with Peter, but still hadn't done it. After everything that had happened, how could Frank ask him for any kind of favor?

"You coming?" asked Jack as he and Albert stood to go get some food.

"I'm not really hungry," said Frank. "I'll save your spots."

After Jack and Albert left, Frank looked out into the forest and wondered what Peter was doing. He resolved that after dinner, he would go speak to him; he had to report back to the commander in the morning.

A light breeze rustled the trees. It stopped after a moment and left him in near silence, except for the muffled chatter of the soldiers in the distance. He looked back and saw that the food line had only just begun moving, Jack and Albert bringing up the rear. Frank was quite alone. Eyes downcast, he recalled the song Peter had sung the day they met and, within the safety of his solitude, risked humming the tune he couldn't get out of his head. His barely audible hum broke into whispered words: "Someone to watch . . ."

"Hi, Frank."

"Peter! Hi. I . . . I was just . . . thinking about you. It's been a few days, since . . . since . . . How are you? How's Terrie?"

"I'm okay. And Terrie is healing really good." Peter walked over to Frank and sat down so close that their legs tapped together, and their shoulders touched. Frank tried to act natural, since he didn't want make Peter to feel bad, but he couldn't help but think, *There's all this space and he sits so close?* He tried to rationalize the behavior, recalling how Peter was with Terrie. *It's completely normal for him to behave like this. After all, he was raised by animals.* But then Peter tucked himself under Frank's arm and wrapped his arms around his waist and hugged him.

Frank blushed and said, "Wha . . . what's that for?"

"Thank you for saving Terrie."

"Oh, it . . . it was nothing."

"It was everything." Peter hadn't let go yet, and Frank felt self-conscious. He tried to give a quick squeeze and a pat on the back to imply the hug was over, but Peter just squeezed more.

It's normal for him, Frank reminded himself.

Frank had only ever gotten hugs like this from Eliza and his mother. It was full and sincere, not the unemotional, macho, pat-on-the-back that he exchanged with Jack or his uncle. This hug was a genuine expression of affection. If he was honest with himself, it was nice, and he was tempted to return the embrace. But then he saw Jack and Albert making their way back and felt a sense of anxiety.

Peter sensed the shift in Frank and asked, "Are you all right?"

"Of course," Frank smiled, trying to act nonchalant. "It's just that I was . . . I was just, um, just getting ready to . . . to go and . . . get some food!" He pulled free of Peter's hold, sprang to his feet, and asked, "Can I get you anything?"

Peter looked up at Frank, confused. "Sure. Just no meat."

Just then Jack and Albert returned, Hawk and Joss trailing behind them.

"Oh, hey, Peter," Jack greeted.

"Hi, Jack."

"How ya doing?"

"I'm okay. Hey, thank you for saving Terrie."

"It was nothing. I'm glad we could help."

Frank waited for Peter to give Jack a hug too, but he didn't. There was an awkward pause as everyone became aware of him standing there. Jack even looked at his brother and asked, "What?"

Frank looked from Peter to Jack, his mind muddled. He felt honored that he'd gotten a hug and Jack hadn't, which made him feel embarrassed again. He stepped in a couple of directions, not sure which way to go, muttering "Nothing. Nothing. I . . . I'll . . . I'll be right back," then dashed toward the dinner line.

Jack watched Frank rush off, then exchanged an inquisitive look with Albert. Peter glanced at Joss and added, "Thanks to you, too . . . ?"

"Joss," answered Joss, "and Hawk here helped too."

Peter nodded at them both and they returned the gesture. They seemed subdued, not in their usual jovial spirits. Jack figured that although the events of Seth's attack had affected them, their restrained behavior wouldn't last long. "Peter," he said, "I'd like you to meet an old friend of mine and Frank's: Kirk Larson."

"Oh, please, just call me Albert."

Peter looked at him curiously. "Albert? Why'd he call you *kirk*?"

Albert smiled and explained, "*Kirk* is a title."

"Yeah, I've heard it before," said Peter, looking at Albert as if he might sprout fangs at any moment.

Unfazed by Peter's reaction, Albert asked, "Have you? Where?"

"I . . . don't remember." Peter looked away quickly.

It was clear to Jack that Peter *did* remember but didn't want to say. Albert must have noticed this too, because he kindly glossed past it. "Well, my *name* is Albert, which you may call me if you wish. And you, Peter—if I may call you that—I've heard much about."

Peter looked back at him. Then with even more suspicion asked, "How old are you?"

Albert smiled at Jack and said, "He *is* good," then turned back to Peter. "How old do you think I am?"

"Looking at you, I'd guess you were somewhere between Frank and Jack. But you seem . . . older."

Albert nodded, "Quite a bit, actually. I have a condition that slows the rate of my aging."

Peter replied, "Oh, okay," as though no further explanation was needed.

Albert and Jack laughed. "You're right, Jack, he *is* a unique one." Peter looked affronted, but with a wink Albert assured him, "That is quite a good thing, young man. What about you?"

"What about me what?"

"I've heard you're cloudy about details of your past. Do you know how old you are?"

"Not exactly," said Peter, "but at least twenty-one."

The group looked stunned. "No way," exclaimed Hawk. "*Maybe* you turned like, eighteen—*recently*. But you can't be twenty."

"The Kodiaks started keeping track of my age early on. It was one of the few human traditions they honored."

"Well, they figured something wrong," said Joss.

Peter's nose wrinkled, and he said, "Well, when they started counting, I was already old enough to walk, and that was twenty-one years ago." Peter wrapped his arms around his legs. "What difference does it make anyway? The bears, they don't care about age. Sure, things like experience come with it, so the others will listen to the ones who've been around longer." Peter looked at them pointedly and said, "But they aren't afraid to be wrong. They admit it, even in front of someone who's younger. They're wise enough to *know* when they don't know all the facts."

"And what if the younger one is untruthful?" Albert asked sagely.

Peter didn't miss a beat. "Animals don't lie. Humans do. And if an older bear was already defying age, I don't think he'd be so skeptical seeing something similar in someone else."

"Touché," said Albert, smiling.

"What are we talking about?" Frank asked as he rejoined the group. He sat back down next to Peter, leaving ample space between them. "Here you go, Peter," Frank smiled, handing him a tray of food. As Peter took it, he scanned the gap between them.

Albert continued, "So, Peter, as I said, I've heard a lot about you. I read the file and learned how you joined our little mission. But those were dry, lifeless reports, so I'd love to hear the story."

Frank shifted uncomfortably. Jack turned to his brother and asked, "You all right?"

"Yeah. Yeah, I'm fine," Frank replied, focusing on his tray.

Peter began the tale, explaining about life with the bears, which Albert found fascinating. He told them that the Kodiaks had gone hunting, leaving him alone for the afternoon, so he decided to have a bath, which was when Frank found him. He laughed, recalling how he hadn't even noticed Frank because he was so into the song he was singing.

"Singing?" Jack turned to his brother. "You hadn't mentioned that."

Frank began choking on his water. Sputtering between coughs, he explained, "Well, I *cough* I didn't want to *cough cough* well . . . embarrass Peter."

Peter looked confused and asked, "Why would I be embarrassed?"

Albert offered, "Music is a lost art to our nation, Peter. Most of us couldn't even think of a tune to whistle if we wanted."

"Well, that's dumb," Peter stated, inspiring a chuckle from his companions. They had gotten used to and appreciated his candor. "Singing isn't as lost as you think. There's plenty of it in the outer regions. I was singing one of my favorite songs. I sing it all the time."

"Why's that?" asked Albert.

"The tune is pretty, but the words . . . I don't know how to say it. I just really like them. I like the . . ." He faltered for a moment, trying to find the right term, ". . . the 'story' of the song. Does that make sense?"

"Makes sense to me," Jack offered. "It's always a treat to hear music. My favorites in Oakmoor were usually the songs that had a tune and words that worked together. And there always seemed to be a theme or tale or," he nodded to Peter, "'story' to them."

"Yeah. And the story . . ." Peter continued, "it's so much like mine."

"Ah, you relate to it," Albert said.

"*Relate*?" Peter cocked his head.

"You *connect* with the song. Its story is similar to your own."

"Yeah," agreed Peter, nodding his head.

Frank began, "Well . . ."

"What?" asked Peter.

Frank blushed again. He tried to say in a soft voice to Peter, "It was sort of a girl's song."

"What do you mean?"

Frank glanced around at the group, and continued speaking softly, "The story of the song is being told by a girl. It's a girl singing about a guy." He gave the group a hard stare—especially Hawk and Joss—as if he were telling them this was *not* something to tease Peter about, as he obviously didn't know better. Frank's voice returned to normal volume. "It's okay, I'm sure you were just repeating the song the way you heard it."

Peter's nose wrinkled as he thought about Frank's explanation. "Well, yeah . . . but—"

It seemed Peter had more to say, but Frank took over the story, hurriedly moving past the song and recounting the events of the chase.

Jack, Hawk, and Joss then filled in pieces of the story of Peter's arrival at camp. They laughed at how much havoc one little naked man brought a team of trained warriors. Suddenly, amid the laughter, Peter asked, "What's a monogram?"

"A what?" Jack asked.

"A . . ." Peter thought for a second, "yeah, a monogram. What is it?"

Jack and Frank stared blankly at each other as Albert answered, "There are all kinds of monograms, but traditionally they are initials."

"Initials?" asked Peter.

Happy to explain, Albert clarified, "An initial is the first letter of a word. In respect to your question, monograms are a collection of the first letters of our names. For example, mine is A.R.L., for Albert Richard Larson. *A* for Albert, *R* for Richard, and *L* for Larson. A.R.L. See?"

Peter thought for a moment and turned to Jack. "So you are J.W. for Jack Waramond?"

"I guess so," said Jack, "though I have a middle name—Gabriel. Making me J.G.W."

Peter looked at Frank and said, "And you're Fr—"

"Franklin," interjected Jack, wearing a playful grin.

"Frank," corrected Frank.

"Franklin!" said Hawk and Joss in unison, beaming that they had something new to taunt Frank with.

Frank shot Jack a look of irritation and sighed, "Thanks a lot." Then he looked back to Peter, "F.J.W.—Frank Joseph Waramond."

"And I'm . . ." the disappointment was palpable as he said simply, "P."

"I guess so. Unless," Albert asked, "do you have a middle or last name?"

"No. Just P," Peter reiterated with displeasure.

Albert spoke kindly. "I wouldn't worry about it. We rarely use initials or monograms or anything like that anymore. Royalty are the only people who really bother with them."

Peter looked dissatisfied, as if he wanted more answers. "So why would someone add their initials to someone else's?"

Albert was able to fill in some blanks. "Ah, I see. It's actually a very old custom. Like I said, we rarely do much with names these days other than identify people with them. But long ago, when people got married, the woman took the man's last name as her own. The custom died out over time. Now we take our mother's last name. The only people who do it anymore are royalty. Like our queen when she married the king, before she died, or the princess when she married the prince."

Without warning, Jack shot up from his seat and stormed away.

Albert looked around, bewildered. "Was it something I said?"

Frank got up, "No, he's just . . . Excuse me," and chased after his brother. He caught up with him just out of earshot of the group. "Hey, what's the problem?"

"Nothing. Just . . . I need a minute."

"No. What was that?"

Jack paused, "I just . . . the . . . eh."

"Jack, what?"

"When Albert said . . . 'married' . . ."

"So?"

Jack looked angry with himself. He sighed, looked at Frank, and said, "It's just . . . Eliza."

Frank groaned, "Oh, Jack." He looked back at the group. Albert was still talking with Peter, who was now scratching the dirt with a stick. Turning back to his brother and adopting a tone as if he were explaining that one plus one equaled two, he said as evenly as possible, "Jack, it's time you faced the fact, Eliza chose Jason."

"No, she didn't," growled Jack. "She married *me*, because she loves *me*." Frank remained silent. "Don't look at me like that. I'm not crazy."

"How should I look at you, Jack?"

"Listen," Jack grabbed Frank by the shoulders and with a desperate look in his eyes, his voice straining with the effort to stay calm, he explained, "Jason forced Eliza to marry him. I don't know how, but he—"

"Jack!" Frank pulled away.

"He did! He's not who everyone thinks he is."

"He's the prince and future king of Idoless!"

Jack threw his arms in the air and turned away.

Frank stood in silence for a minute before he responded. "You know, I never believed any of the rumors about you. Until now. You really did it, didn't you? That night . . . you tried to kill him."

Jack turned and faced his brother. "No." He took a deep breath, his head tilted back as he exhaled toward the stars. "He tried to kill me."

Frank began to argue the point but thought better of it and chose to challenge Jack instead. "All right, he tried to kill you. And then what?"

"No, not that night. That night I went to confront him about it. I went to ask him, face-to-face, man-to-man, how he could do that to me. Don't get me wrong, we did fight, but then," Jack got quiet, "then Eliza showed up."

"And?"

Jack seemed like he was trying to say something but couldn't.

"What did she say, Jack?" Frank demanded.

"She said she wanted Jason . . . But it isn't true, she—"

"Jack, it *is* true. She told me so herself."

Jack stared at Frank in disbelief.

Frank explained, "Eliza and I have spent a lot of time together since you left. She told me that it was one of the hardest things she ever went through, choosing between the two of you." Frank took a breath. "I'm so sorry. I never should have brought you back." He considered his brother for a moment, then seemed to come to a resolution. "I'll go to the commander tomorrow morning and tell him you can't—"

"No!"

"Jack, it's all right. I didn't realize how wounded you were, but I understand now. I get it. I've never loved someone like you've loved Eliza. I've wanted it, but . . ." Frank stopped when he felt a tear rolled down his cheek.

Jack argued, "Do you really think Church would . . . would let me leave? If . . . if you even, tried . . ." Despite Frank's efforts, more tears began to stream down his cheeks and Jack could obviously see. No longer concerned with their dispute, Jack took a step toward him. "Frank?"

With a great sniff, Frank composed himself, wiping the moisture from his eyes, and tried to use the gruffest voice he could muster. "We can't have everything we want simply because we want it. Sometimes the things we want are . . ." his voice broke, and he stopped. Tears welled up once again, but he willed them not to fall.

"Frank, I—"

Frank raised a hand to stop Jack. He lowered his gaze and let one drop fall and hit the ground. He took a deep breath and managed to finish, ". . . wrong."

The brothers stood there looking at each other. Frank knew he was weirding Jack out because even *he* was weirded out. He couldn't understand why he couldn't control these tears. He used to cry a lot when he was younger and had been harassed for it— not just by kids, but adults as well. His uncle, who was the closest thing to a father figure he had, never said so specifically, but it was clear he didn't think it was appropriate behavior for boys. Eventually Frank had stopped crying so easily, but it was still a tender subject all these years later. So when Jack apologized, Frank snapped at him, "Stop, just stop."

"No, I've been a huge pain, and—"

"Look, I know you're hurting."

"Yeah. And so, obviously, are you."

Frank disregarded Jack's concern and persisted, "And you know I care for you. But you've got to stop letting your feelings get the best of you." Then he looked Jack in the eyes and spoke with a voice full of sympathy, "Or I'm going to have to step in."

"I'll try."

Jack began to walk away but stopped when Frank said, "I mean it, Jack. You're my brother and I love you, but this mission is too important—more important than a broken heart. We're going to start moving again soon. If I don't think you can handle it, if I think you're going to be a threat to the mission, I'll personally put you on a transport home."

Jack gave a lifeless smile and said, "You can try, but Church would never let you." Then he walked away.

Frank sighed. He was annoyed that after all that, Jack would still bring up his distrust about Commander Church. He rubbed his eyes and went back to the fire.

Peter was gone, and he realized he still hadn't talked with him as Commander Church had asked. In fact, everyone had gone except Albert, who had his head bowed in some kind of meditation but looked up as Frank approached.

Frank winced, "Sorry, Kirk Larson, I didn't mean to disturb you."

"Don't be silly, Franklin, you didn't disturb me. And again, it's Albert. So, is Jack all right?"

Frank sighed, "Ah, he's fine. He's just got a royal stick up his butt." And though Albert didn't react, Frank immediately felt guilty and said, "Sorry."

"Don't apologize—I'm sure that would make anyone irritable." Frank returned Albert's grin, but his eyes were still red and itchy. Albert noticed and asked, "Are *you* all right?"

Frank knew there was no hiding it. "No, Kir . . . Albert. I'm not." He thought about the advice he'd just given Jack, about not letting emotions get the best of you. He put on his best smile and said, "But I will be."

"Is there anything you need to talk about?"

"No, that's all right." Frank wanted a distraction, so he looked around and asked, "Where'd Peter go?"

"Oh, he saw you and Jack were going to be a while, so he went to check on the bear," Albert explained. "He's really quite a remarkable young man."

"Yeah, he's a good kid."

"Well, I wouldn't say 'kid.'" Albert recounted the story Peter had told them about his age.

"He's twenty-one?" Frank marveled, going silent.

"Probably older." Albert measured Frank with his eyes. "You look . . . relieved?"

"What? Oh, no, no, I'm just . . . surprised. Wow, I thought he was . . . I don't know, younger."

"Indeed, he's not all he appears. But who of us are?" Albert paused before adding, "He seems rather tied to you."

"Yeah, well, we kind of bonded early on."

"Because of the singing incident?"

"Oh, no." Frank cleared his throat, "No, it was Vergo and some of the others. They treated him like some kind of prisoner of war. And interrogated him like one." Albert gasped, and Frank shook his head. "I mean, he wasn't guilty of anything except having information we needed. I was just nice to him when no one else was." He told Albert about the deal he and Peter had made. "He didn't have to agree to help us . . . I wouldn't have blamed him if he hadn't. And now, after what Seth did . . . I don't know."

"I think he'll still aid the mission—if anything, to impress you." Frank didn't know how to respond to that, so he smiled at Albert, as if to imply that it was a nice thing to say, but not a reality. "And with that," Albert concluded, "I think I'll leave you for the evening. I should get some rest. Good night, Franklin."

"Good night, Albert." Frank watched the kirk walk away and was about to head to his own tent when he saw what looked like the letters *PW* scratched on the ground. When he looked up, Peter was standing before him. "Oh, Peter! Hey."

Peter glanced back and forth, never looking him fully in the eyes, but told Frank, "I just got done talking with your leader."

"Commander Church?"

"I told him I would still help."

Frank couldn't contain his smile. "Peter, that's . . . thank you so much!"

Frank's happiness seemed to only aggravate Peter. He mustered up his nerve and explained, "I told him it was on two conditions."

"Oh?"

"The first is that I would only go if *you* wanted me to."

Frank felt butterflies in his stomach at that, and said, "Of course I do." Peter eyed him, as though he wanted more of an explanation. Uncomfortable, Frank added, "Idoless needs this mission to be a success."

This answer seemed to only frustrate Peter all the more. "But . . . do *you* want me to go?"

More butterflies.

"Of course." Peter eyed him again. "I . . . want to see the mission succeed . . . for Idoless."

"But do you want . . . *mind* me being around?" asked Peter.

"Why would I mind?" said Frank, "You're . . ." His stomach turned somersaults. "You're great."

That made Peter smile some, but there was still trepidation in his demeanor, like he didn't believe what Frank was saying. "Well, that's good, because the other condition was that I get to stay with you the whole time."

CHAPTER TWELVE

TRUST ISSUES

The next morning, Frank felt uneasiness hanging in the air. All the distractions—Peter's dramatic appearance, the attack by the Kodiaks, and Seth's insubordination—had taken the focus off the actual mission. But last night, Commander Church had brought it back to the forefront when he addressed the soldiers and explained the full nature of the operation, confirming what many had already suspected: they were going into Death's Province.

The news had hit the men hard; some looked terrified, while others ranted in anger, but Frank was certain all the reactions masked the same thought: they'd just been sentenced to death.

After they finished breaking camp, the soldiers gathered. With Jack by his side, Frank stood at the head of his platoon but could see Peter and Terrie a few yards away. Peter was pacing around as the bear stared back defiantly. After one great huff from the bear, Peter threw his arms in the air and walked over to join Frank. Terrie followed.

Peter said irritably, "He's coming with."

Jack asked, "Is that a good idea?"

"No, it isn't," answered Peter, looking directly at the bear. Terrie huffed again. "But he won't listen to me."

Terrie had only been back on his feet for a couple days, so Frank objected with genuine concern, "I don't know. I really think it would be better if—" Terrie looked right at Frank and gave an unmistakable growl. "If he stayed extra close then."

Terrie seemed content and grunted a sound of agreement.

Hawk and Joss, who seemed to be the only two unfazed by the ominous destination, joined them. Hawk said, "Hey, Jack," and then nodded to Peter, "Kid." He turned to the bear with a straight face and said, "Frank." Then he turned to Frank and gave a dramatic gasp of feigned surprise. He looked from Frank to Terrie and, with a grin, said, "Oops."

Neither of the Waramond brothers got the chance to respond before Commander Church called out to them. "Jack. Peter. Please join me."

Peter grabbed Frank's hand, "Not without—"

"Forgive me. And Lieutenant Waramond."

Frank slipped his hand out of Peter's and stood at attention. He didn't feel right, receiving special privileges just because of his relationship with Jack and now Peter. "Sir, if I'm needed back here . . . ?"

The commander responded, "Your presence makes both our guests happy, Lieutenant. So, you are needed *here*."

Reassured by the commander's genuine tone, Frank did as he was ordered.

The company traveled most of the day, stopping only for a brief lunch. The terrain grew increasingly difficult. With no trails, the soldiers had to rely on tracking devices that lost signals easily in the heart of the forest. Then, just after noon, they stumbled upon something quite unexpected: a woman. The slim figure was laying facedown directly in their path. Jack rushed to her, but

Mike yelled, "Jack, don't touch her!" Jack ignored him and proceeded. Church barked, "I order you to stop!"

Jack almost laughed at the command as he pulled her up gently and asked, "Miss, are you all right?" He turned her over and was taken aback; the woman was beautiful. Or she would have been, if she weren't so dirty and beaten. She had wavy, strawberry-blond hair and smelled almost fruity. "Miss? Miss?" Jack tried to shake her awake lightly. He opened his canteen and poured a trickle of water in her mouth, which she drank instinctively.

After a moment, she sputtered and coughed, "Too . . . too much!" She pushed the canteen away and moaned in pain as she pulled herself into a seated position.

Jack helped her up. "Easy, easy. Not too fast."

"Th . . . thank you." She gave a start when she looked up to see the rows of soldiers, Commander Church, Peter, and the great bear.

"Don't worry about them," Jack assured her. He put a finger up, moved it back and forth and watched her eyes follow it. "It doesn't look like you have a concussion. What happened to you, Miss . . . ?"

"Sarah. Sarah Cassidy," she answered, holding her head.

"What happened, Sarah?"

Sarah groaned as she tried to stand. "It was pirates. They took me from my village, and—oh!" Jack caught her as she began to fall over. "Th . . . thank you. I . . . I'm so sorry. I only just got away. I must have . . . passed out." Her eyes filled with tears and as she fell against Jack's chest she whimpered, "They'll realize I'm gone soon."

His arms instinctively went around her as he comforted her. "Don't worry, they can't hurt you anymore."

"There are pirates all the way out here?" Church asked, scanning the area.

"It wouldn't surprise me," said Jack. "It's far from any kind of authority, and it's not like they'd have to go into Death's Province, even if they could."

Sarah started. "Death's Province?"

Jack tried to calm her. "Don't worry. We're headed that way, but we're not that close. We'll have someone escort you out of here to safety."

The commander chimed in, "Don't promise things you don't have the authority to deliver, Jack. We need everyone we've got."

Sarah's eyes teared up again, "W . . . what? You're not going to just leave me, are you?"

Jack gave Church a look of disgust and argued, "Come on, Mike, we can spare *one* soldier. It won't make a difference to our troop, but it would to Miss Cassidy here."

Sarah began to cry, "No . . . please. The pirates . . . they're monsters! They did horrible things to me. I . . . I can't . . . you can't leave me alone. When they realize I'm gone . . . One soldier won't be able to keep me safe." Church sighed in frustration. Still in Jack's arms, Sarah said, "You . . . you could take me with you. They wouldn't dare attack the army."

"What? No," said Jack. "We really *are* heading to Death's Province. That's no place for you."

"Please," she begged, "please, just don't leave me! I don't want to be left alone." She burrowed deeper into Jack's arms.

"She's lying."

Peter stood nearby with his arms folded across his chest. Frank and the others gawked at him. Jack looked up, half in shock. Even Sarah stopped crying, confused by what was going on.

"What did you say?" asked Jack.

"There's *no one* out here—especially not pirates. They don't come to these parts . . ." he looked at Frank and said firmly, "ever." Peter looked at the woman in Jack's arms and said definitively, "She wants to come with us."

It was as if all the sound was sucked out of the air and Jack's ears rang with warning. He looked at the woman in his arms, who was now smiling. "Hmmm," she said. "Didn't see that coming."

"Wha—?" huffed Jack, as Sarah spun from his arms and kicked him in the chest, knocking him down. She retreated with a nimble cartwheel followed by a backflip, landing skillfully on her feet as she assumed a fighting stance that looked more like a dance pose; she stood with confidence, arms elegantly extended and legs planted, spread as much as her dress allowed. Jack met Frank's eye, both men immediately recognizing it as one of the fighting forms their mother had taught them.

Commander Church drew his sword and pointed it at the woman. "You've got to be kidding. You're outnumbered, three hundred to one. Give up!"

Sarah wiped her face, and the bruises and blood smeared; it was all fake. She gave a girlish laugh, flashed a charming grin and said, "You give up? Perfect. It saves us the effort of kicking all of your asses."

"Us?"

Church had barely uttered the question when a figure fell from the trees, landing with a thud that shook the ground. The warrior looked nothing like the soldiers of Idoless. He wore armor forged of thick metal plating that had been painted red. Curved horns, one longer than the other, jutted out of his helmet, creating a sort of crescent moon and spikes studded his shoulders and knees. A surprisingly high-pitched voice came from the figure, nodding to Sarah, "Plan B?"

"Yup, yup," answered Sarah with a grin as she tore off the outer layer of Idolessian-style clothing she wore, revealing tall black boots, tight red leather pants, and a white blouse, cinched by a vest that pushed out her breasts and exposed cleavage.

"They're from Lithostone!" shouted Church. The soldiers drew their weapons.

Jack asked, "How do you know?" as he picked himself off the ground, rubbing his chest where Sarah had kicked him.

"Look at the other one's armor—it's an old style, but it's Lithostonian." He turned to the two unlikely warriors. "I repeat, you are severely outnumbered. I strongly suggest you surrender."

Sarah and her armored partner glanced at each other and then gazed back at the mass of soldiers before them. With a giggle, Sarah shrugged and winked at Church—then she and her companion charged the Idolessians.

The soldiers were apprehensive about fighting a woman, and Sarah capitalized on their hesitation. What she lacked in size and strength she made up for in skill and aggression. At one point, Jack took her on head-to-head, which confirmed his suspicion about her fighting form. Years of training with his mother in the same form had prepared him, which she seemed to notice and enjoy.

Sarah's partner was the opposite in style, but more than equal in accomplishment. He had none of Sarah's nimble agility, but he possessed a supernatural strength. When he struck his opponents, they didn't just fall, they were thrown. The soldiers piled on top of him, but he flung them off with a single effortless swipe of his arm. For some time, Terrie was—despite Peter's cries of protest—the only one who put up any kind of fight with him.

In the end Sarah and her partner's prowess could not compensate for being so outnumbered and eventually they admitted defeat; putting themselves at the mercy of Commander Church who immediately had them bound.

Ivan Lane reached for the helmet of the armored warrior, who bucked and strained to keep the helmet on, but his supernatural strength seemed depleted, and the binding made it impossible for him move much. The general grabbed the helmet's horns, one in each hand, and yanked upward. Those close enough to see the warrior stood dumbfounded for several seconds.

She had a heavy brow and the wide jaw of a man, but there was just enough femininity to mark her as a woman. Her hair was the same color as Sarah's, and it even seemed like it wanted to twist in the same way, but it hung lifeless off her head. Despite all the mannish qualities, Jack could see a resemblance to Sarah.

Church must have seen it too because he asked, "Sisters?"

"Yes, sisters. Twins, actually," replied Sarah.

Hawk chuckled and remarked cruelly, "So what happened to her?"

Sarah shot Hawk a dirty look and snapped, "She has a name. It's Sophie."

"You don't need to talk about me like I'm not here," muttered Sophie.

Commander Church considered the Cassidy sisters for a moment, then turned to confer with the high-ranking officers.

Jack knew Frank was wondering just as much as he was where Sarah had learned to fight like their mother; her moves weren't standard Lithostonian, that was for sure.

He glanced over at Church and the generals who were deep in discussion about the sisters. So, he made eye contact with his brother and raised his eyebrows in Sarah's direction. Frank glared back, warning him it wasn't the right time. They went back and forth with their wordless argument until Peter, who had watched the whole exchange, asked Frank bluntly, "Why can't he talk to her?"

After a moment's consideration, Frank sighed in defeat.

Jack sauntered over to Sarah and, in a hushed tone said, "Um, excuse me."

Sarah flashed a smile and said without as much hush, "Well heeelllllooo, Sexypants."

Jack glanced back at Frank and the others. "Yeah, uh, hi. I just wanted to ask you about your um . . . your fighting style."

Sarah mocked his efforts to be quiet and whispered back loudly, "What about it?"

Annoyed, Jack continued, "Well, where'd you learn it?"

Sarah gave a snort. "Well, the form I learned, but the flair is just natural." She extended her leg up with toes pointed.

"So, in Lithostone?"

His disinterest in her flair deflated Sarah, and she dropped her foot to the ground. "Yeah. Why?"

"Is it like, a standard fighting form in Lithostone?"

Sarah's eyebrow lifted, and with an impish grin she answered, "Nope, it's for a very select few." She leaned closer and whispered, "So, where'd *you* learn it?"

Jack didn't answer; he just walked back to Frank to report his findings.

Church ordered the company to set up camp there; they'd get back on course in the morning. He also informed them that by the end of the next day, they should arrive at Death's Province.

Sarah and Sophie were given something to eat, then tied to a tree where the commander interrogated them himself with hand-selected soldiers who were . . . unexpected.

Frank braced himself for the conspiracy theories he knew this would inspire in Jack. And as if on cue, the moment they were alone Jack began in on him. "You have to admit, it's odd. He turned away two of the generals, but asked a private to stay?"

Frank wouldn't hear it. "It's not our call, Jack. He's the commander. He can have anyone he wants with him." Frank proceeded to remind Jack of their talk the previous night and how he'd agreed to be better.

Jack brushed him off and proceeded to excuse himself. Frank smelled something fishy and called after, "Jack—What are you thinking about doing?"

Jack smiled as he backed away. "Nothing. I just gotta . . . you know, *go*."

Frank snorted. "Isn't that the same excuse you used to sneak away from Church back at the castle?" He was about to chase after his brother when he noticed Peter hunched over Terrie, who was lying flat on the ground, his breathing labored. "Is he okay?"

"No," replied Peter. He placed his forehead against the bear's. "Terrie is being very stubborn." The bear huffed in reply. "You can't do that, Terrie. You're hurt. What would I do if something happened to you? You're all I have left."

Frank asked gently, "Not that anything *will* happen to him, but um . . . if it did . . . what about the rest of the Kodiaks?"

Peter continued to pet Terrie, who fell asleep. "When I . . . agreed to help you, I . . . I sort of gave up my right to be a part of the pack."

Frank was shaken to hear his suspicions confirmed. "Peter! Why would you ever agree to that?"

Peter looked up at Frank. "We made a deal."

"Yeah, but to give up your home . . ." Frank let the thought hang in the air. He couldn't fathom what made Peter do it.

With a long face, Peter explained, "It was going to happen eventually. The Kodiaks have tried to get me to stay with humans before. Whenever it didn't work out and I went back to them, they made it clear then that it was only temporary. So, when you showed up . . . it just made sense."

Frank knelt next to Peter. "What about Terrie?" He motioned to the animal, careful not to touch him.

"You can pet him," said Peter.

"What?"

"You're afraid to touch him, but it's okay." Peter continued caressing the bear, showing Frank how easy it was.

Frank reached over and put his hand over the bear's bristled fur. He lowered his hand and . . . "It's so soft!"

Peter explained, "Yeah, all the Kodiaks are like that. People think their fur is rough, probably because of how it bunches up and looks all spiky."

Frank rubbed Terrie's neck and back, feeling the even rhythm of the bear's breathing. Absorbed in the moment, Frank absentmindedly chuckled to himself. "My beard's the same It looks bristlier than it is."

Taking the comment as an invitation, Peter reached over and touched his beard. Frank flinched and stood up.

"What?" asked Peter.

Frank reminded himself that Peter didn't have the same kind of boundaries as most people. And his own personal space bubble was, admittedly, larger than most. "Nothing. Nothing." Hoping to change the subject, Frank asked, "So, um, what about Terrie? Can he go back to the Kodiaks?"

Peter looked at Frank, perplexed for a moment, but moved on. "Yeah, being a bear, he can go back. But he's . . . well, you've seen. He's stubborn. He's the one that found me and raised me the most. I don't think he'd ever leave me."

Just then, Frank noticed Jack popping out from behind a tree, waving at him. "Uh, excuse me, Peter."

Without looking up, Peter said, "It *is* soft."

"What is?"

"Your beard."

"Oh . . ." Frank chuckled timidly, then walked to Jack, who looked anxious.

Jack began, "All right, now don't be mad, but—"

Frank crossed his arms, "What did you do?"

"Nothing! Well . . ."

Frank shook his head. "Jaaaack . . . ?"

"Here's the thing. I *was* going to try and eavesdrop on Church and the sisters." Frank drew an exasperated breath, but Jack cut him off, "But I thought about what you said, how I told you I was going to try and be better, and I meant it. So, I let it go. But then I really did have to, well, *go*."

"Get to the point, Jack."

"I was on my way back to you when I came upon Church talking . . . privately with one of the soldiers." Frank rolled his eyes and threw his hands up in frustration. Jack implored, "Really? A secret conversation doesn't seem at all suspicious to you?!"

Anger surged through Frank, and he struggled to keep his voice at a whisper. "How many times do I have to say it? What the commander does is *his* prerogative! If he and the commanding officers want—"

"It was just him and that private he had with him interrogating the sisters," interrupted Jack. "Who is that guy anyway? He seems familiar."

"Who? Private Marks?"

"Marks? Like . . . Commander Ryan Marks?"

"Yeah, he's related to him somehow. Church was Ryan's protégée. And before he retired, Ryan convinced Church to get—Al, I think his name is—to get Al a good position."

"Well, I don't care who his family is. It was just *Private* Marks talking with *Commander* Church. Look, I wasn't there to eavesdrop, and I didn't stay, but I couldn't help but hear some of what they were saying as I left." Jack paused, waiting for Frank to request more.

Begrudgingly, he said, "Go ahead."

With a stoic expression, Jack said, "I heard Church say that things were 'back on track' and 'going according to plan.'" Arms still folded; Frank scrutinized him. Jack added, "I didn't listen to any more. But still, I thought . . . thought you ought to know."

Frank processed the information, then asked, "What's with all the paranoia, Jack? Why do you distrust the commander so much?"

Jack felt completely stuck and was unsure how to answer. He wanted to tell Frank what he'd overheard Church say back at the castle, but to do that he'd have to reveal his knowledge of the castle's secret passages. And Jack knew that Frank—ever the good soldier—would tell Church about the passageways the next time he saw him. No, he just couldn't bear to give that up . . . not yet. So, he took a deep breath and tried something different. "The night I left . . . the *reason* I left . . ." Jack exhaled and ran his fingers through his hair. "I don't know how to say this without sounding crazy. I know I've already given you every reason to think I was."

Frank urged him on. "It's okay, just say it."

Somberly, Jack proceeded. "How much do you know about my last mission? The first time I went to Death's Province?"

"It was classified. Still is."

"Yeah, well, that's because there *was* no mission."

"What do you mean?"

Jack's gaze followed the path the company would be taking the next morning. His hands involuntarily clenched into fists. "Once inside, it didn't take long for me to realize that everything I'd been told about that place, all the reasons I'd been sent in, *everything*, was a lie. It's a death trap and nothing more." Jack's face hardened remembering the chaos and death. "Most of my team was killed in the first few hours inside. The first were shot by our own manic crossfire and the rest got picked off, one after another. Every one of them was killed." Then Jack stood tall. "But like all my missions, I survived because I had something to live for. Some*one* to live for."

"Eliza?"

Jack nodded. "She was like . . . my beacon. No matter where I was sent, no matter how dangerous the task, I always found my way back to her."

"But how'd you actually get out of the Province? You said everyone was killed. Without the wizard, who opened the door for you . . .?"

Jack shook his head. "Maybe the doorway was weakened by our entrance, or maybe, though I doubt it, one of the gods helped me. I don't know what it was, but I was determined to get back to her. So, I . . . *pushed* my way through."

"What?"

"It almost killed me. After I got out, it took me weeks before I was able to travel. And since everyone thought I was dead, I was on my own. It was a long, difficult journey, but I made it, because I had that beacon." Jack felt his heartbeat quicken as he recalled the memory. "And after all that, what do I find when I get back, but that my beacon . . . my *wife*, is marrying another man."

"Come on, Jack, *wife*?"

"Yes, *wife*. I told you, Frank. We married each other on the island."

Frank replied carefully, "On the island? So, you weren't . . . *really* married. Not legally."

Jack looked disappointed. "A legal document doesn't make a marriage real, Frank. What's real is our love, and the promise we made to each other. I mean, sure, if we could, we would have done it the usual way. But we couldn't. So, we did the best we could with what we had. And when it was done, it was done; I was her husband, and she was my wife."

Jack saw the look of doubt on his brother's face and gave a sad laugh. "I can't blame you for thinking that way. It's what everyone thought when we first got back, especially Eliza's father. We disagreed . . . but figured we'd humor him and get 'properly' married. We looked at it as a formality; just a legal extension of the promise we had already made on the island."

"But Jack, why don't I know about any of that?"

"I didn't have time. You were sent on assignment right after we were rescued. And by the time *you* were back, I was reinstated in the army and sent on a mission of my own. And I wasn't about to tell you all this in a letter. How could I?"

"You know you didn't have to wait for me, if that was the case."

"I know." Jack paused, trying to steady his breath. "But there *was* no time. I was sent on my first mission before we could even get the paperwork filed. And when I got back, I was sent on my next assignment even faster. The time Eliza and I had together grew shorter and shorter between each assignment—I barely ever saw her! Every time we began to make headway in planning the wedding, I was sent away again."

Jack closed his eyes and saw Eliza in his mind; not the princess, but the woman he had fallen in love with. "Looking forward to the day we could finally be together got me through each mission. It was because of Eliza that I achieved all I did. She made me a hero. She got me through all my battles. She got me out of Death's Province. She got me home." Jack's face fell. "And she married Jason."

"Jack . . ." Frank whispered, "everyone thought you were dead . . . I mean, that place—"

"Of course, you thought I was dead. And if I had died, I would have been *thrilled* at the prospect of my wife and best friend winding up together. Except . . ." Jack trailed off.

"Except?"

With a haunted tone Jack said, "I remember my first night alone in Death's Province. Realizing . . . accepting . . . I wasn't going to make it out. I thought about all the people important to me. Mom had died while I was on the island, but there was still you, Eliza and . . . Jason." He frowned. "And you know, for a second, I actually hoped he and Eliza would wind up together. But that's when I knew."

"Knew what?"

"I wasn't *supposed* to come back from Death's Province."

"That's a pretty serious accusation, Jack."

"But it's true! That mission was the *eleventh consecutive assignment* I was sent on. Eleven! No soldier gets assigned more than three consecutive operations without some kind of break, let alone eleven! And each mission, my companies got smaller and less skilled. We were never given enough resources to feasibly succeed, and I was the only common factor on each team. I tried complaining, but my protests all fell on deaf ears." Jack laughed remorsefully, "And the group assigned to me for the mission into Death's Province . . . they were a bunch of kids, Frank, barely out of the academy. Look at us now, headed to the same place with a company of three hundred experienced men. I had a team of twenty-five recent graduates and a drunken wizard. We weren't supposed to succeed; we were supposed to die." He looked pointedly at his brother. "So, you'll have to forgive me for not being the most trusting person."

Frank sighed. "That's quite the tale, Jack. I'm touched that you trusted me with it, really. And you need to know . . . you need to hear . . . that I don't doubt a word of it. I believe everything you said." He smiled kindly. "I don't think you're crazy. What you went through . . . I can't imagine what it was like. Eleven consecutive missions . . . That alone would be enough to push anyone over the edge." He paused, struggling to continue, but then said, "I'm just not sure I agree with your conclusions."

"Then explain it to me, Frank. Give me an explanation that makes sense."

Frank reasoned, "It's just . . . you're one of the greatest warriors Idoless has ever known . . . the greatest of your time, at the very least. Why would the army want to have you killed? Why would anyone want to have you killed? It just doesn't make sense. Even if someone in command wanted you dead, no one would have the kind of clout to make it happen."

"It wasn't just *anyone*. That's what I've been trying to say—it was Jason. He was jealous from the day Eliza and I fell in love, and he wanted her for himself."

Frank's face knotted with doubt. "There has to be another reason, Jack. I mean . . . he was your best friend."

"Excuse me." Commander Church's voice made Jack and Frank jump. They had gotten lost in their conversation and hadn't noticed his approach. Jack wondered how much he'd heard, while Frank stood at attention. "It's gotten quite late, and we need everyone at their best tomorrow, so I suggest you two get your rest." He excused himself and headed back.

They knew Church was right. They didn't want to go into Death's Province tired and slow. Jack gave an annoyed groan and started back, but Frank stopped him.

"I just have one last question, Jack." He hesitated, as if he wasn't sure he was ready for the answer. "It's just . . . the last time you went into Death's Province, you said you had Eliza to live for. You basically said you wouldn't have survived if not for her."

"Yeah?"

Frank scratched the back of his head. "So, um . . . given the way things are now . . . why are you going back in?"

Jack exhaled noisily. "We really need to get to sleep."

"That's not an answer."

"That's because I don't have one, Frank. Look, don't worry. I don't have some kind of death wish. It's for her. Everything is for her. Even now, I'm still doing all this for her." Jack could tell that wasn't enough for his brother. "I'm going to see this mission through. I just want to make sure that however this turns out, it's for the right reasons, and that the people I love will be safe."

That seemed to satisfy Frank, and they started back when he turned to Jack suddenly and said, "One last thing. Let's say you're right, and you were sent on those missions to be killed. That *can't* be happening this time, not with Commander Church. He hasn't sent you off to die, he's here with us himself. So maybe you don't have to be so suspicious of him."

"I'm sorry, Frank, but," Jack paused, "right now, you're the only person I trust."

"Then trust me when I tell you Church is a good man, and he is trying to do what's right."

"All right. I'll try."

9 Years Ago

571 AR

A re you serious?"

Eliza giggled, "Yes, Jack. I said it . . . and I meant it."

Jack whooped and kissed her again. Oliver, who stood on the branch of the nearest tree, gave a disinterested, "Meh."

Though she was still giggling, Eliza hushed him. "Shhh, Jason might hear!"

Jack took Eliza in his arms and held her. After a moment, his cheek still resting on her head, he murmured, "You know, we can't keep this a secret from him."

"I know." She tucked her head against his chest. "But it took Jason so long just to get over the fact that we're stuck here."

"He's a lot stronger than you give him credit for, Eliza."

She pulled away, just far enough to look Jack in the eyes. "He's incredibly strong, Jack, but this . . . If you and I . . . if we let him know about our feelings for each other . . . That's telling him . . ." She sighed and let her head fall back against Jack's chest. "It's telling him he's the third wheel. It's telling him he's going to be alone . . . forever."

"What?"

Eliza pulled away. "Jack, we missed our chance with the pirate ship. And the army . . . they're not coming for us. You and I accepted that long before Jason. It's been, what, three years now? Even if they were looking for us, they've given up by now."

"Maybe. But I bet Frank is still looking for us and will keep looking until he has proof that we're dead."

Frustrated, she grumbled, "Frank would understand what I'm trying to say."

"No, I get it. If you and I are together, it means Jason doesn't get anyone."

"You say the words, but you don't seem to understand what they mean." She pleaded, "Put yourself in his shoes."

"I get it. It's sad and unfortunate, but that doesn't mean—"

"It's more than sad—it could be devastating. I know it may have seemed like I didn't care about guys back in school. But that didn't mean I didn't want to fall in love. I was just patient for the right person." She gave Jack a meaningful gaze that made him blush. "But I didn't want to spend my life alone."

"You won't, Eliza." Jack took a step toward her. "You have me."

"Exactly, and you have me. But who will Jason have?"

Jack tried to calm her. "Eliza, I think you might be overreacting." He reached to take her back in his arms, but she pushed him away. As if he was coming to her defense, Oliver flapped down and perched on her shoulder.

"I would think that with Frank as a brother, you'd understand this better, and maybe have a little more compassion," Eliza said.

Oliver gave a supportive, "Meh."

Jack's eyebrows furrowed. "That's the second time you've mentioned Frank. What does he have to do with this?"

"Well, obviously he could relate to what Jason will go through."

"Meh, meh," Oliver sympathized.

Jack thought for a moment, trying to figure out what Eliza was getting at. "Frank's situation is nothing like Jason's. He's on the mainland. I know he hasn't had much luck with women, but he's a great guy, and eventually someone will see that."

Eliza looked stunned. She stopped short and scrutinized him for a moment, then in a flat voice said, "You don't know."

Oliver mimicked Eliza's sentiment. "Meh?"

Jack blinked hard and said, "Don't know what?"

"I . . . I'm sorry, I thought you knew."

"Wait, knew what?"

Eliza shook her head. "I can't say. He obviously didn't tell you for a reason."

Oliver agreed, nodding. "Meh."

Jack waved his hands around, "Whoa, whoa, just what are we talking about here? I thought this was about Jason having to spend the rest of his life alone."

"Yes, but—"

"So what does that have to do with my brother?"

"Jack, I can't. I promised."

"Meh!"

"Hey, he's *my* brother." Suddenly he snapped at Oliver, "And what are you agreeing with? You haven't even met the man."

Oliver slunk around Eliza's shoulder with a dismissive, "Meh."

"And finish your words. Cats *meow*. Not this half-assed *meh* business." He returned his focus to Eliza and implored with a calmer tone, "Eliza, he's my brother."

"Yes, and it's worse knowing that he felt he had to keep it a secret from you."

Jack threw his arms in the air, "Keep what a secret from me?"

Before Eliza could answer, they both turned toward the sound of footsteps. "What's going on here?" Jason said, approaching the arguing couple.

Jack and Eliza stepped away from each other, as if they'd been caught in an embrace rather than an argument. "Jason!" Eliza exclaimed. "We were just, um . . . we were . . ."

Growing stern, Jason puffed out his chest, looked at Jack and asked, "Are you teaching her to fight again?"

"No, I promised I wouldn't, and I haven't."

"So why are you two hiding over here?"

Jack began to explain, "We just didn't want to upset you."

"Upset me?"

"We were talking about Frank," blurted Eliza.

Jason shook his head. "So? What does that have to do with me?"

Eliza was silent.

Jack explained, "She was just worried about you."

Jason's eyes narrowed. "Why?"

"Jack . . ." Eliza pleaded.

Jack appreciated her concern, but he couldn't see why she was so worried. "Here's the thing, Jason. Eliza and I have . . . well we've sort of found that we have a bond."

"Okay . . .?" said Jason.

"I love her, Jason."

Jason smiled, shaking his head, "And . . .?"

"No, it's not like it was in school. I'm . . . I'm in love with her."

Jason chuckled, "Okay, I still don't—"

"And she loves me back."

Jason looked back and forth between Jack and Eliza and put everything together. He opened his mouth as if he wanted to say something, but nothing came out.

Eliza couldn't find her voice either.

Jack felt the awkwardness and broke the silence. "We were . . . that is, Eliza thought maybe, given the situation we're in, the news might, you know, bum you out."

Jason seemed to snap awake. With an exaggerated smile he said, "And why would it do that? My two favorite people . . . are . . . together."

Eliza's voice was full of sympathy. "Jason . . ."

"No, no, Eliza—I know what you're thinking. I'm all right with it."

Jack said, "See, Eliza? He's fine."

"I'm fine," Jason assured her, smiling brightly. "Really."

Jack put an arm around his best friend's shoulder and squeezed. He then added, "And she's just agreed to marry me!"

After a noticeable pause, Jason smiled and said, "Wow. But . . . how are you going to do that?"

"Well, it won't be on paper or anything, but . . ."

Still smiling, Jason said, "Yes, well—congratulations."

Jack heard the change in Jason's voice. It was almost genuine, but it carried a patronizing edge. He asked, "What does that mean?"

Jason shrugged. "What? It means congratulations . . . it means I'm happy for you."

"No. You aren't."

Eliza interjected, "It's not like we're going to do it now."

Jack turned to her, surprised. "We're not?"

"Eliza, don't worry about it," Jason said, feigning disinterest. "You two do whatever you like—and have fun."

"Hey. This is serious," Jack insisted.

"I'm sure, I'm sure. Look, if you don't mind, I'm tired and should get to bed." Jason waved a hand dismissively through the air and headed back toward the cave, calling over his shoulder, "I'll see you both in the morning."

Eliza and Jack stood there motionless. When Jason was out of sight, Eliza smacked Jack on the shoulder and through clenched teeth said, "Do you have no tact?"

Oliver stretched his neck out and yapped, "Meh!"

"Ow. Hey! What'd I do?"

Eliza put a hand to her forehead. "Just . . . never mind."

Jack took her hand and pulled her close to him. "Eliza, he had to find out eventually."

"I know." Eliza bit her lower lip and looked off in the direction Jason had left. "I was just hoping we could find a better way to break it to him."

Jack took Eliza's face in his hands and tilted her head up toward his. "He's my best friend. I've known him pretty much my whole life. Trust me. He's happy for us."

"Then what was with his tone?"

"Well . . . that was . . ." but Jack couldn't answer.

"Exactly. Deep down, he knows he should be happy for us—and he probably wants to be. He might be our friend, but he's also human. And this . . . *us* . . . on this island . . ." Eliza trailed off.

"I know he was upset . . . and I'm trying, but I just don't see what's so bad." Jack looked in the direction Jason had gone. He thought for a moment and turned back to her. "I taught you to fight a little. Would you teach me to understand?"

Eliza's face lit up with a warmth that made Jack's stomach turn upside down. Not wanting to spoil the moment, he whispered, "What?"

She shook her head, smiling. "Just by asking, you've already begun to understand. And that's one of the reasons I love you, Jack."

"I love you too, Eliza," he said, and kissed her.

Jason's mind was reeling as he walked carelessly past the cave.

Of course, he'd noticed a change in Jack and Eliza these past few months. Deep down, he knew something was going on, but he thought—or maybe hoped—that he was mistaken. But now it had finally happened. It was done. Jack had won.

And he said they were getting married?

Jason wondered why they even bothered calling it that.

Does that mean he'll be calling Eliza his wife now?

I suppose he will.

Jason didn't know how long he'd been walking, but he found himself at the edge of the pond close to the cave, a tree branch hanging just above his head. Without thinking, Jason drew his sword and slashed it. The branch hit the ground with a crash. He stared at the damage he'd done for a minute, and realized he was struggling to breathe. He glanced up and on the trunk was an engraving of a heart, with Jack and Eliza's names on it.

How long has that been there?

He knew he should be happy for them, but all he felt was . . . he wasn't sure what he felt. Without warning, Jason blindly swung his sword at anything in his path. He severed tree branches, sliced through tall bushes, and kicked over small saplings.

Why would she choose him?

He's a great guy.

We look alike, like similar things—we even have similar names! He and I are practically the same person. . . except I'm royalty! What's so special about Jack?

Maybe it was just luck.

So if Jack hadn't survived the crash, would she be marrying me now?

"Dammit!" he hissed at himself, stopping his onslaught on the foliage. He dropped his sword and fell to his knees.

Jason knew that if his father could see him, he'd be disappointed, throwing a temper tantrum like a child. Of course, as the prince he could just claim any woman he wanted for his wife. His father had claimed his mother that way, and she was a good woman. But Jason didn't want to claim anyone. He wanted someone to want him, the same way it seemed Eliza wanted Jack.

In a final fit of rage, he picked up one of the branches he'd cut off and hurled it into the pond. It splashed in the water and then floated to the surface, bobbing up and down, down and up, its ripples diminishing as the water calmed. He stared at the branch, watching it drift across the water's surface.

Jason had an epiphany.

It seemed so obvious. He didn't even know why they hadn't tried it yet. Sure, at first they had been preoccupied with the pirates, and then they had assumed they'd be rescued any day. But the pirates were dead and gone, and it was clear to him now that no one was looking for them.

It was time to take matters into his own hands.

It was time to build a raft.

Chapter Thirteen

Opening the Door

Like everyone, Frank woke early the next day, apprehensive of the undertaking ahead. Looking around, it seemed no one had slept well, except maybe Albert, who didn't seem to appreciate the danger they were facing, for he smiled and tried to lighten the men's spirits. The soldiers ate their rations solemnly, and shortly after daybreak they were on the move.

Peter led the way. Occasionally, he'd leap into the trees to get his bearings. He rarely left for more than a few minutes, but Church didn't like it, as he had to halt the company each time and wait for Peter to return.

This stop-and-go pattern continued throughout the day when, close to sunset, Peter told Church to stop, and once again leaped into the trees. The men waited for him to return, but this time he didn't. As the minutes passed, Terrie grew agitated. The bear's grunts became louder and louder, until Commander Church barked at Frank to calm the bear.

"Sir?" Frank said.

"You're the one who has a way with Peter. Get that bear to settle down, it's upsetting the men!"

Frank turned to Terrie, who was rocking back and forth and grunting angrily. He tiptoed up to the bear and spoke softly. "Hey, um, big guy." Terrie grumbled at his approach. "I, ah . . .

I don't know if you can understand me or not . . . you seem to understand Peter, so . . . um, we need you to calm down."

If Terrie understood him, he didn't show it. He just kept rocking and seemed to be teetering on the edge of leaving. Where he would go and what he would do were questions Frank didn't want answered. The grunts grew louder.

The commander chided, "Lieutenant!"

"Working on it, sir." It was obvious to Frank that the commander was on edge, but he felt it was a little unfair of Church to expect him to control the bear just because of his rapport with Peter. He gave it his best effort, but the bear ignored him. After another glare from Church, Frank snapped, "Terrie, you're not the only one who's worried about him, now shut up!" The bear stopped and looked at Frank, stunned. Frank continued, in a hushed but forceful tone, "We're going to find him, but we can't do it with you carrying on like a maniac."

Oddly enough, that seemed to do the trick. Terrie relaxed and walked alongside Frank as he returned to the commander.

"Remarkable," Albert marveled.

A half hour passed, and Peter still did not return. Silence enveloped the soldiers, and a strange sense of exposure permeated the area. Church had the soldiers spread out, shifting from the lines they had been traveling in, to their assigned platoons.

Observing the troop movement, Terrie turned to Frank for reassurance. Frank nodded at him, hoping that his own uncertainty was undetectable. Then they heard him. The sound was faint and distant, but it was unquestionably the voice of Peter shouting, "Frank! Terrie!"

Both Frank and the bear flinched, but Church raised his hand. Frank obeyed, waiting for orders while Terrie roared and charged in the direction of Peter's cries. Church signaled for everyone to draw their weapons and be ready. Peter's voice called out again: "It's a trap! It's a trap!"

Church grumbled, "We're late. Someone beat us here!"

"But how?" asked Private Marks. "We had the boy. He's the only one who knows where the entrance is. How could anyone beat us here?"

General Lane scolded the private for talking out of turn. "And where do you get off calling him 'the boy'? You've got to be about the same age."

Commander Church frowned at Marks and said evenly, "Know your place, Private." He then addressed the group. "I don't think they know where the door is, but they must realize how close we are to the borders of Death's Province. I'm thinking they've been following us, waiting until now to take him."

"The commander is right," Lane declared. "They must realize we're closing in and don't care if we know they're coming anymore."

Moments later, a sergeant commanding the rear arrived at Church's side, breathless from the run. "Sir, we have confirmation, the pylon barrier net has been broken."

"Pirates?" hoped General Anderson.

Church looked at him gravely, for they all knew that wasn't the case. He asked, "None of our scouts saw them?"

"If they're from one of the other nations," General Lane reflected, "secretly on our lands, unregistered, they know what they're doing and how to stay out of sight."

"Wait. Is this all just one group?" asked Jack.

Private Marks asked, "Why?"

Jack elaborated, "Someone's in front of us *and* behind us?"

Just then two more sergeants delivered news.

General Lane spoke up, "Sir, scouts report sightings of an additional cluster of armed men coming at us from the right flank."

General Anderson followed, "And the left. We ... we're surrounded."

Shocked, everyone turned to look at Church. He looked down and sighed, then raised his head and informed them, "I don't have time to go into the particulars, but we haven't been racing just *one* group to get into Death's Province first."

As it dawned on him, Frank exhaled in a barely audible whisper, "The Secret War."

Jack was dumbfounded. Back in Oakmoor Cove, Church had told him that Eliza's father stumbled onto something that upset another party. The photos Church had shown him implied some kind of personal vendetta connected with Hershel, which was what was putting Eliza in direct danger. He tried to piece the old information together with the new. The fact that multiple armies were going after this thing told Jack something more was going on than Church had led him to believe. He turned on the commander. "You told me it was *one group* we had to beat to this thing!"

Church retorted, "Think of it as a group of groups, if you must."

Jack's eyes blazed as he approached Church. "You told me——"

Frank pushed Jack back and said, in a hushed tone, "Not now, Jack."

"What? You knew about this?"

Commander Church sprang into action, announcing to the group, "We don't know the numbers we're facing, but if these groups infiltrated our borders undetected, they can't be very large. We can defeat them in detail or trick them into fighting each other." He gave orders to the generals, who in turn, sprinted away, splitting platoons off from the larger company. The platoon at the center remained under Church's command.

Then, from ahead, Terrie's roar pierced the air, followed by the sound of branches breaking. The enormous bear burst through a wall of foliage with Peter on his back. The bear wasn't so lucky, sporting several new gashes on his face and sides. Mercifully, the stitching on his wound from Seth still held.

As Terrie and Peter got closer, Jack saw their pursuers—which meant they were in range for return fire. Seconds later Church ordered rounds of explosive arrows, which slowed the approaching forces appreciably and helped Peter and Terrie return safely. Unfortunately, this volley of crossfire had attracted the attention of the surrounding infiltrators, and skirmishes began breaking out from every side.

Terrie skidded to a stop next to Church as Peter hopped off and ran to Frank. "The place you're looking for—it's in that direction, just past the next two hills!"

Frank's face reddened when Peter delivered the news to him instead of the commander, but Church didn't care. He'd gotten what he wanted, and he ordered the men of his central platoon in the direction Peter had indicated. Most of the company charged forward while the remaining squads battled with the surrounding invaders.

Jack felt useless. He looked around and assessed the situation. The left flank of Idolessians faced forces from Mechina, wearing uniforms of navy and silver. "Knowledge is Power" was the nation's motto, signifying their worship of intellect. The

Mechinans had the fewest soldiers on the field, relying heavily on their mech-men—robotic soldiers—that could endure, and deliver, more punishment than a human ever could.

On the right flank, were the rough warriors of Lithostone. Wearing crimson and relishing in hand-to-hand combat, the Lithostonians formed the largest group that the Idolessian soldiers faced. Knowing that their Lithostonian prisoner Sarah Cassidy had learned the same fighting techniques as his mother, Jack took a moment to scrutinize their fighting style. It displayed brutal savagery, reminding him of Seth more than his mother or Sarah. When a handful of the Lithostonians broke through the right flank and headed for Church's platoon at the center of the action, Frank broke away to stop them. Jack took two steps to go help his brother when he felt Church's hand grasp his shoulder. "No, Jack! You stay here with me!"

Jack was about to contest, when the sounds of screeching and swooshing came from behind. They turned around to see the rear guard of Idolessians battling a scary-looking lot. Dressed in black with accents of rusty orange, these warriors kept their faces hidden under hoods and masks, leaping out of the shadows and vanishing into them just as easily. They fought as if in a taunting dance, elusive and always just out of reach. Known by most as the Order, the warriors of Phlogiston preferred charms and spells to weapons and armor. It gave them a speed and lightness of foot that other warriors could not match.

Owing to their elusive methods, there was no way to know how many members of the Order were there, except for the three warlocks who paraded in the open, each riding a different creature. One sat astride a rare black unicorn, and another rode a griffin. While these creatures were impressive, it was the leader's animal that stopped the Idolessians in their tracks. He sat perched on a small, wingless dragon with powerful back legs and shorter, wickedly clawed front arms. It had scaly avocado-colored skin, and plumes of feathers sprouted from the back of its head and elbows.

The Idolessian soldiers volleyed rounds of arrows at the Order, but an invisible shield protected the warlocks. Any arrows that breached the shield dissolved to dust as they passed through it. One Idolessian came too close to the shield, and as he swung his sword, his weapon and forearm disintegrated the same way. He stood screaming in pain, clutching his shortened arm, until one of the warlocks raised a hand and blasted him with emerald lightning, killing him.

The Idolessians did have one advantage: Eli Warren, the greatest sorcerer of Idoless. Eli boldly stepped from his position of relative safety next to his son and sent an energy blast of his own at the Phlogiston warlocks. The searing blast of auburn light slowed as it penetrated the protective shield and fried the wizard on the unicorn. The other two warlocks scattered, falling back.

As the peripheral battles raged, Commander Church and his platoon barreled down the middle of the battlefield, contending with the forces of Bionova blocking their way forward. A cluster of Bionovian warriors blazed toward them, and Jack noticed something unnatural about the way they moved. As they got closer, some began running on all fours. That's when it dawned on Jack. He called out, "They're hybreeds!"

Most Idolessians knew the Bionovian soldiers had drug-enhanced strength and stamina, but they had only heard rumors of the hybreeds. They were people whose genes had been spliced with those of animals, rewriting their DNA to give them characteristics of specific creatures. It was a practice exclusive to Bionova, and just one of many examples of the nation's reputation for tampering with genetics.

Upon hearing Jack, Church sent a handful of soldiers to stop the creatures. When a hybreed that resembled both man and jaguar slashed the face of an Idolessian, Jack couldn't take it anymore. He drew his sword and stepped forward to face the creature. Church shouted after him, "Jack, no! I said, stay here!" But Jack ignored the commander and dashed forward into the field of battle to block the path of the creature.

Once face-to-face, Jack and the jaguar-man circled each other. Jack internally marveled at the creature's appearance. Its ears jutted from a furry face sprinkled with dark spots, and its smooth, pink nose sat atop firm white jowls. The creature wore a grey and turquoise Bionovian uniform, but it held no weapon. Then again, it didn't really need one; sharp claws an inch long protruded from its stubby fingers, and it had the fangs of a big cat, which Jack saw glint in the sunlight when the creature yowled at him.

Jack got tired of waiting and, with a grin, whispered, "Here, kitty, kitty."

Roaring, with claws raised, the creature charged.

Jack's sword managed to shear off one claw, sending it spinning into the bushes lining the forest. The hybreed leaped into the air effortlessly. Jack swung his sword overhead but couldn't connect with his opponent. The jaguar-man slashed Jack's arm then kicked him in the stomach with both feet.

Jack hit the ground with a thud.

At that moment, the jaguar-man looked back at Church's group and spotted Peter at the center of it. Baring its razor-sharp teeth, it opened its mouth and let out an eerie scream that was both human and animal, calling to the rest of its ilk, "There! The boy!"

Hearing the call, the rest of the hybreeds abandoned their individual fights and careened toward Peter. Terrie, who had been standing by Peter's side during the skirmish, charged at the creatures and inserted himself into the fight.

Jack heard Peter cry out in protest and saw him use the opening the bear had made to chase after his colossal friend. Church tried to grab him, but Peter had been too quick. So, the commander ordered the platoon to refocus its defense on Peter.

Frank had been where he was most useful: battling the Lithostonians, using his proficiency in hand-to-hand fighting. But when he heard Church's call and saw what was happening, he was close enough to dash over and block Peter's path, shouting, "You can't go over there! They'll take you again, or worse!"

"But Terrie!" Peter wailed.

"I'll help him, but I can't do it if I'm worried about you." Frank's words sobered Peter. "Now please, go back to the commander's side, where you'll be safe!"

Peter did as he was asked.

Frank strode toward the line of hybreeds, drew his broadsword, and quickened his pace. Running at full stride, he raised his weapon and cut through the line. He didn't stop to fight anyone. He ducked and dodged, swinging his sword at any creature he passed as he made his way to Terrie, clotheslining the last, who was part reptile of some kind. While the other hybreeds continued to focus on Peter, the reptile took Frank's assault rather personally and doubled back after him.

Frank didn't realize the lizard-man had been right on his heels until he heard a clamor behind him. He turned to find his brother had tackled it and was now wrapped up with the lizard.

Noticing his brother's bloody arm, Frank started back, but Jack shouted, "No, go! I got this!"

Trusting Jack's judgement, Frank nodded and continued toward Terrie, who was contending with three hybreeds alone.

The bear crushed one under his weight while the other two clawed their way on top of him, teeth and claws sunk deep in his flesh, blood matting his fur. Oblivious to Frank's approach, one of the hybreeds leaned back to take another ferocious bite—but lost its head to Frank's sword. The hybreed beneath Terrie lay in a crumpled heap, leaving just the one on his back, which Terrie was now able to shake off. It hit the ground hard but rolled back to its feet. Its body was squat and wide but dense with muscle—maybe part pit bull.

With Terrie's blood trickling down its face, the dog-man growled at Frank and the bear. Wiping the defeated lizard-man's blood off his sword, Jack joined them.

Recognizing his odds, the dog-man stepped back. Jowls flapping, it barked, "You won't get to it! It will be ours, or it will belong to no one!"

Frank glanced back and saw Peter was safe, standing next to the commander. The last of the hybreeds was falling to its death at the hands of Church's platoon. Frank smiled at his brother who was noticing the same thing. They both turned back to the dog-man.

Then, with his trademark cockiness, Jack replied, "Yeah, good luck with that."

The pit bull snarled in rage and retreated to the left, heading deep into the forest.

Being close to the forest and away from the main battlefield, the Waramonds had a moment to regroup and check on Terrie. Large gashes covered his body, and the stiches in his side had opened. Despite this, he mustered the strength to limp alongside them.

They made a slow procession back and joined the commander, who sighed with relief, "Jack, thank the gods." Then he said sternly, "You know, Peter isn't the only person we need here. I trust you'll remember that you have a larger purpose and shouldn't be out there in battle!"

"Are you *kidding*?" exclaimed Jack. "I don't know if you realized this, but we're fighting all the other nations of Terra Firma! We need every soldier we can get."

Frank put a hand on his brother's shoulder and, with sympathy in his eyes, repeated Jack's own words to him: "Jack, you're not a soldier anymore."

Jack didn't have a chance to respond, but it didn't matter. Despite the Idolessian efforts, the other four nations were closing in on them, making it too difficult for him to get back into the battle even if he'd wanted to. Nevertheless, Church's platoon had gotten past the first of the two hills, and they were now ascending the second, where Peter had said the door would be.

Church turned to make sure the wizards were close and told General Lane to have them prepare; they'd be needed soon.

"Wait—what about Peter?" Frank exclaimed. "We can't take him in with us!"

"You . . . you should do it," suggested Jack. "Someone needs to get him to safety."

"I know you want to protect me, Jack, but wake up! You can't expect me to stay behind—it's chaos out here."

"And as bad as it is here, it's even worse in there!"

"Meaning you're going to need all the help you can get!" argued Frank.

"He's right, Jack," Church interceded.

Jack scoffed but didn't say more.

Frank turned to the bear. "Terrie, do you think you have it in you to get Peter out of here safely?"

Terrie grunted and nodded.

"You're sending me away?" Peter cried plaintively.

Frank reasoned, "Peter, you can't go in there with us. It's too dangerous."

"But I . . . I want to stay with you."

Just then, Eli Warren and the other wizards stepped forward. They looked rough—they had bruises and wounds, and their number was one fewer. As they moved past, one of them looked at Church solemnly and said, "This is still a bad idea. Whatever it is you want in there could *not* be worth all we've lost today."

Church remained stoic. "We need to succeed now more than ever."

"Ever the excuse for escalating violence," the wizard sneered.

"Enough!" said Eli, stepping forward. "It's time." He turned to Peter. "Now, where is it, boy?"

Peter's nose crinkled. "Boy?" he responded with irritation.

Frank nudged him. "Just answer the man."

Peter pointed brusquely. "Between those two trees, *old man.*"

Eli glanced back at the other wizards, and they all walked toward the trees.

"This is it," Church muttered to himself. He looked oddly excited as he turned to his generals. "Lane, you'll be coming with us now. Anderson, you'll stay outside and take charge until I return. We're bringing in only the troops we have near us now." He pointed at the twenty-plus soldiers around them.

Jack said, "We were supposed to be going in there with over a hundred men!"

Ignoring him, Church continued, "Hold these forces back until we get in—and we'll see you when we return."

General Anderson saluted. "Yes, sir." Without another word, he turned and began shouting orders, calling for a defensive line to be formed around the team entering Death's Province.

Suddenly, a brilliant light flared between the two trees Peter had indicated earlier. The soldiers shielded their eyes, and the sounds of battle died out for a moment. The Idolessian wizards all faced the doorway, unfazed by the blaze they'd just kindled. Each had his hands stretched toward the doorway, which was now outlined in rich yellow light, muttering ancient spells.

Moments later the battles resumed with a heightened sense of urgency. Knowing the Idolessians were close to entering the Province, the other armies became desperate, frantically attacking from multiple sides, which brushed them up against the boundaries of Death's Province. The invisible dome surrounding it rippled with distortion as soldiers bumped into it. Though it could not be seen, the barrier was rock-solid, and the soldiers, unaware of its presence, ran into it and fell to the ground in a heap, just as if they'd run into a brick wall.

Eli looked away from the portal just long enough to instruct his son: "Get ready." He reached to the ornate scabbard at his waist and pulled out the golden sword he and the other wizards had prepared for this moment.

Meanwhile, Church put his hand in the air and marched to the head of the line, leaving Jack, Frank, Peter, and Terrie at the tail. He signaled for the soldiers near the portal to prepare to enter. They gathered themselves and focused on the commander. Frank turned to Peter. "All right, Peter, this is it.

When we start moving, you need to break off in that direction. Terrie will take you to safety. Don't look back."

Tears rolled down Peter's face. "No. I . . . I can't."

"You have to Peter. You can't go in there. You're not a warrior." Frank looked at Terrie. "I trust you'll get him out of here."

The bear grunted in affirmation.

The light in the portal returned brighter than before, filling what appeared to be an arched doorway. There was a suction of air around them, rushing past and into the light. It soon grew so strong that those closest struggled to remain standing. The wizards' robes waved and flapped, but they stood as if rooted in the earth. After a moment, Eli lifted the golden sword and plunged it through the light, leaving a gaping cleft in the luminous barrier, as if it were nothing more than a curtain that had been cut. Nothing was visible inside, but the air screamed past them into the opening, stronger than ever. He tossed aside what was left of the sword, its tarnished and melted remnants useless. Eli's voice cut through the whiteout: "Now! We only have a short time before it seals again! Don't look at the light. Keep your heads down and follow me! Go!"

The group charged forward, Eli and his son leading the way.

Peter snatched Frank's hand. Uncharacteristically, Frank didn't contest it; it felt right, especially now, and anyway it would make it easier for him to push Peter away when the time was right. The closer they got; the stronger the portal's pull grew and the louder the wind's howl became. "All right, Terrie!" hollered Frank, and he shoved Peter away.

But at that moment, the pit bull hybreed bounded from the trees, soaring toward Jack and the others. Terrie shouldered his way into its path and as the hybreed tackled him, Terrie slammed back and rolled through the Idolessians. Before Terrie and the hybreed even hit the ground, the vortex of Death's Province swelled one last time to suck those closest to the portal inside.

The soldiers.

The wizards.

Jack.

Frank.

And Peter.

CHAPTER FOURTEEN
DEATH'S PROVINCE

The morning sun peeked over the horizon as Jack looked around Death's Province, his senses keyed up. From this side of the barrier, he could see where they'd just come from, but the people and sounds of battle had vanished.

As for Death's Province itself, it looked . . .

"Normal," observed a soldier. "It's normal."

"What'd you expect?" asked another. "We saw it from the other side."

"I don't know, I guess I just expected it to look . . . different," said the first as he looked around.

A general murmur of agreement broke out. If this was Death's Province, it really wasn't so bad. Jack waved his hands to get their attention and put a finger to his mouth, so they'd all be quiet. But the more they looked around and saw only tall grass and trees, the less anxious and louder they became.

Jack ran to Church, who was hunched over his father and the other wizards, who were all lying on the ground. Church said, "They're all out cold."

In a hushed voice, Jack said, "The same thing happened to our wizard the last time I was here. They'll wake up in a minute with bad headaches. But they won't wake up at all if we don't get everyone to *shut up!*"

He must have recognized the urgency in Jack's voice, because Church signaled for silence immediately.

Now the only sounds came from Peter, who pressed his fists against the invisible wall, demanding to return for Terrie. Frank stood next to him, at a loss for how to help.

Jack and Church approached them, and in a quiet, calm voice Church said, "I'm sorry, Peter. We can't go back until we've completed the assignment."

"B . . . b . . . but, Terrie! He was so hurt!"

Jack leaned toward Frank and whispered, "I understand he's upset, but we *really* need to keep the volume down. We only have a little time before," he looked around, "we only have a little time."

Peter continued to sob.

With a gentle smile, Frank explained, "We want to be here for as short a time as possible, Peter. The quicker we complete our mission, the quicker we can get out." Talk of getting out seemed to relax Peter a little. "Okay?"

Peter sniffed, "All right, Frank."

"Come on." Frank and Peter joined Jack and the commander, who were conferring with one another. The commander lifted an eyebrow. Frank said, "We're all good, sir."

Church nodded. "Peter, this is a very dangerous place, no matter what it looks like now. You need to stay calm and close. You can't go running off like you did before. If you do, we're not waiting for you. Do you understand?"

"Yes."

"Good. Stay close to Frank." The commander looked at Frank. "He's your responsibility."

"Yes, sir."

Church waved the platoon in close and held out a hand toward Jack, who took the floor. Jack took a deep breath and in a hushed voice began. "The first thing you need to know is to *be quiet*. I know it doesn't look bad here and now, but this is temporary. Once we start moving, it's going to get really bad, really fast. And the more noise you make, the more . . . *things* you'll attract."

At that moment, the wizards began to stir. Church gave a signal for all the soldiers to hold. He and Jack helped the sorcerers to their feet. While holding his head, Eli murmured, "It worked? We're in?"

Jack quietly addressed them, "I know your heads feel like they're about to split open. But if it's anything like the last time, that should go away fairly quick and—Albert?"

Albert Larson was mixed in among the wizards, also regaining consciousness. He hoisted himself up, using his staff for support. "H . . . hello, Jack."

"What are you doing here?"

"I don't know. The battle was happening all around, and . . ." Albert saw the commander looking at him with irritation, "I was just trying to stay out of the way. Next thing I knew, I was caught in that force and pulled in with everyone else."

"Well, I'm sorry," said Jack, "but you're going to have to come with us now. Just stay in the center of the group and keep your head low." Jack turned to Church. "Let's get on with this. The sooner we get going, the sooner we can get out of here. We do know where we're going, right?"

Church took an antiquated silver pendant from around his neck and opened it like a locket. Inside was a delicate needle, and Church pointed in the direction it indicated. Jack took a breath and continued his instructions to the group. "No messing around. We're going to get what we came for and get out. You're going to be following me and doing whatever I say." The soldiers' eyes sought out Commander Church. "Don't worry, I'll be working in tandem with the commander. Besides, he's the one with the . . . ?"

Church said, "Let's call it a compass."

"He's the one with the compass. So that's it. This is your one and only chance to ask questions."

A hand shot up, and Church nodded at the soldier who then asked, "What about those girls?" He thrust his chin toward the Cassidy sisters who stood at the far back of the group. Sarah flashed an ironic smile and wiggled her fingers on her bound hand in a petite wave, while her sister, Sophie, just stood there.

"What in Hades . . . !" hissed the commander. "How did you two get in here?"

The sisters both shrugged and said in unison, "We followed you."

Church scowled at the Cassidys, trying to decide what to do with them. Finally, he ordered, "Tie them to that tree over there."

Sarah's lighthearted attitude broke. "Wait, what?"

"Quiet," replied Church. He glanced at Jack, likely expecting dispute.

Jack just threw his hands in the air and said, "It would be more humane just to kill them now. I mean, if something comes this way . . ." He shook his head.

Mike glared at the women again, and Jack wondered what caused his dilemma.

Al Marks said, "We can't leave them here."

General Lane pounced. "You have zero say in the matter, *Private*."

"No, he's right," agreed the commander. "We . . . can't leave them behind. Not here."

Jack looked at Frank to see if his brother noticed the peculiarity of a private addressing a commander so boldly, but Frank just stood at attention, waiting for orders.

Peter, however, was watching with misgivings written all over his face. This reassured Jack, and he tested Mike. "Again, if it were anywhere else, the situation would be different. But in here, we're in enough danger as it is. We need to know we can trust each other."

"We can help you!" Sarah exclaimed, looking desperately to the commander. Her tone was one of bewilderment, as though there was something being left unsaid.

"Yeah, we'll be good," added Sophie.

"Help us? You mean help yourselves to the weapon." General Lane drew his sword and held it at Sarah's neck.

An explosive crack shocked everyone into silence.

Seconds later, a giant, toothy bat fell from the sky and landed on the ground, flopping and twitching. Everyone turned to see a terrified soldier at the back of the formation, a smoking pistol in his hand. He looked back at everyone, taking in the glares of disbelief.

"You call that *quiet*?" Jack rasped.

"It . . . it was c-coming right at me," the soldier stuttered. "I didn't even think."

A roar reverberated from the woodland ahead of them, and the treetops began shifting, as if a large beast were moving through the forest toward them.

"Yeah, that's very clear." Jack dashed to the soldier who'd fired the gun and snatched the weapon from his hands, announcing, "If anyone else has a gun, just drop it now! They key in on noise!" He threw down the weapon. The soldiers looked horrified and turned to the commander, expecting a counter order, but Church said nothing. Jack said as loudly as he dared, "We have to go *now*. Every creature within miles will be drawn to that gunshot." Sarah and Sophie stepped forward in desperation, but before either could say anything, Jack pulled his sword and cut their bindings. "At the first sign that either of you are trying anything fishy, I'll kill you myself."

And with that, he sprinted ahead, sword in hand, leading the group toward the compass' bearing.

After crossing the field of tall grass, the vegetation of Death's Province suddenly became so thick it was like passing through a wall. And on the other side of that wall, they found the Death's Province they'd expected: a hot, swampy wasteland where dark, rotting foliage hung lifelessly from gnarled branches. Within moments, fist-sized insects with thick exoskeletons and barbed pincers swarmed the soldiers, who swatted at them with their swords. To avoid contact with any larger creatures lurking in the shadows, Jack attempted to guide the platoon through sunlit patches of the swamp. When that was not possible, Eli and the other wizards created globes of flame to light the path and keep predators at bay.

This group was doing well, better than Jack's first team . . . But an hour in, they lost their first two men. One soldier thoughtlessly stepped into a patch of shade, when gray, oily hands with long fingers and curled talons snatched him by the legs and dragged him into the darkness. The soldier's scream, followed by gruesome crunching sounds, motivated another to try and save him. He dove into the darkness, sword poised for action—but all that followed was more screaming and crunching.

Eli sent his globe of flame into the shadows. The light exposed a humanoid creature, two heads taller than an average man, with rotting, gray flesh and gangly limbs. The beast clung to a tree trunk by one spindly arm and held the second soldier by the head as it ravenously bit flesh and bone. Blood dripped carelessly onto another of these creatures below, which was devouring the first soldier. After a few seconds under Eli's flame, the creatures bared their fangs and scurried into the darkness, leaving what was left of the two soldiers in a bloody mound.

Before the platoon had time to process what had happened, Jack urged them on and quickened the pace. It wasn't quick enough, though, because the screams had drawn the attention of an enormous, bipedal reptile. The ground shook as the creature stomped toward the shadows and emerged with its jaws clamped around the remains of one of the dead soldiers, who dangled by a leg like a rag doll. The reptile flipped the body in the air, catching it in its mouth; it chomped a few times, then swallowed the meal whole.

The beast sniffed the air this way and that, until it was looking in their direction. Its dark beady eyes narrowed as its nostrils flared. Jack cursed under his breath and rasped, "Run!"

The group bolted, hearing the creature snarl as it thundered after them. As if on cue, two more dragons joined the pursuit. The first came on foot, a different breed with a long, snakelike body and stubby limbs. The second dropped from the sky, its wings stirring the putrid air around them. The beasts snapped at each other, vying for dominance, and eventually they fell to fighting with each other, forgetting their prey altogether.

At first Jack felt lucky they'd been able to put distance between themselves and the dragons. But with the large predators gone, a multitude of smaller creatures exploited the situation. Snarls, hisses, and eerie hyena-like laughter radiated from every direction as they ran.

Several times Jack heard voices behind him cry out in pain, and he knew another of their number was gone. He tried to block out the screams and kept running, but when he heard Albert cry out, Jack skidded to a halt. He turned and saw his friend splayed out on the ground, having tripped on a tree root. Vermin veered toward the easy prey. Jack couldn't help himself and leaped in Albert's direction, ready to rush to his friend's aid . . . but the creatures all just stopped at Albert's feet and gazed at him. One leaned close and sniffed him. Then they all left to join the chase of the soldiers.

Jack put out a hand to help his friend up. "What did you do?"

As he rose to his feet, Albert replied, "I . . . I honestly don't know."

The two men hurried back to rejoin the platoon, which found itself cornered at the edge of a cliff. In front of the platoon, Jack could see the wizards had formed a line to shield the others, blasting the approaching beasts with fire and energy bolts, but for every creature they eliminated, two or three would appear in its place. Jack was able to take out a few of the beasts from behind as he and Albert rejoined the group.

Anxiety high, Jack turned to Church. "Please tell me we're at least headed in the right direction!"

Church opened the locket and observed the needle. "Yes . . . well, mostly. We need to make our way down there," and he pointed down the cliff. Fifty feet below was an enormous algae-covered lake, lined with ancient evergreens on its sandy banks. "We've got to get to the other side of the lake, and then continue northeast."

"Great," Jack moaned.

General Lane joined their conversation. "Can't we just jump down? The water looks deep enough, and it's not so high."

Jack nodded toward the commotion. "Look behind us, General. Do you think the waters of Death's Province are any safer?"

"What about the wizards? Couldn't they transport us down?"

Eli shouted back to them, "Transportation spells like that are too complex to pull off in this chaos. We wizards could maybe transport ourselves, but not the whole group. But if you can hold off this shit storm, we could create a ramp to slide down."

Jack exchanged glances with Commander Church and General Lane. Before he could say he thought it was a good idea, Sarah spoke up. "Can I make an offer?" Everyone looked at her. "Once a day, Sophie can access great power. You saw it—she gains superhuman strength and becomes nearly indestructible."

General Lane retorted, "You ladies shouldn't even be fighting. It's against our laws—"

"Ugh!" Sarah groaned, rolled her eyes and raised a hand to silence the general. "When she does it, she's a living weapon."

"It only lasts for about an hour," warned Sophie.

"We won't need an hour," said Church. He called to Eli, "Father!"

"We heard, just fucking do it!"

Sophie pulled down her helmet's shield and slammed her fists together, triggering a small burst of sparks and a surging hum, like an engine powering up. Sophie charged at the creatures and began kicking, slamming, and pounding anything close enough to her. Some, she even punched clean through, which was a gruesome but impressive sight. Based on what he was seeing now, Jack could tell Sophie had been holding back when she'd fought the platoon before.

Once Sophie had run past them, the wizards ceased their offensive strikes. As if performing a well-rehearsed dance, they turned, pointed their hands to the lake's far shore and shot beams from their palms, creating a magical ramp of light. The structure retained a faint glow after turning into what otherwise looked, to Jack, like glass. The act took all of ten seconds, and the wizards immediately returned to their offensive strikes as the first line of men slid down the steep ramp, landing roughly on the sandy bank. When the second set went, the ramp made a distinct cracking sound.

Jack looked at Peter and said, "You should have gone already."

Peter retorted, "I'm supposed to stay with Frank."

Frank suppressed a grin, which caused Peter to smile. Then he said, "All right, stay close, we'll go shortly."

"Just don't wait too long," one of the wizards cautioned. "I don't think the chute will hold much longer."

"What?" exclaimed Jack.

"It's not supposed to. Besides, we don't want any of this following—"

Distracted, the wizard was suddenly knocked over by an enormous doglike creature with tall ears and milky, dead eyes. Five other beasts of the same type quickly followed and began tearing the sorcerer apart. Both the Waramonds shouted, "No!" But then another dog bounded over the carnage and careened toward them and the remaining group.

Frank shoved Peter down the slide and shouted at Jack, "Go, we'll be right behind you!"

"Frank, are you—?"

"Go!"

Jack dove onto the ramp with one other soldier. All the way down, he could hear it crackling, and he watched in alarm as every few feet shards broke off, dissipating into glittery light particles. Once he hit the shore, Jack rolled to his feet and immediately joined Peter, scanning the edge of the cliff, looking for Frank. Time stretched on too long, and Jack began to panic until he finally saw the wizards throw themselves down the ramp. Just after the wizards hit the shore, Frank and the final two men tumbled after.

Jack shielded his eyes, trying to keep track of Frank's descent when movement on the cliff caught his eye. Another one of the doglike creatures appeared. It leaped high in the air, pouncing on the chute. The force was too much, and the slide shattered into a million pieces that all vanished in a flash of sparkling light, sending Frank, the dog, and the two other soldiers splashing into the lake below.

Emerging from the murky water, the group began paddling toward shore. Suddenly, the doglike creature and one of the other soldiers disappeared, and in their place lurked four large, dark green crocodile-beasts with lumpy backs and long, pointy snouts studded with rows of teeth, rolling over each other in a feeding frenzy as they devoured their kill.

Frank scrambled as one of the creatures veered toward him, but it was difficult for him to maneuver in the water, his heavy broadsword making his progress slow and awkward. The harder he tried, the slower he seemed to move. Everyone was shouting at him and the other soldier in the water, "Don't stop!" and "Keep going!" Frank looked almost annoyed with them. He drew his sword and jabbed the beast to keep it away.

Suddenly, a tentacled beast burst from the depths, knocking the crocodilelike creature aside. Leading with his sword, Frank tore into the appendage. The beast gave an ear-piercing scream as it recoiled and sank back into the depths, a cloud of red blooming where it had been seconds before.

Jack watched in helpless horror when another tentacle burst from the water and wrapped around his brother's torso. Frank's body jerked and then was dragged completely under the water.

The other soldier was closer to the shore, but he wasn't close enough. The crocodile-beast that had lunged for Frank zoned in on him. It opened its chops wide, ready to strike when Sophie, who had finished above and jumped off the cliff, slammed into the monster, crushing it beneath her feet. Jack ran into the shallow water to meet her as the soldier scrambled out. Pointing to the water, Jack hollered desperately, "Frank! Frank! He went under, right there! Right there! Save him. Please, please save him!"

Just as Sophie turned to where Frank had been pulled under, there was a gurgle and spurt a few feet away. Everyone watched as Frank emerged looking royally pissed, clutching his sword, which was dripping blood and guts. He sloshed to shore, trying to splash off the muck and waterweed that covered his body, cursing the whole way.

Just as Frank reached Jack, Peter pushed past and threw his arms around him. "I thought I'd lost you." He hugged Frank so tightly the water and mud squished between them.

"Hey, hey. Okay. I'm all right." Frank patted him awkwardly. "It's all right. I'm all right." But Peter didn't let go.

Unable to get around Peter, Jack threw his hand out to shake Frank's. "I'm glad you're all right, bro."

Frank shook Jack's hand and gave him a meaningful grin. "All right, come on, let's get out of the water." He pulled Peter off, and they clambered ashore.

Having scanned the area, Commander Church felt they were safe for a moment and gave the team five minutes to regroup before moving on.

To their surprise, a groomed path that appeared clear of danger stretched ahead of them. But when they begin down it, Jack understood why. They'd barely made it three yards when they approached a mud slick. He looked on the sludge with dread and demanded they go around.

Church asked, "What's wrong? I don't see anything."

"This is a mudbaby pit."

"A mudbaby? What's that? I've never heard of them."

"It's just what I called them."

"Well, what are they?"

Trust me, you don't want to know."

Aside from the time added by the detour, it hadn't been a bad decision; the trek was still easier than the terrain they had already covered, and they didn't see any monsters. But the lack of creatures only made Jack more nervous. Commander Church asked what his concern was, and without looking at the commander, his eyes peeled for any sign of movement, Jack replied, "When I was here before, it was like it was back up there—nonstop mayhem."

Church offered, "Yes, but it's not like you covered the entire Province. Maybe we're just in a less-inhabited—"

"Mike, if there are less-inhabited areas, it's only because there's something else in that territory worse than what we've encountered so far. And the sun will be down soon, which only brings out more."

Less than an hour later, Jack's words were validated. Moments after the sun sank below the horizon, they did come across something else.

A woman.

She leaned casually against a tree, examining her perfect fingernails. She was tall and slim, and the black dress she wore hugged her figure. A long slit on the skirt exposed her shapely legs, and the dress's snug fit emphasized the soft curves of her hips and breasts. The women's back, arms, shoulders, and neck were all exposed, revealing smooth, milky skin.

Jack was more than suspicious about this woman. She was far too clean for anyone in the wild, let alone in Death's Province . . . let alone *living* in Death's Province. He tried to get the soldiers to turn around, but the presence of something so human—so beautiful—didn't instill in them the fear it should have. When he saw that it was too late, he drew his sword.

The woman sauntered up to the group and scrutinized the men, flashing her dark eyes and running her hands through her long, jet-black hair. Ignoring Jack's aggressive posture, the women spoke to Albert, of all people. "Hello," she purred. Fear in his eyes, Albert hesitated and looked to the commander.

Church stepped toward the stranger and responded, "Hello."

The woman looked at the commander, then back to Albert. She considered the kirk, as if he were a puzzle she couldn't figure out. They all stood there, not saying anything. Finally, the woman grinned, and as if she were having a pleasant conversation with someone in a shop, said, "You're new here."

"Indeed," replied Church.

"How'd you get in?"

"We have wizards with us who forged a key."

"Wizards. Interesting." She noticed Sarah and Sophie at the back, smiled, and muttered, "Mmm, you have women in your group. How . . . progressive." The pale woman tittered, then said, "I never heard of anyone *wanting* to get in here. Are you planning on staying?"

"No. We're just . . . visiting," the commander replied.

The woman looked around. "I must say, it's not exactly the nicest place to visit."

"No, it isn't," Church agreed.

"How long are you staying?"

"Not long. We're just here looking for—"

"Yes, I know exactly what you're here for!" the woman snapped. For a moment, her eyes seemed to flare yellow. She recomposed herself quickly and then, with soft laughter, said, "Forgive me."

Commander Church looked back at the platoon, then glanced at Jack, who still stood with his sword bared and ready. He looked to his father, who just shrugged, then turned back to the woman and said carefully, "Certainly."

She assumed a cool tone and said, "I'd like to offer you a proposition."

"What kind of proposition?"

"I know where you are headed. I can get you there and back to the boundaries of this place safely."

"That's very generous of you," said Church. "If you don't mind me asking, what's in it for you?"

"Oh, nothing much," said the woman. "I'd just be grateful if you took me with you when you left."

Eli interjected, "That is indeed very generous, but—"

The woman's face contorted with rage, momentarily appearing inhuman, her eyes glowing yellow as she snapped at Eli, "You stay out of this, *sorcerer!*" At her sudden, violent transformation the rest of the soldiers reached for their weapons.

Her face already back to normal, she scanned the men and said smoothly, "I understand your apprehension. If I'm in here, you figure I must be evil. But I assure you, I was trapped here by accident," she looked at Eli, "by one of *his* kind."

"I don't think it's a good idea," Eli said as he raised his hands, electricity crawling between his fingers. The other wizards followed suit. "She's oozing with mystical energies, Michael. She's not even remotely human."

At that announcement, all the soldiers tensed.

The woman stood there, unimpressed. She addressed Eli. "So? If you knew where your powers came from, you might not be so quick to judge." There was venom in her voice, but she was calm. "We are on the same side, you and I."

"Not fucking likely," Eli replied.

"So be it," she muttered. "If you won't take me with you . . ."

After a pause, without warning, the woman transformed. Her eyes turned yellow, her ears grew pointed, and her brow ridge thickened. She sprouted fangs, and her arms and fingers elongated, claws emerging at the tips. She leaped at the wizards, landing in the middle of them, and slashed at Eli, her claws tearing into his side.

The other wizards hurled energy blasts to defend Eli, but that only seemed to make her angrier. With an animalistic snarl she bounded onto one of the wizards, biting him in the neck. She swilled the sorcerer's blood in a great gulp and drew back, exclaiming with ecstasy, "It's been so long since I've had human blood!"

"She's a *vampire?*" Jack exclaimed as everyone scrambled.

"Not like any vamp I've seen," observed Frank.

Seeing his father attacked, Church reacted impulsively, throwing his own fire at the vampire. She staggered under the blows but shrugged off flames that would have melted stone. The soldiers attacked, but she was too quick.

"Fools!" shrieked the vampire as she grabbed a soldier by the collar and snatched the sword from his hands. "I am the first! The original! Do you think you can destroy me?" She tore into the man she held, tossed him aside like a pile of trash, then spun and whirled, lashing and biting at anyone she could reach.

Frank had pulled Peter away from the carnage but with his eyes off the battle, he was oblivious to the fact that he was now in the vampire's path. Jack lunged toward Frank, trying intercept, but he was too late. The vampire plowed into Frank, opening her jaws to clamp down on his neck, but stopped short when she saw his necklace. She hissed, spat, and screamed at the sight of the small *t*-shaped pendant on the cord. Frank figured out what was happening, pulled the necklace clean off, and thrust it at the beast, which seemed to alter her form even further. She snarled thunderously then grabbed the body of a wizard and dragged it away as she fled.

Jack asked, panting, "What did you do?"

"I didn't do anything. It was Mom's necklace." Frank held it up and looked at it. "I know vampires don't like lowercase *t*'s, but they aren't even part of the standard equipment when apprehending one these days. They usually just cause 'em to flinch or look away at best. I've never seen anything like *that* happen before."

"Huh," mused Jack.

"Yeah."

"She said she was the original," said Albert slowly.

"What's that?"

"The vampire. She said she was the *original*. I'm thinking that . . . symbol," Albert pointed to the necklace. "Perhaps it meant more in an earlier time, and therefore has a greater effect on something from that era." He studied the charm avidly, and suddenly his eyes flashed with excitement, as if he understood something about it. "You say this belonged to Hazel?"

"Yeah, why?"

They didn't have time to discuss it. Peter came out of his hiding place and clasped Frank again, complaining, "I don't know how much more of this I can take."

Frank pulled Peter off, promising he was fine.

Eli, on the other hand, was not fine. He was the only wizard to survive the attack, but the gash in his side bled freely. He placed a protection spell on it, containing it, and assured everyone he'd be all right to travel.

Jack assumed they were still in the vampire's territory, which kept other creatures away, so they kept Frank's necklace out, to keep *her* away.

With the vampire's threat gone, Church commanded the men to continue toward their destination. Despite marching in near total darkness, the men were greeted by an unearthly glow as they crested a hill. In the growing light, they could see a volcano rising from a deep chasm. Vapors billowed around its peak, swirling with the colors of a vibrant sunrise: pastel blue, violet, pink, and orange, all dusted in a golden glow.

Frank murmured, "It's beautiful."

And it was. They all agreed, pleased to see something so lovely and pure in a land so full of ugliness. But no one was as pleased as the commander. He gave a satisfied smile as he looked at the compass and said, "We made it." Then he led the way down to the volcano's base.

Jack had assumed it would be illuminated by the radiance above, but instead, they found themselves surrounded by a lifeless veil of gray. The light danced above them, but as soon as they lowered their eyes, the gray swallowed the hues. In the drab light, Jack observed pillars of dark stone dotting the land. Between the pillars, the land was flat and covered in sand so fine it absorbed sound.

Every now and again, Jack did hear something that sounded like a flag flapping in the wind . . . except the air was stagnant, and there certainly were no flags. The sound always seemed to come from somewhere just out of the line of sight. And the closer they got to the volcano the more frequent the flapping sounds became, whipping right behind them or just over their heads.

Apart from the ominous flapping, the whole place remained unnervingly quiet.

After walking for several more minutes, Jack began to catch glimpses of the creatures making the noises, but he didn't know what they were. At first, he thought his mind was playing tricks on him, or that the unusual lighting was creating an optical illusion. But when he turned to look at the other men, he knew from the stunned looks on their faces that they, too, had seen something. The apparitions were the same pale gray as the surroundings. And it *was* waving cloth he was hearing; but all he could see were glimpses of gray material whipping by.

"They sort of look like children dressed up as ghosts under bedsheets," Church whispered. "Larger, of course, but otherwise, I'd swear that's what I was seeing."

"Yeah, except kids dressed like ghosts are cute," grunted General Lane. "These things are freaking me out."

Church asked Jack, "What are they?"

Jack shook his head. "I didn't see them last time."

Church reasoned, "Whatever they are, they haven't done anything ye—"

Suddenly they heard someone yelling. "No. No. No! Get off me. Stop. Get off. No. Stop. NO!"

Everyone stopped dead and looked around, trying to figure out who was shouting. "Dan," someone offered. "It's Dan. Corporal Fredrick."

Identifying the missing soldier didn't help; it just made the group more desperate to find him. It was hard for them to determine from which direction the screams had come. Then the cries of struggle turned into a long, bloodcurdling scream that became more and more muffled.

They searched frantically, coming to a small clearing where they finally got a good look at the creatures. Seven or eight of them huddled together, like a pack of wolves over a fresh kill. Hovering, they were tipped down over their prey, wriggling and squirming in place as they feasted. Jack couldn't see what the ghost creatures were gathered over, but since Dan's screams had stopped, he had a pretty good guess what, or who, it was.

One soldier yelled bravely, or perhaps stupidly, "Hey!"

Instantly, the creatures' heads popped up from their meal, and the beings became utterly motionless; even the dangling fabric stopped moving as they glared back at the Idolessians. They *did* look like people with sheets draped over them, their faces expressionless white porcelain masks, chipped and cracked, with black, cavernous spaces where the eyes belonged.

A swishing sound from behind caused the soldiers to turn. One of the beings hovered just behind them, staring with its lifeless face. It flew away almost as quickly as it had arrived, making the flapping sound as it went. They turned back to where the others had been, but only the body of Corporal Fredrick remained.

Dan didn't look as Jack had expected. He wasn't ripped apart, bloodied, or bruised in any way. In fact, he didn't show any signs of injury, aside from those he'd received on the trek getting there. The creatures hadn't been actually eating him. But his body was frozen in a sort of horror, tensed and contorted. His hands were at his face, mouth open wide as if he were still screaming. Jack felt for a pulse but found none.

One of the sheet-figures boldly floated up to one of the other corporals, Cameron Hewitt, who skipped back to put some distance between himself and the thing. Oblivious to everyone else, it calmly followed him, gliding effortlessly. Cameron continued to back away, but then another one approached him from behind, moving in the same tranquil way.

When close to Cameron, the beings began to shake the way the others had around Dan's body. He drew away and the shaking stopped, only to begin again as they caught up to him.

"Stop it!" hollered Cameron. "Get off!" He swiped his sword at one, and it moved out of the way quickly, before swooping back and resuming its trembling once in range. "Get off me!"

Cameron began going to the other men for help. Jack and a couple of others tried slashing at the specters with their swords, but they flickered out of the way and resumed pursuing Cameron. Clearly unnerved, Cameron tried to assure everyone it wasn't as bad as it appeared so he wouldn't be left alone. "It doesn't . . . they don't hurt . . . but . . ." he swiped with his sword at the specter in front of him, but the two behind shook more violently the closer they got. "I don't feel anything. Just get them off me. Get them off!" Then he began screaming as two more of the phantoms swooped in and shook over him, all their heads faced inward, once again looking like a pack of animals feeding on a kill.

As the platoon watched in nausea and dismay, a new ghost creature appeared and floated toward Sergeant Andrew Young. He instinctively backed away, but the process had begun again. Jack looked up and saw more of the creatures descending upon them. Commander Church shouted, "There's more. Retreat! Just go, run to the mountain!" He hurled flames at the creature, but the phantom skipped out of the way.

"But what about——?"

"We can't do anything for them—just go. Now!"

Everyone scattered, but Jack ran to help Sergeant Young, who was still being followed by the phantom. Jack and Young swung their swords, but it was futile; the apparitions would shift just far enough away, and then proceed calmly back on course. "Go. Just leave me," Andrew said bravely, as another of the beings came up behind him, beginning to quiver.

Jack called, "Frank! A little help here!" Frank was at Jack's side in seconds, Peter trailing right behind.

Frank, Andrew, and Jack encircled Peter, and began swinging their swords. While one was swinging, another would be winding up, so that there were no windows for the creatures to get past. They moved as a group all the way to the volcano.

"How long do you think we can keep this up?" asked Frank.

"I'm not sure," Jack said. "They don't seem to tire."

Soon, they reached the edge of the volcano, with the rocky wall behind them and only the creatures in front. To their left came a call from the commander: "Here! Everyone to me. There's an opening into the volcano, and they can't enter!"

Jack and Frank gave each other the shortest of glances and said over their shoulders to Peter and Andrew, "Run!"

The creatures followed and had just begun to catch up when the four men lunged through the opening. They spun around to continue warding off their pursuers, but the creatures had vanished.

Andrew shook both of the Waramonds' hands. "I owe you guys."

"Think nothing of it," said Jack. Frank nodded in agreement.

"What were those things?"

Jack answered, "I don't know. I didn't run unto them last time I was here, thank goodness."

Frank suggested, "Maybe they're only around this volcano."

"Could be."

Sergeant Young peered out the opening of the cave. "Whatever the case, I hope I never see them again."

"Everyone all right?" asked Commander Church.

Everyone looked around, trying to remember how many should be there. How many had they lost?

There were sixteen survivors in all: Commander Church and his father, Eli; General Lane; the Waramonds; the Cassidy sisters; Albert; Peter; Hawk; Joss; Al Marks; Andrew Young; and three other soldiers. They'd lost all the other wizards, as well as thirteen soldiers—almost half of the group.

Heavyheartedly, Church addressed the team. "This has been a difficult journey. We've lost a lot of good men. But I promise you, their sacrifices were not in vain." He smiled. "We've made it."

8 Years Ago
572 AR

Jason leaned back against the trunk of a palm tree, his toes buried in the warm sand. Coils of dried vines sat beside him as he braided them into thick ropes for holding the raft together. The work was repetitive and mindless, and his thoughts drifted to Jack and Eliza. In order to escape the lovebirds, he'd been working on the raft every day for months now, only stopping to sleep or eat. He couldn't help but feel annoyed.

Why would they think that I'd take a break for their little "ceremony"? The sooner I get the raft done, the sooner we can get off this island.

He stood on the shore, washed the dirt and grime from his hands, and splashed some water on his face. Once he felt presentable, he took a moment to admire his work before leaving.

Jason was determined to make more than just a floating rectangle; it needed to be a seaworthy vessel that could endure waves, storms, and gods knew what else. And once they launched, they had no way of knowing how long they'd be at sea. To this end, he constructed a small shelter on the raft, to protect them from the elements and store their rations.

He thought back to when he'd begun working on it, and all the time he'd put into it since. He marveled at the structure—and realized that he had Jack and Eliza to thank for the progress. They'd left him alone, with the time necessary to build it.

Neither Jack nor Eliza had uttered a single word of complaint since Jason began working on the raft, though he no longer helped with any daily chores. Jack and Eliza provided food, gathered firewood, and kept a sleeping pallet for him in the cave, though lately he'd taken to sleeping on the beach.

It was just another way that Jason had tried to create more space between himself and them. He knew they were going out of their way to be kind—Jack had been true to his promise not to train Eliza to fight any more, and they were always ready to help him with the raft in any way he needed. But that didn't help; just looking at them together was harder than he wanted to admit, and the rest somehow made it worse.

Jason gave the vessel one last glance before heading for the cave. Near the entrance, he veered onto a path that skirted the mountain, eventually leading to a ledge. Eliza and Jack had constructed a ladder to make the climb easier, and as Jason stepped off the last rung, he found Oliver at the top, with his grumpy little face puckered around the single fang jutting out of his closed mouth. "Meh."

"Hello, Oliver."

Eliza was hanging a garland of yellow and orange tiger lilies that grew all over the island—the kind she'd taken to wearing in her hair these days. Today was no exception. Hearing Jason's voice, she turned and dashed over to greet him with a hug. "Jason, you're here!"

"I said I would come, didn't I?"

"I know, but Jack and I weren't sure you'd be interested in being a part of this. But I'm so happy you came."

"Meh," Oliver groaned as he flapped past. He landed on a wall of tall boulders, one of which was draped with sailcloth they had salvaged.

Jason looked around. "Speaking of Jack, where is he?"

"He'll be here soon. He just went to get something I forgot."

He looked at the draped boulder. "What's this?"

"You'll see," she winked. "It's a surprise."

Jason looked around and took in the view. From here, almost the entire island was visible. There were hardly any clouds, and the few dotting the sky provided a comfortable shade. At this elevation, ocean breezes could reach them without being so overpowering that they felt like they'd be blown away, and the cords of flowers swayed hypnotically in the gentle wind. Jason felt his shoulders relax as he took a deep breath, appreciating the peaceful scene. He turned back to Eliza, but she was gone. "Eliza?"

"Up here." She was climbing atop the pile of boulders where Oliver had perched. "Come on up. Sit with me while we wait for Jack."

Behind the boulders, he found an assembly of large rocks forming a makeshift stairway that led up the back. Once he was all the way up, Eliza smiled and patted the surface next to her. "Come. Sit." His breath caught in his throat, and Jason did as he was asked. "Jack and I come up here a lot."

Jason heard waves crashing on the shoreline in the distance. A flock of toucans burst from a thick patch of trees and soared over their heads. He took another cleansing breath. "I can see why. It's very um . . ."

"Calming," Eliza finished.

"Yeah," he agreed, and felt himself smile.

"Have you eaten anything yet today?"

For a moment he had the urge to lean in and kiss her, but fought off the impulse and answered, "Umm . . . yeah. I'm sure I must have."

She grinned. "No, you haven't. You never eat unless we bring something to you. Come to think of it, I haven't eaten yet either! I've been a little distracted." She gave a little squeal of excited laugher. "Jack and I prepared some stuff to eat after we're done, but here, split this with me." She pulled an orange from her skirt pocket, tore away the peel, split the fruit in two, and handed him half.

The two of them sat in silence for a minute, enjoying the fruit. Jason realized he was still grinning. He couldn't remember the last time he had genuinely smiled. "So, today's the big day, huh?" Jason popped another wedge in his mouth.

"Yup."

"Why'd you wait so long? I mean, it's been months since you guys told me you were . . . together."

Eliza smirked as she pulled another segment from the fruit. "My dad told me that the months after he and Mom got engaged were some of their favorite times together. They were meeting each other's families, preparing for the future, and just spending time together. I wanted to do the same thing . . . as much as I could, anyway." She smiled and shrugged. "I know it doesn't make a lot of sense. But what about our situation does?"

"No. I get it." Jason couldn't remember the last time he'd felt so connected to another person. There was just something about being with Eliza this way. He couldn't help but think that if strangers saw them now, sitting together, sharing an orange, they'd assume he and Eliza were together. He liked that feeling, and knew it was the source of his contentment. "Sometimes, just being with the one you love is enough."

"Hello?" Jack's voice reached them as he crested the ledge.

"Up here, hon!" said Eliza. As she and Jason scampered back down, she asked, "Did you find it?"

"Yeah. Took me a while—it wasn't where you said it was."

"You should have just let me go and get it."

"It's all right, I had something else to take care of." Jack handed Eliza a small device and gave her a peck on the cheek.

"What is that?" asked Jason, looking at the device.

Jack answered, "It's something Eliza salvaged from the pirates. She's been tinkering with it for weeks."

Without looking up from her work, Eliza stated, "It's a tattoo writer."

"Oh." The men said in unison, underwhelmed.

The tattoo writer was a small black box with a digital screen on the front, above a series of buttons and two dials. On the side there was an empty slot where small discs could be inserted, and the bottom had a small shield over a laser that served as a needle.

Jack and Jason watched Eliza as she stared at the little screen and worked the dials. Jack broke the silence. "Sooo . . . what did you need that fo—?" Eliza shushed him. He looked at Jason and shook his head.

"There, found it!" She exclaimed. "So, this device is really kind of neat. See, I think you can program it to create any design you want. I figure if you have the design on a disc, you can put it in here and then, voilà!"

"Okay?" said Jack.

Eliza continued, "The device does have a few standard designs on it, but that's only good if you like pirate stuff—cutlasses, anchors, or skulls and crossbones. But you can also create your own designs using this screen and the control pad here. I can only manage simple geometric shapes and lines, but I'm sure it could do more."

"That's great. Very neat." Trying not to sound too insensitive, Jack inquired, "And what does all this have to do with our wedding?"

"Well, we were talking about it being unfortunate that we don't have rings, so I got the idea . . . what if we tattooed them on?"

Jack's face lit up. "I like that! It's better than rings of gold or silver. Maybe not as valuable."

"But that's not what's important," agreed Eliza.

"It's more significant," said Jack. "It's permanent. It says that as long as we live, we're together, and nothing on earth can separate us."

Ecstatic that Jack understood and felt the same way, Eliza leaped in the air and into his arms. Forgetting that Jason was standing there, they kissed, but caught themselves. Eliza looked at Jason. "Sorry."

"Don't apologize. It's a lovely sentiment." He looked at the device and asked, "How's it still have power?"

"I found some extra batteries. We didn't salvage anything else that needed power, so . . ." her face scrunched, and she spoke carefully, "I figured it'd be okay?"

Jason shook his head and said, "It's fine, Eliza."

"But that's not all," she continued shamelessly, "While I was playing around with this thing to see if I could make the ring tattoos, I started to experiment with it and I . . . well, I kind of designed a symbol for us."

Eliza skipped past the dumbfounded men to the shrouded boulder and yanked the drapery off. There, on the surface of the rock, she had etched a simple but elegant image. It was a triangle pointing up, with a circle in the center; inside the circle was another triangle, pointing down.

She explained, "The triangles represent you two, and the circle is me. Jack, you're at the center of my life," she said as she touched the triangle in the center. "And Jason—my prince, my friend . . . you are our base." Suddenly she became quite sheepish again. "When we were first shipwrecked on this island, it felt like a death sentence, but the three of us came together and made it work. And there are times I've been happier here than I'd ever been back on the mainland." She looked to Jack and their eyes locked for a moment. "And so, for that . . . ." she took Jason's hand, "for both of those things . . ." she took Jack's hand as well. "And for so much more, I am grateful."

She hadn't asked yet, but both the guys knew where she was going. Jason extended his right hand. "Do mine first."

"Then me," said Jack.

"Meh," hollered Oliver, soaring down to be included.

They all laughed.

Soon, the three of them had the image imprinted on the backs of their right hands.

After, they fell silent, and Jack, admiring the decoration on the back of his hand, stepped forward. He looked out at the ocean and said, "You know, growing up, I heard people describe their wedding day as the happiest day of their life. I thought it was a sweet sentiment, but I didn't get it." He looked at Eliza, "Until now." He started to laugh. "I don't know what I'm supposed to say. I just know how happy I am. I'm happy like I've never been before." Jack looked at Jason and teased, "Jason, buddy, I know you've poured your heart and soul into that raft, but a part of me hopes it doesn't work."

Jason could feel his face start to twitch, but he caught it; he knew Jack didn't mean that literally.

Jack closed his eyes, took a breath, and began, saying the first thing that came to mind. "My mom used to tell me and Frank stories when we were kids. She told us about the gods, of course, but later she hinted that there was something more. She told us stories where humans didn't come into existence under the gods' watch. Something—or someone—else made us. Made everything." Jack put his newly branded hand out and motioned at the world surrounding them. "The Grand Designer, she called him . . . her . . . it. Whatever it is, it's different than the gods. Not just more powerful, but superior in every way, right down to its very being. They were only stories—"

"Good. If the gods thought she intended otherwise, they'd smite her for blasphemy," chortled Jason.

Jack laughed. "Yeah, but I believed them. Well, want to believe them. I mean, I look around at everything, and . . . well, I can't believe it's all just here by chance. I can't believe someone as wonderful as Eliza could just be an accident."

Jack paused for moment and then said, "I don't make it a secret that I'm not terribly impressed with the gods." Eliza and Jason both flinched, half expecting a bolt of lightning to strike Jack dead. He saw their looks of fear and smirked. "They have to care about us to be listening. But that's my point. This . . . *Designer* . . . if it's real, it's listening right now."

Eliza smiled at Jack's speech the same way one might smile after hearing a poem they didn't understand. "That sounds lovely, Jack. But, um . . .?"

"I just want you to understand how much my heart is in this, Eliza. I don't think they care, but if the gods are the best I have, I make these vows for them. But if there is something more out there that does care, I make these vows for it to hear." Jack grasped Eliza's hand and faced her, "I take you as my wife. I promise to be true to you through good or bad. If you're sick or healthy." He grinned and said, "I know you don't like being taken care of, but I will always keep you safe." Eliza playfully slapped him across the arm, and they laughed. Jack sobered. "I really do, Eliza. I don't ever want to lose you. I will love and honor you for as long as I live."

Eliza wiped tears from her eyes. "I guess it's my turn now, huh? I don't know if I can compete with that." Her voice cracked and got higher pitched than normal. She scoffed, annoyed with herself for being so emotional. But Jack smiled like he loved it. "Jack, I made you wait a long time, until I knew I was ready. I just want you to know that the wait was worth it, because I can say without a doubt in my heart or mind that I love you. This Designer you speak of sounds beautiful. So, to honor you, I make this promise to it, the same as you. I take you as my husband. I swear to be true to you, no matter the situation. I don't care if you're healthy or not. I will always love and honor you." Then she gave him a wicked grin, "And I'll keep you safe, too." Jack hooked his arms around her waist and pulled her close. "I swear it. Only death will part us."

They stood there and gazed into each other's eyes, relishing the moment. Jack mouthed, *We did it*, and Eliza nodded.

Jason was trying to be a good sport, but realized he'd turned away. Jack and Eliza had been too involved with each other to notice, but he forced himself to look back. Then, if only to get things moving again, he cut in, "What are you waiting for? Kiss her!"

They did as instructed, and Jason glanced away again.

After, Eliza and Jack tattooed their ring fingers with delicate bands of black ink. The three of them then strolled back down to the caves, where Eliza and Jack had a feast laid out—fruits and vegetables of every kind they'd ever found on the island. After they'd had their fill, Jason said he wanted to work on the raft a bit more, adding, "I was thinking I'd sleep on the beach tonight. It's nice out. And that way, I can get an early start tomorrow."

Jack and Eliza both knew he was offering them privacy for the evening, and they gratefully accepted the gift. He ambled to the mouth of the cave, then turned back. "This was really lovely. I'm very happy for you both."

Jack and Eliza thanked him but were already lost in each other's eyes.

Jason intentionally took a longer route back to the seashore; he needed time to process. He would never admit it out loud, but he was jealous. He still wasn't sure how Jack had managed to win Eliza's affections. Over these last three years, Jason had developed strong feelings for Eliza himself, and he was certain her feelings had grown for him as well. *Obviously not as strong as her feelings for Jack*, he mused bitterly. But still, he was sure there was something more there than mere friendship between him and Eliza.

Jason found himself pondering again what would have happened if Jack hadn't survived the shipwreck. *Could Eliza and I have had a chance?*

He thought about the future.

Could we still?

The whole time, his mind kept going back to those minutes he'd spent with her earlier, sharing the orange. He'd give anything to have that kind of feeling all the time. Jason shook himself. *Get over yourself—it's done. They're married.*

Jason walked a couple more yards, and as he approached the beach, a thought crept in. *Well, not actually married. Not legally.*

His mind argued with itself.

It doesn't matter that it wasn't legal. Not to them. To them, it's official. They're married.

But what if she changes her mind? It's technically not too late.

She won't change her mind. This is Eliza. She wouldn't have done it if she hadn't meant it.

Yes, but she said herself, nothing about our situation makes sense. Under the circumstances, maybe . . .

Maybe . . .? Just let it go.

Jason looked at the fresh tattoo on his right hand and thought how he'd rather have the band around his left ring finger.

I want what they have.

Once we're home, maybe I can find it.

He'd been standing on the shore struggling with his internal dialogue for several minutes before he registered what he was seeing. He gazed across the beach, seeing the remains of his raft. It had been torn to pieces, scattered across the shore. Some of the parts were so far away that they were being pulled out into the ocean by the tide. *More pirates?*

He ran to where his tools and sword lay. He drew his blade and looked around to see if the culprits were still around. Then he reasoned, *If it had been pirates, wouldn't they have seen this sword and taken it when they were destroying the raft?*

If it hadn't been pirates, then what was it?

Wild animals?

We haven't seen any kind of animal that could do this kind of damage on the island.

If not wild animals, then what, or . . . who?

Jason didn't want to think it, but his mind kept going to Jack.

He wants to stay. He said he hoped the raft wouldn't work.

Jack wouldn't do that to us.

Wouldn't he? He's happy here.

But I'm not. Even if he wanted to stay, that doesn't mean he'd keep me from leaving.

Wouldn't he?

CHAPTER FIFTEEN

A WEAPON, OF SORTS

The soldiers stood at the mouth of the cave and looked down a long, dark hallway. At the far end, faint amber light softened the darkness. "The proverbial light at the end of the tunnel," said Jack. Frank chuckled in agreement.

No one else said anything; they were all either gazing at the glow at the end of the hallway or watching Church, waiting to hear his orders.

Commander Church ordered General Lane to stay with the soldiers, guarding the entrance as well as Sarah and Sophie. Church turned to Jack. "Would you like to come with me? I believe you've earned it."

"Only if Frank—"

"Jack, don't!" exclaimed Frank. "Sir, don't worry about me, I—"

"No, it's all right, Lieutenant. You've been a tremendous asset. You've earned it as well." Church glanced around him. "Peter, if it weren't for you, we wouldn't be here. So, you're welcome to join us too, if you'd like. Lieutenant Waramond can continue to watch over you."

"Okay."

Albert stepped forward. "I know I haven't really earned anything, but I would be very interested in coming along, if you'll permit me."

Commander Church considered him for a moment, and then shrugged. "As long as you keep up, that's fine with me." Then he turned to Eli. "Father, how are you doing? Are you ready for this?"

Eli staggered forward, still weak from his injuries. He gave a pained smile. "You just try and keep me outta that fuckin' cave."

"All right, then. Let's go."

Commander Church led the small group down the hall toward the light. At the end, they stepped through a narrow opening into a canyon bursting with lush foliage. Vegetation grew everywhere within, spreading across and even up the sides of the walls before reaching the mouth of the volcano. A small brook trickled in the distance and birds flew overhead. It appeared to be daytime, though Jack knew it was night outside, but there wasn't a sign of a lamp or torch.

Jack followed behind Church as they cautiously ventured toward the center of the cavern, which was dominated by a handsome tree. Its limbs branched out wide and proud and, like its trunk, they curved and bent, curling like corkscrews. Deep reddish-purple fruits dangled amid small citrus-scented flowers, whose petals had hints of warm colors that seemed to shift and change, as if a light breeze were passing by making way for a new wash of pigment. The group stood speechless and marveled at the tree, in awe of this place.

"It's strange," said Jack. "But I . . . I feel . . . good. Refreshed, even."

"Yes," agreed Church. "There's something soothing about this place."

"I wish Terrie was here," said Peter wistfully.

Albert didn't look as refreshed as everyone else; in fact, he looked rather sick. His skin was nearly grey and sweat beaded on his forehead. "It's hard to believe this exists inside a place so terrible," he muttered as he wiped the sweat from his brow, ignoring Jack's concerned glances.

Suddenly Eli cried, "What the fuck?" He opened his tunic. The gash from the vampire was still there, but it looked as if it had been healing for weeks.

Church ran to his father. "How did you do that?"

"Wasn't me. As we walked into this place, I could feel the protective spell I placed on my wound lifting. Now there's . . . this. But, now that I mention it . . ." Eli thrust out his hand. When nothing happened, he put both hands out, face fixed in concentration. Nothing happened again.

"Father?"

With a mixture of intrigue and apprehension, Eli said, "My . . . my magic. It . . . it's . . ."

"Gone," came a voice from behind.

All the men whipped around. Mike, Jack, and Frank drew their weapons but eased when they saw the owner of the voice. A stooped man in simple white robes stood before them, gripping a book in one hand and a crook in the other. His white hair gleamed in the cavern's surreal light, and a long, thin beard covered a face draped with wrinkles and a wide smile. He continued, "There's no access to the kind of magic you use in here."

"Then how did this happen?" asked Church, motioning to his father's side.

The man chuckled, "I didn't say there wasn't supernatural energy here. Just not the kind you're used to." He chuckled again. "And if you don't mind my saying," he looked at Eli's healing wounds, "what's here is a bit better."

Church grinned at the others, satisfaction radiating from him. Jack could hardly blame him. Already, the powers here were proving to be unlike any he had seen before. Church faced the old man once again. "So, who are you?"

The old man laughed. "Where are my manners? My name is . . . is . . . well, now. I haven't used it in so long I daresay I've forgotten!" He thought for a moment, then asked, "What would you like to call me?" The men looked at each other, dumbfounded. "Well? Come now, don't be shy."

"Um, how about . . . Bob?" offered Frank.

"Delightful!" exclaimed the man. "My name is Bob. Welcome to where I live."

"Thank you," the commander replied with caution and slight confusion.

Bob asked, "Can I offer you anything? Are you hungry? Thirsty?"

"Yes, please!" Peter replied eagerly, then stepped back. "I mean . . . if that's okay?"

"Of course it is, young man," said Bob. "Please follow me." With a skip that most men his age couldn't have managed, Bob led the group down a gentle slope to a clearing with the greenest grass Jack had ever seen. A line of woven baskets filled with bread, fruit, and vegetables sat along the side of a large log next to the brook they'd been hearing. Bob showed them some carved wooden bowls they could fill with the water and then told them all to help themselves to whatever they wanted.

They dug in. With a hint of embarrassment, the commander offered, "I'm so sorry. We shouldn't impose on you like this."

"Don't be silly!" Bob asserted. "It's been so long since I've had company, I'm delighted to share what I have with you! Good, isn't it?"

Engrossed in the feast, the men could only nod in thankful agreement. Jack marveled that no one, himself included, was concerned that this could be a trap. They all intrinsically trusted

Bob. As the men ate, Church told Bob who they were, and about the others waiting at the entrance. Bob insisted on having the rest of the group join them, so they went to gather the rest of the team.

When the second group entered the cavern, they were greeted by a flash of light. The soldiers looked around to figure out what had happened. Puzzled, their focus finally landed on the one piece of the scene that didn't quite fit: Sophie.

A few pieces of her armor had fallen off, and what remained hung loosely on her limbs; she looked like a child trying on an adult's clothes. She pulled off her helmet, revealing thick strawberry blond hair that twisted and flowed just like Sarah's. As a matter of fact, except for the beauty mark on her upper lip, she looked exactly like Sarah—an identical twin.

Sarah gaped at her sister, jaw hanging open. She murmured, "Sophie . . . how?"

"I . . . I don't know!"

"Oh my!" exclaimed Bob. "You had *quite* the spell on you, didn't you?"

The sisters looked at the old man. Sophie hung her head in shame as Sarah snapped at him, "What do you know about it?"

"Nothing," replied Bob. "Just that the kind of magic you're used to out there doesn't work in here."

A note of hope rose in Sophie's voice as she dared to ask, "Is this permanent?"

"Only as long as you're in here," answered Bob.

There was no hiding Sophie's disappointment. She frowned and hung her head low.

Bob went to her. "You were just as beautiful either way. Come, come, let's get you out of all that bulk."

They left Sophie's armor in a heap by the doorway, and she cinched her pants so they wouldn't fall off. She tied her shirt in a knot around her waist, exposing her belly button, and rolled up her sleeves.

Some of the men were watching shamelessly, staring at her like dogs drooling over a piece of meat. Even General Lane gazed at Sophie like he'd never seen a woman before.

Sophie began moving her hands to cover the portions of her exposed body while Sarah told them to keep their eyes to themselves, or she'd pluck them out.

Bob whispered to Sophie in a soothing tone, "Ignore them, dear." He then spoke to the group. "Can we agree, as long as you're here, you'll follow my guidelines?"

Mike took charge. "Yes, of course. Your house, your rules."

Bob nodded, "Good. Then as long as you are here, you will treat each other with respect. And I mean *everyone*." Bob glanced toward the Cassidy sisters.

"Understood." Mike glared at the men and ordered, "Keep it in your pants."

Just as they were finally ready to move on, they realized Private Al Marks stood at the threshold of the cavern, unwilling to enter. Mike called back to him, "Al?"

Al answered nervously, "I, um . . . I think it's best if someone stands guard."

Church strode over to Marks, and the two had a private but animated conversation. Turning back, Mike said, "Yes, that's good. Stay here, Private Marks."

Bob tried to argue, "That really isn't necessary."

"I'm afraid it is," replied Church as he glided passed.

Soon the entire group, minus Al, was together again, eating and drinking as if they were attending a festive social gathering. Jack couldn't stop thinking about how surreal this whole situation was. Hawk and Joss assumed their jester status. They even got Frank to chuckle—*very* surreal. After a while, almost everyone forgot where they were.

Commander Church stepped forward, offering a hand. "Bob. Thank you so much for your hospitality. We are truly in debt to you."

Bob beamed at them all. "Think nothing of it, nothing at all." He shook the commander's hand. "You're welcome to stay as long as you like."

"That's very kind of you, but I'm afraid we don't have that kind of time. We're actually here for a reason."

"Yes, I know what you're here for," replied Bob.

"You do?"

With bright eyes, Bob answered, "Yes, of course. You're here for the sword, aren't you?"

Church and his father exchanged glances, then Church tentatively replied, "I believe we are."

Bob smiled. "Very well. Follow me."

General Lane stayed behind with the soldiers, while the first group—made up of Jack, Frank, Peter, and Albert—followed Mike and Eli. They walked along the brook, arriving at the wall opposite the doorway they had used to enter the cavern.

Bob stepped aside and pronounced, "The Armor of God."

Amid the foliage that grew up the rock walls, Jack noticed gaps that formed six niches. Albert gasped and stood stock-still, while Jack and the others slowly approached the wall. Framed by the branches and flowers growing around it, each niche displayed an elaborately carved image of a piece of armor. Put together, the six pieces comprised an entire suit. The first depicted a belt, the next was a breastplate, then what looked like a pair of sandals, followed by a shield, and then a helmet. The sixth and last opening didn't have an engraving. Hanging by a set of roots emerging through the wall of the cave was a shimmering sword. It had a double-edged silver blade, a golden hand guard and pommel with an ivory grip covered in engravings.

In the wall just above the sword Jack read an inscription:

FOR THE WORD OF GOD IS ALIVE AND ACTIVE.

SHARPER THAN ANY DOUBLE-EDGED SWORD,

IT PENETRATES EVEN TO DIVIDING SOUL AND SPIRIT,

JOINTS AND MARROW;

IT JUDGES THE THOUGHTS AND ATTITUDES

OF THE HEART.

Church approached the sword and passed his hand over it, not yet daring to touch it. With wonder and awe he whispered, "The sword of the gods."

"Ah, no," Bob corrected Mike, "Not of the *gods*. This is the Sword of the Spirit," he pointed to the inscription on the wall, "signifying the word of God. The one true God."

Mike looked at Bob with confusion.

Albert dashed past him for a closer look at everything. First taking in the wall of inscriptions, then after looking at the book in Bob's hands, he gasped, "It . . . it's real!"

The commander spun on the spot. "What? You knew about . . . *this?*"

Albert looked as if he were dizzy with wonderment. "No . . . no. Not *this*, exactly. Not the sword. I mean, I've read about it. The armor. But I . . . I thought it was metaphoric!" He looked at Jack in desperation. "But it's real. I was right, it's all real!"

"Hey, slow down," said Jack. But then he noticed something peculiar. "Albert, your hair . . . there's gray at your temples!"

Too obsessed with the discovery to respond, Albert began to ramble. "This . . . changes everything. Everything!"

Frank went to help Jack keep Albert on his feet. "Easy, Albert. Take it easy." He took one of Albert's arms, while Jack held the other.

The brothers helped Albert sit down on a nearby log. He seemed to be teetering on the verge of a nervous breakdown, randomly exclaiming, "It's real!" and "Changes everything."

"Kirk Larson, pull yourself together!" bellowed Commander Church. Albert snapped back to reality and looked at the commander.

Church continued in a calm but stern tone, "Please explain. *What* is real? What changes everything?"

Albert was out of breath and sweating, like he'd just run a race. He looked around at the men, collecting his thoughts. "I . . . I don't even know where to begin."

"Take it slowly. You say, 'it's real.' What is 'it'? *What* is real?"

"Not, exactly *what* . . . but *who*," said Albert.

"Who?"

"God."

"Which god?"

"No, not god—God." At Church's blank look, Albert tried to explain. "God. The one true God, as Bob put it. *The* God. Not the god of the seas. Not the god of the sky. Not the god of knowledge, or love, or war. Not *a* god . . . *The* God. The Creator of all . . . of everything."

Everyone except Bob looked confused; Albert wasn't making sense. Jack and Frank glanced at each other. Their mother had told them stories about something like that. She called it something different, but still . . .

Church said, "Kirk Larson. There is no such deity. Don't you think we'd know about a god like—?"

"Not *a* god—*God!*" shouted Albert, standing to his feet. "When I was inducted as a kirk, I received access to a vast collection of ancient texts that the kirks only speak of among themselves. One was an ancient book about the beginning of humankind, all the way back to its creation. More importantly, the whole book is about our Creator and His actions."

Bob chuckled and said, "Sounds like you already had access to the Sword of the Spirit!" Jack didn't understand what he meant, and he and the others waited to hear more, but Bob remained silent.

"That's impossible," Eli interjected. "If there were any such documentation, the Wizard's Council would know about it. Most everything was lost when the gods returned and reshaped the earth."

Peter chimed in with a confused, "Whuh?"

"You've never heard the story of the gods' return?" Frank asked. "Short version: Almost six hundred years ago, the world was shaped differently, with land fragmented all over the planet. There was no magic, just technology. For thousands of years, the gods didn't show themselves. As time passed, people came to think of them more as legends. But then, one day, they came back. And when they did, it was with retribution."

Peter's brows furrowed in confusion, and Frank clarified, "Vengeance. They were angry we'd forgotten them. To punish us, they dropped great portions of land beneath the sea and brought up others, leaving the world with only one landmass: Terra Firma. Billions of people died when that happened, and much was lost. Humankind was able to rebuilt itself with the knowledge of *what was* as a foundation . . . that is, we were lucky we didn't have to start from scratch."

"It didn't help that afterward, the gods started fighting with each other," Jack added with a note of loathing. "Constantly bickering with one another, trying to determine who was the strongest and deserved the most worship from the survivors."

Frank noted, "But they stopped that around the time the nations began to split."

Peter listened to every word with astonishment, when the commander cut in. "We don't have time for history lessons. The point is," Mike rounded on Albert, "if there *were* a god as powerful as you say, it would have made itself known long ago and set itself up as ruler of all."

"Not so," said Bob. "You see, when God created us, He gave us something special." He smiled. "Free will. We're free to do whatever we want. And even though God *deserves* our worship as our Creator, God would rather we offered it because we wanted to, not because we had to—unlike those other beings you call gods, who demand it."

"That's ridiculous," said Eli.

Peter spoke up. "No, it isn't. The Creator . . . *God* . . . is real."

Eli raised an eyebrow at Peter. "And how would you know? You grew up in the fucking wild."

Peter crinkled his nose, offended by Eli's demeaning tone. "I can tell you that the animals know there is a Creator. Just look around you! Look at the land, water, and sky. That doesn't just happen."

Eli gave a puff of irritation. "Yeah, and the gods control those things as easily as you or I breathe the air."

"But can they create life?" asked Peter.

"Excuse me?"

"They're powerful, and can do all kinds of amazing things, but can they create life?"

"Of course they can. With their return came magic that had been lost for eons. Magical creatures and beasts long extinct were reborn because of them."

"Not shape creatures. Can they make life? Can they make . . . ung . . . I don't know how to say it." Peter started pointing at and grabbing his chest, as if he were trying to point out something that was inside of his body. "Me . . . not my body . . . *me*! The part that leaves our bodies when we die. My . . . my . . .?"

Albert offered, "Your soul?"

"What?"

"Your soul," Albert repeated. "The word you're trying to find. It's called your soul."

"Okay . . . soul. Can they make a soul?"

Eli shifted uncomfortably. "And how would the animals know anything about this 'God'? It's not like they have one."

"Yes, they do," argued Peter.

"No. They don't. They're like any other monster or beast."

Peter turned to the group. "They do. They just have different kinds of souls than us . . . simpler souls."

Eli countered, "This child doesn't know what the fuck he's talking about."

At the word *child*, Peter's face flushed, and his fists clenched.

The commander cut in. "It doesn't matter!" He sighed loudly. "What matters is that we found this." He gestured to the sword hanging next to him and wrapped his fingers around the hilt. "We can figure out the rest later. Right now, let's see what it can do." Mike took hold of the sword and pulled.

It didn't move.

He inspected the weapon to see what fastened it to the wall, but he couldn't see anything. The handguard barely rested on the vines and looked as if the slightest breeze could blow it off its perch. Yet when Mike grabbed hold again and pulled, the weapon still refused to budge. He put a foot on the wall for leverage and pulled with both hands, but the weapon remained inexplicably fixed in place. Panting, he let go and gasped, "Father, do you think you could release it with some kind of spell?"

Eli reminded Mike, "I don't have any magic in this place." But he took hold of the weapon alongside his son, and they both threw their weight back to try and release the treasure. When it failed to move, Church glared at the sword, then asked for Frank and Jack's help. All four of them pulled on the weapon at once, but nothing happened. Even Albert joined them, but the sword remained immobile.

Peter decided to try. There wasn't much room for him, with five grown men in the way but he stretched his hand through a gap between Jack and Mike.

Through gritted teeth, Church grunted, "Peter, stay out of the way."

But as Peter's fingers brushed the hilt, the sword fell perfectly into his hand.

The sudden release sent the four others falling backward to the ground. They got to their feet and encircled Peter, admiring the dazzling weapon. Church reached out and demanded, "Here, Peter." Church took hold of the sword and instantaneously the blade and its golden handguard crumbled into a fine dust that floated to the ground around them. Shocked, the commander stood with just the hilt in his hand. He turned to Bob and snapped, "What is the meaning of this?"

Bob shrugged, "Perhaps it *is* metaphoric." He shook his head and smiled, with a sigh that suggested it was quite an enjoyable riddle.

"Perhaps? *Perhaps?*" bellowed Commander Church. With the hilt clutched in his fist, he strode toward Bob. "What do you mean, *perhaps?* The sword was right here! I saw it! I'm holding the remains of it!"

Jack and Frank intercepted Church. "Whoa there, Mike," said Jack. "Take it easy."

"How can you tell me to take it easy? We came all the way out here. Lost all those men. For . . . for *this!*" Mike held up the hilt of the sword, which unexpectedly flew from his grasp, and soared through the air straight back into Peter's hands. A dazzling light blinded them momentarily, and when their eyes adjusted, they saw the entire sword shimmering as if brand new. Peter looked up at the magnificent silver blade. Then, just as abruptly, it was gone again.

Church rounded on Peter. "What happened? How did you do that?"

Peter dropped the hilt on the ground as if it had burned his hands. "I . . . I don't know!" He backed away and stood by Frank.

Church knelt to pick up the hilt where it lay on the ground. Cautiously, he reached out for it, but as soon as he touched it, the handle sprang back into Peter's hand again. "What are you doing?" demanded Church.

Peter, who looked more stunned than the rest of the group, cried, "I told you. I don't know." He turned to Frank and handed him the hilt. "Please, just take it. I don't want it."

Frank walked it over to the commander, but before he got to Church, the hilt sprang out of his grasp and back to Peter again.

Church pleaded, "Bob, please explain what's happening. The boy—"

"Boy?" Peter objected.

"Peter," Church corrected, irritably. "He isn't even a part of all this. He lives in the wilderness, for goodness' sake. And has no need for a weapon of this nature!"

"And you do?" asked Bob.

"He doesn't understand," Church persisted.

"Doesn't he?" Bob looked at the inscription on the wall, reading the final line. "It judges the thoughts and attitudes of the heart."

Eli grunted. "Are you're saying the sword, of its own volition, goes to Peter because he believes in this 'Creator of all' god bullshit?"

Bob shrugged, his face revealing that he thought this was a very good possibility.

"That is the *dumbest* fucking thing I've ever heard."

With one of his chuckles, Bob asked, "Is the sword going to *you?*"

Church looked ready to attack Bob, when a crack of electricity flooded the air. Light flared, and the group went silent as a human form fell from the light's wake. The figure that landed looked something like the Cardinal, though, Jack noted, dressed simpler than the man he had fought. This man wore a red double-breasted jacket with a belt cinched around it. His simple cape had black trim that implied the feather outline. Instead of a helmet and hood, he wore goggles over a mask, under a wide brimmed hat with a red feather tucked in its band.

Jack and Mike drew their swords. Frank just stood dumbfounded.

"Freeze! You're under arrest," bellowed the commander. He glanced at Frank, "Lieutenant? Raise your weapon."

Frank didn't appear to even hear the commander.

Bob chuckled and remarked to himself, "Now, this is interesting!"

The Cardinal seemed stunned at the sight of the men—the Waramonds in particular. "Oh my," came a murmur from the Cardinal, revealing that he was actually a she, wearing padding to bulk herself up to look like a man.

"Take off your mask," ordered the commander.

Without complaint, the Cardinal pulled off the hat and yanked off the goggles and facemask.

Jack lowered his sword in disbelief and gasped in unison with Frank. Commander Church looked at both of them. "What are you doing?"

The woman was pretty, but otherwise ordinary looking. Hanging around her neck on a shiny gold chain was a small *t*-shaped pendant, identical to the one Frank wore. Her hair was the same reddish hue as Frank's beard, and her eyes were the same hazel as his as well.

"M . . . Mom?" stammered Jack.

"*Mom?*" echoed Church looking back at Eli and Albert. "This is Hazel Waramond?"

"It is," confirmed Albert.

Jack and Frank walked slowly toward the woman, barely daring to trust their eyes. Hazel walked toward them with the same kind of trepidation. Once in arm's reach, with tears rolling down her cheeks, Hazel reached up and put a hand on each of her sons' cheeks, as if to verify what she was seeing was real. "You're alive," she muttered to Jack. Frank grabbed hold of one of her shoulders, while Jack cupped the back of her head. After a moment, satisfied that they weren't hallucinating, they threw themselves into a massive hug.

Frank stammered, "How can this be? M-Mom . . . you, you're . . ."

With a gentle smile, Hazel hushed him. "Oh, my boys, look at you. So grown up." Hazel brushed away her tears and put a hand on Frank's chest, looking at his decorated uniform, "Franklin . . . so handsome. You look just like your father. Look, you're a lieutenant now! I'm so proud." She took the *t*-shaped pendant hanging from his neck between two fingers, eyes beaming as her smile widened. "You found your brother and brought him home, didn't you?"

Frank nodded, unable to speak and she wiped a tear off his face. Hazel turned to Jack, taking in his lack of uniform. "Jack . . . my, look at all that hair! And you've found your way out of the military," she said, not with disappointment but with joy. "I have to confess I'm surprised, but you have so much more to offer this world than just being a warrior." She then took in both her sons. "Oh, you both do!" and embraced them again.

Jack felt a lump in his throat. To hear these words of praise from his mother—and she had no idea of all that he'd been through. Everything he'd had and lost: his rank, his wife . . . his way. "Mom. How is this possible?"

"I think we'd all like to know the answer to that, *Cardinal*," Church interjected, his sword still pointed at Hazel.

Jack said, "Mike, relax. This is our mother."

"I know, Jack. But she's also the Cardinal, who happens to be an enemy of Idoless. And forgive me, but isn't she supposed to be *dead*?"

The brothers had lost themselves at the sight of their mother, and now came back to reality.

"Yeah, Mom, what's going on?" Frank inquired, particularly perplexed by her attire.

"No, she's not the Cardinal," Jack stated, looking at Hazel's outfit. "At least, not the one I fought."

Hazel looked shocked. "What? You fought with a Cardinal?"

"But it wasn't you. Was it?"

Hazel smiled, "I think I would remember fighting one of my sons."

Abruptly, Frank exclaimed, "Mom's the Cardinal! Mom's the Cardinal!" and fell to the ground as if something had swept his feet from beneath him.

Jack and Hazel ran and knelt beside him. "Franklin, are you all right?"

Panicking, Frank looked at his brother and said almost desperately, "Jack, Mom's the Cardinal." Then he looked at his mother as if the last few minutes had never happened. "Mom . . . you . . . you're . . . ?"

"Yes, my boy, I know." Hazel took Frank's head between her hands and kissed him on the forehead. "Oh, I'm so sorry I did this to you."

"Did what? Mom, what's wrong with him?" asked Jack.

With disappointment, she answered, "I must have put a spell on him at some point."

"A spell? You can do magic?" Jack thought about the evidence on hand, and everything that was happening. "Are . . . are you . . . a sorceress?"

"No, Jack, I'm not. But I do have a few magical devices at my disposal. One of them can alter someone's memory. And I must have used it on Frank, even though I can't imagine why I would. Maybe he found out I was the Cardinal and I had to do this to him," Hazel theorized, as if she were a detective solving a case. "Now that he's finding out again, the mental wall the spell created is crumbling."

Then Bob said, "Actually, the spell was probably eliminated when he entered the cave, and seeing you just reminded him."

When Hazel saw Bob, she beamed. "Oh, hello, Bob!"

Bob looked surprised, but grinned. "I know you? And my name really *is* Bob? How about that?" He laughed.

Then she also noticed Albert. "Hello, old friend."

Albert smiled and waved.

"Wait, slow down." Jack shook his head. "Mom, just what is going on?"

With sympathetic eyes, Hazel looked at her son and suddenly her body flickered, as if she were a computer monitor changing frequencies. She pulled out a golden ball from her jacket pocket, revealing a device covered with seams and tiny bolts. Two small windows revealed gears and cogs turning inside. A portion of the sphere flattened where there was a dial, and after looking at it, she tucked the ball away and muttered, "Oh dear, less time than I thought. I wasn't counting on seeing you boys . . . it's slowing me down and my mind is all messed up." Hazel then turned to the commander. "Mr. Church?"

Mike stepped forward.

"Oh, I'm sorry," she looked at his uniform and the gold oak leaf, clearly taking him in for the first time. "*Commander* Church." Hazel paused, taken aback by something about Mike. Her eyes narrowed with curiosity. "I trust you have the sword by now?"

Confused—but interested since the attention was back on the weapon—Mike answered, "Yes, we have the sword. Well, sort of," he looked at Peter.

"That's right," she said, like she was recalling something, and said, "Don't worry, it'll work itself out."

Flabbergasted, Church said, "What? But it's . . . *attached* to him somehow."

"Yes, but just for now."

With exasperation and disbelief, Church echoed, "Well, for how long?"

"Don't concern yourself with that. Just make sure to hang onto the Mechinan compass you have. It will lead you to any piece of the armor within a nation's borders."

"Any piece . . . ?" Mike's eyes lit up as it came together in his mind. "There's more!" Church looked back at the place the sword had come from, gazing over the other engravings. He turned back to Hazel and said, "This sword is only a sixth of the weapon, isn't it?"

Bob chimed, "Well, a weapon of sorts."

"It's the Armor of God," Hazel stated. She flickered again and cursed. "Look, I'm here to tell you, the sword is needed to get the breastplate." Hazel then turned back to Jack and Frank, "Oh, I do hope I'll get to see you two again. It's wonderful seeing the men you've become. I'm so proud of you both." Tears returned to her eyes.

Frank pleaded, "Mom, you don't have to go." Hazel gently placed a finger against Frank's lips to stop him.

Jack joined in. "He's right, Mom. This could be like a second chance for us."

"Wait," exclaimed Church. "You haven't explained anything."

She flickered again, "I know, but I'm already out of time and I told you what I was here to tell you. I'm so sorry I got distracted by my boys." She turned back to her sons. "Yes, I do have to go. I don't have a choice. It'll happen any moment."

"No!" shouted the brothers and Church.

A *ding* sounded from the gold sphere in Hazel's jacket.

Suddenly Hazel looked as if she'd just remembered something and sputtered to Bob, "When we meet, I have doubts. Use that!" Then she spun to face her children and said, "Oh, I love you so mu—!"

Then with another flash of light, Hazel Waramond was gone.

Chapter Sixteen

SAFE PASSAGE

Well," Bob exclaimed with a clap, "that was all very illuminating." And he turned to leave.

"Wait!" cried Jack. "You know our mother?"

"Not yet, but she seems lovely. Can't wait to meet her."

Jack and Frank chased after Bob along with the others. Mike kept begging him to stop and explain things, but Bob seemed quite focused on whatever it was he was doing. "Sorry, I really need to hurry, not much time," he explained, like it was all very simple. He laughed, saying more to himself than the others, "All this time waiting, and now suddenly I have to hurry!"

"You don't have much time until what?" asked Albert.

Bob answered plainly, "Until I die." He seemed rather excited by the notion.

His statement took the Idolessians off guard and they followed in muddled silence.

After a brief but unusually quiet hike, Bob led them to a sheltered alcove that he'd transformed into a living space. Books and baskets lined makeshift shelves, and along the alcove's back wall sat a bed frame fashioned from tree branches. Its straw-filled mattress held neatly folded blankets on top.

Bob pulled a knapsack from one of the baskets and set it on the bed. Next, he removed his sandals and put on a pair of military-style boots. As Bob tied the laces, Church pushed for more information, "But the sword . . . what's so special about it? What can it do? Does it cut through anything?"

"I suppose," Bob answered absently as he finished tying the second bootlace. When he stood up, the boots were hidden under his long tunic.

Eli grunted, "That's nothing special. I don't know a substance I can't cut or blast through with the right spell."

Bob shrugged and began to take clothing out of the baskets and stuff them into the knapsack. From one of the baskets, he pulled out a long shawl and hung it over his shoulders. He replaced the rope around his waist with a belt, again military in style, and tucked the shawl under it, leaving enough slack so he could lift it over his head like a hood. With his task completed, he turned to face Church. "You already know it's more than a sword."

"Yes, exactly. This is supposed to be a weapon of . . . wait." Church stopped, and it was clear that the wheels were turning in his mind. "The Armor of God . . . could it *kill* a god?"

"Oh, it has."

When he could speak again, Eli asked, "How . . . the fuck do you know?"

"I saw . . . well, I *did* it, actually."

Bob continued with his preparations, but for everyone else it felt like the air had been sucked out of the room for a moment.

"Wait, what? When?" Albert blurted.

"Oh, that was a long time ago. Around the time the five nations were created."

"That was hundreds of years ago," remarked Frank.

Bob chuckled again and rolled his eyes with a *Yeah, it was* look. "When we killed the . . . *god*," he said cynically, "it marked the beginning of the nations." He stooped to pull a box from under the bed. Out of the box, he removed two objects and a pouch that jingled. The first object was a small wooden compass-locket similar to the metal one Church had. Upon seeing the one Bob was handling, Church clutched his own. He looked back at Bob, who gave him a knowing wink and asked conversationally, "Are there still five nations?"

"Yes. Yes, there are," answered Church.

Bob checked the contents of the pouch before placing it and the locket in the knapsack. "Hmm, there were five of us. I was the one who did the deed." He lifted his chest. "I may not look it now, but I used to be quite the warrior. But we all worked together to make it happen. Once the gods realized we had the power to destroy them, they were much more amenable to conversation."

Bob turned his attention to the second object, which looked very much like the device Hazel had used. The gold orb had windows revealing clockwork inside, and there was a dial as well as a button located above a keyhole. Bob set it on the bed, gave it a little pat, and continued, "Frankly, the others and I didn't want to hear any of it—those beings don't have any right to the label of *god* just because they're superhuman. But before we could do anything about it, we were betrayed by our own people. The gods promised them riches and power if they split up the armor and the five of us were imprisoned with the various pieces, cursed to watch over them ever since."

"You remember all that, but you couldn't remember your name?" asked Peter.

Bob burst into laughter, then explained, "I remember what I need to, young man." Then he turned to Frank, "It hasn't been so bad. I was given this remarkable place to live. Everything I need has been provided for me—plenty to eat and drink, books to read, and time to think. Especially time. You age slowly here . . . very slowly, oh my, yes. It's very difficult to get hurt, and even if you do . . ." Bob pointed to Eli, whose wound had now completely healed. "Don't get me wrong, it took me some time to adjust, but eventually I saw it for the blessing it was."

"Blessing?" asked Eli.

"Yes, blessing."

Frank asked, "But didn't you miss your home?"

"No. But there's a good reason for that: my wife was allowed to come with me. Being near her always felt like home to me, no matter where we were." He paused for a moment and looked at his hands. "Before we got here, she was dying of cancer. The healers could do nothing for her. But this place cured her."

"Where is she?" asked Jack.

Bob sighed. "Aging slows here, but it doesn't stop. I lost her some time ago."

"Oh, I'm sorry."

"Don't be. We got to spend hundreds of years together. Now, here." Bob reached in the pouch set at the top of the knapsack, then turned to the men and held out a sphere that couldn't have been much bigger than a walnut. The copper orb was etched with verdigris and had tiny bolts on its seams. Sunk between the seams was a small keyhole, and dangling from it was a fine chain attached to a miniature key. "This will help you get out of the containment field."

"What is it?" asked Commander Church.

"We call it a hopper."

"I've heard of those," Eli said enthusiastically. "But I thought they were all gone."

"They're not *all* gone." Bob eyed his knapsack.

"No one's been able to redevelop them." Looking at the bag hungrily, Eli asked, "How do they work?"

Bob held up the ball, took the key, and aligned it with the keyhole, being careful not to put it in as he explained, "Put the key in and turn it. You'll hear a winding-down sound. A moment later there will be a *click*. Make sure everyone who's going is in physical contact with each other and facing the direction you want to hop. Then simply leap in the air. Once you're off the ground, it will transport you a short distance—over a pond, to the other side of a wall, or even . . ."

"Past a magical barrier," finished the commander, as he took the hopper from Bob.

Bob smiled and gave him a nod. "Only one use per hopper, so make it count."

Jack turned to Church. "Wait. Are you saying you didn't know how to get us out of here until now?"

Church exchanged an uncomfortable glance with his father, then replied, "We had good reason to believe there would be a way provided once we had the weapon."

Jack balled up his fists. "Good *reason*?"

Bob laughed uncomfortably, "Okaaay, I think that's my cue to go."

"Go?" cried Commander Church. "You can't go! You haven't—later, Jack—you haven't really explained anything yet. The sword, how do we work it?"

"You can't just wield the power of the Word with one simple explanation," said Bob as he cinched up his knapsack and threw it over his shoulder. "You need to learn it first. Understand what it is you have."

"At least tell me how to . . . to *detach* it from Peter," said Church with a growing desperation.

"Hazel said you'd figure it out." Bob picked up the golden orb, pulled out a key, and inserted it into the ball.

Church breathed out of his nose irritably. "Fine. We'll figure it out." Bob began winding the key, and Mike became even more desperate to keep him from leaving, "But . . . what about the rest of the armor?"

A winding sound came from the device in his hand. "What about it?" Now a quiet but clear *click* sounded from the ball.

"Bob, wait!"

Bob took a deep breath, preparing to leap, when he suddenly stopped himself. "You know, there was something I was going to tell you . . . hmmm." Everyone waited in silence, then he said, "I can't remember. Oh, well. Couldn't have been that important." He winked at Peter, and a moment later Bob pushed the button above the keyhole and sprang in the air, disappearing in a flash of light. The instant he was gone, a rumble shook the cavern, causing some of the plants and trees to drop leaves, which crumbled to white ash upon hitting the ground.

Commander Church, who turned this way and that, clearly trying to process the information he had, ignored the tremor and turned to Eli. "Father . . . how far can those *hoppers* take you? He can't be too far, can he? We can go after him."

Eli looked unsure, "Not far, but I don't think he used a hopper. The device he used was different. I think it was either a jumper or skipper."

"What difference does that make?"

"Well, they're like hoppers, but they have greater capacities for travel. They can take you farther and even, if the legends are true, through time."

"It makes sense, actually," said Albert. He turned to Jack and Frank, "I'll bet that's what Hazel had. It's the only explanation that fits."

Another tremor, larger than the first, surged through the cavern. It wasn't so big that it knocked anyone off balance, but Frank collapsed to the ground anyway.

Jack ran to his brother's aid. "You all right, bro?"

Frank clutched his head, doing all he could to keep himself together. He whispered, "Jack, she died."

"What? Mom? Well, yeah, Frank she—"

"No, you don't . . . I mean . . . I was there when she died. I helped . . . I mean, I didn't know it was her . . . we captured the Cardinal. But before . . . before I knew . . . it was too late, she was, was . . . already . . ."

Jack could barely find the strength to ask the question. "Are you saying . . . did you . . . ?"

"I . . . I can't remember, Jack, I . . . I can't . . . can't remember!" Frank's eyes were as wide open as they could be, but his pupils were tiny. He began to hit himself on the head. "What did I do? What did I do?"

Jack knelt down and grabbed his brother's hands to stop him. "Frank! I don't know what happened. But there is no way—do you hear me? *No way*—that you would ever have hurt Mom if you knew it was her. This whole Cardinal business is screwing us up. Besides, if Mom had been caught and discovered as the Cardinal, don't you think we'd have heard about it?"

It seemed to help a little. Frank still looked befuddled, but Jack's reasoning made sense. "Yeah . . . that's true."

"You got screwed over with this spell and things are rushing back at you. Just give it time before you jump to conclusions. We'll figure it out, okay? Hey, Frank—okay?"

Frank looked up at Jack and, in a soft voice, said, "She died in my arms, Jack."

"Then she died with someone she loved and who loved her."

Frank forced a smile. "I'm sorry. This is . . . this memory spell . . . it . . . it's messing me up."

"I'm sorry, bro. But I meant what I said. We'll figure this out together. I promise."

A much larger rumble rippled through the cavern. This time large branches and even rocks tumbled down, disintegrating into ash as they hit the ground. To answer the question they were all thinking, Eli Warren said, "I think I know what that dimwit forgot to mention before he left. I think without him here, the imprisonment spell is deteriorating, and the cavern along with it. We don't have much time before this place comes crashing down."

Church ordered Frank, "Time to get up, Lieutenant."

Concerned only with his brother, Jack protested, "A little sensitivity would be nice. This is serious, Mike."

"Which is why I hadn't said anything until now. But we need to hurry, before we're all crushed."

Coming to the commander's defense, Frank said, "Back off, Jack." He picked himself up off the ground. Jack would have been concerned if he hadn't been expecting that reaction. *At least he's regained himself,* Jack figured. Frank squeezed Jack's shoulder. "Hey, I appreciate it. Really. But the commander is right."

The rumbling began again, more violently than before.

"We really should hurry," said Albert.

They retraced their steps back to the wall of the cavern where they'd gotten the sword. Unexpectedly, Church stopped and shot a blast of fire from his fist. "Father, with Bob gone, that spell has been broken, and whatever was disrupting our magic before is gone. Can you capture an image of the wall?"

Eli understood, and he stepped in front of the wall with his hands raised. He closed his eyes and muttered a spell; the wall appeared to spring right up to where Eli was, then began to fade, revealing itself to be a copy. The fading duplicate wall then shrunk down into a tiny marble that hovered in the air before Eli. He took it and crammed it into a pouch on his belt. "Got it."

Instead of coming and going, the earthquake had become one long, unbroken tremor. Frank still seemed a little flummoxed from the breaking of the memory spell, until he had to pull Peter out of the way of a piece of the cavern wall that fell from above them. The group found the others, and Church ordered them to get out.

They sprinted back to the cavern entrance. With the spell broken, Sophie had returned to her former appearance so she collected as much of her armor as she could, reentering the tunnel in a rush. Jack noticed that Al Marks, who was still waiting, seemed to be restraining himself from asking how things had gone, but as he ran by Church simply barked, "Later." Jack glanced at Frank, hoping that maybe he'd seen or heard it too, but he hadn't.

Jack took one final glance back at the cavern before joining everyone. The falling rubble obstructed his view, but he thought he saw a flash of light in the spaces between falling rocks, and there was Bob, wearing his wide smile, just standing there as if nothing were happening. Then he disappeared in a cloud of gray ash. Jack blinked, trying to decide if he believed what he'd just seen. But there was no time to think about it, so he joined the others.

As they neared the exit, someone shouted, "What about those things outside?" They took the risk and threw themselves out before the mountain imploded. No one stopped running though; they knew they needed to put space between themselves and the mountain, not knowing how far its destruction would go. The group stopped once they'd made it well past the edge of the volcano's base. They looked back with awe as they realized that the volcano had disintegrated into the same fine, ashen sand that had once surrounded it.

As the ash slowly settled, the sun broke on the horizon. Not wanting to waste any daylight, Church rallied the group. "Good work, everyone. We got what we came for." There were a few muted cheers, and a couple of the soldiers clapped. "We only have one thing left to do: Get out of here alive." Church prepped everyone on how the hopper worked, so that once they reached the barrier, they could get out as fast as possible. Hawk and Joss were amused that the group was going to have to jump in unison, thinking it would be a funny sight to see. Eli warned them they should take it more seriously, explaining that he didn't know what would happen to anyone who wasn't off the ground with the others. "It could seriously fuck you up," he told them earnestly. The smiles of the few who were laughing at Hawk's jokes melted away.

The journey out was much easier than they expected. They kept waiting for the first monster to creep its way out of the shadows or come storming at them from the depths of the forest, but nothing happened. Even the insects were nowhere to be found. All they had to contend with was the difficult terrain. They retraced their path almost exactly, but they didn't encounter the remains of even one of the men they lost. Patches of ground where someone had fallen were stained dark with blood, but no bodies remained.

As they neared the doorway, everyone moved faster. Jack tried to keep them reined in, but because the sun was beginning to set, he felt the speed they were gaining from the excitement was worth any risk. The sooner they got to the exit, the better.

Just when they began to relax, they finally saw something: a gangly, gray creature sat watching them from the cover of a tree. It was far enough away that it didn't directly threaten them, but something about the way it just watched them was . . . eerie.

At the sight of the beast, they slowed their pace.

Shortly after, someone saw another one—and then another, and another. Jack wondered if the gray beasts had always been there, and the Idolessians were only noticing them now, but in other instances, he could see them slither into place. The monsters kept their distance, but their numbers escalated with each step the soldiers took. And it wasn't just the lanky creatures anymore; the other beasts they had encountered earlier joined their ranks.

"Can't be more than a few hundred yards before we reach the outer ring where the doorway is," Jack whispered to Mike.

"I know, but it's not like we can make a break for it. With this many of those . . . things, we'll be overtaken and annihilated before we even make it a few feet."

Al Marks interjected, "If that happens, take the weapon and go, Mike. We'll hold them off while you get out." The commander shushed him. "No, you need to get out with it! That's all that matters."

"I said shut up!" hissed Church.

While he didn't know what it was, Jack felt certain that something decidedly odd was going on—and Al Marks was in on it. Before he could put his finger on it, a raspy, seductive voice interrupted Jack's thoughts. "Hello again."

It was the vampire. She'd resumed her human form and stood before an impenetrable wall of monsters.

"Hello," answered Church.

In a pleasant tone, the vampire said, "Fancy running into you ag—leave it!" She pointed at Frank, who was reaching under his shirt for his necklace.

Frank looked at the commander, who softly confirmed, "Leave it." But something about the nod he gave conveyed to Frank that the full statement was, *Leave it . . . for now.*

Her casual smile returned along with her friendly tone. "Excellent. I was thinking. We got off to a bad start before. I'd like to start over. I'm sure we could reach some kind of arrangement."

"What did you have in mind?"

The monsters were licking their chops, anxious to dig into the soldiers, but they were resisting. Acting as if the beasts weren't even there, the vampire said, "For you to take me with you outside the barrier of course."

"But what do we get out of it? If I recall, the original deal was that you would escort us through the Province safely. We're nearly out now."

Now the vampire acknowledged the mass of creatures around her. She looked around at all of them, and even patted a goblin on the head as if it were a pet. "It seems to me that you could still really use an escort. Tell you what: I have someone here to plead my case for me. He's an old friend of Jack's."

"What?" wheezed Jack.

"His name is Charlie. He'll tell you what a fine, upstanding lady I am." The vampire turned to the mass of creatures behind her.

Out of the ranks of beasts stepped a slim man with freckles and short red hair. He looked like he was about Peter's age or a recently graduated cadet. He wore a uniform that looked just like the ones the Idolessian soldiers were wearing, except that he wasn't wearing a beret. The top button of his tunic was undone, his sleeves rolled up like Jack's—and his skin had the same milky quality as the woman's. He stepped right up next to the vampire and said, "Hey, Jack. You look older."

Jack moaned, "Oh, Charlie."

Mike looked at Jack with horror in his eyes, "Is this man from your old platoon?"

Jack nodded. "He was a good kid. They all were. But we were outmatched by this place."

Charlie continued, "Please, Jack. Things don't have to get ugly. Just let her out"

Jack didn't respond.

"Come on, Jack. It's me, Charlie."

Jack grimaced. "You may look like him and you may sound like him, but you and I both know you aren't Charlie."

"Yes—I am. Being a vampire isn't like you think. I'm still me."

Frank whispered, "Same old vampire lies."

"Same old vampire hearing," responded Charlie with a confident voice. He resumed his meeker tone, continuing, "See? Lilith just improved me so I could survive here."

"Lilith?" asked Jack.

"Yes," said the woman. "That's my name."

Charlie explained, "She's not like the vampires we know out in the world—she's ancient. The first of us. You don't know what it was like for me, Jack. In this place, alone. But she saved me. She doesn't deserve to be trapped here."

Jack could see they were at an impasse. If the soldiers tried to fight their way through, they would surely be destroyed; but he was confident Lilith wasn't imprisoned in Death's Province by accident, and to set her free seemed . . . dangerous at best.

"You have a deal," said the commander.

Jack hissed, "Mike, no!"

Mike glared at him. "We don't have a choice, Jack! Look around you!" Jack opened his mouth to respond, but Mike continued, "We don't have the time to argue." He turned back to Lilith, "You guarantee our safety as long as we take you with us?"

"You have my word," she responded with an unnerving smirk.

"What about all your . . . friends, here?" asked Mike, looking at the horde of monsters. "Aren't you concerned that some of them will get jealous that you get to leave, and they have to stay?"

"Oh," Lilith smiled, "we've all been in here together for some time, and they all know who the biggest dog is." She scratched under the chin of one of the gray beasts.

"Okay, then. Let's go." said Church, striding confidently toward the wall of creatures. Once Lilith joined him, the horde parted.

In less time than it would take to cross a street, they breached the thick outer ring of trees and brush. Without the forest enveloping them, they could see the full moon shining down and lighting their way. It almost felt peaceful as they crossed the swath of tall grass. Charlie and the rest of the Death's Province inhabitants remained at the forest's edge to watch.

With an air that sounded as if she were making small talk, Lilith asked, "So, how do we get through?"

Church answered, "We have a magical device that will transport us out."

"What, like a hopper?"

"Do you know how they work?" asked Church. Lilith nodded. "Then you know," he said with a swift glance to Jack, "that we only have one shot at this."

Jack hoped Mike was trying to pass him the message that they weren't going to let her out.

"I understand how they work," she said curtly. Then she asked, "Which of you has it?"

Keeping a cordial tone, Church answered, "With all due respect, that's classified." Lilith smiled sweetly to keep up the pretense of civility, though Jack saw her hands clench into fists.

As they approached the entrance, Jack moved stealthily behind his brother and untied the cord that held the *t*-shaped pendant. Frank realized what was happening a second too late. He couldn't say anything, at the risk of causing a commotion, but his eyes warned Jack that he shouldn't try anything. Jack wanted to explain that Church wanted him to do this—Frank would be more comfortable with it then—but he had no way to explain it all, so he just winked.

"Well, this is it," said Church.

Jack inched next to Lilith, noticing the hungry look in her eyes as she gazed toward her freedom.

Much to Jack's chagrin, Frank followed him.

Church pulled out the hopper. "Everyone ready?" He looked pointedly at Jack, then inserted the key. He began winding until the hopper clicked audibly. "Everyone: place your hands on the shoulders of the people next to you." The group did so, standing in staggered rows, making a sort of net; everyone except those on the outside of it had their hands on two different shoulders. That way, if they accidentally let go of one person, they'd still make it through.

Being on the outside, Jack placed his hand on Lilith's cold shoulder; she gave him an evil smile. He felt a hand on his own shoulder and turned, expecting to see Frank, but found Peter instead. Frank was behind him, with his hand on Peter's shoulder and fear in his eyes.

"On the count of three, we jump," announced Mike. Everyone remained quiet, but it was a nervous, dead silence that came with the tension of the moment. "One." Jack looked at

Frank. "Two." He could do nothing about it anymore; it was now or never. "Three."

They all leaped in the air, but as Jack did so, he flung the necklace in front of Lilith. She recoiled but attempted to grab as many people as possible. The chaos ended with a blinding flash of light.

Jack waited impatiently for his eyes to readjust to the dark. He understood just enough of what had happened to feel both relieved and horrified. He had succeeded; Lilith was still inside Death's Province—but so was he.

He'd dropped the necklace in the commotion, and with his eyesight restored he scrambled around on his hands and knees searching for it. Despite the full moon, Jack struggled to find the tiny charm amid the brush.

"Lose something?" growled Lilith, as she rose to her feet. Jack didn't answer, he just continued to search. A moment later, he heard the horde of creatures storming toward them. Lilith sauntered toward Jack. "I don't have much time to make up my mind before my *friends* arrive and tear you apart. I must decide if I'd rather watch it happen," she reached down, clutched Jack by the throat, and raised him off the ground with one hand, "or do it myself."

Jack drew his sword, but Lilith batted it away with one hand. He kicked her and tried to pry himself free, but she was too strong.

The thunderous approach of the beasts grew louder.

Jack prepared for the end, but he hit the ground instead.

As he regained his senses, Jack heard Lilith screaming and found her right forearm on the ground in front of him. Next to her stood a stunned-looking Peter, holding the sword from the cave, its blade glinting in the moonlight.

There wasn't time to think. Jack stood up and reached out. The sword sprang from Peter's hands and into his own. He spun around with a great slash, severing a goblin's head from its body. He then swung at Lilith, who jerked away and flew off into the night.

"She can fly?" Peter said in shock.

The monsters rushed at them, but they quickly realized the sword gave Jack the advantage. A few tried to go for Peter, but Jack pointed the sword at them, and a beam of light shot out turning them to dust. Once that happened, the fight became much easier, and Jack chased the horde back into the forest with little effort.

When he was sure they were all gone, he lifted the sword to marvel at it, but in a blink the blade was gone again, leaving him with just the hilt. Just then, black smoke drifted into the space between him and Peter, and Lilith materialized out it. She looked livid. "You may have prevented me from leaving, Jack, but you are trapped here with me."

He had no idea how the sword worked, but he raised the hilt and bluffed, "Yeah, well, I have a little protection. Or didn't you notice me kicking the asses of all your friends?" He looked at the stump where Lilith's hand should have been. "And it did a pretty good number on you too. Think it'll grow back?"

Lilith's eyes yellowed, and she sprouted fangs. She hissed at Jack. "Yes, well, let's see how well it does against your old friends." Then she dissipated into mist again.

Jack rejoined Peter, who asked, "What did she mean, 'old friends'?"

"I don't know."

But then he saw them: the soldiers who had in died in Death's Province. Their bodies lurched from the forest shadows, lumbering toward Jack and Peter. The soldiers bore the horrific wounds that had caused their deaths, blood still seeping from some. But there were other uniformed bodies as well. They were thinner and more decomposed, but Jack recognized the men from his original platoon.

None of the approaching figures were the people they had once been. "Zombies," breathed Jack.

"What are zombies?"

"They're the reanimated bodies of dead people." Peter looked at him as if he didn't understand, so Jack added, "They aren't alive. They . . . they don't have their souls. They're the worst kind of plague. All they want to do is eat the flesh of the living. If they bite you, you die, and your body will become one of them as well. If they don't eat you completely first."

With disgust, Peter exclaimed, "That's horrible!"

"I've only faced them once before, back in the army. They can only be created with the darkest of magic." Jack gazed at the hobbling creatures headed toward them and sighed, "Which this place is full of."

"Are you all right?" asked Peter.

Jack couldn't help but laugh, "Of course not. We're trapped—"

"That's not what I meant."

The utter futility of the situation clawed at Jack's mind. Turning to Peter, Jack saw kindness and understanding in his eyes. Before he even realized what he was doing, Jack blurted out the words that had been weighing on him from the moment he had walked into Death's Province. "Why am I here? Why did I survive this place before, only to have my life go to crap? Now I'm back and stuck again, and we didn't even get the weapon out!" He looked out at the zombies inching closer. "I should be one of those things! But I'm alive! Why?" Jack's voice broke with emotion, and he turned away from Peter.

"Destiny," answered Peter. "You're here for a reason."

Exasperated, Jack said, "How on earth do you even know a word like that?"

The zombies were almost upon them.

"I've heard of it." Like it somehow proved something, Peter extended his arm and offered Frank's necklace. He must have found it.

Jack didn't take it. "Well, you've heard wrong. There's no such thing. If there is, I just missed it before and am fulfilling it now," and dropped the sword hilt to the ground.

Peter looked down at the hilt. His eyes then flickered from the doorway to the approaching zombies, and then back to the hilt again. He said, "Let's find out," then picked up the hilt and dashed toward the doorway. "Let's get out of here," said Peter, then turned and raised the hilt in the air.

8 Years Ago
572 AR

Eliza stormed up to Jason and said, "Can we talk?"

It sounded more like an order than a request, so Jason put down the parts of the new raft he was working on. "Um, sure. What's up?"

"You and Jack."

Oliver soared past, and perched on her shoulder and agreed, "Meh."

Jason picked up a hammer and began working on the raft again, "Eliza, maybe you should just drop it."

"No," she said with a stomp of her foot. When Jason looked up, he saw Eliza's stony expression daring him to contradict her. "This whole situation has escalated way too far. You're mad at him, and now he's mad at you for being mad at him."

Jason dropped the hammer he had been using and spun to face Eliza fully. "He's mad at me? He has no right!"

"Seriously, Jason, do you really think Jack destroyed the raft?" asked Eliza. "You know it couldn't have been him! We were together the whole day."

"Not true. There was a chunk of time when it was just you and I up on the mountain. He could have done it then."

She reasoned, "But you know as well as I do that he didn't."

"I don't know what he's capable of anymore." Jason picked up the hammer and tried to resume his work.

"He even offered to help you build the new raft."

Jason snapped, "I don't want his help." He stopped pretending to work and just leaned on the new raft. "He flat out said he hoped the raft wouldn't work. And I get it. He's happy here. He has everything he could ever want."

"That's not true."

Jason looked up at Eliza and said, "He has you."

An uncomfortable silence settled between them, but Eliza ignored it and tried to carry on. "There has to be another explanation."

Jason crossed his arms. "You know what? You're right. I was the only other person alone with it, so it was probably *me* who did it! That's probably what Jack thinks."

"Of course not," said Eliza. He knew she was lying, or at least not telling the full truth. Five years stranded on the island with her had made him an expert on her tells, and her downcast gaze left no doubt.

"Jason, I'm not trying to figure out who did the damage right now. I'm just saying we shouldn't be fighting with each other, because we all know it wasn't any of us."

"I . . . I know! It's just, nothing makes sense! And you and Jack are so happy here." Jason struggled to find the words—and the courage—to ask what he really wanted to know. He uttered a few sounds, but his voice failed him. "Eliza, do you . . .?"

Eliza took Jason's hand, "What? What is it?"

Jason looked down at her hand then blurted out the question that had been rattling in his mind ever since the wedding: "Do you even want to leave?"

Eliza considered him for a moment, and then looked down at their joined hands. Her touch had released his anger with surprising speed, and he felt his shoulders relax. Without any trace of accusation in her voice, Eliza quietly said, "Are you asking if I destroyed the raft?"

"No," said Jason. "No, I know you didn't. You couldn't. And . . . and I know Jack didn't either. But it's like I said . . . you're both so happy here."

With a genuine tenderness in her voice Eliza said, "I am happy here, Jason. But it's a very selfish happiness."

"So . . . what does that mean? Which do you want—to stay or to leave?"

"It means I want to stay *and* leave."

"Fine, but if you had to pick one, if you were given the option . . . if you had to choose—"

"Jason." Understanding bloomed on Eliza's face. She must realize he wasn't talking about the raft or about leaving or staying on the island. She looked bravely at him and said, "I already did choose."

Jason slumped back. "I . . . I know . . . I know . . ."

"Jason, I'm so sorry."

"No, it's fine." Jason laughed under his breath, and it sounded hollow even to his own ears. "I should have just claimed you at graduation, before we ever boarded the damn ships."

Eliza smirked at him and said, "And how well do you think that would have worked out?"

They both laughed for a moment, relieving the tension. Jason was glad she knew he wasn't serious. If he had been, he knew his face would be sporting a red mark in the shape of her hand, and the sand would be marked with her footprints leading away.

Then Eliza turned to Jason with a serious expression and said, "We've shared so much here—you're always going to have a special place in my heart."

He didn't think he'd ever be able to say what he did next, but things had gotten so open and honest between them, he felt like, if there was ever going to be a chance for him to ask the question, now was it. "Eliza . . . if things were different. If, say, it was only you and I who'd survived . . .?"

"Don't, Jason. We can't think about 'what ifs.' If Jack hadn't survived, I mean sure, things *could* have been . . ." Eliza paused. Jason could see her mind working, choosing her words carefully. After a moment she continued, "different. But I can't say how they *would* have been. This is how they *are*." Jason began to turn away, but Eliza stepped in front of him. "What I *can* tell you is that you are a remarkable person—far better than the arrogant boy you were in school. You are going to be an amazing king."

Jason looked Eliza straight in the eyes and said, "If I'm a better person, it's only because I knew you." Eliza blinked and stepped backward. Jason reached out to catch her. "Whoa, are you all right?"

Eliza shook her head and muttered with a sort of disbelief, "You and Jack really are a lot alike."

"I know, we look like each other, but—"

"No, no," Eliza snorted, "Not that."

"Then . . .?"

"Nothing. But when we get home—"

"We?" asked Jason.

"What?"

"You said, when—*we*—get home."

"Yes, Jason. *We* are going to fix the raft. Make it better than it was before. And *we* are going to get off this island." Eliza shot him a friendly but serious look. "Are you going to be all right?"

With a smile and a sigh, Jason said, "Yeah."

Then she inquired, "And Jack . . . are you still mad at him?"

"No. I told you; I know it wasn't him. Look, I'm sorry if I was . . . if I—"

"It's okay, Jason. This whole thing was bizarre. I gave up trying to figure out who and how, and I just want to move on." When Jason looked into her eyes, he knew she meant it. "Now, I'm going to go and get Jack, and we're all going to get to work on that raft." Eliza gave him a hug and left.

Jason stood there for a moment, thinking.

She wants to leave the island.

Don't make anything out of it.

I'm not. But still . . . she's not as happy here as I thought. She wants to leave.

CHAPTER SEVENTEEN

NOTHING, IF NOT A MAN WHO LIVES BY THE RULES

Not yet ready to accept that Jack and Peter had been left behind, Frank kept searching through the soldiers to see who had made it out. But it was true: they weren't there.

Mike Church screamed in rage as he blasted the barrier of Death's Province with flames so hot they glowed white. A few paces to his right, Eli was desperately rummaging around in the dirt till he found the remains of the golden sword used to cut into the barrier. He picked it up and began humming an incantation to it. After a moment, he slashed at the doorway with it, but his efforts only created ripples of distortion on the shield.

Frank saw General Anderson emerge from the forest, take in what was happening, and approach the commander with trepidation. "Sir?"

Church turned and barked, "*What?*"

Anderson went to attention, "Sir! All the foreign forces have been sent packing, and we're tending to the wounded now. Sir."

"Good . . . good work, General. We . . . we . . ." Church looked to his father, who had just tried the sword again, but threw it to the ground when it didn't work. Church turned back to General Anderson in disappointment. "Unfortunately, we—"

Suddenly, a slash of light radiated from the barrier's entrance next to Eli, who backed away in alarm. It wasn't anything as extravagant or dazzling as when the Idolessians had broken into Death's Province earlier—no blinding light or noisy winds—just a modest gash that glowed faintly. Through it, Frank could see a herd of zombies approaching. Without warning, Jack and Peter charged through the opening, and with a zip of light, it closed on the arm of one of the undead, snipping it off like shears cutting a flower stem. As it closed, Frank thought he heard a woman's scream of fury, but with a fading echo, it was gone.

Jack stood before the mass of soldiers, almost as surprised to be there as everyone was to see him and Peter.

Peter looked up at him, smiled, and said, "Destiny."

"Mission accomplished!" exulted Commander Church.

Everyone whooped and cheered as they encircled Jack and Peter. Al Marks wormed his way through the crowd and asked Jack with a sort of desperation, "You still have it, right? The weapon, you *do* have it?"

Jack didn't want to answer; he'd had enough of this mystery. He tapped Peter's shoulder to make sure he was paying attention then turned to Church and asked, "What's the deal with Private Marks? Why does he keep behaving like he has some kind of authority in this?"

Clearly not expecting such a question, especially amid the celebrating, Mike gaped at Jack. "He . . . he doesn't. I'm sure he's just . . . concerned that everything we all just went through wasn't a complete waste of time."

Jack looked at Peter, whose face was full of suspicion. He looked up at Jack as if he wanted to tell him something, but Jack just shook his head, essentially saying *Later*.

Frank broke the moment when he threw his arms around his brother and lifted him off the ground. "Jack! Thank the gods!" He turned. "And Peter—!" Peter looked eager to receive the same treatment, but Frank just gave him a grand handshake and pats on the back. "I was so worried."

"I was worried too," said Peter. "Worried I wouldn't see you again. You're my favorite person I've ever met." He then took the initiative and gave Frank a hug.

"Wow, um, thanks, Peter. I . . ." he patted Peter's back a couple more times, then pulled away. "I think you're pretty great too." He then moved out of the way to allow others to congratulate Jack and Peter on their safe return.

Moments later, Commander Church called for everyone's attention. He explained that there would be a full debriefing once they were back at the castle, but the important thing was—gesturing at Peter, who held the sword hilt—they'd gotten what they had come for. He told them to keep celebrating and take a well-deserved rest for the night, but come morning, they'd make their way back to the base camp and then straight home.

When the soldiers scattered to enjoy their night, Jack found Frank to tell him about Al Marks and Church. Before Jack could get a word out, Church himself followed by Marks and the high-ranking officers marched up to them. With a note of panic in his voice Church asked, "Where's Peter?"

Jack shrugged, "I don't know, he was just here. Why?"

With a tone that suggested it was obvious Church hissed, "He still has the sword."

"He needs to be put under constant watch," said Marks.

General Lane offered, "Should I put together a search party?"

Frank said, "I think the question you should be asking is where's Terrie?"

"Terrie?" asked Church.

"The bear," clarified Jack.

"Oh, right," said General Anderson, and his face fell. "He was amazing. After you all entered the Province, he annihilated that hybreed who attacked you, and sent the Bionovian contingent packing all by himself."

Frank's face fell and he asked, "He wasn't looking so good when we went in. Is he okay after that kind of fight?"

"He was still breathing when I last checked him, but well, none of us knew how to care for him. He finally just fell in a heap over there just beyond that hill." Anderson pointed. "We've been trying to keep him as comfortable as we could, but . . ."

They walked over the hill and found Peter on his knees, the sword hilt lying on the ground beside him, in front of the large, hairy mound that was Terrie. As he gently stroked the bear's muzzle, without even a glance over his shoulder, Peter said in a sad, flat tone, "He's gone."

Frank walked over, knelt next to him, and said, "Peter, I . . . I'm so sorry." He tried to place a comforting hand on Peter's shoulder, but Peter batted it away.

"What do you care?" Then he sniffed and wiped away some tears.

With gentleness Frank asked, "Peter?"

"I'm fine!" he snapped. "The Kodiaks look at death differently than people. We choose to celebrate the lives of those we've lost, rather than lose ourselves in mourning over them."

"Yeah, but you aren't an animal. It's okay if you—"

"No, I'm not crying because of him. Terrie's my family. I love him and will miss him, but he's with the Creator now, and far better off than he's ever been here. These tears are," there was disappointment in his voice, "selfish. I'm just thinking of myself."

Suddenly Commander Church growled, "No!"

He looked as if he were trying to keep an invisible person from taking something away. He had his feet planted on the ground, and both hands outstretched, clutching . . . it was the sword hilt. He must have tried to snatch it up. Slowly, he began to be dragged toward Peter, until the hilt finally flew out of his hands and into Peter's. Church shouted, "How are you doing that?"

"I . . . I don't know!"

Mike's brow furrowed and he said, "Well, it's not safe for you. From now on—"

"Jack's right about you!" yelled Peter, backing away.

"What?" said Mike and Jack at the same time.

"He doesn't trust you, and neither do I." Everyone fell silent. Peter looked at them and began to yell, drawing a small audience of nearby soldiers. "Why don't you people just say what you mean? Why does everyone keep lying?"

Jack gave Frank a light jab to go help, figuring, if anyone would be able to calm Peter it would be him. But this time, it was quite the opposite. When Frank stepped forward with hands raised and said, "Hey, Peter, maybe—"

Peter shouted in his face, "And you! You're the worst of them all!"

Frank stepped back and warbled, "What?"

Peter threw his arms down. "Why won't you just say how you feel about me?"

"Peter, I . . . what?" Frank glanced around nervously at the others.

"You like me."

"Well, sure I do."

"No!" Peter stomped again. "You *like* me."

Frank's face went red, and he said, "Peter, I . . . I'm sorry, but you're upset, and seeing things that aren't—"

Peter grunted. "No, I'm not!" He stormed back over to Frank and bellowed, "I saw the way you looked at me the first time you saw me. And it hasn't gone away—you still look at me like that. But it's not just my body you like. You like . . ." Not having the words, he pointed at his heart, and tried his new vocabulary word, "Me. My soul." Frank stammered out a couple of words, but Peter was unrelenting. "Every time we see each other you're more interested in me than the time before. But you don't say anything, even though it's so obvious you want to!"

"I . . . no, I don't." Frank said, rather defensively.

Peter stomped his foot. "Yes, you do! And it's driving me crazy, because . . . because it leaves me feeling like I'm not allowed to say that I like you too!" He stomped a foot on the ground again. "Why can't I say it?!"

Frank gasped, "Huh?"

Jack heard a snort of laughter, and they all turned to see Hawk and Joss trying to contain their laughter. Hawk sniggered, "I think it's 'cause you look like one of the bears."

Joss was laughing so hard, his only contribution to the joke was mouthing, "It's the beard," between laughs as he flourished a hand around his chin.

Frank growled at them, "Not. Helping."

But Peter demanded Frank's attention. He dropped some of his anger, but none of his passion. "Isn't it obvious? I . . . I've tried to signal . . . to hint that I like you too . . . to let you know.

But then you act so . . . so . . . you don't . . ." Peter balled his hands into fists and shook them around in frustration, "Your words are so different from everything you're *saying*."

Frank tried to speak, but only managed to nervously stammer, "I . . . Peter. That's . . . that is so . . . that's wrong . . . I didn't."

"Why are you lying?" Peter waited for an answer, but he didn't get one. Frank looked around at the other soldiers who were watching the scene while Hawk and Joss just laughed more and more. "I don't understand. What's the problem?"

Frank began to speak rather boldly, "Peter, I'm sorry you got the wrong impression. I think you're great, but that kind of thing . . . that's against the law. And besides . . ." trying not to look at the others around him, he added, "I'm not like . . . *that*."

Peter grumbled, "Who are you trying to convince, Frank? Me, or them?"

"Peter, you're wrong. Now just—drop it."

"Then maybe I should just go. I filled my part of the deal!"

Commander Church warned, "Lieutenant, until we can figure out how to separate the weapon from him, he can't go."

Jack was disgusted with Church as he watched Frank's entire body sag under the weight of frustration. Deep down Jack knew what Peter had just said about his brother was true, he just hadn't allowed himself to see it until now. But after having survived Death's Province for a second time, something was turning inside him that somehow made what was happening with his brother far more important to him than any mission, or weapon, or whatever.

"Take your stupid weapon," shouted Peter, as he threw the hilt to the ground. "I don't want it! I don't want anything to do with you people anymore!"

The hilt lay on the ground. When nothing happened, Church took a few steps, leaned down and picked it up. Still, nothing happened. Everyone stared at Church with the weapon in his hand, waiting for what would happen next.

Everyone, that is, except for Frank, who'd taken the opportunity to slip away.

Jack chased after Frank. He pushed his way through the brush and found his brother in a small clearing sitting atop a boulder. He had his elbows resting on his knees, his head down, and his forehead planted in his hands.

Jack said gently, "Hey, bro. You all right?"

Frank's head sprang up. It was clear to Jack he was trying hard to look and sound as natural as he could. "Hey, Jack. Yeah, I'm good. I just . . . needed a little air. I think I . . . I think I was, um, upsetting Peter, so I thought maybe it was better if I wasn't around." He was only able to look at Jack a moment before turning away in . . . was it *shame*?

"Sure, sure." Jack sat down next to Frank on the boulder. "Poor kid, huh?"

"Yeah, I . . . I didn't realize he felt that way."

"Yeah, me neither," said Jack. "There's a lot of things I didn't realize."

Frank groaned, "Don't."

"What?"

"Just don't. I know Peter has a sort of sixth sense about . . . *stuff*. But he's wrong. I'm not . . . I'm not *that*."

"No, of course not." Jack gave Frank a gentle jab in the ribs. "He's got good taste, though."

Frank tried to laugh, but all he got out was a single, "Ha."

Jack added, "It's just . . . I was thinking, a while back . . . Eliza said—"

"She told you?"

Jack threw up his hands in defense, "No. She didn't tell me anything." Frank started to relax, but this reaction solidified Jack's suspicions. "I mean . . . she started to say something once, because, well, she thought I already knew," he felt Frank tense up again. "*Something* about you. But when she realized I didn't know, she clammed up. I never found out what she was talking about."

"Oh," said Frank. "Well, it's not . . . *that.*"

"All right," said Jack, though it seemed rather clear to him that it was. He felt oddly glad he was finding out about this now. He knew in his youth that he wouldn't have reacted as well. But now, after everything he'd been through, he was seeing life differently.

They sat in silence for a bit, just listening to the breeze. Every once in a while, the sound of Frank's labored breathing overpowered it. It would have been a nice night to sit and enjoy being outside. Looking around, no one would ever think there was any place in the world as awful as Death's Province, let alone so close.

Finally, Jack said, "You know, if it *was* true? I wouldn't care."

"Well, that's very nice. But since it isn't . . ." Frank added stubbornly, "since I'm *not*, it doesn't matter."

"I know. I'm just saying if you *were*, you'd have my support. I just want you to be happy."

Frank looked stunned. "It's not about happiness, Jack. It's about right and wrong." He shook his hands in the air and looked away again. "Which doesn't matter, because . . . I'm not."

"Okay, okay." They sat a bit more, then Jack said, "It's just," Frank sighed, "looking back . . . some of the things you've said . . ." Jack observed his brother, who still couldn't bring himself to look back for more than a glance. "If you were . . ."

"If I were, I would be an even bigger outcast than I already am."

"Frank."

"It's perverted! It's against the natural order of things. Why do you think it's illegal?"

"It's illegal because people don't know any better."

"Oh, and you do?" Frank got up and began to pace.

Jack remained seated, thinking it would show some stability. "No. I don't know. I just . . . I just know that finding someone who feels the same way about you that you do them . . . to love someone . . . If you can find that, you should take hold of it and never let go. Screw what anyone else thinks."

Frank stopped pacing, but he kicked a spot in the ground over and over, processing what Jack had said. "Yeah, but it isn't love we're talking about. It's just a warped, perverted—"

"No. It *is* love we're talking about." Jack kept looking right at Frank, even though Frank still couldn't bring himself to look back for more than a couple of seconds at a time. "Frank, I know you."

Frank muttered, "Obviously not that well."

They both gave the smallest of chuckles.

"What I mean is, I know that you aren't just . . . looking for sex." Jack looked at Frank squarely. "Or am I wrong?"

"No but—"

"You were never that kind of guy. You're a romantic. You've always been looking for love."

"Yeah, well, I won't ever find it, thanks to this . . . perversion," said Frank miserably.

"Is it a perversion? Maybe it just . . . is," reasoned Jack. "Does someone else tell you what your favorite color is? Your favorite food? We like what we like. Some guys are attracted to a woman because she has big boobs, or they like that she's a brunette, or her shape, or whatever. It's only after that first connection that we really get to know them. You happen to like something a woman can't offer." Then he said, "And Peter . . . I guess he's pretty cute—"

"Stop!" Frank put up a hand in the air, while covering his eyes with the other. "Argh! Just don't. Quit trying to make me feel better about this." He took his hand away from his face. Tears were welling up in his eyes, but he resisted letting them free. "When we first found him, I felt so repulsive. He's so young." Frank grunted, "I feel like one of those kirks who molest their acolytes."

"Sure, he's young. But seriously, there was never any question that he was of age."

"He's like—fifteen years younger than me, Jack!" Frank swatted the branch of a nearby tree and watched its leaves fall to the ground. "I should be locked up."

"You aren't being fair with yourself. Show me one of the older soldiers who doesn't look at younger girls like that."

"Yeah, well, that isn't right either."

"Maybe." Jack went quiet for a moment. Frank grunted, which suggested he felt he'd won the argument. But then Jack said, "Do you remember that family I visited on the way out of Oakmoor? Philip and Maria?"

"What about them?"

"Well, Philip is like, nineteen years older than Maria."

Frank shrugged, "Yeah, but they're—"

"What, a man and a woman? We aren't arguing gender right now, Frank. We were talking about age. And Philip and Maria are just one example. I've seen many couples who have large gaps between their ages, and I bet if you let yourself, you could too." Suddenly, Jack's eyes widened, "What am I thinking? Frank, Mom and your father had like, eleven or twelve years between them."

"Fine, Jack, you win—age doesn't matter," said Frank, though his attitude suggested Jack hadn't proven anything.

"And as for the kirks, I've always thought the reason so many of them did those things was because they took that ridiculous vow of celibacy."

Frank looked scandalized. "Jack, they're devoting themselves to something bigger than sex!"

"Don't misunderstand me: I respect them for that kind of devotion. And I think there are some people built to handle that kind of life. But mostly I've found that people need companionship, and I'm not talking just about physical stuff. When we try to contain that need, even if it's for a noble cause, it can come bubbling out through the cracks in twisted ways."

"See . . . you *do* think it's twisted."

"No. I think what those particular kirks have done is twisted. Doing those kinds of things to children, who didn't understand or have a choice in the matter—*that* is twisted. But I think if the kirks had been allowed some proper companionship to begin with, maybe they would never have preyed on those kids the way they did."

"Get to your point, Jack."

Jack paused, letting silence fill the space between them. After a few moments, he said in a calm voice, "I guess my point is, there's a difference between a person's actions and their nature." Frank looked unimpressed, so Jack took a beat to reconstruct his argument. "When a husband and wife are 'together,' it's a good thing, right?" Frank nodded. "But if a woman is raped by a man, it's bad. The 'act' is the same, but it's not the genders of the people that dictate which one is good and which is bad. So why are you letting gender dictate who you're attracted to now? I mean, are you telling me that what those kirks did would have been all right if they'd done it to young girls?"

Frank kicked the ground some more. "No, of course not. But . . . what if . . . ?"

"*What if*, what?"

"What if there isn't a good version? What . . . what if . . . what if it's . . . if it's just . . . is just . . . is . . ."

Jack pushed, "Is what, Frank?"

"Evil?" With that, the wall finally broke. Frank began to cry, and it quickly turned into outright blubbering. Jack stood up to go to his brother, but Frank pulled away, keeping his distance. "What's *wrong* with me? Why do I . . . why? What is it? Am I sick? Am I broken?" Jack would take steps toward him, but Frank stepped away, keeping him at arm's length. Trying to move further away, Frank stumbled and fell to his knees and bawled, "I don't want this!"

Now Jack could get close enough to rest a hand on his brother's shoulder. He just stood there like that for a couple of minutes, letting his brother weep. Frank took deep, struggling breaths between sobs. Once he calmed down enough to regain some control, Jack knelt down and said to him, "Frank, I don't know why you feel the way you do. But don't assume that it's wrong just because people tell you it is. People are wrong all the time."

Frank looked disgusted. "Argh! Why are you trying to talk me into it? It isn't normal, Jack. It isn't *natural*." Desperately, he added, "It could be like the vampire curse—I'm just a shell, with a monster inside pulling my strings. I could be possessed or something."

"I don't think this has anything to do with the mystical, Frank. There are ways of detecting that, and there have been enough people dealing with . . . what you are. I'm sure that if it was supernatural in nature, we'd know by now. Besides, if you were cursed or possessed, you wouldn't be struggling with this, you'd just be doing it. It seems to me it's just a part of you. And all you're doing right now is fighting who you are."

"Who I am?" spat Frank. "Jack, just because it's a part of me doesn't make it right. Would you say the same thing about a murderer—that killing is all right just because it's a part of who he is? People do all kinds of bad things, but you can't justify them as good just because they're 'part of who they are.'"

"So, who chooses what's good and bad, Frank? I've killed people. Doesn't that make me a murderer?"

"That was in war."

"To me, a kill in battle is murder to the family of the man whose life I took. Who makes the rules that one kind of killing is acceptable, while another isn't? You? Me? Some dude on the street? How about the king, or maybe the chancellor? Is it the same person deciding one kind of love is wrong while another is not?"

"I don't know who made the rules, Jack. But they're in place for a reason," stated Frank. "They're designed to protect us."

Jack was angry, mad that his brother had been led to feel this way about himself. "From what, love? If people fall in love, who does that hurt? What are we being protected from?"

Frank didn't back down. "Hey, you haven't been living with this the way I have. It's easy for you to say, 'Just do it, be happy.' But that's not the way things work. We can't always have everything we want, Jack." He paused like he didn't want to finish, but then did, "Otherwise, you'd be with Eliza."

Frank flinched lightly; he'd probably expected Jack to explode after a statement like that. But it didn't surprise Jack, considering the way he'd been acting the whole mission. Instead, Jack said calmly, "You're right, Frank. She didn't choose me, so I can't have her just because I want her. But if Eliza *had* chosen me, would it have been wrong for me to accept that love? Peter likes you, Frank. Deny it all you want, but you like him too. Who knows if it's love . . . but don't you owe it to yourself to find out if it is?"

Frank stammered, "Jack, I can't. We're not meant to . . . people are designed to be a certain way."

Jack sighed. "Frank, the only thing that makes us all the same is the fact that we're all different. Sure, we have our similarities— it's how we connect with each other. How we find our friends, and," he added pointedly, "our mates." He thought for a moment, then declared, "And . . . and I think someone who's crippled deserves to be able to walk!"

Frank asked, "What? What does that have to do with—?"

"Their legs are broken, but that doesn't mean it's wrong for them to find a way to move through the world. So, in your situation, even if things aren't how they're *supposed* to be, you need to do the same." Jack grabbed Frank's shoulder and said, "Maybe something inside of you isn't working the same way as with most people, but that doesn't make it wrong for you to . . . *find a way to move through the world.* None of us are perfect. We're all flawed and broken in our own ways. And it's not wrong to want someone to share your life with. Having that doesn't hurt anyone." Jack finished, "You're my brother. You're the only person I have left in this world, and I want nothing more than for you to have that kind of happiness. Who cares if it's not 'normal'? If you can find it, if you can find love, even if it's with another man . . . then so be it."

Frank stood up and dusted himself off, then said, "That all sounds really nice, Jack. You make a passionate argument. And maybe it would make me feel better if not for the fact that, evil or not, it's forbidden." Wiping the remains of tears from his eyes, Frank said with a hint of bitterness, "It doesn't matter what you think. It doesn't matter what I feel. No one cares."

"But if—"

"It doesn't *matter*, Jack! It's against the rules. And I am nothing if not a man who lives by the rules." Jack felt tears stinging his eyes as he sought out his brother's face, but Frank refused to meet his gaze. "Now, let's get back to the rest of the group. We've wasted too much time talking about this as it is."

Jack didn't try to argue anymore. He figured that for as long as Frank had been living with this, one heart-to-heart wasn't going to change things, no matter how much he wanted it for him. But that didn't mean he was going to give up.

They lumbered their way back through the brush. As they approached the campsite, Frank stopped.

"What is it?" asked Jack.

"Nothing. It's just . . ." Frank breathed a groan, "Hawk and Joss."

"Oh. Yeah."

"They're going to be a nightmare."

"I know it's easier said than done, Frank, but you just can't let them get to—"

They both heard it at the same time: the sounds of a fight. Without thinking, they ran back to the campsite. When they leaped onto the scene, they came across Commander Church barreling down on a cornered Peter, screaming, "What is the secret? Tell me, you insolent—!"

"I told you I don't know! It just keeps coming back to me. I'm not doing anything!" Peter shoved Church off and began throwing punches.

Commander Church refused to relent. He deflected each punch Peter threw at him, and then knocked him to the ground. Peter lifted himself up, grabbing hold of his head, blood trickling through his fingers. Church was back over him lifting a fist high in the air, a fist that suddenly lit on fire. "Maybe the only way to separate it from you is to separate *you* from *it*." He then began to bring the flaming fist down on the youth.

Frank caught the commander's arm, pulling him off Peter, "Sir, please. He's not doing anything on purpose."

Stunned from being manhandled, Church dropped his fist, and the flame went out. He glared at Frank. "Stand down, Lieutenant! This boy—!"

"This man has lived up to his part of our deal," stated Frank. "He got us into Death's Province, just like he agreed to. And then some. He lost his best friend in the ordeal."

"But he—!"

"Should be let go. That's what we agreed to. We need to follow the rules." He looked down at Peter on the ground and put out his hand to help him up. "Because I am nothing if not a man who lives by the rules."

"Yes, but the situation has changed," contended Church. And he began to reach for Peter again.

Frank pushed himself in front of Peter. "But the *deal* hasn't. I made Peter a promise, and I heard you agree to it." Frank folded his arms. "Hitting him isn't the answer to the new situation. If you want to make a new arrangement, *ask* him. Otherwise, you're going to have to go through me to get to him."

Jack stood next to his brother. "And me."

Fire burned in the commander's eyes—literally. But the Waramond brothers stood their ground. After an intense moment, Mike's eyes returned to normal. His face contorted with regret. "You're right." He looked to Peter, who was peering out from behind Frank, "Peter, please accept my apologies. The situation is . . . after having survived that place . . . I know it's no excuse, but I'm sorry. I'm so sorry." He tried to plead his case to Peter while Frank stood between them, an unmoving wall. "That artifact you have is the whole reason we're on this quest. So many men lost their lives for us to have it . . . I don't want it to all be for nothing."

Peter leaned further out. "I told you; I don't know why it keeps coming back to me."

"I understand that. Would you please stay with us a bit longer? Just until we can figure out how to . . . separate it from you."

Peter stepped out fully from behind Frank, to stand next to him. "Do you promise not to hurt me?"

The commander pledged, "I promise, no harm will come to you."

Peter stepped forward and put out his hand, and they shook. He then turned to give Frank an approving smile; but all he saw was Frank's back as he marched over to a log in front of a fire and sat down, very much alone. He positioned himself so that his back was facing where everyone else would sit.

Church announced to the crowd that had gathered, "I may be your commander, but even those of us in leadership positions need to realize when we're in the wrong. I own up to my offense, but it's time to move on. Eat something and get some sleep. It's going to be a long day tomorrow."

As everyone began to sit down around the fires, Jack saw Peter begin to make his way to Frank but stopped him. "Hey, Peter. I think we'd better leave Frank alone for a bit."

"I don't understand, Jack. Why is he like . . . ?" Peter began, but he couldn't quite finish the question.

"Come have a talk with me."

Peter glanced at Frank, but agreed, following Jack to another part of the campsite. Along the way, Jack could already hear whispers being exchanged between the soldiers. Some were about the confrontation that had just occurred, but all pretty much featured Frank in some way. It didn't even matter if it was true or not; Frank's secret was out, and once they got back to the castle, it was only a matter of time before everyone knew . . . Lieutenant Frank Waramond is gay.

CHAPTER EIGHTEEN

THE REAL WORLD

As the soldiers made their way back to the base camp, their glances and snickers made Frank's face burn. He did everything he could to ignore them, and the most effective way to do that was work. He took on all the extra responsibilities himself and made up new ones when needed. A couple of jobs he did alone, because the soldiers assigned to help him realized they had *something else to work on* at the same time. Frank knew it wasn't true, but he gladly let them go. Burying himself in his work also gave Frank a good excuse to keep his distance from Peter.

Frank had been wrestling with his attraction to men for years. The only person he'd ever admitted the truth to was Eliza, but that was only because she had figured him out. His saving grace was making a career in the army; while he might be attracted to some of the soldiers, none were about to reciprocate, so all he had to do was keep his feelings to himself. And he'd managed to do just that for years with no one the wiser.

Those thoughts flooded his mind during the two-day trek back to the base camp. There, Captain Vergo and the skeleton crew had prepared for departure by stowing all the equipment and dismantling all but one of the control rooms inside the transport ships. They simply needed to pack up the returning men's gear, close the single control room, and then they could begin the ride back to the castle. "No more marching!" cheered

Hawk and Joss together. "Time to start taking it easy," added Hawk, as they made their way around the legs of the transport vessels.

Frank ducked for cover behind another of the transport's landing legs, waiting to find out which of the ships they were going to be on—so he could avoid it. Since Peter had outed him, he'd managed to keep a distance from the two clowns . . . so far. He wasn't about to get stuck with them for the ride home. They likely had plenty of new material they were just itching to use.

"What are you doing?" asked Jack, who had come from behind him.

Startled, Frank jumped and turned to find Jack with Peter. "What? Oh. Um, nothing. I just . . . I . . ." Frank tried to think of a good motive for a grown man to be hiding.

Peter glanced in Hawk and Joss's direction, then asked, "Do the ships have names? Numbers or something?"

"Letters, actually," answered Jack. He pointed at the side of the closest hull, which had a man-sized letter *C* on it. "Why?"

Peter looked at the furthest ship, said, "Save me a spot on *D*," and headed toward Hawk and Joss. He walked right up to them and asked, "Can you two tell me which is ship *A*? Frank is supposed to be on it."

Ship *A* happened to be on the opposite end of the row. Frank and Jack chuckled as Hawk and Joss eagerly led Peter to it.

"Amazing," sighed Frank.

"Yeah, he's pretty cool."

"Don't."

The brothers found a row of three seats on ship *D*. Frank told Jack to go in first, because he preferred sitting by the aisle; it gave him room for his larger frame to stick out. Jack went in but sat by the window leaving a space between them. Frank guessed he was hoping to get him and Peter to sit next to each other.

As Frank sat, he noticed, in the far back, with a couple of soldiers guarding them, sat the Cassidy sisters. Frank had learned, due to all their help on the mission, Commander Church had offered them the opportunity to defect to Idoless, promising a fair trial and that he'd even vouch for them personally.

After a few minutes, the transport's engines began to warm up. As the door started to close, Peter sprang through it. He jostled down the aisle until he found Frank and Jack, whereupon he gazed at the empty seat between them and asked, "Hey, Jack, would you mind if I sat by the window?"

With a hint of disappointment, Jack replied, "Oh, um, sure."

Frank rolled his eyes. *How ridiculous. It's not like this is lunch period at school.* Anyway, Peter would rather sit by the window than him, which he was just fine with. Completely fine. It didn't bother him. Nope. Not at all.

Feeling let down that his plan hadn't worked Jack looked at Frank, who'd pulled his beret down over his eyes, pretending to sleep. Then he turned and looked at Peter, who was engrossed with the view outside the window. And in the silence between them, Jack was alone with his thoughts.

His original plan had been to break ways with the army as soon as they were out of Death's Province. But after everything that had happened, he felt there were too many loose ends that needed tying up before he could leave. The biggest being the discovery that their mother had been the Cardinal. He'd promised Frank they would figure it out together.

Jack's mind raced around with all the possibilities, often derailing just at the notion that his mother was actually his childhood hero. He was so wrapped up in his thoughts, the time passed quickly, and the next thing he knew, the ship was landing.

Amid the chaos of the disembarking soldiers, Commander Church intercepted the Waramonds. He wanted Peter to accompany him to meet with the king, who apparently was impatiently waiting for them on the tarmac.

For the first time in days, Peter looked to Frank the way he had before. Jack could tell Frank wasn't sure how to react. Peter's pleading look had clearly been done on instinct. But when Frank didn't do or say anything, Peter just lowered his head and followed Church obediently.

The shame on Frank's face was unmistakable, so Jack offered, "Come on, let's make sure they treat him all right."

Frank agreed, and they followed.

Along the way, they passed numerous soldiers from the castle who shook Frank's hand, welcoming him back and saying they were looking forward to getting back to their combat training. But they also passed some of the Death's Province troops, who fell silent at the sight of him.

Just then, Major Larry Smith, Frank's student with the walrus mustache and missing ear, approached. He smiled and said, "Lieutenant!" then punched him right in the face, knocking Frank to the ground.

Everyone gasped.

Jack yelled at Smith, "What's the matter with you?"

Even Smith looked shocked. He exclaimed, "Frank! Are you all right?"

"I'm fine. I'm fine," said Frank.

Smith helped Frank up. "I thought . . . oh man, Frank, I'm so sorry. I thought my chances of getting ya, wouldn't get any better than this. But I should have known better. After coming back from . . . from that place . . . I'm so sorry!"

"Don't worry about it, Larry," Frank rubbed his bruised jaw, then chuckled. "You finally got me."

"I don't think that counted."

"Look, Larry, we gotta run, but I'll see you for training this week," said Frank as they continued walking in the direction Church had taken Peter.

"This week? Are you sure you want to start so soon after just getting back?"

Frank smiled and hollered over his should, "Anything to get back to normal life."

"See you then," the major shouted back.

The brothers made their way to Commander Church and the king who was wearing his finest robes and a broad smile. When he saw Jack he beamed all the brighter, "Jack, I don't know how to thank you! The commander tells me you were a true asset to the mission. Exactly what was needed."

Church confirmed, "I'm positive we wouldn't have succeeded without him, Your Majesty."

"I'm . . . glad I could help," said Jack a little awkwardly.

As the king continued his praise, something caught Jack's eye. He glanced up to one of the castle's low balconies and saw a figure shift into the shadows of an overhang. Before he even registered that it was Eliza, he had already said, "Excuse me," and chased after her.

Jack dashed to the side of the castle, running up it till gravity took hold and leaped to catch a flagpole protruding from the side of the building. He swung off it, caught hold of the bottom of the balcony, then heaved himself over the railing. A couple of handmaidens stood in his path, the younger of the two tried to stop him, but Jack pushed past.

He ran down a short corridor, skipped around the corner, and caught up to Eliza. He ran up behind her and said, "You didn't have to spy to find out. I made it back alive."

Just then, the two handmaidens arrived. The younger of the two, a teenager with chestnut-colored skin and a mound of black hair in tight coils, stepped forward. "Princess, I'm so sorry, we tried to stop him, but he—"

"It's all right, Emily," said Eliza.

Jack looked at the handmaiden. "Emily? Not . . . not *little* Emily?"

Emily blushed, then chanced a smile and timidly said, "Hi, Jack."

He looked at Eliza with shock, and she explained, "After she and Frank rescued us from the island, I made sure she was taken care of. I owed her that much after what I did to her family."

Emily countered, "You have to stop blaming yourself, Eliz—" The other handmaiden cleared her throat, and Emily adjusted, "Princess. You had no way of knowing what would happen."

Eliza strolled over to Emily, rested a hand on her shoulder, and said to Jack, "I am her legal guardian now." She looked at Emily. "So, it's all right for you to call me Eliza." She glanced pointedly at the other handmaiden, who bowed her head in response. Eliza went on, "After we got off the island, I made sure Emily got proper schooling. Not long after you left, she graduated, moved to the castle, and has been my assistant ever since." Emily grinned bashfully at Jack, then Eliza requested, "Emily, would you and Sheila please excuse Jack and me?"

Sheila began, "But, Princess—"

With a note of irritation, Eliza said, "I know you aren't supposed to leave me alone. I promise, I'll be fine." Sheila glared untrustingly at Jack. "Or do I need to make my request an order?"

The maidens bowed to Eliza, then Emily dashed up to Jack, kissed him on the cheek, and whispered, "Thank you for saving my life." Then she and Sheila scurried away.

Eliza said, "She's been waiting a long time to tell you that."

Jack and Eliza stood there uneasily, neither sure who should speak next.

Jack felt like anything he had to say to her would just start a fight, and he didn't want to fight anymore. Except . . . "So, I've got a bit of a bone to pick with you."

"Excuse me?"

"You heard me."

He didn't say more. Being in Eliza's presence scrambled Jack's thoughts, and all he could do was look at her and think of the past until finally Eliza asked, "Well?"

"Well, what?"

"Pick away."

"Meh," agreed Oliver.

Jack glared at the cat for a moment, then said, "Why didn't you ever tell me about Frank?"

"Tell you what?"

"You know, that he's . . ." Suddenly Jack became uncomfortable. It only lasted a moment, but in that moment a multitude of thoughts hit him all at once. He didn't want to say *it* too loud. And why not? He tried to justify to himself that it was because he didn't want to out Frank any more than he already had been, but no one was around. He didn't understand; he'd been so comfortable with the idea of Frank being . . . it . . . being *gay* before. He just wanted his brother to be happy. But now that he was back in public, around people again, something was different. Jack wondered what it must have been like for Frank all these years, having to be so careful with his words and not reveal this aspect of himself, and to always feel the way Jack was feeling right now. Having to constantly lie.

That hesitation was enough for Eliza. "Wait, he *told* you?"

When she asked that, it was as if she'd dropped the princess façade and was the old Eliza he remembered. It took him a little by surprise. "Yeah. Well, sort of."

"Sort of?"

"Meh?"

"Oliver, don't help," said Jack. "Yeah, sort of."

"I don't understand." Then she gave Jack a stink eye. "Are we talking about the same thing?"

"We'd better be."

Eliza glared at Jack for a moment, considering him, then a slight smile broke on her face. "He actually *told* you?"

"No, the guy he likes did."

Eliza's eyes widened and she blurted, "WHAT?"

She composed herself as Jack shushed her. Keeping quiet, but sounding like a child on her birthday, Eliza rambled, "He likes someone? And the guy likes him back? Who is he? Is he a good guy? Is he good enough for Frank? I can't believe it happened so quickly. I mean, Frank's so stubborn. You know how stubborn he can be. I never thought, never dreamed he'd even admit . . . let alone allow himself to fall for someone, I mean—"

"So, you two are like, what, girlfriends or something?" Jack was upset. He understood why Frank had kept his feelings secret. But hearing Eliza completely in the know about them . . . it hurt.

Eliza gave him a sharp look. "He's my friend, Jack. My *best* friend."

"I know you two are close, but he's my brother. Why'd he tell you?" He sighed and admitted what really bothered him. "Why didn't he tell me?"

"I don't know, Jack. I'm sure he was just afraid he'd lose you."

"Lose me?"

Eliza spoke seriously, "Look, Jack, I have an uncle who's gay. I'm the only member of my family who even talks to him anymore. He kept it a secret most of his life, but he got to a point where he just couldn't take lying to everyone he loved. So, he told them." Eliza paused then and said, "According to my family, they can't associate with him as long as he's choosing to break the law. And that's the way it is for a lot of gay people. Because of that and other harassments, my uncle was forced to defect to Mechina where he was at least free to be himself. But not everyone has that option." Eliza gave Jack the most serious of looks, "*Of course* he was afraid to lose you."

"So, why'd he tell you?"

"Oh, he didn't tell me. I just . . ." Eliza smirked, "well, I figured him out."

"How?"

"I just caught him at a moment his guard was down. But listen, we don't have time for that." Eliza demanded, "I *need* to hear about this guy. Is he one of the soldiers? I mean, is he gay too? He must be if he told you. But how did you find out?"

Jack gave Eliza some of the finer points about Peter and how he'd gotten involved in the mission. He told her about his uncanny ability to read people and his raw bluntness. After he finished, Jack asked, "So, you're happy about this?"

"Well, not about everyone knowing—Frank must be beside himself—but if it gets him that much closer to loving himself," she thought about it, "yeah . . . I am." She looked at Jack. "I take it you aren't?"

Jack grunted, "I don't know what I am yet. I just wish I had known sooner. I feel bad for him. I just want him to be happy. I want . . ." He wasn't sure if he should say it, but he couldn't think of a better way to put it. "I want him to have . . . what we had."

Eliza's eyes widened and she even gasped, but before she could find her voice, the king rounded the corner, followed by Mike Church, Eli Warren, Captain Vergo, the royal guard, Albert Larson, Frank, and . . . Peter.

"Ah, there they are. I'd almost forgotten, you two are old friends, aren't you?" chimed the king.

Jack realized what he'd done. "Oh, yes . . . King Hawthorn, I'm so sorry."

"Think nothing of it, Jack, nothing at all," chortled the king as he patted Jack on the shoulder. "Come, it's time for supper."

Albert anxiously stepped forward and said, "But my lord, you really need to hear about our discoveries."

The king waved him away. "And those discoveries will still be around after we eat. We need to be properly nourished before doing any serious work. Princess, I trust you'll join us?"

She bowed respectfully. "Of course, Your Majesty. Though I'm not sure I know your entire party." She looked at the group before her, "I know the kirk and the commander, of course." She gave Albert and Mike a regal nod.

Mike returned the gesture and said, "Princess." But Kirk Larson was deep in thought, and only glanced at her in reply.

Eliza turned to Eli, "I'm guessing, Commander, that this is your father, the famous wizard Eli Warren?"

"My lady," said Eli, as he took her hand and kissed it suavely. Mike rolled his eyes.

Eliza looked at Vergo. "Argus."

"It's . . . Captain Vergo," muttered Argus, nodding back curtly.

Eliza smiled at Frank and said his name affectionately, then took in the sight of Peter. She couldn't contain the slightest squeal of delight, "And who is this?"

Frank looked at Jack, then at Eliza, and muttered, "Oh, for Pete's sake." Peter looked up at him and Frank whispered, "No, not you."

Commander Church asked, "Is there a problem?"

Frank stiffened. "No, sir, none at all."

"I'm Peter, Miss Princess," said Peter to Eliza, and he bowed his head like the others before him had done.

Eliza grinned. "A gentleman." She bowed back. "So, you are the man who aided this important mission? Jack was just telling me a little about you." Frank sighed. "You *must* sit next to me for the meal—I would love to hear all about you."

"I think we would all like to hear about this mysterious young man," agreed the king. "Come, come." And he led the way to the royal dining room.

A week later, in the cave, atop one of the wings of his airplane Frank wiped sweat from his brow with the back of his hand, which was the only part of his body not covered in oil and grime. He locked the last nut in place with a wrench, then grunted as he got to his feet, saying to himself, "I think that's it."

He crossed to the open hatch on top of the fuselage and climbed down the ladder inside the craft, then entered the cockpit. Next to an exposed section on the control panel sat a section covered with new buttons and controls. Frank flipped one of the switches and looked out the side windows. He heard a light humming as the engines came to life and the propellers shifted, swung forward, and then stopped. "Aw, no." The humming became sporadic, and smoke rose from the engines. Frank flipped the switch back and the propellers jerked forward, fanning out to their original state.

He threw the wrench to the floor and stomped out of the craft. Walking to the end of the dock, he crouched down and splashed some water on his face. The coolness felt good, and it made him realize just how hot he'd gotten. He lifted his head back and took in a great gulp of air. He'd already removed his outer shirt earlier, but now he pulled off his undershirt and used it to wipe the sweat off his face. Just then he heard Jack calling, "Frank, you in here?"

"Yeah, over here."

Jack found his brother and said, "Working on the plane, I see."

"Yup."

"I thought you had combat training to teach?"

Frank headed back inside, "I did. This morning."

"Oh." Jack followed.

Frank went back in the cockpit, threw his gross wet undershirt on the pilot's seat, grabbed his main shirt and put it on unbuttoned, got down on the floor, and began fiddling with some wires underneath the console.

Jack continued, "I thought you had some of those private lessons too."

"Oh. Yeah, I don't think I'll be doing those anymore."

Jack sat in the copilot's chair. "Why not? I thought you enjoyed teaching those classes."

In a nonchalant way, Frank said, "Well, it was an easy decision. All my pupils dropped their lessons."

"What?" huffed Jack. "*All* of them?"

"Don't worry about it. These things happen."

"Yeah, but . . ."

Trying to sound upbeat, Frank said, "It's all right, Jack. It's going to give me lots more time to work on the plane. I already finished setting up the plumbing for a shower, sink, and toilet this morning. Now I'm working on a little something extra I'm adding to the engines, although they're giving me some trouble." Just then, a spark flew from the dashboard. Suddenly a small fire erupted and he smacked it with a rag to smother the flame.

"But you gave lessons earlier this week. What changed?"

Frank sighed. "I don't know."

Jack wouldn't let it go. "Did they give a reason? I mean, it's not very—"

Frank slapped the rag on the ground. "Look, Jack, just drop it, all right?" Then he went back to work on the controls.

"It's just . . . It seems odd that they'd *all* have something else to do."

Sighing, Frank looked at his brother. "Think about it, Jack. We've been back six days now—long enough for word to get out about me. So of course no one wants to have 'special private lessons' anymore with Lieutenant Faggot."

Annoyed, Jack said, "You don't really think they would all—?"

"Of course they would. Half of the soldiers that quit were probably afraid of me trying something on them, while the other half was afraid what the first half would think of them if they stayed."

"I'm sorry, Frank."

"Don't be." Frank leaned back and resumed his work. "I'm fine."

Jack eyed Frank suspiciously, but he must have decided not to push anymore and switched the subject. "So . . . I've been doing some digging about Mom."

Frank hoisted himself back up and reengaged in the conversation. "You did? What'd you find out?"

Jack pulled out a piece of paper. "Well, I found her employment records, and it looks like she began working at the castle right after she had you. Which confused me, because I thought she met your father here."

"She did," said Frank. He took the page from Jack and examined it.

"But if these records are accurate, she had to know him before."

Frank looked up from the form. "Now that you mention it, Mom never talked much about her past, just Dad's. I don't know anything about her family. I guess I always just assumed she was born in the castle, the daughter of another maid or something. But if she didn't start here until after I was born . . ." He thought about it. "Where'd she come from?"

"It doesn't say anywhere in her records. But it's a good starting point. I thought maybe we could ask some of the older maids about her. It might give us a direction to look next."

"Yeah, that sounds like a good idea," Frank responded, more perky than he'd felt in a while.

"So, how about I help you finish up here, and then we head back up to the castle and start?"

"Actually," Frank flipped a switch and all the power running through the plane shut down, "I can leave it as it is."

"Are you sure?"

"Yeah, it's not like there's anything that will get ruined if I don't finish now. Let's go." He wiped his hands on a rag, but then looked himself over, "Eh, do you mind if I stop at the dorms first, so I can take a quick shower and put on some fresh clothes?"

"Not at all."

On their way back up to the castle, the Waramond brothers discussed some of what they might ask the maids, and Frank recalled what he could of their mother from his childhood, but nothing was coming to him. "Probably because of that bloody *spell*," he complained.

When they ran out of theories, the conversation shifted to small talk. Jack told Frank he'd taken Peter to see the griffins earlier that day, and how much they had taken to him. "He probably understands them better than most."

As they reached the castle grounds, Frank asked casually, "Where is he, anyway?"

"He's with Eliza. She wanted to get him some new clothes and stuff since he's staying here."

"Staying?"

"Yeah. Well, until they can get that spell figured out that's keeping the sword bound to him. Don't worry, he'll probably leave once they do."

"Don't," huffed Frank.

"Don't what?"

"I know what you're trying to start. It won't work, and I don't feel like arguing with you right now."

"I don't know what you're talking about," Jack said evasively. "I know you want him to leave, so—"

"I don't want him to leave," sighed Frank.

"So, you want him to stay?"

"No, I . . ." Frank stopped walking, and Jack turned around to look at him. "I told you I don't want to argue."

"Well, what *do* you want, Frank?"

Frank put a hand up to his forehead, covering his eyes, and moaned to himself, "You're as bad as Eliza." Frank lowered his hand and looked at his brother. "What do you want me to say, Jack? Do you want me to admit I'm lonely? Fine. I am. Do you want me to say I like Peter? Fine . . . yes, I like him. A lot. He's sweet and kind, and sincere, and amazing and . . . and . . . yeah," he muttered with embarrassment, "I think he's cute."

"And he likes you too," said Jack.

"But what good does that do me, Jack? We can't fall in love, get married, and live happily ever after. It's illegal! As much as I'd like it to happen, it never will. It's easy for you to say just do it, but I'm the one who has to deal with the consequences. So will you just stop pushing?"

Appreciating Frank's candor, Jack said, "I'm sorry, Frank. Really, bro, I don't mean to pressure you."

"Thank you," breathed Frank.

They continued their walk back to the castle and were almost there when Jack asked, "How *do* you do it?"

"Do what?"

"Well . . ." Jack hesitated, then explained, "you know, the word's out. Rumors are kind of traveling around. I had a few guys flat out ask me about you. Asked if you were . . . you know."

"Oh?"

"I didn't know what you wanted me to say, but I assumed you'd rather it was kept quiet, so I lied and told them you're straight as an arrow."

"Thanks," said Frank flatly.

"It sucked."

"What did?"

"Lying like that. Having to cover up something I don't even think is that big a deal to begin with. What's it like for you? I mean, you're surrounded by soldiers . . . I know what they're like. What do you do when they're all going on about how hot some woman is or something?"

"I don't know. Most of the time I don't really have to say anything. I just laugh with them and let their assumptions do the rest."

After a slight pause Jack said, "That's awful."

Frank shrugged.

"What about when you see someone *you* think is attractive? I mean, the other soldiers can go on and on about wanting to 'get some of that' or whatever. Even the classier guys will at least say 'wow.' What do you do?"

They were getting close to the castle entrance which made Frank begin to feel uncomfortable about the conversation topic. No one was around them at the moment, but soon someone could be. "I don't know, Jack. I try and avoid it."

"How can you avoid it? You're surrounded by men—you're bound to find some of them attractive. Do you even allow yourself to appreciate that?"

With a hushed voice, Frank answered, "I just kind of ignore everyone."

Jack looked confused.

"It's hard to explain. I mean, obviously I see everyone, but I sort of remove myself. I see and acknowledge that people are there, but I kind of mentally keep to myself."

"Huh," grunted Jack. "And I thought *I* was the one who ran away."

"Hey, now. I do what I have to, in order to stay right."

Jack just looked at him. "It isn't *right*, Frank. It isn't fair."

"No one said life was fair, and this," said Frank, opening a door, "is the hand life has dealt me."

With building passion, Jack asked, "Frank, even if what you feel *is* wrong, how does it make everything you do to cover it up right? I mean, if you shut yourself off from the world, are you even really here."

Frank's eyes darted around; they were now inside the castle, and people milled around everywhere. He pulled Jack aside and whispered, "Look—I never thought you'd know about . . . *this*. I never dreamed you'd know about it and still be cool with me."

"Frank, of course I'm—"

Frank put up a hand to stop Jack, then said, "I want you to know I really do appreciate it. But please," he looked around to make sure no one was listening, "just drop it."

"It isn't right," Jack stated again, but he said it in a way to imply it was the end of the talk . . . for now.

They reached the hall that led up to the entrance of the lieutenants' dorms, where they found a small group of people waiting for them: Eliza in a lavender and green variegated wig that matched her gown, along with Oliver on her shoulder, Emily and two other handmaidens, a couple of soldiers, and a dignitary behind. Eliza lit up at the sight of Frank, and she pranced toward him as quickly as her constricting outfit would allow, her small party trailing behind. On instinct, Eliza almost leaped into Frank's arms for a hug, but upon seeing how dirty he was, she stopped herself. "Oh my, Frank. Where have you been?"

Frank looked down at himself, having forgotten just how filthy he was from working on the plane. His shirt was still unbuttoned, his belly exposed without his undershirt. He pulled the flaps of his shirt together and held it shut. "Oh, hey, Eliza. I was just, um . . . working on something."

She snickered, "Obviously."

"Meh," agreed Oliver, who had flown up to a nearby statue and perched upon it.

Eliza's eyes flicked up at Jack for a moment, and she gave him a nod. "Hello, Jack. It's good to see you again."

Frank was surprised. That she sounded . . . well, not sincere, but less sarcastic than he'd have expected. Jack must have felt the same because he replied in an almost respectful tone, "Princess."

Eliza and Jack glared at each other a moment, but not to be detained from her purpose, Eliza broke into a grand smile and began her story, barely stopping to take a breath. "Anyway, Frank. Peter and I have been spending the day together. He told me all about himself, the bears and Terrie, and how he helped with the mission, and about you, and just all kinds of stuff."

Frank mustered, "Well, that's great. I'm glad you two had a good time. But as you see, I need to get cleaned up."

"Wait, there's more. At lunch, Peter told me about some of the combat he went through on the mission. He told me how he got in more than one scuffle, and confessed he felt some frustration with the results."

Confused Frank said, "Okaaay?"

"Well, I told him how you taught combat training classes here at the castle."

Understanding began to wash over Frank but he didn't let on. "Oh?"

"I told him how good you were. While I know he can't join one of the regular classes with the soldiers, I know you also give private lessons so I thought maybe you could make some time to help him." Eliza gave him a hopeful look.

Jack put a hand on Frank's shoulder and said, "Frank, weren't you just telling me about how you'd had some space in your schedule open up?"

Eliza's smile broadened at the news.

"Ah, um . . ." Frank shook his head then said defiantly, "Actually, the thing of it is, I've moved on to a new project." He gestured at the state of his clothes. "I'm just not sure I have any time for lessons anymore."

"Are you sure?" Frank hadn't noticed Peter being there but recognized his voice in an instant. "I'd really appreciate the help."

Frank paid closer attention to the people in Eliza's group now. The man he thought was a dignitary, was actually Peter. He'd shaved off the scruff from his face, his mop of curly hair had been trimmed, and the princess had outfitted him with new clothes that fit him properly. The pants were baggy, but intentionally so, cinched by his boots. He wore a fold over tunic with a cloth belt under a long, dark sleeveless vest with thick golden colored pattern and trim.

Taking in the sight of Peter, looking so tidy, so . . . handsome, Frank gave an involuntary gasp. Jack and Eliza's eyes met. She giggled. "Oh yes, I almost forgot, we cleaned Peter up a little. Do you think we did a good job?"

Peter stepped forward.

Frank stammered, "Yes, um, yeah, he um . . . he looks . . . good." Frank shook his head again then said, "I mean, you look . . . that is, it works for you . . . that look, I mean."

Peter blushed, "Thanks, Frank." Then he looked down and his eyes widened and his face melted in a way that said he liked what he saw, just as much as Frank liked seeing him.

That's when Frank realized he had absentmindedly let go of his shirt, which fell open exposing his ample belly. Frank snatched his shirt flaps and closed them again.

"Sooo?" purred Eliza.

"What?" asked Frank, as he snapped back to reality.

Eliza put an arm around Peter's shoulders and put her head next to his. "So, do you think you could help Peter out?"

In a daze, Frank murmured, "S-sure."

Eliza asked, "Would tonight be a good time for the first lesson?"

"Yeah, all right."

With a single clap, Eliza squealed, "Great!" then asked, "The usual room?" Frank just nodded. "I'll bring Peter there around seven."

Peter put out a hand to Frank. "It's a deal."

Frank chuckled with embarrassment but took his hand and shook it.

With that, Eliza, Peter, and the others headed down the hall. Frank stood there stunned, then asked himself more than anyone else, "What did I just do?"

"You joined the real world for once, Frank." Jack nudged his brother toward the dormitories. "Now come on, you should get cleaned up before the lesson."

Frank followed Jack distractedly for a moment, then stopped and exclaimed, "Wait. We were going to go talk with the maids about Mom."

"We have plenty of time for that. This is more important."

Frank began to move, but pouted, "I wasn't even thinking. I just looked at him and I was . . . was . . ." He stopped moving again.

Jack shoved his brother on. "You were being human." At those words, Frank stopped and looked at Jack with frustration. "Frank, you are *not* the first person to get swept away by a pretty—or handsome—face."

"I need to be stronger than that," Frank demanded.

"Fine, be stronger," said Jack, downright pushing his brother forward.

Suddenly Eliza came scuttling back, skidding to a stop, grabbing ahold of her wig to keep it from rolling off her head. With a grin still on her face, she said, "I just have to say, that was probably one of the cutest things I have ever witnessed in my entire life!" Then, just as abruptly, she scurried off before either of the brothers could respond.

Frank grumbled, "It's not funny, Jack."

"I don't know, it *was* pretty damn cute."

"Oh, shut up."

7 Years Ago

573 AR

After six months of work, the new raft rested on the beach nearly done. During that time Jack and Eliza theorized about what had happened to the original raft. Eliza clung to the idea that its destruction might have been supernatural, a way for the gods to punish them for Jack's irreverence at the wedding. Jack, after letting go of the theory that one of the pirates had survived, developed a more practical theory, which involved animals. Jason remained silent during these discussions, and Jack and Eliza both feared he secretly still held Jack responsible. After months of debating, however, they began to accept that whatever had destroyed Jason's first raft would likely remain a mystery.

All that was left on the new raft was finishing the sail. Jack and Jason had spent most of the morning scraping bark from a tree trunk that would be the mast. Their arms ached from the effort, and they both stopped to rest. The men didn't say a word; they just leaned against the nearly completed raft and gazed out at the ocean. They were hot and sweaty, welcoming the breeze that blew across the beach and cooled them.

Then Jack said, "I hope Eliza gets back with the water soon. I'm parched."

Jason nodded. "Isn't it fascinating the way the world works? Here we are thirsty, and we're staring out at millions upon millions of gallons of water—but we can't drink any of it."

"It'd actually make us thirstier," confirmed Jack.

"It's fascinating."

The two friends watched the waves rolling up on the shore, listening to the calming roar.

A few minutes went by before Jack said, "The raft is looking pretty good. You should be proud."

"*We* should be proud. It's better than the one I was building myself. I owe you and Eliza. Thanks, man."

"That's big of you to say, Jason. Thank you. And now, after all this time, it's finally almost done," said Jack. He stared out toward the ocean again, his thoughts drifting back in time. "How long has it been since we first got here anyway? Four years?"

"Four years, five months, and three weeks—give or take a day or two."

Jack muttered, "Four and a half years. Wow." Then he chuckled. "Truth be told, I stopped trying to keep count after the first two went by."

"Yes, well, you were . . . distracted," said Jason as a shadow passed over his face. "Not that I can blame you. It's been wonderful having Eliza here."

"Yeah, she's great." Jack agreed. "And I'm not just saying that because she's my wife. Just her being here has made this island more than bearable."

With significance in his voice, Jason said, "I can't think of anyone I'd rather be stranded on a deserted island with."

"She's the best," replied Jack, feeling a strange sense of déjà vu.

"Perfect, really," returned Jason. Figuring Eliza would be back soon, Jack was going to let the moment pass, but then Jason chuckled and said, "You'll have to race me to the court when we get back home to *actually* marry her."

Jack tried to laugh with him, but something about the way Jason had said that seemed almost . . . sincere. "Okay, seriously, you know she's with me, right?"

Jason chuckled, "Of course."

All traces of laughter had disappeared from Jack's voice as he said, "Seriously. You understand?"

"I said I did," answered Jason, but he seemed unable to wipe the mocking smile from his face.

"You said it . . . like you didn't mean it. I'm sorry, but I need to hear you say the words, Jason. Say you understand that she's my wife."

Jason sighed. "Look, the truth is, I don't know what she wants."

"Well, I do."

"I'm sure."

"Stop that."

"Stop what?"

"Stop talking to me like that. Like you know something about her I don't."

"Sorry, Jack." Jason placed a hand on his shoulder. "I didn't mean to get you worked up."

Jack brushed the hand away, "And now you're trying to act like I'm the one being irrational or something, when you still haven't answered me."

Jack felt Jason study him for a moment, then finally said, "She wants to leave, Jack."

"What?"

"Eliza. She's not happy here like you. She's made the most of it, but she wants to go home."

"Jason, we're all going home. Sure, I'm happy here, but I'll be happy wherever I am, as long as it's with her." With pity in his eyes, Jason looked away, which only made Jack angry. "And she feels the same way."

Jason snapped, "It's not like you two are really married."

"Jason . . . you were there. You saw it. She and I—"

"Come off it, Jack. That wasn't real, you two were just playing."

"We made do with what we had," protested Jack. "But that didn't make it any less real."

Jason huffed and looked away, muttering under his breath.

"What was that?" asked Jack.

"Nothing. Listen, just forget about it, all right?"

"I will," said Jack. "After I've heard you say it. She's *my* wife. Say it, Jason."

Jason looked back with an anger Jack had never seen on his best friend's face before. Though his heart hammered in his chest, Jack refused to let Jason intimidate him and didn't look away, only repeating, "Say it."

"Don't you give me orders!" raged Jason. "Don't forget who I am!"

A faint buzzing filled Jack's head as he responded, "I haven't forgotten. You're my best friend . . . who's never pulled rank on me before."

"I won't be spoken down to like some kind of idiot!"

"Fine, I won't speak to you like one if you stop acting like one." The buzzing grew louder, and Jack wondered if he was losing his mind, but he refused to stop until Jason acknowledged him. "So just say it, Jason. I need to know you understand."

The two stared at each other. Then, without warning, Jason cocked his fist in the air in one fluid movement and aimed for Jack's face. Jack ducked to the side, deflecting the attack. "Jason! What are you doing?"

Jack's sudden movement left Jason off balance, and he rolled to the ground. When Jason rose again, he emerged with a pistol in his hand, aimed at Jack. Jason looked at the rusted barrel, its few remaining bits of polished metal shimmering as it reflected the sun's rays, and then he dropped the weapon as if it had shocked him. He looked at Jack. Neither man knew what to say. The punch was one thing, but Jack was shocked that Jason would actually draw a weapon on him. "I . . . I just—" began Jason.

Before he could explain, Eliza burst from the jungle behind them, yelling as she dashed past, "What are you two doing? Don't you hear it?"

"Meh!" screamed Oliver, soaring past.

Both Jack and Jason were snapped out of the moment, and Jack suddenly realized the buzzing sound wasn't in his head, it was the sound of . . . "A plane. That's an airplane!" He looked up and saw a large, old army seaplane soaring overhead.

Jack and Jason darted after Eliza, who was now on the beach, firing a flare into the sky after the aircraft. Once they caught up to her, she said, "Sorry, I'd have been back sooner. I got the stuff from the cave and was almost back when I heard the plane. I dropped everything and ran back to get the flare gun."

"I'm glad you did," said Jason with remarkable calmness.

Eliza looked stunned. "I'd have thought you guys would be more excited. You especially, Jason. I figured you would be running to the cave to get the flare gun yourself. But you both were just standing there like a couple of statues. What were you doing?"

"Nothing," answered Jack.

The plane circled back, clearly in response to the flare.

"They saw it," cried Eliza, "they saw it!"

The plane swooped down, positioning its pontoons for an ocean landing. Once down, it approached the shore, and then came to a stop in the distance.

"That is one old aircraft," said Jack. "When was the last time the army used prop planes?"

Jason continued to gawk at the vessel floating on the water. "They use them, just not for anything important. Once Mechina started trading with us and we got some real technology, they stopped producing that style of plane."

The trio stared intently at the plane. It was too far away for them to see inside the cabin clearly, but there was definite movement within it.

"I wonder who it could be," said Eliza.

Without thought, Jack replied, "It's Frank."

Jason and Eliza spun around to look at him. Jason asked, "What are the chances your brother would just happen to be out here?"

Jack smiled. "This didn't happen by chance. Frank would never give up trying to find me."

At that moment, one of the side doors on the fuselage opened, and a girl with dark skin popped her head out.

Both Jason and Eliza turned to Jack, eyebrows raised. "It's Frank, huh?" asked Eliza with a smirk.

Jack shrugged.

The girl tossed out a small object that burst to life as it hit the water, taking the form of a lifeboat. The girl turned inside the plane for a moment then jumped into the raft. She held a rope fastened to the plane in one hand and an oar in the other. Someone in the plane tossed a second oar to her, and she began to chop into the water, heading toward shore.

"What's a girl that age doing way out here?" murmured Jack.

It took her some time, but when the girl was close enough, in youthful excitement, she couldn't help but begin to wave at the trio. Mindlessly, they waved back. Oliver, perched on Eliza's shoulder, yawned.

Once the girl neared shore, Eliza recognized her. "Emily!" Emily couldn't answer; she just ran up and gave Eliza a hug. Eliza began to laugh and cry, then laughed some more as she held the young girl.

"Who's Emily?" Jason asked.

Jack explained, "She and her family were on the ship with us the night we were attacked. I helped get her to safety before . . . well, before everything went bad, and we were separated. Apparently, she survived."

Emily pulled away from her embrace with Eliza and regained her voice, "There were seven of us who survived. The morning after the attacks, the army showed up and rescued us all."

Eliza asked, "But how did you manage . . . ? I mean, the plane!"

Emily looked at Jack. "Your brother, Frank. Anytime he got leave from the army, he'd borrow the plane and we'd go looking for you."

Jack and the others looked back at the plane floating out on the surface of the water, and in the doorway stood the unmistakable frame of Frank Waramond. He gave a great wave when he saw them look in his direction. Even from the distance, Jack could see Frank's smile through his thick beard.

"Are there anymore survivors? Is anyone else here?" asked Emily.

"No, it's just us," responded Jason.

Emily stared at him with a funny look on her face. After a moment, it hit her: "You're Prince Hawthorn!" She bowed. "The king will be so pleased! He mourned for so long."

Trying not to sound surprised, Jason asked, "He, he did?"

"Oh, yes. Everyone was surprised by how hastily he announced your passing," explained Emily, "even before the first round of search parties came back. Everyone assumed it was because he was in shock and so upset by your death. But you're alive!"

Jason grabbed the lifeboat to position it to go back to the plane and said, "Well, what are we waiting for? Let's go!"

Jason and Eliza joined Emily in heading for the lifeboat. But Jack stood rooted to the ground, looking back at the island. He looked up the shoreline and at the raft they'd been working on for the last few months. Oliver flew overhead, trying to catch up with Eliza, and Jack thought of the day they'd found him . . . their first kiss. He looked at the jungle where it had happened, and then up at the mountain that poked up through the trees. From where he stood, he could just make out the place they'd had their wedding ceremony.

Jack looked down at his tattoos. He couldn't help but feel like they were leaving their home.

Realizing that Jack had not joined them, his friends walked back up the beach to make sure he was okay. "Is there something you need?" Emily asked.

Jason was in no mood to wait and said, "There's nothing back there we can't replace back home."

It was true; there was nothing back there that they needed. But what he wanted was to remember the island exactly as it appeared right at this moment.

Jack and Eliza looked at each other. He sighed and couldn't think of anything else to say except, "I love you."

"I love you too," smiled Eliza.

He smiled back and said, "All right, then let's . . . let's go home!"

Chapter Nineteen

A Cardinal Reveal

It was nearly seven o'clock. Frank paced around the workout room. He made a mental note to stop by the maintenance room after the lesson, because a couple of the lights had burned out, creating a dark spot at the room's far end. The butterflies in his stomach wouldn't stop. "I'm just teaching a lesson," he told himself as he continued to pace.

The chamber had large mirrors along one wall, and he found himself checking his hair, which he'd combed a part into. He stopped himself, practically slapping his own hand away. "I've done this hundreds of times for countless others." Then he mumbled, "Why am I talking to myself?"

Just then he heard a knock at the door, and he muttered, "I think I'm going to throw up." Then, as naturally as he could—though his voice cracked a little—he called, "Come in."

Eliza strode into the room with Peter and her usual cluster of handmaidens trailing behind. She smiled at the sight of Frank. "Here we are. Peter, it's been a pleasure spending time with you today."

"Thank you, Princess. Thank you for everything," said Peter. "The new clothes and the haircut are great."

"Think nothing of it. You're always welcome to come and see me for anything. If you need help with something, or just need to talk, my door is open to you."

"Thank you, milady," said Peter with a respectful bow.

Eliza nodded back politely, then said, "Have fun, and I hope you learn a lot." Eliza waved to Frank and mouthed the words *See you*. The flock of maidens stood by the doorway waiting for her, and a couple of them were looking on the scene with a sort of disapproval. Eliza saw their sour faces and asked sternly, "Is there a problem?"

"No, my lady," they both said, looking to the floor.

It seemed clear to Frank that news about him had reached ears beyond the soldiers. Speaking in an unnaturally loud voice so all could hear, he nervously offered, "Um, Princess, if you'd like, you could . . . er, stay and watch. It's not like this is anything but a lesson." He gave a weak chuckle.

Eliza grinned. "Sorry, Frank. It's just the two of you."

Frank stammered, "If it's because it's so dark in here, it's only a couple of lights out. I could run and get—"

"It's not that, Frank. It's because I wish to attend the hearing of those sisters who came back with you from the mission." She continued to usher the group through the door.

Frank reasoned, "Oh . . . oh, shouldn't Peter and I be there? They may need our testimonies."

"I spoke with the commander earlier, and he assured me his statement would be all they require. But if it turns out that you're needed," Eliza said, "I'll let them know where you are."

As Eliza shooed the last couple of handmaidens out the door, Frank tried one last time: "Ah, say, speaking of the commander . . . shouldn't Peter's guards be here? To protect the weapon and all."

Eliza turned back. "Oh, the guards are just outside the door here. I figured you two don't need them distracting you. Bye!"

Frank watched the door close, then turned around to face Peter and awkwardly said, "Well."

Peter said, "You don't need to worry so much."

"W-what do you mean?"

"You're so nervous. I'm not . . ." Peter sighed. "Jack and Eliza explained how things are. What the laws are. How *you* are."

"Oh?" grunted Frank, annoyed and curious about exactly *how he was* according to Jack and Eliza.

"This is just a lesson," Peter clarified. "That's all I'm expecting."

With that, Frank drew upon the years of experience he had containing his feelings. He'd grown adept at visualizing a container and putting everything he wanted to hide within it. Then placing that container, sealed and in the furthest reaches of his chest, where it was easiest to maintain and control. He did that now, took a deep breath, and said, "All right, then. Let's begin."

Peter took off the long sleeveless robe of the outfit Eliza had gotten him, so he'd have an easier time moving around. He folded it and set it down in the corner of the room, placing the sword hilt on top of it. He joked, "I hope it stays there."

Frank began the lesson by asking Peter why he wanted training, and what he was hoping to get from it.

Peter answered, "I want to be able to defend myself and the ones I love." He went on to list all his defeats on the mission. Commander Church beat me down quickly. I couldn't fight that jerk . . . what was his name—Seth? Even you, that first night we met, you had me on the ground before I even knew you were there. I mean, every time," Peter moaned with frustration, "every single time, I fought someone, they defeated me without any effort."

"Not so," Frank said. "That first day, remember the commotion you caused? An entire platoon of soldiers had a hard time holding you down." Peter shrugged in reply. "And when we were in Death's Province, you knew I had to watch out for you, so you stayed close but never got in my way."

Not impressed, Peter said, "Yeah, but that isn't fighting."

"It's part of it," said Frank. Peter crinkled his nose with doubt. "No, really. Becoming a skilled fighter begins with understanding who you are—your strengths and your weaknesses. Those times you were defeated . . . well, first of all, you were fighting people who've had a lot more combat experience than you. The proper course of action would have been to retreat."

"But what if I *can't* run? When that Seth guy had Terrie . . ." Pain filled his voice when he mentioned Terrie's name, "I couldn't run."

"We're getting to that. So, those times you fought—what if you had utilized some of what you did when you did run?" inquired Frank.

Peter's nose crinkled again. He started to say something, then stopped to think about it. He mulled it over for a moment, and finally said, "Huh?"

Frank chuckled. "I've noticed something about you. When you follow your instincts, you're actually naturally skilled. But when you *try* to fight—that's when you have problems." Frank stepped back and drew his broadsword and swung it around once, as if he were blocking an attack, then followed through with a slash toward an imaginary opponent. He turned to Peter and asked, "Did you see what I just did?" Peter nodded. "Okay, now you try it." Frank handed him the weapon.

Peter was muscular, but Frank's sword towered over him, and his arms sagged under its weight. He examined the weapon, noting its unusual pommel, and asked, "What's this?"

"In the army, when you get your license as a trainer, you're given a pinecone patch to signify it." Frank leaned a shoulder at

Peter, showing him the pinecone design that looked a lot like the end of his sword. "And as a reward, we get to choose an item with the trainer's pinecone on it. I chose this sword. I wouldn't have been able to afford it otherwise, and it . . . well, that's part of what I want to show you. Go on and try what I did."

When he tried to swing the sword around, Peter couldn't control it with as much precision as Frank had; the weapon was just too big for him. As soon as he finished, Peter knew it was a poor imitation. With a determination to get it right, he began to try again.

Frank stopped him. "Wait. Wait. Here—try this." He retrieved a different kind of sword that he'd brought along. It was the kind that Jack and most of the other soldiers carried. The blade was much shorter, with a slight curve. The guard and grip were a bit more modest as well. They traded weapons. Peter swung the new sword with ease and comfort. He smiled at Frank, who grinned back. "Easier, right?"

"Yeah."

"It's great to know different moves, but you need to know how to apply them to the person you are and utilize your strengths. This sword," Frank held up his pinecone broadsword, "it's more suited to me than you. You're much lighter and faster than most." Peter swung the sword around again and added a little jump to make the slash attack. "Very good. Like I said, you're a natural. I'd even venture to say you'd excel with a different kind of weapon altogether. Anyway, *now* let's talk about fighting forms."

"Forms?"

"Yup. There are many different forms of martial arts fighting, and within each form there are a variety of subforms. I'm going to start by teaching you the basic one taught in

Idoless's academy. It's a good basic form that works for most. As you progress, I'll show you others."

"Progress? I get more than this one lesson?"

"Oh, um . . . well, yeah. I mean, one lesson won't teach you much." Frank could tell that even though Peter had promised him this was nothing more than a class, he was still excited about getting to spend more time together.

Frank wrestled with himself.

For most of the mission, he figured Peter had connected with him solely because he'd been kind to him. But now that Frank knew there was more to it, it left him with a new feeling. A feeling he didn't know how to put inside the container in his chest.

"Anyway," Frank continued, "the different forms can be mixed, of course." Peter had actually said he was attracted to Frank. And it seemed to be true; no one had ever looked at him the way Peter did. "But as you use them . . ." In the mirrors he saw his sizable frame, dwarfing Peter's thin, fit body and felt embarrassed. ". . . make sure you keep in mind not to let the form dictate what you do. It's *you* who dictate the . . . why do you like me?" Peter looked stunned. It was a question birthed from this new uncontained feeling. And because it wasn't properly contained, it found a way out. Frank immediately tried to reverse course. "I . . . I'm sorry. I shouldn't have . . . I didn't mean to—"

"Why wouldn't I? You're kind, and brave, and talented, and you, you look . . ." Peter struggled to find words, but he gestured at Frank's body; the body only moments ago he was feeling embarrassed about. Finally, Peter finished, "You're the manliest, most sexy person I've ever met. You're amazing."

"But . . .? No, I'm sorry, it was inappropriate of me to ask. I've just never had anyone . . . no one has ever . . . anyway, let's continue."

"But Frank—"

"No, I'm sorry." Frank unlocked the container and slipped the new feeling in. "That was my fault. It won't happen again. This is *just* a lesson." Then proceeded to show Peter the beginning fighting stance.

If Frank hadn't been so distracted, he might have noticed that someone else was in the room with them. Someone who'd broken the far set of lights earlier, so he could hide in the darkness of the rafters. Someone dressed all in red, who was now making his way through the shadows to the sword hilt Peter had set down.

Meanwhile, in another part of the castle, a guard ushered Eliza to a seat at Sarah and Sophie's trial, which had already begun. Commander Church was laying out how the team had encountered the sisters and questioned them about their task as it was given to them by Lithostone.

Sarah did most of the talking, with her usual perky charm. She was very vocal about how they'd been sent *because* they were women. "They figured Idoless's prejudice against women would help us sneak past your defenses." She then giggled, "Believe me, we didn't count on getting found out so quickly."

Jeers and hisses from the crowd demonstrated their disapproval while Eliza felt a twinge of jealousy for the Cassidys. For women to be sent on such a dangerous mission and respected as warriors was unheard of in Idoless.

The commander spoke openly about what the women were guilty of, but everything they'd done for the team also peppered his narrative. He closed by citing himself as an eyewitness, signifying his credentials, and making a personal plea to the king who was mediating the hearing himself. "Your Majesty, these women saved the mission numerous times," said Church. "I'm certain that if they hadn't been there, I wouldn't be standing before you now. They deserve a second chance and are interested in finding that chance here in Idoless. We now leave the decision in your gracious hands."

King Hawthorn had remained silent throughout the testimonies, listening to what Mike and the Cassidys had to say. Now he just stared at the two women. His eyes flickered back and forth between them and occasionally to the commander, who stood bold and confident of the case he'd made. Finally, the king said to the women, "Within these very proceedings, it was brought up that women aren't allowed in Idoless's army. It's against the law for women to do any fighting at all. Do you two understand that?"

Sophie nodded while Sarah tilted her head and said, "Sure, whatever."

King Hawthorn chuckled to himself. "Charming." Then he spoke to the room as a whole. "You have all heard the case Commander Church has made. I wish to know, does anyone have anything else, positive or negative, to say about these defendants before I make my decision?"

Though Eliza knew some of the people in the room disagreed with the case Church had made, no one dared to challenge it. The room remained silent for several minutes. "Very well. Then as the king of Idoless, I declare you both cleared of all charges." He then instructed the sisters, "As defectors, you aren't free to go yet. There are other procedures you must go through." He smiled, "But that's mostly formality and busywork. I welcome you to Idoless as its newest citizens."

The Cassidy sisters hugged each other, happy with the outcome. They were the first defectors to Idoless in some time. In the past, people had come for the freedom of worship it offered; it was the only nation of the five that gave the option of worshipping the god of one's choice, or even none at all. But still, no one had defected there in a while, let alone women. So, for that, the Cassidys received some applause.

Eliza strode up to the sisters to personally congratulate and welcome them, offering to help them with the transition to a new home. When she saw Sophie properly, she could tell what had happened to her: a spell gone wrong. "Oh, you poor thing. You were impatient, weren't you?"

In shock, Sophie answered in a whisper, "Y-yes."

Sarah grew more serious than usual. "How did you know?"

Eliza put a finger to her lips to imply they shouldn't say too much with so many people around. In a conversational tone, she said, "I can't make any promises about the results, but I promise to do what I can to help you fix it."

Sophie moaned, "You can't fix it. We've tried everything." She dared a glance at her sister, but Sarah looked away, telling Eliza she was more than just familiar with what had happened to Sophie . . . she was involved.

Just then, several soldiers arrived to take the sisters away to begin the process of becoming Idoless citizens. Eliza told them, "We'll talk." Then she watched the Cassidys as the soldiers escorted them from the chamber. They kept glancing back at Eliza until the door they were taken through shut.

"Jealous?" came the voice of Jack from behind.

Eliza spun around, "What?"

"Are you jealous of where they came from?"

Of course she was. "Of course not," she replied.

"Riiiigggghhhht," said Jack, not bothering to tone down his sarcasm. "The only nation ruled by a queen, where women can join the armed forces, are free to fight if they want, and have an equal voice with men . . . if not greater."

"Yes, women have more freedom in Lithostone in some ways than they do here, but there are other freedoms lost in return. Frankly, I'd rather be thankful for what I have than mourn what I don't," said Eliza. "And besides, no one ever said Idoless can't change."

"Always the revolutionary," chuckled Jack.

Eliza's eyes narrowed and she thrust a finger in his chest, pushing him backwards. "Listen, buster, as we've just covered, a woman's opinion doesn't count for much in Idoless. But I am in a unique position here. The only woman in this nation who *does* have any kind of say is the queen. She can make changes. Good, positive changes. So in time, I'll be able to—"

"So that's it? That's why you left me? For power?" asked Jack.

Between gritted teeth, she responded, "You assume too much."

Jack remained cool. "Hey, sweetheart, I haven't assumed anything. I was there that night, remember?"

Her voice remained steady, but tears began to roll down Eliza's face. "Oh, I remember. I remember you leaving."

Just then, Eliza realized just how *not* alone they were. Their argument was gaining the attention of people still trickling out of the chamber as Emily and the other handmaidens were watching with alarm. Jack glared back at them all, and said, "Don't judge what you don't understand."

Eliza sniffed, "That's rich coming from you."

"What's that supposed to mean?" asked Jack. "My wife married my best friend. What was I supposed to do? Stay and be the godfather of your children?"

The comment stung. She tried to defend herself. "It's not . . . it wasn't like that, Jack."

"So explain it to me. What was it like?"

Eliza finally broke, "I thought you were dead!" She exhaled, "Dammit, Jack!" and spun around so he wouldn't see her cry.

Jack looked to the ceiling, cursed himself, and mumbled, "This isn't going to work." Speaking louder he said, "This . . . us. Being here, together like this, it's not going to work." He sighed. "Look, I wasn't even going to come back after the mission, but I did because of some stuff with Frank. But the more that I think about it, that stuff . . . it's all in the past. And digging up the past isn't always a good thing." Jack paused, then said, "Tomorrow, I'll head back to Oakmoor Cove."

At those words, Eliza's tears stopped, and she looked back at him. "I just need to know one thing . . . I need to understand." She regained her composure, but even so, she had to focus herself to ask the question. She took a large breath through her nose and let it escape through her mouth, then said, "I get why you left. You loved me. You loved me so much, and after everything that happened . . . that night . . . your state of mind . . . What I said was too much, so you left. But . . ." Eliza looked in Jack's eyes, "If you loved me *that much*, why did you keep accepting those missions?"

"Eliza, I didn't have a choice."

"I get it. You had a tremendous sense of duty—it's one of the things that makes you who you are. But it doesn't make sense. If you loved me so much that the thought of losing me would make you give it all up, why would you keep taking all those missions to begin with?"

"What? No. You don't understand. Eliza, when you're a soldier, you don't have a choice. You can't refuse orders." She forced her face to remain blank, intentionally making Jack justify himself further. He explained, "When you enlist in the army, you stay until your time is up or you lose your pension. Then you either retire or sign up for another call. But I didn't retire early, I deserted in the middle of my call. Technically I should have been arrested and court martialed. You can thank King Hawthorn that I wasn't."

Eliza stammered, "No, you . . . Then why . . .?"

Jack explained, "I was sick of it. Getting sent out on mission after mission, without any rest, never getting to see you. I was this close to pulling out early and losing my pension just to be with you. But then I was sent to Death's Province, by Jason. That's how I realized." He looked at Eliza squarely. "Jason was trying to get me k—"

Suddenly alarms blazed.

Frank had begun to relax, falling into his usual comfort zone as a trainer. If he were honest, though, this class was still different. He was teaching and Peter was learning, but they were having fun. He'd never laughed so much in any of his other classes.

They'd just begun to move on to basic defensive moves and blocks when the sword hilt flew across the room into Peter's hands. "What the—?" said Peter as it slapped into his palm.

Frank and Peter turned to where the hilt had come from, only to see the Cardinal chasing after it, already nearly upon them. Frank shoved Peter away and stepped forward, throwing a punch. The Cardinal wasn't interested in him though; he hurtled over Frank, going after Peter.

Frank reached back, caught the outlaw's cape, and gave a jerk. The thief fell to the ground, but swiftly jumped back to his feet. Frank looked him over, trying to remember how his mother was dressed back in Bob's cave. This outfit was similar, but different. This guy didn't have the double-breasted jacket, and he wore a hood like the Cardinal Jack had fought, but no helmet—and it looked like it was a man. But his mother had padded herself to hide her gender as the Cardinal, so he couldn't help but wonder . . . "Mom?"

The Cardinal tilted his head like a dog not understanding something, but then he unleashed on Frank, throwing kick after punch after kick. Frank ducked and dodged the assaults, but he held back, afraid his opponent might be his mother.

Peter called, "Frank, it's not your mother. It's—no!"

It wasn't normal for Frank to get distracted in a fight, but when Peter spoke, Frank looked at him—and the Cardinal took the opening, spin-kicking him right in the stomach. Frank felt all the air leave his body, and as he gasped to get it back the Cardinal made another attack. This time he struck Frank in the face, sending him backward into the mirrored wall, which cracked in a spiderweb pattern. Frank hit the ground with a thud, as small pieces of the mirror fell around him.

The last thing he heard before blacking out was Peter shouting with concern, "Frank!"

Peter began to run, but in a crimson blur the Cardinal was upon him. The bandit kicked Peter, launching the hilt into the air. The thief darted after to catch it, but the hilt turned in midair and sailed back to Peter, who was on the ground recovering. The Cardinal stood stunned for the briefest of moments, but dashed back at Peter, kicking the hilt from his hand. They watched it soar across the floor of the room, but this time the Cardinal didn't chase after; he just stood and waited.

The hilt turned and skipped across the floor back to Peter, but the Cardinal intercepted it. He looked as if he were playing a game of tug-of-war using an invisible rope against an equally unseeable opponent. Finally, he let go, letting the hilt return to Peter, who caught it on purpose for the first time. With forced bravery, he yelled, "You can't have it! Not while I'm alive!"

At those words, the Cardinal reached under his cape behind his back and drew two short swords with serrated blades. He charged Peter with a sort of bloodlust, swinging the swords in the air and dropped them down on Peter, but they stopped with a *clang* that shook the room.

Peter had instinctively used the hilt to block the blow, and when he did the mystical blade had appeared, stopping the Cardinal's swords effortlessly.

The Cardinal pulled away to regroup.

Moments later, Peter looked down at the hilt and realized the blade had vanished again. He tried to hide his shock by assuming a posture like the one Frank had been showing him, holding the hilt at the ready, pretending he had complete control over the weapon.

The Cardinal's head tilted ever so slightly, analyzing Peter. He sheathed one of his swords and began to stalk toward the young man.

Peter tried to sound threatening, but the fear in his voice was evident. "S-s-s-stay back. I-I'm warning you!" The Cardinal prowled closer. "I said, stay back!" But his threats meant nothing to the cloaked figure. He kicked Peter, knocking him on his back. From the ground, Peter began to lift the hilt, hoping the sword would work again; but the Cardinal stepped on the arm that was holding the weapon. Peter winced in pain. The Cardinal raised his weapon and began to drop it down on Peter, when Frank's broadsword deflected the blow with another *clang*!

A small trail of blood rolled down his forehead, but Frank looked all right otherwise. He grumbled, "You didn't really think this wasn't going to happen, did you?" Frank raised his sword, flinging the Cardinal's blade away from Peter as he stepped protectively between them, ready for combat. "Let's go, then."

The Cardinal lunged forward, slashing repeatedly. Frank deflected each attack but marveled at the Cardinal's skill. His movements suggested he was young and spry, but he had the prowess of someone who'd been fighting for years.

They crossed blades a few more times, when Frank finally knocked the sword out of the Cardinal's hand. Both of them breathing heavily from the combat, Frank and the scarlet bandit glared at one another. Frank asked, "Who *are* you?"

The Cardinal didn't answer. With his free hand, he reached under his cape and brought out two small pellets. Moments after he threw them, they exploded into clouds of thick smoke, filling most of the room.

Peter shouted in fear, "Frank?"

Frank reached over, grabbing his shoulder, and said, "Stay close. We're going that way." He pointed toward the door, and after walking blindly for a moment they passed through the smoke and could see again. The door to the room was open—

and just outside of it were the bodies of Peter's guards, bloodied and dead. Frank told Peter, "Stay here," then dashed out the door in time to see a red cape whipping around a corner at the end of the hall. Frank slammed a button on the wall and rushed after, as lights flashed, and alarms began to sound.

Though he wasn't gaining on him, Frank always kept the Cardinal within his sight. The longer they ran, the more soldiers joined the chase. As they closed in on the Cardinal, Jack joined the chase. "What's going on?"

"Cardinal."

"Mom?"

"I hope not." Frank glanced to his brother, but Jack was gone.

Frank knew they had the Cardinal when he was forced to turn down a dead end. When he and the other soldiers rounded the corner, it was to find a heap of red on the ground lying before Jack, who was dusting off his hands.

Frank was dumbfounded. "Where'd you go?"

"Huh?" asked Jack. "Oh. I, um, took a short cut."

"How'd you—?"

"I just figured he'd head this way."

"Down a dead-end hall?"

Jack's eyes darted around, and he just said, "Um, yeah."

Frank was stunned but shook it off. He marched over to the Cardinal and detached the bandit's belt. As he did, a couple of the other soldiers sniggered. "I'm disarming him," he snapped, then growled, "Grow up." The Cardinal's second sword fell out as Frank pulled off the belt full of smoke pellets and other weapons. He kicked the serrated sword away and handed the belt to one of the corporals.

Frank checked for other hidden weapons, but only found an odd-looking bracelet. It was covered in intricate details and had a clear stone imbedded in it. It didn't seem like a decorative piece of jewelry, which is why he stopped trying to remove it when the Cardinal, still reeling from Jack's knockout blow, muttered, "N . . . no, please . . . Will die without . . ."

"All right, but if it turns out to be dangerous, or some kind of device to help you escape, you'll wish I *did* kill you. Now let's see who you really are." He tugged off the hood and mask. "Marks! Private Al Marks!" Frank shook his head, "I don't understand. You're the Cardinal? Why?"

Marks had regained his senses, but he didn't respond. Frank shook him. "Answer me!"

Marks just grinned.

"Maybe we should ask the commander," said Jack. "I'm telling you Frank, they're up to something together. Marks and Church both, and who knows who else?"

"That's enough," demanded Frank.

"Yeah, Jack, that's enough," echoed Marks mockingly.

Jack glared at Al. "I don't know what you think you're up to, but—"

"You're right, you don't know anything!" spat Al, then said to Frank, "Can we go now? This conversation is boring me."

Frank handed Marks off to the other soldiers, ordering him to be locked up. Jack wanted to see him all the way into a cell, to make sure Al didn't try anything. Frank agreed, and told Jack he would join them, but needed to check on Peter first.

Frank returned to the workout room. Two new guards stood outside the door while other soldiers were clearing the scene. He asked them, "Where's Peter?"

"Inside, sir."

Frank went in, and at the sight of him Peter lit up. "Frank! I was so worried." Peter ran to him but stopped short. It was obvious he'd intended to hug Frank, but restrained himself, likely to respect Frank's feelings. Still, Peter was so bothered by the whole ordeal he had to grab ahold of his own arms, settling to hug himself.

"I'm all right, Peter, don't worry. We caught the guy." Frank tried to give Peter a little comfort by patting his shoulder. That's when he realized Peter was trembling. He spoke as soothingly as he could. "Hey, it's all right, Peter. It's gonna be all right."

"I-I'm sorry. I was j-just really nervous. I-I know i-it's selfish, b-but I don't think I, I could handle it if . . . if you were killed too."

Too? Thought Frank. Then he realized . . . *Terrie.*

A soldier called in the room, "Lieutenant Waramond, the commander wants to see you at the holding cells right away."

Frank jumped. "Right. Please inform him I'm on my way."

"Yes, sir."

"I gotta go, Peter. I'm sorry your lesson got ruined. Can I give you a raincheck?"

Peter crinkled his nose, "The rain checks what?"

Frank chuckled. "No, a 'raincheck.' It just means we'll make it up later."

Peter released a hand from holding himself and stretched it out to Frank. "It's a deal."

Frank chuckled again, "Deal," and shook Peter's hand. Peter was visibly shaken up, but now Frank could feel he was downright trembling.

Frank wanted to fix everything. This remarkable young man had been torn away from all he knew, lost the closest thing he had to a family, and was shoved into this world that he clearly wasn't comfortable in. And he was certain that everything Peter had given up and gone through was for him.

His instincts told him something that could help comfort Peter, but he wasn't sure if it was appropriate. There was no time to think about it, though; the commander was waiting for him, so he had to either do it or not. So, he focused himself, checked the container in his chest, and wrapped his arms around Peter.

Frank thought, *I've hugged Jack countless times; this is exactly the same.* He felt Peter's body tense, clearly trying to control his emotions. He gave Peter a few pats on the back, showing it was over (like men do when they hug) but Peter just held on, his head pressed to Frank's chest. He heard a sniffle and felt Peter's body convulse; he'd begun to cry. Gently, Frank said, "Hey. Hey, it's okay." The next thing Frank knew, he wasn't patting Peter on the back; he was just holding him.

"I'm s-s-sorry," blubbered Peter.

"It's okay. Everything's going to be okay." After Frank said that Peter ever so gradually melted into his arms, becoming something far different than any hug he'd ever shared with Jack. The thing was, it didn't seem . . .

Is this wrong? It's just a hug. If it isn't wrong, at what point does it become wrong? And if it is wrong . . . why?

They pulled apart and looked at each other. Peter's eyes were red and swollen from crying. He reached up and scratched Frank's thick beard and said, "Thanks, Frank."

Frank tilted his head, leaning into Peter's hand. He thought how nice it felt . . . too nice! Frank pulled away, "N . . . no problem. I . . . um, I need to get going. I'll see ya later. The guards will take you to your quarters."

Frank went out the door and dared a glance back at Peter, who waved good-bye.

As Frank strode down the crowded castle hallways, he could feel the container in his chest crack. He felt like everyone could see it—the container and what was inside. He felt like it was written on his face, and he was scrambling to find a way to hide it.

He was nearly to the holding cells when he had to stop. He ducked into a hidden alcove and stood there for a moment, thinking how he didn't have time for this, the commander was waiting for him. But he just couldn't bring himself to move.

His breathing had become labored, and all he could think was, *Why can't I just be normal?* A few tears fell from his eyes and Frank whimpered to himself, "Why?"

And with that, the container shattered.

It lasted a minute.

For the first thirty seconds, he allowed himself to weep. He was on the edge of blubbering, yet he had to be careful not to draw attention to his hiding place.

In the thirty seconds after, he straightened up, wiped the tears from his eyes and face, forced himself back out into the hall—and began to create a new, stronger container.

CHAPTER TWENTY
A Traitor Among Us

Since the day Jack had agreed to leave Oakmoor Cove and come back to the castle, he had been enjoying his freedom as a free agent. In the mission to Death's Province, he involved himself where he pleased, or not at all. "I'm not a soldier anymore," he'd kept reminding his brother. But for the first time, he was missing his uniform and rank.

He and the other soldiers had brought Al Marks to the holding cells, but once there, he was kept out of the proceedings. The commander showed up and hurried right in. Jack tried to follow, but Church said, "This doesn't concern you, Jack," as the door slid closed between them with a hiss.

Jack shouted after Mike, "The crap it doesn't! I helped capture him!" Two guards forced him back, stepping between him and the doorway. He knew Mike and Al were up to something and presumed the Cardinal ruse was part of it. His first instinct was to eavesdrop on the conversation taking place between Mike and Al, but the detainment sector was one of the few places in the castle that *didn't* have the secret passages running through it. Frustrated, Jack paced the parlor of the detainment center.

Just then, Eliza rushed in, her brown and pastel blue wig was crooked, and her dress disheveled from running. "Is it true? The Cardinal has been captured? Is it true?"

"Yeah, we caught him," said Jack. "Why do you care?"

"What? I don't. I mean, the Cardinal has been stealing from the castle for a year now. I'm just curious who it is."

"It's Marks."

"Who?"

"Marks—Private Al Marks."

One of the guards gave a cough, implying Jack shouldn't be sharing information.

Jack spun on him. "She's the fucking princess! I *think* she can be trusted."

The guard didn't react, but Eliza tilted her head in disapproval. "Jack, please. I don't think that's necessary."

He wasn't listening. Through the windows of the control booth Jack could see the holding cells. Guards crowded the booth, however, and Jack had to crane his neck to peer around them. Occasionally, he caught a glimpse of Al, who sat with his hands shackled to a table while Church paced around him shouting. Jack wondered if it was an act, or if Church was just mad that Marks hadn't accomplished his task.

Before Jack could finish his thought, Frank rushed past, not even realizing he and Eliza were there. Jack called after him. Startled, Frank looked back. Jack was about to talk about the situation, but he noticed Frank's eyes were red and swollen. "Are you all right?"

"Not now, Jack."

Remembering that Frank had just been to see Peter, Jack argued, "But, Frank—"

Frank spun around and roared, "I said, not now!" and went inside.

Jack and Eliza both stood there stunned and silent. With an awkward sort of quietness, they both sat down on a nearby bench. Finally, Jack broke the silence. "I shouldn't have—"

"Neither should I," said Eliza. "He isn't ready."

"He'll never be ready, Eliza. We shouldn't have played a game with his life like that." With disgust, Jack grumbled, "What was I thinking, encouraging him to . . . putting him in that kind of situation."

"You said it yourself—you just want him to be happy. That's all either of us wants for him."

"Did he look happy to you?" Jack interlaced his fingers, rested his arms on his legs, and lowered his head, sighing, "All we did was torture him."

"I'm not trying to justify whatever happened to Frank. But what you call torture . . . that's his life, Jack. Every day. Every single day, he's expected to pretend like he's fine. Pretend like he's just like everyone else. Except he has to act like he's not interested in a relationship, while still coping with being lonely . . . when it would be so easy, so simple, for things to be all right for him if people would just let go of their prejudices. If they could just stop hating people who are different from themselves."

Jack crossed his arms and leaned back against the wall, "Yeah, well, I don't see that happening any time soon."

"It isn't right. It isn't fair."

Recalling that he'd said the same thing to Frank not that long ago, Jack replied, "No one said life is fair. That's what Frank said to me. And it's true. Believe me, I know it."

Side by side, they sat and waited in quiet stillness.

Then Eliza broke the silence. "For years now, I've been thinking about what I'd say to you if I ever saw you again. Year after year, I thought, *Any day now, he'll be back and I'll tell him.* But you didn't come. So, each year, I'd revise my speech." She paused. "Then, after five years, I think I'm finally ready to let go . . . and I hear you're coming back for some insanely dangerous mission. And I knew. Right away, I knew. You agreed to it because of me."

Jack couldn't argue, but before he could reply, Eliza continued, "Then I learned you were going to come here first. So, in my mind, I began to rehearse again." Eliza's voice mellowed and she sounded like she almost relished reliving the memory. "Oh, how I planned and prepared for everything you could possibly say to me," she looked at Jack, her voice fuming, "and how I would tell you off for leaving m . . ." She faced forward again, "for leaving."

Jack wasn't sure what to say. He'd be lying if he said he hadn't had similar scenarios playing in his mind for all these years. He began to respond, but she wasn't finished; she raised her hand to stop him. She leaned in so the guards in the room couldn't hear her say, "I know what Frank is going through, because every day since you left, every single day, I've been expected to lie the same kind of way. I have to pretend like I'm fine. Like I haven't lost my husband. Pretend like I'm in love with someone I'm . . ."

Eliza gave a great dry sob then explained, "I knew Jason was manipulating the situation, but I never knew how far back it started . . . I never realized how far he was taking it, until . . ." She cried out suddenly, "Oh, Jack, I didn't know! And that night, I was trying to protect you . . . I thought he was going to kill you unless I—!"

Suddenly all the guards stood at full attention. Jack and Eliza both looked at the entrance as King Hawthorn arrived. Captain Vergo followed him, along with an array of royal guards. He looked to his right, seeing Jack and Eliza, and said, "Good evening, Princess, Jack." Noticing the tears in Eliza's eyes, he asked, "Is everything all right?"

Eliza rose to her feet, curtsied to the king, and explained, "I'm fine, Your Majesty. We were just reminiscing. I guess mixed with all the excitement . . . with the capture of the Cardinal . . . I just lost myself. Please forgive me."

"Oh, Eliza, think nothing of it. Poor girl," cooed the king as he tenderly wiped away one of her tears. "Such delicate creatures."

Despite the tension, Jack couldn't help but think, *Eliza is anything but delicate.* He'd never known anyone as strong as her; it was one of the things he loved about her.

The king excused himself, and Jack swung around to face Eliza again. They studied each other, not sure if they should try to pick up where they'd left off. Finally, Jack put out his hand. "I can't take this anymore. Come with me."

Shocked, she asked, "What?" He didn't explain; he just took her hand, pulled her out of the parlor, and led her down the hall. "Jack, what are you doing? Where are you taking me? Jack?"

He led her to an out of the way alcove for privacy. Jack's eyes scanned the hallway to make sure no one saw them as he pulled Eliza in. "Jack what are you doing?"

He pulled Eliza toward him, and his heart raced. Having her in his arms again, the years melted away. Eliza looked up at him, and everything around him, his past and present, it all disappeared. He looked in her eyes and felt he could live there.

Jack kissed her, and to his amazement, Eliza kissed him back.

After a moment he whispered, "Let's run away."

"W-what?"

"I'm leaving again," he said in a low voice. "But this time, you should come with me."

"Jack, I-I can't. I mean . . . Frank—"

Filled with excitement, Jack said, "We can take him with us. And Peter, too. Maybe in time, they'll—"

"Jack, you're talking crazy."

"No, Eliza. This is the sanest I've ever been. We can run away. Run away and live happily—"

"Don't you dare say 'live happily ever after'! This is not some fairy tale. This is life!" Despite her cool logic, she lunged toward him, and Jack felt her lips against his own.

After a moment, Jack pulled back from her. They stood face to face, arms around each other as they had done so many times in the past. "I don't understand you." Before she could respond, he leaned down to kiss her again.

Eliza pushed Jack off, "No. No. I'm sorry. We can't."

"Yes, we ca—"

"No, Jack! We can't." She pulled away and tried to adjust her clothes and hair. "I am the princess of Idoless. Do you really think if I disappeared, they wouldn't come looking for me? And you'd be accused of kidnapping me."

"I didn't say it would be easy, but it can be done." He waited for some kind of reaction from Eliza. When she just gawked at him, Jack groaned. "I've only been back for a short while, and I'm already sick of it, Eliza. All of it. The secrets. The lying and double-crossing. The people. Eliza, you and I, we've paid our dues. It's our turn to be happy." Then he tacked on, "It's Frank's turn."

He could see the hunger in Eliza's eyes. Maybe she wasn't saying it, but she was interested. But something held her back. "No, it'll never work."

"I did it before. I got away."

"And five years later they found you," Eliza overruled him. "I'd be content anywhere with you, Jack, but we can't live our lives always looking over our shoulders."

Desperate, Jack persisted, "Then we'll find somewhere better than Oakmoor. We'll defect to another nation. We'll . . . we'll find another island."

"Jack, enough!"

"Why not? Give me *one* good reason we should stay?"

She didn't respond at first, and Jack made an *I told you so* sort of sound. But then she said, "What was it you said before—'Life isn't fair'? If we left, maybe we would be happy. But I have a responsibility beyond my own happiness. What about all the lives I could improve as queen? I could make the world a better place. We both could."

"So, what? You're going to stay with Jason? After all he's done? You're going to stay with the man who tried to murder your husband?"

Eliza replied quickly, "According to everyone, including the law, *he* is my husband."

Jack saw the regret dart across her face as soon as she said the words, but it was too late. They snuffed Jack's passion. With deep sadness, he asked, "Who are you married to, Eliza? Me or him?"

"I . . . I don't know."

"You don't? Well, I'll tell you. You're married to *me*. You made vows promising yourself to me, just like I did to you."

"But we have no proof that it ever happened. Meanwhile, Idoless has records—and witnesses—to prove I'm married to Jason."

"I don't care about *records*. What we promised each other was real, Eliza. It was as real as any other marriage in Idoless. So, I ask again: who are you married to?"

"I love you, Jack."

"That doesn't answer my question."

"Well, it's the best I can do right now!"

Jack considered her. He remembered all the things she'd told him, about how much saying *I love you* meant to her, and how seriously she took those words. It gave him a glimmer of hope.

But her refusal to answer his question concerned him. "Something bad is coming, Eliza, and I'm sick of being the one who always has to deal with it."

"If you're right, then I *really* can't leave." She stood in silence for a moment, then her face softened, and she added, "And neither should you."

Jack had reached his limit. She had stripped him down to his core, and all that remained was to simply tell her how it was for him. "I love you, Eliza. I have always loved you, and I always will. I pledged my heart to you, and you will have it until the day I die. But there is no way I can stay here and 'make the world a better place' while my wife is with another man. I can't do it. I just can't. So I'm leaving." He took a step forward, so they were sharing the same space again. He took her hand, looked into her eyes, and said, "I want you to come with me."

"Jack, I ca—"

"Just think about it. I'm not going to . . . I won't leave like I did before. Look, tomorrow at eight o'clock the king is throwing another a feast, to celebrate our success in Death's Province. I have no interest in attending it. I'm going to leave an hour before it's scheduled to begin." Jack cupped Eliza's cheek in his hand. "If you want to come with me, it'll be the perfect time to go. Everyone will be busy getting ready. With any luck, no one will even realize we're gone until it's too late, giving us plenty of time to gain a good head start." He thought for a moment and looked around the alcove. "I'll come back here, to this spot at seven o'clock, and wait for you. And I'll tell Frank about it tonight. Hopefully, he'll be with me."

"Jack, I . . . I can't. I'm under constant watch," argued Eliza.

"So where are all your watchers now?" When she didn't have a reply, he smiled and said, "You are an amazing, resourceful woman, Eliza. When you want to get away from them, you can."

He went up to her, reached up, and gently pulled off her wig. Her real hair tumbled down and fell over her shoulder. The person before him was no longer the princess. Now it was just Eliza, the girl from the academy and the woman from the island he had fallen in love with.

"Jack, that doesn't change—"

"Just promise me you'll think about it."

"Jack."

"Not now. Tomorrow. Seven o'clock. I hope I'll see you then, because . . ." Holding her there he rejected all the negative feelings he'd held onto all these years, and he kissed her like it was the day they married. "If you aren't here tomorrow, this is the last time you'll see me. I love you, Eliza."

And with that, he left her standing there holding her wig.

Jack went up to the lieutenant's dormitory to wait for Frank. This recent development with Eliza had all but evaporated his concern about what was going on with Mike Church or Al Marks.

He hadn't brought much from Oakmoor, but he didn't want to lose his nerve to leave, so he pulled out his bag to start packing. He set it on his cot and opened it up to refill it with what he'd brought, and was surprised to find something new inside, waiting for him: a large envelope with his name on it.

He recognized the tidy handwriting as Frank's and pulled the flap back so he could retrieve the contents. Inside were two sheets of paper. The top one was a letter which read:

Jack,

You have no idea how much I've enjoyed having you back these past few weeks, bro. Even though we can't seem to stop finding things to argue about, having you in my life again has been a treasure, and I've been happier than I have been for some time. There are a couple of things I wanted to say to you, but I wasn't sure I'd be able to say them right in person, so I wrote them down.

First, I wanted you to know, the way you reacted when you found out about my "stuff" surprised me in the best way possible. I should have trusted you earlier, but it's not easy living with these feelings and always being afraid of how someone would react if they found out. Your reaction gave me hope for a better world. Eliza has been trying to encourage me to "be myself" for some time now. She wants me to be an example and show the world that people like me aren't the degenerates and perverts they assume we are. She thinks if I did, others like me will follow suit. I wish I were as brave as she wants me to be, but I'm not. However, with people like you showing acceptance, it will make it easier for the next generation of people like me to be brave. And if that happens, maybe in time they won't have to live in hiding, lying to the ones they love. And then, maybe, they could even have the kind of happiness I won't. You're making the world a better place, Jack, and Mom would be proud of you. I know I am.

Secondly, I need to ask you a favor. I know we talked about solving the mystery of Mom and the Cardinal together, but I also know how hard it is on you being here. I know you won't be staying much longer. When that time comes, please don't say good-bye to me. I'm honestly not sure I can handle it. In light of all that has happened, I actually considered asking if I could go with you, but it's better if I stay. While I can't be the example Eliza wants me to be, I think I can still do some good here. If all the good people of Idoless leave, things will only get worse. I'm not saying that to try and guilt you into staying or anything. After all you've been through, I just wanted you to know that I understand. And while I'll miss you, you have my support.

Good-bye brother,

Frank

P.S. The second page is a little going-away gift. It's not a surprise—we talked about it before. I hope you like it.

Jack lifted the page to expose a fresh drawing Frank had done of their mother. It was like the one he'd already done for himself, but something was different about this one. Jack couldn't put his finger on what it was, but somehow Frank had captured the look in her eyes that made Hazel Waramond anything but plain.

He sat on the cot and reread the letter, lamenting that he hadn't even gotten a chance to ask Frank to leave with him, but was already told "no." He scanned the letter a third time, reading aloud, "If all the good people of Idoless leave, things will only get worse."

That was basically the same thing Eliza had been saying.

His desire to run away with Eliza weakened. All the important people in his life felt this sense of responsibility to make the world a better place. Eliza didn't love Jason. But being his wife had given her a position of power, and she was planning on utilizing it. Frank had every reason to leave; the world he'd built for himself was crumbling around him. Jack could tell he was doubling his efforts to finish his airplane so he could make a smooth exit when it was time, yet he was staying to "do some good" first. Jack looked at the drawing of his mother and recalled the stories he'd heard as a kid about the Cardinal. Thievery aside, the Cardinal was a sort of champion for the weak and poor.

And with that, Jack felt sure Al Marks was *not* the real Cardinal.

Just then, he heard the outer door opening. He threw his stuff back under the cot, then folded and crammed the letter with the drawing into his pocket.

A moment later, a tired-looking Frank entered the room.

Jack tried to look natural, but he knew he wasn't doing a good job of concealing his emotions. Frank picked up on it right away. "What's up with you?"

"Nothing."

Frank looked him over, and said, "You read it."

Jack lied in the sincerest voice he could muster, "Read what?" Frank's brow furrowed as he measured Jack. "I . . . I was just curious about what happened with Marks."

Frank stared at him a moment longer then sighed, which Jack hoped meant Frank believed him. "I don't know what's going on with him. He didn't give us anything useful. He respects Commander Church, so he would at least respond to his questions, but the few times I tried asking anything he just gave me this smug grin, like he was better than me or something . . . or like he knew something I didn't."

"So, you didn't get anything out of him?"

"Not right away. Vergo showed up with the king and spent some time with him."

"Yeah, I saw them," said Jack. "I suppose with Vergo's methods . . . Does Marks still have all his fingers and toes?"

Frank sniggered. "Don't get me wrong, I think Vergo goes farther than I deem appropriate in an interrogation—but you can't deny he gets results."

"But you said Marks didn't say anything."

"He didn't." Frank opened the top button of his tunic to give his neck some breathing room. "Nothing useful, anyway. I thought Marks was being insolent with me until I saw the way he was with the king. When they showed up . . . if looks could kill, they'd have dropped dead on the spot."

"He was disrespectful to the king?"

Frank raised his eyebrows, "He *spat* on him."

"No way!"

"Way. That's when the king let Vergo go to work."

Jack shifted on the cot. "But you said Vergo didn't get anything useful out of Marks. What *did* he get out of him?"

"Well, let's see. He didn't specify, but he made a couple of comments that could be interpreted as him having some kind of cause he's fighting for. But what crackpot doesn't have a cause?"

"A cause?" Jack spoke aloud. "So, he was trying to kill you and Peter to get the weapon for this . . . cause?"

"That about sums it up."

Jack pondered the information for a moment, then changed his tone. "So, um. You and Peter . . ."

"Nothing happened, Jack," Frank said firmly.

"No, ugh, I just wanted to apologize for pushing you into it. I shouldn't have done that."

Frank waved a hand in the air, "It's all good. I've had to . . . control my feelings before."

It hurt Jack to hear him say that. He thought about how he felt for Eliza, and how it would be if what he felt for her was considered wrong. "So, how *is* Peter? I haven't seen him since before your lesson."

"He's shaken up, but I think he'll get through it. He's had a lot piled on him so quickly. Add an attempt on his life . . . it would freak anyone out. But if anyone can deal with it, it's him. Anyway, he can't get much safer than he is now."

"Oh yeah?" asked Jack. "They put more guards on him?"

"Yeah." Frank smiled with an air of relief. "Including Commander Church himself." Jack's stomach dropped as Frank continued, "Until we've figured out how to break the spell binding the weapon to Peter, the commander has decided he'll stay by his side 24/7." Jack started to say something when Frank put up a hand. "Jack, I don't want to hear it."

"Frank, you need to hear me out."

"No, Jack. I know you've had some conspiracy theory about Church that's been brewing since the day you got back. But the commander is a good man."

Jack thought a moment, then said, "I'll make you a deal. I won't say a thing about Church or any of my theories. Just let me show you something, and then—I promise you—you'll want to hear more about what I know." To help convince Frank, Jack offered, "I won't say another word about Church until you ask me to. Just please . . . for Peter's sake, let me show you."

Frank exhaled noisily. "Fine. But it better be good."

Peter looked around Mike Church's quarters with wonder. Three levels divided the large room into sections. At the highest point, atop a handful of stairs, sat a large, comfortable looking bed. A few steps below the sleeping area a modest kitchen occupied one of the corners. At the lowest level, where Peter stood, a couple of chairs, a sofa, lamps, and end tables formed the living room. Cabinets placed against the walls held personal artifacts and trophies. Church kept the apartment neat and tidy.

He appeared to have a place for everything, and everything was in its place.

The only thing out of place was a cot set up in the living area.

Commander Church excused the last of the guards, and as the door slid shut behind him, turned to face Peter. "I hope you'll be comfortable."

Peter looked at the cot and set the hilt on it, knowing it was the only reason he was there. "It looks nice," said Peter, trying to seem at ease with the situation. "Thank you."

Commander Church glared at Peter for a minute, then began to move into the room. "I know you don't trust me, Peter. I'm sorry for what I've done to give you reason not to."

Peter didn't respond. He just walked around the room, looking at the different artifacts and banners hanging from the walls, moving to counter Church and keep space between them.

Mike took off his beret and set it on the small kitchen island. "Would you like something to drink?"

"No, thank you."

"Do you mind if I have something?"

Peter crinkled his nose, "What difference does it make if I care?"

Mike grinned. "I was just being polite." He removed a bottle from the fridge and two glasses from a cupboard. "If you change your mind, there's a glass for you." He filled one glass, took a great gulp from it, set it on the counter, and refilled what he'd just drunk. Mike ambled over to the couch and sat down. He took a smaller sip of his beverage, then closed his eyes and leaned his head back.

"Are . . . are you going to sleep?" asked Peter uncomfortably.

Mike kept his eyes closed, but answered, "No, but I am resting. It's been a long day." He opened one eye and looked at his guest. "Please, sit. I'm not going to hurt you." Peter sat stiffly in the chair farthest away from the commander. They sat in silence for a minute, then Church said, "So, you're fond of Lieutenant Waramond."

"Um, yeah."

"Men aren't my thing, but even if they were, I'm not sure I see the appeal. Don't get me wrong, I respect him as a soldier. But for *romance*? Why him?"

Defensively, Peter explained, "He hasn't done anything. I like him, but he doesn't like me the same way."

In a much more jovial tone than Peter had ever heard from him before, the commander said, "Oh please, Peter, of course he does."

"I-I don't want to get Frank in trouble. I know it's wrong here . . . I mean . . . illegal, to be—"

"Peter, I'm just trying to make small talk." Mike opened his eyes and leaned forward. "I'm not trying to get you or anyone else in trouble. I know Frank hasn't *done* anything. And even if he had, I wouldn't care. What he does on his own time makes no difference to me." He leaned back and closed his eyes again. "I know plenty of gay people. As long as what they do doesn't affect me, I don't see any reason why I should disturb their lives."

Even though he knew something was going on, Peter could tell that Mike at least meant what he was saying . . . even if he was only using the fact to placate him. Regardless of his concerns, Peter's curiosity got the better of him. He took the opening and asked, "So why is it illegal?"

Mike took another sip of his drink, then answered, "I don't know the reason. It was decided a long time ago."

"B-but people can . . . if they want to? I mean, you, you said, you know gay people?"

"Yes, I do," replied Church. "It's a secret, of course. But I know dignitaries, as well as a general and a colonel, who are gay.

I even happen to know that one of the Cassidy sisters who just defected to Idoless is gay."

"How do you know about all of them?"

"Some of them, I stumbled on their secret. While others, like the general I spoke of, took a risk and entrusted me. He needed my help, or risk getting caught by the authorities—or worse, his wife."

With a flat voice, Peter said, "Oh. So, you don't know any . . . any *couples*?"

"No. I suppose not." He looked at Peter slyly. "But rendezvous can be arranged. I've helped that general a few times. I could do the same for you. Make it so you and Frank—"

"No, thank you."

"But I thought—?"

"I'm not interested in just . . . mating," groaned Peter. "Besides, I told you. He isn't interested in me like that."

The commander responded with a cunning grin, "And I told you, he clearly is. But even if you're right, it's like I said, he's a good soldier. He'll do what I tell him."

Peter sniffed, "How romantic."

"I thought you wanted him?"

"I don't just want sex with him," stated Peter. "Sex is a part of love, not the other way around."

"I'm just trying to help you, Peter."

"Thank you, but I don't need that kind of help."

Exasperated, Mike sighed, "Well, what *do* you want?"

"I want . . . I want to leave."

"Fine, go," snapped the commander. He got up, drained his glass, and walked over to the counter. "There's the door."

Peter didn't think, he just darted for the door. He'd gotten used to the hilt and was ready for it when it flew from the cot, across the room, and into his hand. The commander moaned, probably because he was hoping it was going to be left behind.

Peter pressed a button on the wall, and the door slid open with a hiss. He'd anticipated facing guards, but instead standing in the doorway was Mike Church's father, Eli Warren, and next to him, still in his scarlet Cardinal robes, was Al Marks, who sneered and said, "Hello there, young man."

Peter gasped and fell backward into the room, landing with a thud. The two men entered and sealed the door behind them.

Mike sighed, "You didn't exactly give me much time."

Al pointed at Peter and questioned Mike, "You were letting him leave?"

"I was trying to win his trust," argued Mike. "But that isn't very likely now, thanks to you showing up."

"Where was I supposed to go once your father got me out of there?"

"Anywhere but here," answered Mike.

"Don't you talk to me like that!" demanded Marks.

"Shut up!" bellowed Eli. "You're bickering like a couple of fuckin' kids."

Mike apologized, "You're right, Father. I'm sorry."

But Marks was still fired up. "Why is the boy even still alive?"

Mike answered, "I'm not about to kill him if I don't have to."

Marks complained, "We've tried all our other options." He grabbed a knife from the kitchen, and he headed toward Peter. "You were right the night we got out of the Province. The only way to separate it from him is to separate *him* from *it*."

Mike jumped in front of Al. "No! We haven't tried everything yet." He turned to Eli, "Father, if it's a spell of some kind that binds the weapon to Peter, could you break it with another? Or maybe transfer it to me?"

"Or me," added Marks.

"You?" asked Eli.

"Yeah, me. Why not?"

"We decided at the beginning that once we had the weapon, it would be handled by Mike. You said yourself he was the best choice."

"And he still is. But I couldn't do it when we made that decision. But now, thanks to your spell . . ." He raised his arm and shook the bracelet on his wrist. When he got no reaction, he said, "I just meant if I had to, I could do it."

Eli looked at Marks doubtfully, then turned to Peter. "Don't be afraid."

Peter snorted as he gazed at the knife in Marks's hand.

Eli looked back at Marks and barked, "Put that shit away!" Marks reluctantly put the blade down, and Eli turned back to Peter. "I'm sorry for all this, but we just don't have the time to explain."

He put one of his hands just over Peter's head. He closed his eyes and concentrated, his brow creased as if he were trying to think of an answer to a question. Peter tried to pull away but felt an invisible force holding him in place. Eli raised his other hand. It acted like a magnet, pulling up Peter's hand that gripped the sword. Peter's hand hovered just under Eli's for several minutes until finally Eli released him.

"Father?"

"Nothing. I didn't see any kind of spell that I could break or alter. Something was there, but it was unlike any spell I've ever seen. Maybe it's the same kind of magic we experienced in the cavern. Whatever it is, it'll take some time to study before I can even attempt to break it. It ain't happenin'. Not here. Not now."

"I know how to break it," spat Marks, raising the knife once again.

Eli flicked his hand, and the blade flew from Marks's hand and stuck in the side of the kitchen island like a dart. "What is with your bloodlust?"

"It's not bloodlust. It's decisiveness."

"I find it interesting you're so willing to do the deed, though. Perhaps you hope the one who kills the boy is the one the weapon will attach itself to next?"

Marks countered, "I'm just taking a page from your son's playbook—the 'hands-on commander.' The point is, we're out of time, and we need to act."

"He's innocent," retorted Eli.

"And that is unfortunate, but one life lost compared to hundreds of thousands is an easy sacrifice for me to make!"

Eli turned to his son for assistance, but Mike was at the kitchen island putting his beret back on. He then pulled the knife from the island and said, "He's right, Father. It's only a matter of time before they realize Ryan isn't in his cell." Mike strolled across the room, each step heavier than the last. "I learned something tonight that complicates things even further than we imagined. The king can't be allowed to have the weapon, and this might be our only chance to get him while his guard is down." Peter was still lying on the floor. With everything happening, he hadn't been able to bring himself to move. Mike stood over him and raised the knife. He looked regretful, yet absolutely decided as he said, "I'm sorry, Peter."

At first Peter thought defiantly, *Fine. Good. I can't wait to die and be done with all this. Maybe I'll see Terrie again.* But then his mind shifted to Frank.

He rolled backward and sprang to his feet as Mike brought the knife down with such force the blade broke when it hit the spot Peter had just been.

Peter thought of his single lesson; Frank's voice rang in his head, "That first day, remember the commotion you caused? An entire platoon of soldiers had a hard time holding you down . . . Becoming a skilled fighter begins with understanding who you are—your strengths and your weaknesses . . . those times you fought—what if you had utilized some of what you did when you did run?"

Marks reached for him, but Peter leaped in the air and bounced off his chest, landing on the back of the couch.

Peter began to leap, hurdle, and pounce through Church's quarters, never stopping for a moment, just as he had the day Frank first found him. Peter entered the kitchen space, leaped and grabbed hold of the light fixture hanging from the ceiling and swung from it, kicking Al in the face. He bounced back into the living room and grabbed Mike's trophies from the shelf, hurling them indiscriminately at the men.

Suddenly, a glowing force field raised him in the air. With nothing to provide leverage, all he could do was squirm as he hovered.

"Excellent, Father," applauded Mike.

Al Marks wasn't in the mood to waste any more time. He snatched a sword off the wall and charged.

Just as Marks was upon Peter, a cloud of thick smoke burst around them.

Sounds of scuffling came from within the cloud, and Marks flew out of it. He hit the floor at Mike and Eli's feet with a crash. Al picked himself up, wiped blood from the corner of his mouth, and spat. A tooth clicked as it rolled across the stone floor.

As the smoke slowly dissipated, it revealed a red-hooded figure with a cape and helmet with a black visor.

The real Cardinal.

"You only got me because you took me by surprise," taunted Marks. "You won't be so lucky a second time." The Cardinal didn't answer; he just looked over his shoulder at the large window behind him.

All three men shouted, "No!"

But it was too late. The Cardinal grabbed Peter and pulled him from the force field, then threw himself through the window.

Mike, Eli, and Al all ran to the edge of the window and saw that the Cardinal and Peter had landed safely eight stories below.

"So, he can't fly," said Eli.

"What?" asked Mike.

"Everyone thinks he's a ghost or something, but he was swinging on a cord." Then he said definitively, "The Cardinal is human."

"Then where'd he come from?" asked Mike.

Eli just shrugged.

"Shouldn't we go after them?" asked Al. "Eli, can you get me down there? Maybe a—"

"No," interrupted Mike. "It's too late for that now."

"Too late?" gasped Al. "What was the point of going into Death's Province to get the damn thing if we're just going to let them run off with it now?"

"Listen, our hand has been forced, and we need to act fast," said Mike.

"Yeah, and whose fault was that?" retorted Al.

Mike huffed. "You're blaming me?"

"You were going to let him go, and now look—he's gone."

"That again," grumbled Mike. "I *wasn't* going to let him go. But we wouldn't even have had to worry about any of this if *you* hadn't gotten impatient and tried to kill him and then get yourself caught in the first pla—"

"Enough!" roared Eli. "Mike's right. It would be good to have the weapon in hand, but we still don't even know how to work it." Al was about to retort when Eli added, "And neither does anyone else. We can get it later."

"Right," agreed Mike. "Al, you're forgetting the goal of the mission. It was to get the weapon, yes. But the more important goal was to make sure the king wouldn't."

Begrudgingly, Al agreed, "I suppose."

"Though it's ahead of schedule, we have the resources for the next part of the mission." Mike paused and looked at his comrades. "Let's kill the king."

Just then, with a thunderous boom, the door burst open. Four soldiers, followed by the Waramonds, stormed in, all with their swords drawn. The king strode in the room, looked sadly at Mike, and moaned, "Oh, Commander Church, I'm *so* disappointed."

Mike Church looked almost peaceful as he replied, "Not as disappointed as you're going to be." He addressed the soldiers in the room, "Now."

Suddenly, three of the soldiers turned, quickly killing the fourth. And just like that, all the swords that had been pointed at Mike, Eli, and Al were now pointed at Jack, Frank, and the king.

5 Years Ago
575 AR

J ack crept down the secret corridors of Castle Idoless. He kept finding himself trying to be quiet, which was ridiculous. The only person he could possibly run into would be the only other person who knew about the corridors besides himself, who also happened to be the exact person he wanted to see right now: Jason.

He and Jason had spent their childhood in these corridors after having found them by accident. Every morning after breakfast, if he didn't have chores to do, Jack would dash to Jason's room, which housed one of the access points into the secret passages. And that access point was where Jack was headed now.

He had nearly reached the doorway where so many of their childhood adventures had begun when he stopped for a moment, pulled out the wrinkled notice, and read it for the umpteenth time.

King Thomas Saulomon Hawthorn

is pleased to announce the marriage of his son

Prince Jason David Hawthorn

to

Lady Eliza Bella Nickolie

Then, like all the other times before, he crumpled it up and threw it to the ground, leaving it behind like the trash it was. And, like all those other times, he went back to the wadded ball of paper, picked it up, flattened it out, and caressed Eliza's name with his finger. It had been so long since he'd seen her. He hadn't even been able to say good-bye before leaving for his mission to Death's Province.

It had taken him more than three months of traveling on foot to make it back to the castle. The whole time he had been driven by the fact that Eliza must think he was dead, and he didn't want to put her through that sorrow any longer than he had to. After all, she was how he'd gotten out of the province—she was his beacon home.

He had envisioned her on the other side of the magical barrier, reaching for him. And so, he went to her. It had felt like all the flesh on his body was being torn off his bones, but his love for Eliza had kept him pushing past the pain to get to her until he burst out the other side.

He'd arrived on the outskirts of Juniper City to be greeted by the marriage notice, proudly hung on a message board for all the townsfolk to see . . . confirming his theory as to what the mission had really been: a scheme to get him killed.

In hindsight, Jack could now clearly see what Jason had been doing. The prince had ensured Jack's speedy return to the army, but not out of friendship. Jason wanted Eliza for himself. That's why each mission was more dangerous than the last with fewer resources each time. Jack was certain; all the missions had been attempts to get him killed.

He took the smallest of pleasures in the fact that they had all been unsuccessful—and how much that must have frustrated Jason. And soon, he would learn even this, his most desperate attempt, had failed. He remembered how Jason had even manipulated him into feeling like it was his choice.

"No, Jason, not again!" Jack threw his pack to the ground and some clothes fell from an opening. "Do you realize I've been on ten missions in a row now? Ten! And these . . . kids I got saddled with last time, they're all just a bunch of recent graduates. They mean well, but they don't know what they're doing out there. I don't know who thought it was a good idea having a lieutenant lead a bunch of greenhorns, let alone on a mission like that. It was sheer luck that we—"

"Don't be so modest, Jack. You are the greatest warrior in Idoless. Possibly the greatest we've ever known. I know you've been . . .

taken advantage of, but that's only because you've produced such astonishing results."

Jack knelt down and began cramming the clothes back into his pack as he explained, "Don't thank me, thank Eliza."

"Eliza?"

"Yeah, with her I have reason to survive—something to fight for. I like to think of her as," his tone softened, "my beacon home."

Jason paused, shook his head and replied, "Well, it's worked, because look at you now. Only a few years back in service and you're already a lieutenant."

Jack stood up. "Yeah, and if it wasn't for that stupid promotion I would have already said something. But I've had enough. I'm out."

"Out?"

"Yeah, out. It's not worth it. I'm withdrawing from the army early. I won't get my pension, but Eliza and I were content on the island with no money. As long as I'm with her, I'm good." He turned toward Jason. "Do you realize how long it's been since I've even seen her?" Before Jason could answer, Jack threw himself onto a nearby bench and grabbed his head between both hands. "Most people still don't even know she and I are married!" He leaned back pinching the bridge of his nose and then, almost as an afterthought added, "Except maybe Church."

"General Church?"

"Yeah, he was the lead on one of my assignments. I told him all about the island and . . ." Not to be dissuaded from the issue at hand, "And now you want to send me out again?"

Jason sat next to Jack and explained, "Oh, not me. I've been pointing out how unfairly you've been treated, and that you've more than earned a break. So, when this new mission came up, I told Commander Marks flat out, it wasn't happening. Honestly, you weren't even supposed to hear a single word about it."

"Jason, you met me and the remains of my team on the tarmac! You told us we only have an hour to get cleaned up before heading out again."

"Them, not you.

"What?"

Jason gave a weak smile and replied, "I got you out of it."

"What? Really?" Jack shot to his feet.

"Maybe it was selfish of me, but . . . you're my best friend, Jack. But the mission is quite urgent, and I still need to get the team assembled to go."

Jack looked around then asked, "And you're really sending these greenhorns?"

"Unfortunately, yes. Our resources are stretched very thin, but we must act fast."

"Why?"

Jason raised a stack of files he was holding. "This isn't pirates, or some skirmish with one of the other nations. It has to do with something in . . ." He looked around to make sure no one was listening, leaned in and whispered, "In Death's Province."

Jack gasped, "What? But I thought Death's Province was some sort of prison the gods created to contain the worst creatures on the planet."

"That's just the legend. I even did some of the research myself to make sure the intel wasn't a mistake. The province *is* a prison, but not for beasts. It's meant to contain a group of demigods bent on destroying all of Terra Firma. They'd nearly succeeded about 200 years after the return of the gods, when the wizards of Phlogiston imprisoned them there."

"Phlogiston? They don't give a damn about Idoless. They keep to themselves more than any other nation."

"That was three . . . almost four-hundred years ago Jack; a lot has changed. But that's all beside the point. We've learned that the demigods might be close to breaking free. However, as long as they're in the Province, they have no power. There, they're just like ordinary people and can be killed like them. So, if we act fast—execute a strategic assault on them before they escape—the problem will be solved."

"This is still Death's Province we're talking about, Jason. Not many people have gone in there—but of the few that have, not one has come back. Who's even leading such an operation?"

"That's why I needed to talk to you. Which one of your team do you think has the proper constitution to lead an operation like this?"

Jack stepped back in shock. "Are you fucking serious? None of them!"

Jason huffed, opened a file, looked at some papers then asked, "What about Charlie Garner?"

"No, not him."

"But his file says—?"

"No, he's great. He's probably the best of the bunch."

"Perfect."

"No—Jason, no! You can't . . . you can't do this. They won't succeed. They aren't good enough. Where's Church? Where is . . . I don't know, any other soldier with even an iota of experience?"

"Church is on assignment. They all are. I told you, Jack, we're stretched thin."

"Well, can't you wait for them?"

Jason closed the files and tucked them back under his arm. "No, we can't. I told you; we have to act now."

"Well, you can't!"

"And just what do you suggest I do, Jack? This isn't just for Idoless. It's for all of Terra Firma. We can't let those . . . demigods escape, or it means the end of everyone." Jason stood up, "It's our duty.

"Damn it!" Jack kicked his pack off the bench and his dirty clothes fell out again. He didn't pick them up though. He just stood there with his hands on his hips, staring at the ground. He thought about Charlie and all those young men he'd just fought alongside. They needed him. Idoless needed him. "Fine, I'll go."

"What? Jack, no!"

"I have to." Jack pointed back at the transport and said, "I'm not sending those kids to their deaths!"

Jason didn't respond, he just glared at Jack. After silence that felt like hours, with a forcibly even tone, Jason said, "I'll say this. Commander Marks is getting close to retirement. He's planning on going in a year or two."

"So?"

"Jack, the rank of commander—it's the only rank a person can't earn. The king can choose anyone he wants . . . the person doesn't even have to be in the army. He could choose a dignitary, or just some guy off the street."

"Yeah, I know. What does that have to do with any of this?"

"Commander Marks is lobbying for General Church to take over his position, but the king wants you. I do too."

"What?"

"Oh, come on, Jack, I'm sure you've heard the rumors. The king has known you since we were children. He trusts you. And he's not going to be around forever. So, he'll include me in the decision, so that when it's my time to step up to the throne, I'll have someone at my side who I trust." Jason put a hand on Jack's shoulder and said, "Look, I don't want you going to Death's Province, but. . . If you did go, and the mission was a success . . . no one would doubt your qualifications for the advancement."

Prestige and rank didn't mean much to Jack, but the perks that came with it did. He'd get to see Eliza all the time. He'd get his own quarters in the castle, and she could move in with him. He wouldn't have to go on any assignments other than those he deemed necessary himself. The only trick would be surviving this one.

He thought of Charlie and the others again, and none of that mattered. So, Jack agreed to go.

From that point, everything had moved quickly. Within days, Jack found himself inside Death's Province. Once there, he quickly discovered everything Jason had told him was a lie, and he realized that volunteering for the mission had never truly been a choice. Now, with his entire team dead, Jack thought about the hundreds of other soldiers who'd died on his previous assignments. *Were any of the missions legitimate—or were they all attempts on my life? Were all those men sacrificed just so that Jason could get me out of the way?*

Being manipulated by his best friend hurt, but the thing that puzzled Jack most wasn't Jason, it was Eliza. *Why had she agreed to marry him?*

Jason Hawthorn walked into his study, closed the door and turned on a single lamp. He stood there for a moment and took a deep breath.

Things were finally going his way.

He pulled off his royal robes and threw them across a chair. He then tossed his shoulder strap and belt, which held his weapons, including his new gun, on top of the robes. *The maids can deal with it tomorrow.*

He scanned the room and didn't know what to do with himself. He was too wound up to work. He'd been married to Eliza for just over two weeks now, and today was the best day since the ceremony itself. Eliza had been depressed for some time now, but she was finally coming around. And today—oh, today, they'd spent the whole day together, working out some of the etiquette Eliza needed to know in her new role as princess.

Jason cherished any time he and Eliza spent together. He called their times together "orange days," based on that special moment he'd spent with her on the island atop the mountain. It was such a simple thing, sitting with her and sharing an orange, but he treasured every second of it as one of the best moments of his life.

Remember, that was Eliza and Jack's wedding day.

It wasn't real.

It was their day, and you're making it yours?

They were just playing house.

They pledged their lives to each other.

It wasn't real!

They got married.

She and I are married—for real!

Jack's voice came from the shadows, "Do you always mumble to yourself when you're alone?"

Jason sprang to his feet. "Wha . . .?"

Jack stepped into the light and said coolly, "Hey, buddy."

"Jack? You . . . you're—"

"Alive? Yeah. Happy to see me?"

"O-of course I am! I just . . . didn't realize . . . you . . . when and how did you—?"

"Oh, I just got back tonight. It took me a while to get here on my own. After all, everyone thought I was dead."

Jason searched for words but couldn't find any. He just smiled awkwardly as he gazed at Jack.

"So," said Jack, as though he were starting a conversation on any other day, "what about you? How've you been? Still preparing for the demigods to break free from Death's Province? I'm sure when I didn't return, you knew we had to mount full forces or all of Terra Firma might be overtaken."

Jason giggled nervously. "No, no, y-y-you must have . . . succeeded! Oh, Jack, what you did for Idoless, we must—!"

"Don't."

"Don't?" It took all of Jason's focus to stay rooted to the floor, rather than step back as Jack strolled up to him.

Jack leaned in and said, "Don't try to manipulate this conversation. It isn't going to work. Not again." They just stood there as the seconds ticked by. Then, breaking the silence at last, Jack said, "I have just two questions for you."

Jason tried his best to remain calm and sound natural as he replied, "What do you want to know?"

"I was your best friend, Jason. How could you do that to me—send me into a place like that?"

"I-I don't know what you're talking about. I mean, I got you out of the assignment, but you, you insisted—"

"I know why you did it. In a twisted way, I even get it." Jack began to pace calmly around the room. He picked up a glass orb, looked at it for a moment, then set it back where it came from. "She's amazing. Any man who got to know her the way we did would do anything to have her." Jack paused for a moment, staring at a display cabinet with the only item Jason had brought back from the island: Beauregard's rusty revolver. Jack casually picked it up and examined it, then set it gently back on its base. "She's the best."

Accepting he'd been caught, with a mixture of embarrassment and stubbornness, Jason answered, "Perfect, really."

Jack picked up a small wooden replica of a boat. Instead of returning the model to its base, he threw it against the closest wall and watched it shatter. Then he calmly continued, "So there's only one other thing that I really want to know."

Jason gulped. "And that would be?"

"What did you do to her?"

"I don't—?"

"You and I both know Eliza would never marry you unless—"

"Well, she did, Jack!" spat Jason. "I asked her to marry me, and she said yes, because she loves me!"

"You're a liar!"

"And you're a fool! A fool for thinking someone like her could be happy with someone like you. Maybe on the island you two had a little fun—"

"A little fun?" hissed Jack.

With renewed confidence, Jason thundered, "Oh, come off it, Jack, the island wasn't reality, it was a fantasy you were just playing in! Here, in the real world, she wanted more than you could offer."

The two men slowly circled each other, a new tension building.

"If that's true," said Jack, "then why did you have to kill me? If Eliza and I weren't really married, and she would rather be with you, why would you need me out of the way?"

Jason sighed. "She was too gentle-hearted to hurt your feelings and go after what she really wanted. I just helped her conscience."

"You're full of shit! You think you're in love with her, but you still don't know who she is. She chose me, Jason. Not you. Me. And that's why you needed me out of the—"

"You're just a soldier, Jack. A blunt instrument for me and others with real power to send wherever we need," taunted Jason. "That's the kind of power Eliza wanted. Because of me, someday she's going to be a queen. Not the wife of some worthless grunt, the adopted boy of a servant."

The room went quiet, the only sound their rapid breathing. Finally, Jack spoke. "You say that, but deep down you know that as long as I'm alive, you'll never have a chance with her."

"Then let me get on with my life and die already!" shouted Jason.

He reached toward the chair where he had discarded his belt and grabbed his gun from the holster.

Jack ducked behind a sofa as Jason pulled the trigger twice. Immediately after the shots, sentries posted outside Jason's study pounded on the doors. "Your Majesty? Are you all right? Prince Hawthorn!"

Adrenaline had begun to course through Jack's veins as he hid, crouched behind the sofa. He could hear the pounding on the door becoming more urgent when suddenly an alarm began to sound, and a red light on the ceiling began to blink repetitively, casting the room in an unnerving crimson hue.

Jack couldn't see where Jason was so he reached up, grabbed the glass orb again, and tossed it across the room. It landed with a thud, followed by another pair of shots aimed in the sound's direction. Before silence had a chance to fall, Jack darted in the direction the shots came from, crashing into Jason, knocking the gun from his hand, sending it sailing across the room.

Now they were on an equal playing field.

Seconds later, the former friends launched at each other, moving across the room in a blur. Years of practicing together had made Jack and Jason extremely familiar with each other's strengths and weaknesses in battle, and neither held back as they moved around the room, punching and kicking, knocking over everything in their path.

After another minute of pounding, the guards forced the door open and began to pour into the room. Jack and Jason had always looked a lot alike, and the dark room made it difficult to tell them apart, so the soldiers confined them both. Though restrained, Jack and Jason attempted to claw toward one another until Jason finally used his advantage. "Him. Get him. I'm the prince. I'm the prince! Get him!"

The entire room turned against Jack. The soldiers grabbed and held him allowing Jason to pummel his face and abdomen with no restrictions. A few moments later, Jack could barely hold himself up. His body sagged in the soldier's arms as Jason continued to whale on him.

One of the soldiers standing closest to Jason said gently, "Sire, I think he's had enough. He . . . he isn't a threat anymore."

Jason rounded on the soldier, "He tried to kill me!" Then he hit Jack across the face one last time, stepped back, and adjusted his clothes.

The soldiers continued to hold Jack, waiting for a command from the prince to take him away. But Jason didn't say anything. Instead, he walked over to where his gun had landed, picked it up, and walked back. "Lieutenant Jack Waramond, you attempted to murder the prince of Idoless." He raised the gun to Jack's head and said flatly, "Your sentence is death."

The guards holding Jack looked at each other, unsure if they should contradict the prince, but leaned away, holding Jack at arm's length to not get sprayed by his blood.

"Jason, no!" shouted Eliza from the doorway. She ran into the room and put herself between the gun and Jack. The emeralds covering her long gown sparkled in the dim light, and as she bent to examine a gash on Jack's forehead, the golden tiara she wore atop her black wig with a large lavender braid fell off and clattered to the floor.

Jason bellowed, "Eliza, he tried to murder me!"

"He wouldn't do that!" She touched Jack's face gently. "Jack. Oh, Jack, you're alive! Can you hear me?" Eliza's voice echoed with authority as she barked at the soldiers, "Let him go!"

Startled, they heeded her command and released Jack's arms. He slumped to the ground, and she helped keep him steady.

Despite having been beaten to a pulp, Jack murmured, "E . . . El . . . liza?" He gave a weary sigh. "Ah miss'd you." Then he looked at her, managed a smile, and said, "Yu luk pretty."

Eliza alternated between smiling and crying. "Oh, Jack! How did you . . . when did you . . .?"

"I'll a'ways find ma way back to you, 'Liza. Yur ma wife. Ma beacon."

"Oh, Jack!" she cried. She was gingerly touching his cheek when Jason cocked his gun, the click resonating across the room. She took a breath, then said, "I'm so sorry, but . . . no, I'm not." Jack looked at her with bewilderment. "Jack, I'm happy you're alive . . . but things have changed."

"B-b-b . . . but we're . . . you and I . . . the islan' . . . we got . . . married . . . we—?"

"No, Jack. That wasn't . . . that wasn't . . . real," cried Eliza.

"No. We, we, we . . . you promised, I promised . . . we said it . . . we . . . we meant it."

Eliza began, "It felt like it at the time, but—"

Jason cut in, "It doesn't matter, Eliza, because he's about to be executed for crimes against the nation."

Eliza stood up and faced Jason. "He's a war hero, Jason. You can't have him executed."

"Eliza, he just tried to kill me!"

Eliza tried to reason with Jason, "He survived Death's Province. Who knows what he's been through? He might be mentally unstable."

Jason growled under his breath, "Eliza . . ."

"But you have me, Jason. You—have—me." Then Eliza reached down and picked up the tiara from the floor, returning it to her head as she said very clearly, "Because, I chose you, Jason. I *choose* you."

At Eliza's words Jason's shoulders dropped, and he took a deep breath. After he holstered his gun, a scream pierced the room. Jason and Eliza spun around to see Jack, in his second wind, taking out the soldiers around him. Jason began to retrieve his pistol, but before he had time to do so, Jack threw one of the unconscious men at him.

Looking like a beetle on its back, Jason's limbs flailed as he scrambled to get up, screaming, "Get him! Get him!" But by the time Jason was on his feet, Jack was gone.

Jack didn't use the secret passages again, in case Jason expected it. He ran down the main hallways, trying to remain focused. He was pretty sure he had a concussion, but he didn't have time to worry about that. He just needed to get out of the castle, to get away. But all he could think about was Eliza saying those words: *I choose you, Jason.*

Jack dashed into the lieutenants' dorm, hoping for a moment to catch his breath. Mercifully, no one was there. *Due to the alarms blaring, they're likely searching the castle . . . for me.*

He walked to his bed and cabinet, which had remained untouched after so much time away, grabbed a bag and shoved some clothes in it. He also took a small box he had kept under his bed, which was full of a handful of items that had sentimental value to him, including some drawings Frank had done.

Frank . . .

He ran to Frank's room, found one of his sketchbooks, and tore a page from it. He heard boots tromping in the hallway outside and knew he didn't have much time. Grabbing one of Frank's drawing pencils, Jack quickly scribbled:

Frank,

  I don't know how to say this, but I have to leave. I'm not sure where I'm going, but I'm not coming back. Please don't try to find me. Just know I love you, bro.

~ Jack

He grabbed a spare sword leaning against Frank's wall and then charged his way out of the castle. No one could stop him. He made his way down a few flights. Once he was near ground level, Jack threw himself through a window, scaled down the castle wall . . . and disappeared into the night.

CHAPTER TWENTY~ONE
BATTLE

What is the meaning of this?" barked the king.

Ignoring him, Church ordered, "Frank, Jack, drop your weapons."

Jack felt the familiar weight of his sword in his right hand, his grip so firm he could feel the nubs on the hilt through his glove. Next to him, Frank remained in a defensive stance, sword in his left hand, the right balancing it, poised and ready.

Without moving, Frank spoke. "Where's Peter? What'd you do to him?"

"I said, drop your weapons!"

King Hawthorn took a step toward Church. "It's over, Michael. You'll never get away with whatever it is you're planning."

Mike laughed. "I don't know if you've noticed, but your own soldiers just turned on you. There are men loyal to me all over the castle. All I have to do is say the word, and we take over."

The king grinned. "Then why don't you? What's your grand plan, Mr. Church?"

Marks barked to Church. "This is our chance! Just kill him now!"

Under his breath, Jack said to Frank, "Now," and the brothers swung their swords wide in opposite directions, knocking away all three of the insurgent soldier's blades that had been pointed at them.

Jack knew, before anything else, he needed to take Eli and his magic out of play. He raced between the soldiers, deflecting their blades as he barreled straight at the wizard, kicking him square in the stomach before he could do anything. Eli's aged body doubled over, and he dropped to the ground. Mike shouted with concern, "Father!"

Jack kicked Eli across the face, knocking him out cold, and murmured to himself, "At least we don't have to worry about dealing with magic now," but immediately had to duck out of the way of an enormous fireball speeding toward his head. "Oh yeah." He watched Mike's blazing orb scorch the wall on the other side of the room, and shouted back, "Just a few parlor tricks huh, Mike?"

Mike answered by hurling a second ball of flame at him.

As Jack deflected strikes from one of the three soldiers and dodged fireballs from Mike, he saw Frank knocking out the second soldier, pulling the king past, then throwing him out the door, urging him to safety. "Your Majesty, run. Don't trust anyone. Just get to safety."

"Don't let him get away," roared Marks, who charged after, followed by the third soldier, but Frank blocked their path.

Jack ran to Frank's side to help block the door, wagering that although Mike could easily eliminate him and Frank with one burst of mystic fire, he wouldn't do it because it would also mean killing his followers, including Al, who stood between them.

The gamble paid off. Mike stopped lobbing the fireballs. However, he raised his left hand and spoke into a wristband, "It's time. Execute order 45."

As he spoke, Mike's voice emanated from wristbands that Al and the other soldiers in the room wore. Jack figured anyone loyal to Church was hearing that message now. Right away, his mind raced to Eliza and her safety.

Jack goaded, "So, what's the deal, Mike? Being the commander wasn't enough for you?"

Mike brandished his sword at Jack, "You wouldn't understand if I told you. You're far too selfish. Too focused on your own trivial problems to recognize what's going on around you." Then he ordered his men, "Take them out and get the king."

As the sound of metal clanking against metal began to echo through the room, Jack kept close to Mike so he couldn't throw more fire. "Oh, I see things pretty clear now, Mike. It was *you*, wasn't it? *You* decimated the island, just so you could have those photos to convince me to go with you on your death wish of an operation."

Mike replied coolly, "It didn't take long to find the island. I had the full resources of Idoless at my disposal." Then, in a moment of stillness, said, "I wonder why it took five years to find you the first time? It's almost like they assumed you were dead without even looking."

"What are you trying to say?"

Church took advantage of Jack's pause and advanced aggressively with two of his insurgent soldiers at his sides. The charge knocked Jack off balance, and he fell to the ground. Church brought his sword down toward Jack's chest—but was blocked by Frank's sword as he slammed into both of the insurgents, debilitating one and knocking the other out completely. This allowed Jack to roll through the opening and begin battling Al and the final soldier, leaving Church to Frank.

"I trusted you," growled Frank as he swung his blade around at Church, who got out of the way just in time. "Defended you."

Mike was unable to do more than deflect Frank's continuous attacks. "Frank, I don't want to fight you."

"Jack kept trying to warn me about you, but I didn't listen. I kept telling him what a good man you were."

Mike backed away, "Frank, I wanted to tell you. To include you, but—"

"Include me?" raged Frank, "What, in this?"

"It's the Secret War, Frank. Don't you see?"

Frank snorted, "Yeah? Then where are the other nations?" Mike didn't have an answer. "Exactly. This has nothing to do with the kings fighting each other for power. This is just about a bunch of insurrectionists trying to take over."

"Frank, you have to listen to me . . . try and understand."

"I'll never betray Idoless!"

"Yes, I know," said Mike sadly. "Your blind loyalty is why I didn't include you. You never were able to see the shades of gray between the black and white."

"It's not about black or white, it's about right and wrong."

Mike's eyes flashed with fire, and he roared, "It's always been about right and wrong!" as a wave of heat burst from him, sending Frank recoiling. He took advantage and, with flames trailing from his hands, swung his sword.

Just as Frank had done for him, Jack sprang between his brother and the commander blocking the attack, which sent sparks and glowing cinders flinging across the room.

Jack and Frank now stood side by side, in a showdown with Church, Marks, and the single remaining soldier. The commander's eyes glowed with intensity, and his sword blade had transformed into a coarse, black shaft with steam rising from veins of orange, molten metal that ran along it.

Frank could feel heat radiating from Mike, as though he were a human furnace. It was so hot, both Al and the remaining soldier took a step away from him. Frank noticed a series of dark scorch marks on his brother's sword and said, "Hot."

"Yup," responded Jack.

Mike hurled a ball of flame at them. Each twisted in a different direction, allowing it to fly between.

"Very hot."

"Yup."

"Give up," ordered Mike. "My men are taking over the castle as we speak. If you surrender now, I promise to let you live." Neither Jack nor Frank responded. "Fine, how about I promise no harm will come to Eliza or Peter?"

Just then six new soldiers arrived. Frank relaxed, heaved a sigh of relief and said, "I'm glad you all showed up. Take him into custody."

Jack sheathed his sword and answered Mike, "We'd take you up on your offer, but there's just one problem."

While stowing his own sword, Frank finished, "We can't trust the promise of a two-faced traitor."

But the soldiers didn't move. One even looked to Church and asked, "Sir?"

Understanding in an instant, Frank moaned, "For fuck's sake," and he charged the new men before anyone had a chance to react.

The first he punched square in the nose, then kicked another who was behind him. He drew his hefty broadsword and tossed it to one of the others, who unconsciously dropped his own weapon to catch it. Frank kicked him in the groin and grabbed his broadsword back as the man fell, then used its pinecone-shaped pommel to knock out another.

Everyone still standing swarmed the Waramonds.

Frank maneuvered into position to fight alongside his brother, but Al Marks and the other soldiers swarmed and pinned him against the wall, leaving Jack to face Church alone.

Waves of heat from Mike grew so hot they engulfed the room, causing everyone to stop and look over to see what was happening.

The fight between Jack and Church was growing increasingly intense. With each clash of their swords, portions of the charred outer shell of the commander's sword crumbled to the floor until all that remained was a blade that looked as if it had just been forged, glowing a brilliant yellow-orange, with flames licking the sides. And after one ferocious strike by Church, in a dazzling shower of embers, Jack's sword broke in two. Church followed with a kick that knocked Jack to the ground, defenseless.

Mike spun his sword into a reverse grip, and drove the blade down. Jack barely managed to roll out of the way in time, and Church's strike was so intense it plunged deep into the floor and sent a blazing ring of energy radiating out. The floor crumbled instantly, plummeting everyone to the level below.

There was no fighting as everyone recovered and tried to make sense of what had just happened. The room they were now in was large and expansive, with a high ceiling, and Frank recognized it immediately as the reception hall. Instead of conversations and laughter, the room was now filled with the sounds of coughing and gagging as billowing dust from the collapsed floor above filled the air.

As the commotion cleared, Frank glimpsed a flash of red in the gaping hole above him. The dust-filled air made it difficult to see clearly, but Frank was quite certain he could make out at least one figure poised at the edge of the hole. Moments later the Cardinal, with Peter in tow, swung in on a cord, landing safely on the ground. Peter ran to Frank's aid as the Cardinal checked on Jack.

At the sight of the scarlet bandit, Jack wheezed, "M . . . Mom?"

An electronically distorted voice, neither male nor female, reverberated in response, "No, Jack. I'm not your mother."

Suddenly, Mike Church's voice roared, "I've had enough of this!" He strolled out of a cloud of dust, still clutching his sword, though now it looked like a blade of pure fire, a faint shadow of the original blade visible within. His eyes continued to spark, and now it looked as if his entire body were on fire.

Everyone, insurrectionists and Idolessian soldiers alike, stood rooted where they were, stunned by the sight of Church's startling appearance. Everyone except Jack.

Frank watched as his brother dashed straight at Church, pinching a sword from a soldier's hands as he passed ("Hey!"), swinging it at Mike. But Mike's fire sword destroyed Jack's new weapon after just a handful of clashes. Jack backed off but snatched another sword from yet another unwitting warrior ("Wha?") and continued the fight; but that blade was shattered after only two strikes.

Mike wasn't holding back. He marched toward Jack, with murder in his flaming eyes. Jack spotted an abandoned sword on the ground, snatched it up and blocked the blow Mike dropped upon him. Jack held firm as long as he could, but Mike's sword hissed against his own, finally shattering it, and sending Jack falling back.

Frank felt helpless as he watched Mike stroll over to his brother, ready to deliver, what would surely be a single death blow. He didn't know what he could do, but he had to do something, so he grabbed a piece of rubble and was ready to throw it at Church when the voice of Peter called out, "Jack!"

Everyone turned to see Peter across the room, holding the mystical sword hilt in the air. Frank watched with amazement as, without being thrown, it flew across the room into Jack's hand. As the hilt slapped into his palm, a flash of light filled the room, and the supernatural blade appeared once again. Although it retained the ivory hilt and etchings, it now looked more like the style of sword Jack was accustomed to: a curved blade with a rounded disc for a hand guard.

Mike muttered, "How?"

Frank could see the grin spread on Jack's face just before saying, "Sword of God beats sword of fire."

Jack didn't waste any time and swung the weapon at his opponent, but it went clean through Mike as if the blade were just a hologram. Jack examined the weapon to make sure the blade was really there while Mike, having expected to be split in half, checked himself for any kind of wound.

Realizing he was fine, Church lunged at Jack with a new confidence. Jack instinctively blocked, and the mysterious sword, as solid as could be, didn't let Mike's attacks through.

Frank watched the battle in awe. The mystical sword only seemed to work a little over half the time. Every time Jack reached Mike, the blade passed through him as if it weren't there. It happened again and again, and Frank could see the uneasiness grow on Jack's face.

Jack remembered how in Death's Province, Bob had referred to the weapon as the "sword of the spirit." He pondered if that had something to do with its erratic solidity, and in his mind whenever the sword *failed*, he began thinking of it as "spiriting."

Despite his concerns, the sword protected Jack when he blocked with it. Unlike the other swords, it more than endured Mike's fiery weapon and remained pristine despite the intensity of the fight. It even seemed to shimmer as if there were always a light shining on it.

He wasn't certain, but the sword also seemed to offer him protection from Mike's heat. He didn't feel it radiating off Mike like he had before. And as Mike continued to unleash fire at him, Jack could swear that time seemed to slow and the sword . . . *guided* him to cut through the scorching orb, dissipating it.

Jack slowly began to realize that the more he trusted the sword, the more he was using it as instinctively as he had in Death's Province.

The more confidence Jack gained, the sloppier and more erratic Mike's attacks became. Mike began throwing all kinds of fiery blasts at Jack, but each time, Jack was able to disperse the flames into nothingness.

When it became clear Jack had taken full control of the fight, the flames covering Mike seemed to embody his rage, and in a burst of anger they blazed with fury and engulfed him entirely. Jack could no longer make out Mike's features, just a shadow within the inferno. Mike threw down his sword and raised both hands, shooting a tremendous bolt of fire at Jack.

Everyone in the room recoiled from the indescribable heat.

Everyone except Jack.

When the blast reached him, Jack swung his sword and deflected it back at his adversary. Mike could do nothing to stop it, and it hit him with a blinding light.

Mike screamed "No!" and when the light faded, the heat evaporated—and there was no trace left of Mike Church.

Exhausted, Jack dropped the sword and fell to his knees next to it. The blade disappeared before it even hit the ground, the hilt retaining its new shape.

Finally, one of Mike's men said, "He . . . he destroyed him. The commander is dead!"

Al Marks raised his sword in the air and bellowed, "For Mike Church, attack!"

The battle reignited, but Marks didn't join the fight. Instead, he went straight for Peter, grabbing his collar and shouting at him, "How did you do it? How did you send the weapon to him?" Marks shook Peter violently. "Answer me! You know how to work it. How do I take control of it?"

"Get off'a him!" snarled Frank as he tackled Al.

As they fought, Frank was taken aback by how well Al fought—like a seasoned veteran but with the added agility of his youth. Fortunately, Frank was no novice; he'd been trained by Hazel Waramond, and he didn't hold back. After exchanging a series of blocks and blows, Frank backhanded Al, sending him reeling backward. Marks came right back while one of the other insurgents joined the fight. Frank made short work of the newcomer, but in the time it took him to do so, Al had grabbed a fragment of rubble and smashed it into Frank's head.

The world went black for a second, but Frank didn't allow himself to pass out. He looked up and could see Marks pick up a discarded knife and raise it, ready to finish him off—but then Peter grabbed ahold of him.

Marks broke Peter's grip easily and seized Peter by the throat, thrusting him up against the wall. He raised the knife and said, "I guess we'll have to go back to the original plan."

"Hey!" shouted Frank.

He'd managed to get to his feet and threw a piece of rubble, hitting Al on the forearm that was pinning Peter against the wall.

Al dropped Peter and shook his arm from the sting, but he didn't seem wounded. "Nice try, Waramond," he laughed, "but you missed."

Frank grinned. "No, I didn't."

Al looked at his arm, and then yanked back his sleeve, revealing the ornate bracelet he wore—now with a large dent in it, the stone at the center cracked in two. Half of the jewel fell out of its setting, and Al dropped the knife, fell back clutching the band with his other hand. He began to howl in pain, thrashing on the ground as a windstorm whirled in place around him. Great gusts of wind blew the wreckage and rubble around with Al Marks at the center of it.

As the gales of air billowed out of the bracelet, they seemed to stain Marks with age. His hair turned gray, then white. His whole body thickened and grew muscular but then contracted and shriveled into that of an elderly man. When the winds faded, Al collapsed.

Jack had finally regained enough strength to get up and ran to his brother. He and Peter helped Frank get up and with caution examined Al.

Upon the closer look, Frank exclaimed, "It's Ryan . . . Commander Ryan Marks!"

Suddenly, the voice of Eli Warren emanated from all the insurgents, "Our leaders have fallen! Retreat!" Jack looked up at the remains of Commander Church's quarters above. Eli had a wristband like the one Mike had, and he repeated the announcement into it, "Our leaders have fallen. Everyone fallback and retreat!" The message echoed all around the room from every traitor.

Jack yelled, "Don't let him get away!"

But it was too late. Eli had been fiddling with a small copper-colored device. He jumped in the air and vanished in a flash of light.

With that, everyone began to scatter—some to escape, others to capture.

Jack turned to Frank and asked, "When did he get one of those hopper things?"

Frank shrugged. "He must have pocketed it back in Bob's cavern." He examined Jack. "Are you all right? How'd you not get burned?"

"I think the sword was protecting me." Jack looked at the blood running down Frank's face and asked, "What about you—are you all right?"

"I'm fine." But then Frank winced in pain, grabbed hold of his head, and almost fell over.

Helping him stay upright, Jack said, "We'd better get you to the infirmary."

"We can't. Not in all this," said Frank, referring to the pandemonium of traitors trying to escape.

"We've done plenty today. Everyone else can take care of the rest."

Jack and Peter walked Frank to the hospital wing. After a quick examination, the doctors diagnosed Frank with a severe concussion, and he was assigned a bed. Frank protested, but the doctors said it was necessary. He only agreed once Peter and Jack were cared for as well. They didn't get beds, but they got plenty of bandages.

Frank had to stay for continued observation, but the doctors said he'd be released in time for the feast, provided there were no complications before then.

Jack was shocked. "They're still having a feast? After all this?"

Frank replied, "I guess King Hawthorn's got some big announcement that can't wait. That's what I heard a couple of the doctors saying, anyway."

Jack shook his head, "That is *such* a bad idea."

"Whatcha gonna do? He's the king," sighed Frank in a ho-hum way, as he dug into a cup of pudding he'd been given.

Jack shrugged then stood up. "Hey, Frank. I gotta . . . I gotta go take care of something. You gonna be all right by yourself for a bit?"

"He's not by himself, Jack," said Peter. "He's got me."

Jack glanced at Frank, who had become very interested in the pudding cup and not making eye contact. "That he does, Peter. Thanks." He patted Frank on the shoulder and said, "Bye, Frank."

Frank grabbed his arm to stop him "Wait, what? You aren't . . . ?"

"What?"

Frank let go. "N . . . nothing. That just sounded so. . . um, nothing. I'll see ya, Jack," and smiled awkwardly.

Jack left the infirmary and aimlessly wandered around the castle. He'd told Frank he had something to do, but the truth was, he just needed some time to be alone and think. But minutes turned into hours and soon it was just after six o'clock.

Using a few of his own personal shortcuts, he made his way to the lieutenants' dorm. The air had that staleness it gets when there isn't anyone around. *Likely everyone is heading to the feast or is still in the hospital . . . or fled,* he figured.

Jack thought he heard something break the silence, just a tiny flicker of sound; but when no one came in, he relaxed. He pulled out his bag from under his cot. He had only begun to pack it yesterday, but that felt like weeks ago now. He thought of the letter and drawing Frank had left him; they were both still in his pocket and had been for the whole fight. He didn't dare pull them out to see how wrinkled and ruined they were.

Jack sat on his cot, then reached to the very bottom of his bag, pulled out a shabby old army uniform, and stared at it. The last time he'd worn it was the first time he'd gone to Death's Province.

Why'd I even bring this?

Why'd I even save it?

He'd had it cleaned, but it was still damaged. The shoulder straps were gone, and there were some tears and worn spots. He took out the beret; it was the old style, red with a black band instead of the black with red the soldiers now wore. It looked so old. He gazed at the dogwood leaf pin. He used to be so proud of that symbol and what it represented. But Mike had worn it too. So had Al, or Ryan Marks, and all the others who'd tried to take over Idoless. *What if I hadn't been here to stop Mike? What would have happened to Idoless if they had won?*

What would have happened to Eliza?

Jack's impulse was to find her and drag her away to safety, even if he had to carry her kicking and screaming.

Distracted for a moment, Jack thought he heard something again, but when he looked, no one was there.

He thought back to his days in the academy. The instructors had drilled into them that no one person was more important than any other, that they were all part of a larger cause. They were all part of one body: the body of Idoless. If you were an arm, then be an arm to the best of your ability. If you were a pinky toe, then be the greatest pinky toe Idoless had ever known. The body wasn't whole without all its parts in place, and it didn't do any good if the nose was trying to be the eye or vice versa.

Irritated, Jack threw the beret down on his cot. What body? Hundreds of soldiers had just defected. They weren't even defecting to another nation; just to some cause . . . whatever it even was. Mike had even died for it.

Jack had only been back for a month, and he was already tired of it. Tired of the mistrust, of the betrayal, of the fighting. Tired of people. *How much good can one person do in a world so broken?*

Jack looked at the clock next to Frank's bed which read six forty-five.

Time to go.

Since the attack, King Hawthorn wanted her under constant protection. But just as Jack had suggested she could, Eliza managed to sneak away from her bodyguards.

Carrying her black wig by its large orange and yellow braid, Eliza scurried down the hallways of castle Idoless to meet Jack. She wasn't going to run away with him. She was going to try and talk him into staying.

They would find a way to fix things . . . they had to.

Jack had been right; due to the approaching feast, no one was around, and the absence of an audience gave her freedom to jog as fast as her restrictive dress would allow. However, as she passed a clock on the wall, she noticed it was a quarter after seven; even later than she thought and picked up her speed.

Even though she was late, she knew Jack wouldn't leave without giving her a proper chance to join him—*wouldn't he?*

She ran faster yet.

As she reached the alcove where Jack asked her to meet him, she could feel butterflies in her stomach at the thought that in just a few steps, she'd be seeing him again. But when she reached the alcove, it was empty.

Chapter Twenty-Two
Gone Again

Tugging irritably at the large bandage wrapped around his head, Frank took in the reception hall of the castle. He'd never seen it decorated more lavishly. Yard upon yard of green silk streamers billowed from the rafters. Garlands made of fragrant honeysuckle and hundreds of tiny, twinkling lights covered the room, all likely to hide the damage it had suffered from the previous night's battle. A small stage with a lectern had been set up along one of the main walls, and a pair of large cameras stood nearby. *Cameras?* This announcement must be pretty big. Frank couldn't remember the last time the king had issued a nationwide broadcast.

Just before eight o'clock, a commotion erupted at the entrance to the reception hall as Eliza ambled in wearing a distant expression and a crooked wig. She was immediately swarmed by the soldiers who were supposed to be watching her, along with her gaggle of handmaidens, who attempted to straighten her wig. Only Emily, tapping away on her mech-pad, gave the princess space.

Frank went to Eliza's rescue, redirecting the mob away from her. "Leave her alone. She's fine." Some of the soldiers began to argue with him, complaining about how much trouble they'd be in if the king found out she had been wandering the castle alone. "Well, I won't tell, if you won't," he retorted. "She's here now and safe. So just go and take your positions."

Reluctantly, the soldiers spaced themselves out around the room. Frank shooed the handmaidens away as well, then he and Eliza found a corner of the room where they had privacy.

She looked up at Frank. He thought she wanted to say something, but instead she reached up and gently touched his bandaged head with concern. He took her hand away but didn't let go. He cupped it between both his hands and asked, "He . . . he's gone again, isn't he?"

Eliza threw herself against Frank, and they held each other as she wept.

Eventually, Eliza composed herself and began to mingle with guests as she was expected to. Frank felt an overwhelming desire to protect her and acted as a sort of social shield. His actions were selfishly driven, since she was the only other person who shared his grief from Jack's departure. Frank followed her like an overly protective chaperone, wearing a gruff exterior so no one wanted to talk to her for long. That is, until they ran into Peter.

Without a hello or any other kind of pleasantries, he asked, "Are you all right?"

Frank had become used to Peter's uncanny ability to read people, but Eliza was taken aback. She adjusted and responded, "I'm fine, Peter. Thank you."

Peter looked around, his eyes asking, *Where's Jack?* But he looked back at Frank and Eliza and, as if he knew everything, said, "I'm sorry."

Blinking new tears from her eyes, she smiled at Peter and patted his shoulder, letting him know it was okay.

Later, King Hawthorn ascended the stage, accompanied by Kirk Larson and several soldiers.

The crowd began to simmer, but Peter swooned, "Who is *that?*" He nodded toward one of the generals, a large, beefy man with a thick beard. He looked a lot like Frank, only older.

Frank had conflicting feelings over this. Peter's question was clearly motivated by an attraction to the general, which confirmed to Frank that Peter was legitimately attracted to him. Big and furry wasn't society's norm of good looks, but apparently, Peter truly liked it. The other emotion was awkwardness. The reason the general looked so much like him was . . . "That, umm. That's Joseph Karr. He's . . . well, he's my uncle."

Before more could be said, the king approached the podium. And the lights shifted so he was the only one illuminated. The room became quiet as King Hawthorn began his speech.

"Good evening, everyone, and thank you all for coming. Tonight is an important event for the people of Idoless. In a moment, I have a rather important announcement to make. But I can't do so without first recognizing the original purpose of this event, and that is, to welcome back the heroes from a most dangerous mission and congratulate them on their success."

Even though no one in the audience, beyond those in the military, had any clue what had happened, there was a mild applause out of respect.

"Yes, we owe those men a great debt," the king continued. "Unfortunately, that brings me to another matter. Many of you will be alarmed to find out that last night, Castle Idoless was attacked."

Frank heard gasps from all around the room.

King Hawthorn took a deep, sad breath, then said grimly, "We find ourselves living in a dangerous time, my people. It was a coup, led by Commander Michael Church, assisted by his father, the wizard Eli Warren, and former Commander Ryan Marks. They tried to kill me and take over Idoless."

The crowd gasped even louder than before.

"And thanks to the element of surprise, Commander Church and his followers nearly succeeded." Then the king grinned proudly. "But thanks to the efforts of Idoless's fine loyalists, including the fortunate arrival of," he gestured to his right, "General Karr and a platoon of soldiers returning early from assignment—which gave us the additional reinforcements we needed—we were able to turn the tide."

The crowd cheered much more sincerely now.

The king raised his hands for silence, and as the volume subsided, he continued, "And with that, I have a handful of honors to give out."

King Hawthorn proceeded to give out eleven awards for valor and heroism. Each recipient shook hands with the king, accepted his medal, then went back to his place in the crowd. When the king began to move on, Frank couldn't help but feel a hint of resentment. *That was it? Considering all we had done, how could Jack and I be left out?* That was, until the king called his name and asked him to the stage.

With a wide smile, King Hawthorn said, "Lieutenant Franklin Waramond, you played a very important part in last night's victory. You and your brother saved my life, and my sources tell me you were the one who defeated Ryan Marks personally. A medal of valor didn't seem like enough to me. You get one of course, but more so . . ." Frank saw his uncle behind the king beaming at him as the king pulled out a small leather box and opened it. Inside were two golden sassafras leaf pins. "I hereby promote you to the rank of captain."

Frank took the box and bowed low to the king, thanking him as he flushed with pride. As he rose, he made eye contact with his uncle who gave Frank a proud wink. Heading back into the crowd, Frank couldn't help but feel a small rush at the sound of the applause; he wasn't used to receiving that kind of praise. Eliza and Peter congratulated him enthusiastically upon his return as well.

As the applause died down, King Hawthorn continued, "Just a few more, then we'll move on, I promise." Frank assumed the king was talking about Jack, but the names he heard next were the last two he ever expected. "Corporals Hawk Taylor and Joss Huntsman, please step forward." Both heavily bandaged, Hawk with a cast on his arm and Joss with one on his leg, the two men hobbled forward. The king explained, "After *Captain* Waramond and his brother helped me escape from Commander Church, these two brave soldiers found and protected me. Each almost lost his life multiple times to assure my safety."

Frank's jaw dropped when the king pulled out a pair of boxes like the one he received. King Hawthorn then proceeded to promote both Hawk and Joss to lieutenants; they were now ranking officers.

The room erupted into cheers. Hawk and Joss soaked up the praise. Hawk even threw his casted arm in the air and waved. Once the cheers died out—which took some time, because Hawk and Joss encouraged them to go on as long as possible— the king continued, "As I mentioned, former Commander Marks is in custody, thanks to Captain Waramond. As for Michael Church, he was killed in battle. The remarkable man who defeated him deserves . . . a very special thanks."

Eliza leaned into Frank, who put an arm around her for mutual support as the king scanned the crowd, looking for Jack. Everyone began looking around, curious if this special person might be right next to them. When he couldn't find Jack, King Hawthorn looked to Frank, who shook his head sadly.

Understanding washed over Hawthorn's face. "As I said, he's special. Far too special. Nothing I do or say right now could adequately honor him, and I know he doesn't like attention even though he deserves it. So I'll honor him," the king looked at Frank, "by letting him be."

The king waited for a beat, then continued, "All right, then. On to business. Tomorrow, the recording of what I'm going to tell you now will be sent throughout the entire nation of Idoless." The king paused and took a sip from his goblet, Frank saw a slight shake in his hand as he brought the vessel to his lips. He turned to Eliza to see if she had noticed it too, and her grim expression confirmed she had. King Hawthorn nodded to the men stationed behind the cameras and began to speak.

"Good citizens of Idoless, I have a very important announcement to make; it is quite possibly the most important announcement in the history of our great nation."

Frank could feel the atmosphere of the room shift, becoming silent and focused with tension pulsing from person to person.

"First, I need to lay some groundwork. Things you need to know, to understand, why."

The room remained silent, but the question lingered on everyone's lips: *Why what?*

"I know you are all familiar with the story of the gods' return. For 580 years, we have retold those events so they would never be forgotten. How the gods destroyed humanity's peace, blighting the very land we walk upon. The planet churned with chaos, killing billions. And yet, humanity prevailed, and the continent of Terra Firma became our new land.

"At first, we tried to get along . . . humanity, that is. We were united in the tragedy brought on by the gods; one land, one populace, one nation. But there are many gods, and they are jealous by nature. They competed with each other to determine who was the greatest among them. Naturally, they gained followers and worshippers along the way. Some trying to win favor for safety, others simply submitting to the gods' powers. The point being, we were pulled into the gods' quarrels, ultimately resulting in the five nations of Terra Firma: Mechina, Lithostone, Bionova, Phlogiston, and of course, Idoless. We don't fully understand how or when it happened. Even Mechina doesn't know, and they know everything—just ask them." There were some light chuckles, then the king continued. "In any case, covenants were made, and the nations split. The four most dominant gods were established as the patron deities worshipped by the other four nations, while Idoless ... well," King Hawthorn grinned, "we remained *idol less*."

Frank could feel anticipation sweep through the room. The king was recapping common knowledge. With this kind of introduction, he feared what kind of provocative news the king planned to drop on them.

"As you well know, our citizens are free to worship the god of their choosing, or none at all. In the early days, we were shunned and oftentimes penalized by the gods themselves for not bowing to one of them as the other nations had. Nonetheless, we prevailed and fought our way forward to become a mighty realm, recognized and respected by the gods as equal to any of the other nations.

"That, however, might change because of what I am about to tell you. You see, we have made a discovery. One that I feel *must* be shared with you all.

"We've uncovered evidence of another god: a god more powerful than all the others combined. We've found the records and accounts of the beginning of time as we know it, all fashioned by the hand of this god. The god of gods. *The* God. It was all contained in a book, which the kirks have now been studying fervently."

A murmur broke out.

Having been on the mission to Death's Province, Frank now understood what the king was getting at. Still he questioned why the discovery of a new god, even one so powerful, warranted a national statement.

King Hawthorn called out, "Please, everyone, please calm yourselves. Our investigations are still ongoing. We'll be sharing everything we can as it becomes available. The first step was to share this news with everyone. The message I'm delivering tonight, along with copies of the book I spoke of earlier, will be provided to each Idolessian in the days to come. To show our commitment, the kirks are already adding spaces in their temples devoted to this new god." The king paused and closed his eyes. When he spoke again, power coursed through his words, "To *our* God."

"WHAT?" someone in the crowd shouted. With that, the murmurs exploded into a deafening roar. The people of Idoless took pride in their religious freedom. Despite having the freedom not to, many still worshiped their god of choice.

Finally, King Hawthorn's voice boomed from the stage: *"Listen to your king!"*

The room quieted.

"You must understand: this is *good* news I'm giving you. And I promise you, nothing has to change for you if you don't want it to. Idoless will not be like the other realms; no one will be forced to worship God if they do not wish to. On the other hand . . ." The king stopped and looked out at the room, then directly into the cameras. With boundless passion, he said, "Idoless is the greatest of all the nations. We've grown and flourished despite not having a patron god for nearly six hundred years. But in light of our discovery, well . . . I believe the greatest of the nations, deserves the greatest of the gods.

"Now, as I said, the kirks are already reorganizing their temples. And soon, they will be fully trained in understanding the nature of God, as instructed through the book, available to assist anyone who has questions. Meanwhile, we will be building new temples exclusive to the worship and celebration of our God as He gains more and more followers . . . as I'm certain He will. He already has one," the king grinned, "me."

The citizens gazed at their leader, awed by the endorsement.

"So please, when you have the opportunity to learn about Him . . . and I assure you, everyone will . . . do so with an open mind and heart. That is all for now. Good night."

With that, King Hawthorn and the others with him stepped down from the stage and left the room.

Frank and Eliza looked at each other with amazement. "Wow," said Frank. "I never thought . . . never expected . . ."

"It's good, though," said Peter. "The Kodiaks love God."

"Really?" asked Eliza, "Are the bears in contact with this god? I've never even heard of him."

"Not god, God."

"Isn't that what I said?"

"No, it isn't," stated Peter.

"Well, you'll have to tell me what you and the bears know about him," said Eliza. "I'm not sure I understand why we've never seen or even heard of a god so powerful before."

"Never heard of who before?" came a familiar voice from behind.

"Jason?" Eliza spun around while Frank ("Your Highness!") sprang to attention. Although she smiled, Frank detected a lack of sincerity he'd never seen from her before. It didn't help that

Peter eyed Jason suspiciously. In an even, controlled voice Eliza said, "You're back early from Mechina."

Jason glanced around, seeming to sense the tension, but leaned in, gave Eliza a peck on the cheek, and said, "Yes, well, I'd have been here sooner, but I had obligations holding me back. Fortunately, I sent General Karr ahead—oh, at ease, Frank. I understand he was able to aid in the events that happened here last night. If I'd have known about it, I would have been with him myself."

"Well, you're here now," said Frank.

Jason looked out at the extravagant-looking room. "I heard about this feast, but I'm beginning to feel like it's a bit more than just a party."

"I'll say," said Frank.

Jason waited, clearly wanting to be filled in.

After everything that had happened with Jack, Eliza was battling with her emotions. She decided to try something she learned from her good friend: visualizing a container and putting everything she wanted to keep hidden or controlled within it. The container was covered, sealed, and set in the furthest reaches of her chest, where it was easiest to maintain and control. She took a deep breath and, sounding more like her usual self, said, "You literally just missed it, and . . . well, it's too much to describe. You need to have your father explain it to you. Frankly, I'd like to come with you when you do."

Jason beamed, "All right, we can go talk to him together."

Eliza asked, "Can Frank and Peter come?"

"Frank and who?"

Peter stepped forward and bowed. "Me. I'm Peter, Your Majesty."

"If he's a friend of yours, then of course. It's a pleasure meeting you, Peter."

Eliza grinned as widely as she could muster and said, "Thank you."

Jason then looked to them all and said, "We'll go in a bit, but I have one piece of business to take care of first. I'll find you all when I get back." Jason leaned in to give Eliza another kiss and turned to leave, but then he snapped his fingers and turned back. "By the way, I ran into your uncle."

Shocked she asked, "You saw Uncle Hector?"

"Yes. He sends his love, of course. And we have a bit of a surprise for you." Eliza went silent, waiting to hear what it was. He smiled, "But it'll have to wait. I'll tell you after I get back. Now, if you'll excuse me." Then Jason excused himself and left the room.

Jason walked to the far end of the castle, into a sector that wasn't used often. With each step he took, the smile on his face grew.

There were fewer soldiers posted here than in the more commonly traveled parts. And if it were the king walking past now, they might have been more surprised at the presence of royalty. However, Jason frequented this part of the castle often.

He entered a secluded wing, at the end of which contained a single room with nothing in it except four soldiers posted along an empty wall. One stepped forward. "Sire."

Jason nodded to the soldier and put his right hand on a brick in the wall, while the guard placed his hand on a different brick. The portion of wall between their hands transformed into a doorway. Jason and the soldier entered, and the wall reappeared behind them. The soldier stayed, guarding the door on the other side, while Jason continued ahead alone.

He walked through a narrow opening, which led to a stairway. The further down the stairs Jason went, the rougher the walls became, until it looked more like a cave than a constructed hall.

The steps ended at a small landing, which was lit by torches, though the space was being wired for electrical lighting. The cold, dank space was located deep under the castle, dug into the face of the cliff the castle perched upon, and it was under construction. Crude, narrow slits had been hewed into one wall to let in air, and they showed the night sky outside. Three soldiers at the landing saluted Jason as he arrived.

One of them, a brawny, blond man, stepped forward. Jason addressed him: "General Holden?"

"Mission accomplished, sir."

"There were no complications?"

"No, sir. We did just as you instructed and met no unexpected problems."

"Perfect," said Jason with a smile. "Please, show me."

"Yes, sir." General Holden led the prince to a door that had two men posted at it. He unlocked the door and opened it. Jason stepped inside, while Holden and the others waited outside.

Jason stood there for a moment, gazing at the contents of the room, which was like a smaller version of the castle's treasury. Ancient artifacts and statues stood scattered across the space, and priceless paintings leaned against them. Along one wall, chests of jewels and stacks of gold bars sat on shelves alongside the kind of technological devices available only in Mechina. The adjacent wall housed shelves loaded with bundled paper money, bonds, and deeds. The farthest wall, however, had been cleared out for a very special item.

With a swollen eye and blood trickling from a cut on his forehead, Jack Waramond slumped against the wall, shackled at his ankles and wrists by chains fastened to the wall. At the sight of Jason, he sprang up but was pulled short by the chains.

Jason didn't even flinch. He just grinned at his old friend and said, "You just *had* to come back."

Jack continued to struggle against his bindings until both of his wrists began to bleed from the pressure.

"Did you know that I was just *finally* beginning to accept that you were truly gone? I thought you had left for good. And after all this time, I was coming so close, so very close, to just letting you die in whatever hole you'd dug for yourself."

Jack stopped struggling but glared at Jason through his good eye.

Jason continued, "Oh, how I searched for you those first two years. I spent a small fortune sending soldiers and bounty hunters alike to find you. And you know, there were a few times I think some of them came this close to finding you." Jason pinched two fingers close together. "But I guess that doesn't matter anymore, because you came back on your own."

Jack mumbled something.

Jason took a step toward him. "What was that?"

"Why?" sighed Jack.

Jason gave a great, hearty laugh, "Why?" He crossed his arms, and shouted out the door, "General Holden. Hey Rick, would you please join me?"

Rick Holden was from the same graduating class as Jack, Jason, and Eliza. He entered the room and stood at attention. "Yes, sir."

Jason walked over to him and asked, "General, can you tell me why this man has been taken into custody like this?"

Holden replied, "Because you commanded it, sire."

"Aw, Rick," moaned Jack.

"And you don't need any reason other than that?" asked Jason.

Rick grinned wickedly at Jack and said, "Of course not."

Jason whipped around to face Jack again. "It appears he didn't need any more of a reason than *my* say so."

Jack spat some blood to the floor in response.

Jason grinned. "General."

"Sire."

"Let me tell you why." Jason's smile melted off his face. "Five years ago, this man tried to kill me."

Jack began, "Rick, you know I would do no such—!"

"Oh yes, you did!" bellowed Jason, shaking his fist at Jack. "You were my friend! You were my best friend and you betrayed me! You snuck into my room that night to kill me."

"Don't!" shouted Jack, "Don't you dare try and turn this on me! It was you! *You* tried to kill *me*!"

"I don't recall sneaking into your room in the dead of night."

"I wasn't there to kill you," said Jack. "I was there to ask how . . . how you could do what you did to me." Then he said with bitter mocking, "To your *best friend*."

"I didn't do anything to you," said Jason.

"So what were all those missions, huh? After we got off the island you sent me on mission after mission, each more dangerous than the last. All the other soldiers got to rest, but not me. You sent me on eleven in a row, Jason. Eleven!"

Guiltless, Jason responded, "You were our most valuable warrior, Jack. you don't understand the decisions those of us in command have to make."

"Oh, I understand," said Jack. "Through all those missions, I told myself that Idoless needed my skills. And I was prepared to do anything for my nation . . . for my prince . . . for my *friend*. But each time I came back . . . each and every time, I saw Eliza less and less. Like she was being kept from me."

"Don't try and bring her into this, Jack."

Jack pulled on his shackles until the chains grew taut, "But I have to, Jason, because she's what this is all about, isn't it? You can delude yourself all you want that I'm the bad guy, but the truth is, *you're* the villain of this story. You tried to have your best friend killed, because you wanted his wife."

Jason folded his arms. "Don't be ridiculous."

"You wanted her. You wanted her, but you couldn't have her."

"Shut up," spat Jason.

"Because she was with me."

"I said, shut up!"

"You thought maybe if I was dead—"

"Shut up, Jack! You don't know anything!"

"I knew she'd never choose you while I was around. Because she doesn't love you, Jason. She loves m—"

Jason backhanded Jack across the face, screaming, "Oh yeah? Oh yeah?" He hit Jack again and again. "So why is it she's with me now, and not you, Jack? Or did you forget what she told you that night? She chose me!"

Jack hung weakly from the chains but carried on. "She . . . she said the words. But . . . you know as well as I do . . ." he gave the slightest of sniggers, "by now you probably know better. We both know she didn't *actually* choose you. She would never choose you, because she loves *me*."

Jason roared and went to hit Jack again, but Jack actually used the chains to pull himself out of the way, causing Jason to hit the stone wall behind him. Jack then headbutted him and, even though the chains didn't have much slack, being at such close range, he was able to knee Jason in the stomach.

Rick Holden rushed over and socked Jack in the stomach. Once Jason regained himself, he kicked Jack's defenseless frame. Jack gasped for air, struggling to stand, but in the end had to let himself drape from the chains and just groaned, "Meant to be here."

Dusting himself off and straightening his shirt, Jason recomposed himself. He then announced, "Jack Waramond, you attempted to murder the prince of Idoless. I hereby sentence you to life in prison." Jason waited a moment, taking in the sight of his former friend, hanging from the chains. He reached over, snagged the necklace hanging around Jack's neck, pocketed the souvenir and continued, "Tomorrow, you will be sent to the Zelkova Pits to live out the remaining years of your life."

"Meant to be here . . ." muttered Jack.

"What was that?"

Before Jack could respond, the cliff began to tremble and a blinding light blazed through the tiny windows in the wall, lighting the entire room in brilliant white. After a moment, the trembling stopped, and the light subsided.

Jason muttered, "What the . . .?" as he peered out a tiny window.

Jack just hung there, but droned, "Looks like the wizards were right. Opening the doorway into Death's Province was a bad idea." He lifted his head and looked at Jason, but then let it drop again and continued to mutter to himself, "Meant to be here . . . I'm meant to be here . . . meant to be here . . ."

"You know what to do, Rick," said Jason. "I need to get back up to the castle." And Jason promptly left.

Jack just continued to mutter, "Meant to be here . . ."

To be continued in…

Acknowledgments

God, you have all of me—my failures and my successes. Thank you for making me a nerdy, creative person who enjoyed doing this sort of thing . . . and the endurance to keep going even when it got rough.

There are many people I'd like to thank who helped me along the way of creating this book, from those who encouraged me to "just go for it" when I wasn't sure if I should even try writing, to the folks who read chapters and/or early versions of the book and gave me input.
That encouragement was essential.

Also, I'd like to say a special thanks to
Greg Boyd, Floyd Largent, and Cassie Woodard

And Kate Furlong Conley
The book is better because of your help. I'm so glad you listened to that still small voice. Truly, I can't thank you enough.

Author's Notes

The inspiration for *The Secret War* series grew out of a divergence between the way I was raised and the realities I've experienced in life. I grew up in a conservative Christian family, but as it turns out I'm gay, which has strained my relationships with them, to say the least. Please understand, I still love my family very much, and they love me. They only want what's best for me, we just happen to disagree on exactly what is best.

I could bore you with details of the countless exchanges we've had discussing the finer points of the Bible and homosexuality since I came out, but I won't bother because the result has always been the same—nobody's views have changed. But that makes sense; no person changed my mind to begin with. I believe I'm where I am now because I was blessed with my sexuality. Yes, blessed. I'm glad I'm gay. Having to deal with these feelings forced me to question what I'd been taught, and even if it turns out that homosexuality is a sin, at least now I can claim my beliefs for myself.

See, up until I finally came to terms with my sexuality, I had blindly agreed with my family on the subject, and it troubled me that it took being gay myself to force me to really think about it. I worried what other issues I hadn't thought about, causing me to question my faith and beliefs entirely. After a lot of thought and prayer, I found my way back to faith, but it was balanced by a new outlook.

At that point, I stopped trying to persuade my family to my way of thinking. Who am I to say what is and isn't right? My new goal was, and still is, just to get them to understand me and why

I believe what I do. What God does in their hearts with that understanding is between them and God.

The idea of writing a short story to achieve my goal had been brewing in my mind for some time. I thought, rather than talk about myself directly, maybe I could take my family on a journey with a character; I hoped it would allow them to experience the subject from another perspective. However, while I came up with some of the characters and specific events, I could never come up with a proper story in which to incorporate those ideas. I had no framework, no outline.

Then one day a family member and I were having one of our regular ~~arguments~~ discussions, when the subject of marriage came up. He, of course, maintained marriage is between "one man and one woman," while I argued that gender shouldn't dictate who we're allowed to love. My family member leaned heavily on the legal aspects of marriage, because at that time, gay marriage was a political focal point, and not yet a legal reality. I tried to challenge him with questions about what makes a marriage a marriage, and in a heated moment I created a quick scenario asking, "So, what if . . .?"

"What if a man and a woman get stranded on an island? They live there together for years and fall in love. The island has no legal system and no religious authority figure to declare them man and wife. If these two people committed themselves to each other, in your opinion," I asked my family member, "are they married in God's eyes?" The answer I got was frustrating. He skirted around the issue and got locked up on unimportant details, but ultimately settled on, "Well, that would never happen." And with that, I had my outline.

In my efforts to address all the details he could possibly get hung up on, and because God made me a creative person, the short story grew into a full-length novel. And though the marriage question still applied, the expanded story created an opening for me to add a gay character to address homosexuality more directly. So, I split the man in two . . . into brothers, Jack and Frank.

Once I finally began writing, the story exploded; scenes practically wrote themselves. And while writing one of those scenes—truly, I didn't even mean for it to happen—suddenly I found myself setting up a much larger adventure. I actually spoke out loud at the time, "Well . . . I guess this is a series now." But I didn't question it. It was too perfect. It offered me more time to do things than I could in just one book. I could challenge my family with more questions but also do what I'd wanted from the beginning: express myself in this creative way, to help them understand what I believe and why.

At the risk of sounding melodramatic, the story became a labor of love that I have poured myself into. That said, despite everything mentioned above, I believe the story is actually quite a bit of fun. Everything I told you above is at the story's core, but it's not just the big gay book about being gay, and if you don't want to focus on the religious, social, or political commentaries, you don't have to. Every time the story grew, it made room for more adventure, mystery, and new twists and turns which can still, and I believe do, entertain. That's the first reason I decided to share the story with the world and not just my family. But if it can help anyone, in any way . . . maybe someone else going through what I am . . . perhaps help them communicate with their family in a different way . . . well then, it's beyond worth my while to share it.

About the Author

Keith James lives in Glen Lake, Minnesota with his husband, John, and their dog. He graduated from the Columbus College of Art and Design in 1998, with a major in illustration. After school, concerned with being able to pay the bills, he "got caught up in life" taking what was supposed to be a temporary job. Nearly three decades later, he's found himself unhappily still working a "just to pay the bills job" and not doing art. But he feels ready to get back to doing what he's loved for as long as he can remember . . . art.

To see more of his art visit: *www.thegeekcanpaint.com*

www.ingramcontent.com/pod-product-compliance
Lightning Source LLC
Chambersburg PA
CBHW031733180726

48283CB00005B/1494